Life, Libby, and the Pursuit of Happiness

HOPE LYDA

HARVEST HOUSE PUBLISHERS

EUGENE, OREGON

Cover by Left Coast Design, Portland, Oregon

Front and back cover illustration © Krieg Barrie

This is a work of fiction. Names, characters, places, and incidents are products of the author's imagination or are used fictitiously. Any resemblance to actual persons, living or dead, or to events or locales, is entirely coincidental.

LIFE, LIBBY, AND THE PURSUIT OF HAPPINESS
Copyright © 2007 by Hope Lyda
Published by Harvest House Publishers
Eugene, Oregon 97402
www.harvesthousepublishers.com

Library of Congress Cataloging-in-Publication Data
Lyda, Hope.
  Life, Libby, and the pursuit of happiness / Hope Lyda.
        p. cm.
  ISBN-13: 978-0-7369-1789-6 (pbk.)
  ISBN-10: 0-7369-1789-6 (pbk.)
  1. Public relations personnel—Fiction. 2. Life change events—Fiction. I. Title.
  PS3612.Y35L54 2007
  813'.6—dc22

                              2006035766

Printed in the United States of America

      07 08 09 10 11 12 13 14 /LB-CF/ 12 11 10 9 8 7 6 5 4 3 2 1

Acknowledgments

The creation of a book depends on so much...familial support, inspiration, perseverance, caffeine, solitude, friends, the spirit of possibility, and kind words when deadlines loom. Special thanks to...

Kim Moore—my editor extraordinaire—who catches gaps in my stories or lapses in my judgment without ever laughing at me. Your gift is a gift to me!

Kimberly S., for your connection to the heart of this story and the "Regal Queen," and for your quiet, constant encouragement.

Beth Tallman, who so graciously agreed to meet a stranger (moi) for coffee at Caffe Ladro to talk about the Seattle music industry (and risk parking tickets).

Marc, for your presence in my life.

Many things are possible for the person who has hope.
Even more is possible for the person who has faith.
Still more is possible for the person who knows how to love.
But everything is possible for
the person who practices all three virtues.

—from *The Practice of the Presence of God*

One

The vacuum sound of skateboards approaching at Mach speed caused me to turn just in time for an onslaught of Seattle's fine young citizens on wheels.

"Lady, you look like a dork," said the one wearing a stocking cap down to his eyebrows as he pointed at my head. The umbrella I held over my head served as a sound-intensifying alcove. Dork rang out at a very caustic and offensive range.

"That's a girl," said another as he rushed by me, did a half-twist off of the angled sidewalk and landed with a thud onto the rough street. "Not a lady," he yelled, finishing his move and his thought.

The third charmer looked back over his shoulder and added, "No, that's a creature." They all laughed with adolescent enthusiasm and the surprisingly deep tone teen boys possess.

My street linguistics were a bit rusty, but I was pretty sure that wasn't a compliment. It wasn't until later that I thought to shame them for their use of the word "dork." Wasn't that a put-down from before *my* generation?

I pondered this as I continued toward my usual Sunday morning destination. Moments later I stood in front of familiar, worn, gray-teal doors and reached for the 1920s door handle. I had to pull hard against the force of the morning's wind. I even leaned toward the street to create enough resistance force. *Would I ever get used to this city?* I wondered as the splintered edge of the door snagged the hem of my pants.

"Today would have been a perfect day to sleep in," I said to Nomad the hound dog as I entered the 80 Days used bookstore. I turned to detach my clothing and caught a glimpse of my reflection in the display window. The knotted, sci-fi cone of my curls shaped by a fall gust of wind from Seattle's Elliott Bay hovered above my head like a foreign object. Young bachelor number three was right. I was a creature.

Mr. Diddle, the owner of the narrow and musty establishment, spoke from somewhere above sight line. "What fun is sleeping when there are so many nooks and crannies in the world of literature to explore?"

This was a typical remark from the optimistic man whose stature and attitude were that of a leprechaun. I passed three aisles, turning my head left and then right, and at last discovered Mr. Diddle's lower half at the top of a rusty, standard ladder cleverly and dangerously tricked out with roller skates for wheels.

"I brought you coffee and a jelly donut. If you'd serve coffee and pastries, maybe you would have more customers. And a sign would be helpful."

Nomad trotted behind me, talking a slow yawn chatter while his nails clipped the wood in a friendly rhythm. In minutes my lap and attention would be his.

"My dear, 80 Days exists for those who stumble across a narrow, unmarked entry and have the joy of discovering a new destination. And real book browsers like to have both hands free so that they can reach for a frayed cover instinctively. So they can turn pages without juggling beverages. You found me, Libby. Wasn't the act of discovery part of your fun?"

"Yes, I suppose so. But I was trying to locate another bookstore, which does serve coffee and pastries. I was lost."

With creaks of old knees and ladder rungs, Mr. Diddle descended slowly while nodding. He about-faced to receive his Sunday sacraments and extended a finger past the grip of his paper cup and pointed at me. "You say lost. I say right where you were supposed to be. I may have to wait for my clientele, but they are always worth waiting for. I bought 80 Days from old Mrs. McCready when it was just a travel bookstore, and now it is a little bit of everything. So, you see, a sign would confuse people more. Clearly 80 Days is the name for a travel book store. Which this is not."

"You could change the name," I offered, but then we both shook our head simultaneously and Nomad howled. I sighed my resignation and began to wander.

"What's on the agenda for today? Portugal? Cambodia?"

"Mr. Diddle, you offend me. I do not come to a bookstore with an agenda. That is unconscionable."

"You do research for your travels."

"I explore random possibilities for my travel itineraries. Big difference. My notes are for fantasy trips I'll never take."

"Some day you will. That is why I like that you come here to do your research and type the itineraries. Someone should get use of my computer!"

"I hope your other regulars actually purchase books from you, because I'm indeed a browser, not a doer." Sadly, this was true for every area of my life.

"Not yet, maybe." Mr. Diddle held up his jelly donut and motioned me toward the back of the store, where a crooked door cut in half and fitted with deadbolt locks on the top and bottom halves served as his receiving dock for occasional boxes of used books and even fewer boxes of new texts. He stopped just shy of the last row of shelves and nodded to a stack of white boxes in the far corner. "You'll have fun with those. Good thing you came today. I have a third-party buyer planning to take a peek at this collection tomorrow. These are early 1900s travel guides for England and Spain. Beautiful treasures."

My eyes grew wide. "Maybe this day is shaping up. And to think I almost went elsewhere—"

Mr. Diddle shook his head to cut me off. "Tsk, tsk."

"Not the other bookstore. Just somewhere else," I said, purposely vague.

With a slap of a hand on my thigh, I motioned for Nomad to follow me. I pulled one of the courtesy rag rugs from a pile at the end of the book aisle and carried it to a corner, where I sat down cross-legged and waited for the mass of Nomad to fill and form to my lap.

"You will be here until you need to be elsewhere," Mr. Diddle said, winking and tapping his temple with his finger.

With mock sincerity, I bowed my head slightly to the grown man with a smear of raspberry jam on his forehead. "Such a lofty statement of nothingness, O Wise One."

"Do you want first dibs or no?"

"Yes. As long as they're free," I said while I rubbed Nomad with one hand and retrieved books from the box with other. Taking my time, I opened up the leather covers and let my eyes fall with anticipation onto the ornate title pages: *Travels in Paris, Sophisticated Voyages, Every Ladies' London*. Exquisite line art depicted images of proper women wearing large-brimmed hats, with eyes that looked demurely off the page while they sipped tea from a full-service set. All I could think was, *These women had only a smidgen of the rights and freedom I have now. Yet they saw the world. They experienced the adventure of travel and the warmth of a foreign shore.*

Would I ever go anywhere?

"What have you learned?" Mr. Diddle called out from his back room.

I had seen this so-called office, which housed a typewriter table dwarfed by an old black-and-white television and a roller chair that allowed the sitter to recline on the spring spine to a fifty-degree angle before tumbling backward.

I dropped a book about proper packing for an African safari back into the box. "I'm just starting to look at these."

"No." Mr. Diddle's voice and then body emerged from the office full of self-importance. "About your...um... sticky job situation. You find out this week, right?"

"I find out tomorrow, as a matter of fact." I rubbed Nomad's ears vigorously to avoid further discussion.

"Do not let them roll over you. Your job should not be at risk. You, Libby, are a precious commodity." Mr. Diddle pointed his finger into the air to emphasize his point and returned to his media den. "Let me write you a reference."

I paused as if giving this careful consideration and then broke into my Mr. Diddle impersonation. "Dear Friends and World Rulers at Reed and

Dunson Public Relations. Libby frequents my shop. She is a lousy consumer but a nice gal. Her time spent in the travel section is pretty much a waste because she never has the guts to go anywhere. Please give her a job that will finally afford her the time and money for the vacation of a lifetime because I like her and my dog likes her. Sincerely, the Man Who Does Not Know What PR or Advertising Is."

"I know what it is. I just don't like it," he hollered from the cave. I think I heard his finger stab the air once again above his bald head.

Maybe the reference wasn't a bad idea. It would never get me a raise, but it could get me fired. And I was hoping and praying for one of two things to happen: 1) I would get a pink slip and the subsequent severance package and unemployment would allow me to go on a short-term trip to Italy with pay and benefits or 2) I would get the promotion I have deserved and been denied for three straight years and use my five weeks of vacation to go on a short-term trip to Italy with pay and benefits.

"I have it all planned out," I said quietly.

Howl.

Nomad knew how well that worked for me.

Two

Outlook Not So Good.

Dang.

Don't Count On It.

Crud.

My Sources Say No.

Conspiracy!

I tried to shake my Magic Eight Ball into submission as my mind stumbled along a rabbit trail of questions. Would my reality ever reflect the potential my seventh grade English teacher had seen in me? Could a thirty-year-old declare a different life major? If I end up begging and praying to keep a job I loathe...will I still have a soul?

Very Doubtful.

Shut up, you seventies has-been.

If *Wake Up and Smell the Inevitable* had been in my icon-turned-paperweight's repertoire, it would have surfaced frequently. For more than six months I had ignored talk of a corporate merger circulating the Seattle offices of Reed and Dunson Public Relations. It should have occurred to me that such an event could disrupt my professional game plan. But I was so focused on my personal objectives that I did not read the blatant warning signs—Yuban served instead of Starbucks House Blend at staff meetings, the design department's refusal to reorder business cards, the replacement of annual bonuses with a gift basket of smoked salmon and chocolate-covered hazelnuts.

I had coasted along on my private ship of denial until the day I saw Mave Storm strut her stilettos across the polished maple foyer. She was a high-priced mediator from New York with a reputation for creating the best win-win situation possible. She redecorated her villa in Brazil and the corporation cashed in big on her guillotine tactics.

Visions of my long-overdue promotion drifted toward the unreachable horizon.

Anyone who read the corporate obituaries in the trade publications knew that employees rarely saw a payoff or a paycheck after Mave entered the scene. Her philosophy was to start from scratch, reasoning that those who remained resented the restructuring. She was right. I already felt seething contempt, and *I* was *still* in the running to stay on board with the company I complained about frequently to friends and unfortunate baristas.

So here I was, drowning my denial with consecutive Diet Cokes while watching my corporate fate battled out. I pretended to peruse Bacon's Media Directory at the research desk, but I was really angling for a clear view of Mave facing off with Cecilia Mitchum, vice president of Reed and Dunson (and—if my keen observations proved to be correct—the devil's daughter).

I tried to interpret their body language. I wanted to know if I should:

> a) defer my student loan for a second time
> b) return my recent immediate-gratification purchases
> or
> c) jump off the Space Needle and eliminate a need to
>   mess with options a or b

"Libby, reception keeps buzzing your office. And you have a call on line four." Rachel, Cecilia's assistant, tapped my shoulder with her hazelnut biscotti in passing.

"Not now." I brushed the crumbs off my new, bright red, velvet-is-back, DKNY sweater—my recent "light deprivation cure" purchase triggered by the smell of autumn in the air.

I knew the persistent caller was my sister, Cassie, and I felt guilty for not reciprocating her communication efforts of late. But not guilty enough to take the call. In my neurotic haze of self-absorption, I saw Cass's married-with-children life as the antithesis to my imperfect, single, career-challenged existence.

But did I really want to ponder my position in the success vs. failure equation right now?

Outlook Not So Good.

My mind echoed the piece of junk Eight Ball.

I reflected back on the past five years of caffeinated, long hours slaving for Reed and Dunson. I had ignored my dating clock and spent countless weekends either working, worrying about work, or doodling fantasy escape maps in case I ever ran for the exit instead of the copy room. Shamefully, I put my creative nature aside and accepted the demands of the account executive training program, certain that my obedience would pay off in the form of a promotion.

Of recognition.

Of validation.

Years passed.

Trainee after trainee departed with either promising alternative jobs or depleted bank accounts and plans to move back in with their parents. For me, the latter would be the equivalent of the aforementioned option c.

So I remained.

Inertia was sucking me into the vortex of likely failure. And yet some voice, sounding a lot like an overzealous cheerleader, told me that if I stayed long enough the promotion would be mine. The scene I conjured up of my turning point included me using my in-the-moment phone call to contact a very handsome man. A man who was eagerly, supportively waiting for news of my great job offer...and who had a diamond ring waiting in his sock drawer and an offer of his own. How these miracles would happen, I didn't know. But it was the order of things. At some point I convinced myself this myth was true.

Go. Fight. Win.

Ah, down in front.

My grandmother's rosary beads had a reconditioned sheen thanks to my incessant fiddling. *Please God* (here I go again)...*I'll limit my complaining about Cecilia to just friends if I get a promotion. And if I get that pink slip, may I keep my eyes on the prize of Italy. I'm not good at this praying thing, but if it's okay to ask to find a really nice online flight and hotel package, that'd be great. Thanks. I mean, amen.*

I watched the pipe cleaner-shaped figures with a glimmer of hope. I saw that they broke from their debate to nibble on lasagna and lunch on Chianti delivered from Ciao Cucina. I glared while they crossed off social security numbers from their master list and wiped blood-red sauce from recently plumped lips. I cringed as those alien lips formed my name and blew smoke rings through it while I watched the scene on mute from afar.

My sister's phone number appeared and disappeared on my cell phone, but I couldn't lose my focus. I was a passenger in a driver's ed car—one glance away and my life would come to a messy end. And with de-elasticized, unintentional granny underwear no less.

Hours after the last bread stick was digested, hands were shaken and the divas parted company. I scurried back down the hall to my office and tried to calm my pulse by sniffing the remnants of my vanilla-patchouli candle. A "good luck on your promotion" gift from my friend Ariel.

I should mention she gave it to me before *last year's* review.

I'm so behind schedule.

Five minutes later Cecilia entered without a knock. Typical disregard for anyone. This was the woman who had interviewed me three times within a two-week period and then mistook me for her on call manicurist on my first day. Ah, if only I had understood how that so-kooky-almost-forgivable mishap foreshadowed the relationship to come.

"Libby." Cecilia closed the door with force that suctioned the air out of my dank cubbyhole office. She was adjusting nicely to playing God while slightly tipsy. I acted busy. Very busy. I doodled pictures of the Cheshire cat.

"I have news for you."

Not good or bad, of course. Just news. I looked up at the tall, striking fifty-ish woman who had vacationed at the Desert Rehab clinic as many times as she had been engaged. Four was the last count. The correlating number wasn't by chance. The next husband-to-be who never came-to-be was always claimed during a weak moment in detox.

I drew a big four in the center of the cat's forehead and waited.

"I really went to bat for you. I'm sure you know about Mave's reputation for cleaning house down to the janitor. Who wants to start a major venture with a disloyal crew, right?"

"Certainly." I needed to sound so very understanding.

"She has agreed to my recommendation to keep you on board in a new position." She awaited my gushing gratitude.

I swallowed hard. Pride had such a nasty aftertaste.

"Cecilia, I appreciate your faith in me. As creative account executive I will focus on teamwork. In fact, I look forward to the new challenge." Where did that come from? Had that cheerleader just taken over my very being?

"Well... there was a lot of negotiating done. Like I said, she is a tough nut to crack. She didn't go for *that* position exactly. And, honestly...I don't see you in that position either. You are too analytical for creative..."

I serve this woman for five years, and she still doesn't know me. Or my skills.

Cecilia licked her lips nervously. "There is another exciting, new position I'm sure you will be pleased with."

"Janitor?" I allowed my sarcasm to come up for air.

"Goodness...aren't you funny? No, you will be the assistant to the new senior account executive. They are bringing a very successful AE over from the prestigious head office of Newman Winters in Chicago. Blaine Slater. You'll be working with the best. He came with an amazing endorsement from the headhunter agency Mave swears by." She leaned in toward me and whispered, "And I hear he is divine in the looks department."

But I only heard one word.

Well, two.

"Assistant?" *Headhunter?* I had visions of my shrunken visage swirling from a chime in Mave's villa courtyard as she and Cecilia laughed hysterically, lounging on lounge chairs and doubling up on double martinis.

"To the best." Knowing her news was less than desirable but better than the worst, she slowly backed toward the door. "I've scheduled a meeting next week for you, Mave, Blaine, and myself. We want to take care of our housecleaning before new personnel come on board. Until then it might be good to brush up on…well, assistant skills, I suppose."

Harsh.

My mind flashed to the day I saw Rachel using a steam iron on Cecilia's office drapes. Sweat rolled down her nose as she blew hair out of her eyes. "Apparently an MA degree stands for Masochistic Assistantdom," she had said. Streaks of mascara carved up her face, and we laughed together at her expense.

I looked up from the noose I was drawing around my cat, who now had a 666 stamped above the four. "Thank you, Cecilia. I'll do that."

The door closed. I was exiled from wonderland and trapped forever in never never land. Never never move to an assistant position. Never never accept a demotion graciously from a lush. Never never tell my mother. I unlocked my fingers and rubbed them back to life. Then I picked up the phone to call my sister with the amazingly bad good news.

"You didn't tell Mom, did you?" asked Cass, less out of concern than fear of missing yet another "Look, Mom, no success!" conversation between me and our very driven mother.

"I think I need a weekend to invent a positive spin for this."

"You are the queen of spin. Besides, you might as well wait until Mom and Dad come up next month." Her voice lifted, but she sounded more distracted than supportive. Could be she mentally slipped on the "mom" word and could not recover her balance.

But Cass was a *little* bit happy about my predicament. After all, what would our family do if we couldn't gather together over the warm glow of my life going down in flames? "Yeah, you'd love to witness that confession."

"So sensitive. By then you might have a plan in mind. Besides, Libby, you should feel good. You get to hang on to your job, right?"

"Well, *a* job…not quite mine. I was hoping to get the creative account executive position this month. I'm actually moving down…from assistant account executive to assistant *to* an account executive."

"Case of the Misplaced Preposition?" Cass resorted to our favorite tactic of reducing all less-than-desirable circumstances to a Nancy Drew mystery title. Sometimes it helped.

Not this time. "Good try."

"There are other agencies in Seattle, you know."

"I'll see how this plays out. Besides, I'm fully vested in the retirement fund in ten more months. I don't want to blow that." I knew nothing about my retirement plan. I just wasn't ready to justify staying or going.

"Good thinking," Cass confirmed. Then I heard her sigh heavily. "Don't you dare say it."

"What?"

"The 'I have to think about such things because I'm *single*' spiel. Then you insert crazy logic about how I don't have to worry about money or layoffs or economic decline or nuclear war because I'm married."

"I wasn't going to say...okay, so I almost went there." It was true. After all, Cass was cared for, provided for. It wasn't the life of my dreams, but it was the life she had always wanted, and she got it.

And me? I was enjoying the downhill scenery as my life whizzed by with all its shortcomings.

Libby demoted.

Whoosh.

Libby dating The Man Without a Future.

Whoosh.

Retirement fund-less Libby.

Zoom. Zoom. Woosh.

I looked out my door and saw Jocelyn from personnel hugging Karen from accounting. The firing line had begun. I nudged my office door closed to protect myself from the Storm-induced inferno taking place.

"Oh, no. It's started, Cass. It's like that scene from *Broadcast News*...you know, when Holly Hunter's character tells William Hurt's character how sick she feels inside...watching her coworkers get fired. "

"Right...and he is super practical about it. 'This has happened at every station I have ever been to' or something like that."

"I feel more like Holly than William right now." I watched a few more people cram their personal belongings into pre-labeled file boxes. Some minimum wage temp had possessed the hit list days before. "I didn't realize how lucky I was to hear my bad news. I have no idea how to act in front of these people. What do I do?"

"Try being Holly Hunter on the outside and go share their pain. But be William Hurt on the inside. I know you, Libby. You will start taking on some bizarre responsibility for your good fate and their bad fate. You take on way too much emotional baggage from these kinds of things."

"I did use Grandmother's rosary beads…"

"Do you think you were the only one to pray about keeping a job?"

"No, of course not. I meant that I need to trust in why I'm here for right now."

"Okay. That sounds healthy. Now go be Holly Hunter."

I slipped the beads into my pocket and stepped into my appointed role. My mind had already distanced itself from the anger boiling in my gut. Survival instincts propelled me further into the crowd of the newly unemployed. I carried the right posture of sadness. I added humor where a light moment was needed. I paused thoughtfully when the weight of the loss was too much to bear. But I sensed I wouldn't recognize my own reflection had I caught it in one of the PC monitors being permanently shut down.

It was only four o'clock, but I was determined to leave. "What are ya gonna do, fire me?" I imagined a hallway confrontation with Cecilia. I would laugh maniacally and keep walking. Yes, I would. I quickly gathered my belongings and checked email. I was glad to see a message from my Aunt Maddie. I printed it and dashed for the door. No encounter took place. Most managers feigned urgent phone calls so they could have their backs to the exodus of workers and former company softball teammates.

As I rode the elevator down in silence, my knees shaking, I had a personal epiphany. While I played my assigned roles, the mark where the real me was supposed to stand remained empty. Maybe…maybe it was time to start playing *me*.

And like any epiphany worth mentioning, it scared me senseless.

Three

I stood in front of Chin Chin's smudged take-out window deciding whether to order enough for leftovers. Chang Chin grabbed his dull, dented No. 2 pencil and poised it above the order pad. There was no expression on his face. No customer service pleasantries tickled his features. And though I'm a regular customer, we played out a scene from the Tower of Babel.

"*Just* then noodles," he emphatically announced.

"Well, noodles *and* pork."

"You always get fork with take out."

"Not fork...well, yes, I want a fork. But I want moo shu pork. Pork. You know...a pig." I pushed my nose up in a snout, much to the surprise of his customers seated inside. I had never before resorted to charades, but I thought it would clear up this point of regular confusion. Chang was disgusted...appalled, as though I had just threatened to rub hot mustard in his eyes.

He left.

Kayo, his wife, shuffled to the window to complete my order. Her usual cherub smile was replaced by a constipated frown. She shoved plastic bags at me and shook her head. "You know he has a bad heart," she said with her stern mouth.

Clearly, I had threatened the life of her husband and I was lucky to get a taste of her cooking. That is what her eyes said. And I heard her.

I waddled to the bus station with my hard-earned comfort food rustling against my thighs. Using public transportation is a bit like picnicking on a nudist beach. Everyone knows your business. Anyone paying attention knew that I wasn't in a worthwhile relationship because a romantic comedy DVD rental tried often to escape from my coat pocket, and my single order of ethnic food was draped over my middle finger as I balanced between poles like a solo circus act.

If I wasn't afraid of heights and had not experienced the executive-spread syndrome from years of sitting in an ergonomically incorrect roller chair, I would have seriously considered joining the circus and suiting up in Lycra.

Well, and if I could handle change.

I got off the bus at Kerry Park and joined a couple tourists taking in the view of the Space Needle. My favorite bench for journaling was free, so I plopped down and pulled the printed email from my new Prada leather knapsack—a pre-promotion splurge that after the day's events transformed into demotion debt, the cost of which would be transferred to so many different 1.9 percent introductory rate credit cards that I will have lost the bag by the time it is paid for.

The vegetable chow mein's smoky noodles pulled me from my negative tangent. I eagerly opened the container and dug in. Food. Comfort. A young boy scouting out the area wandered away from his sightseeing parents and came upon my hideout. He stared at me with his baseball cap askew. I was a bad judge of kids' ages, but I guessed he was about seven. He kept staring at me, and I wanted him to vamoose.

"B-bye." I motioned elsewhere. "Oh…hey, it looks like your folks want you to look at the Space Needle. Isn't it cool?"

He wasn't budging. He peered more closely. I was an odd, free-range animal he would describe to his school class during share time.

I did the adult thing. I spit out the edges of my noodles in a most sinister way.

He ran back to his parents with a look of fear. Only once did he glance back at me. His folks handed him the binoculars and ADD boy was immediately mesmerized by the boats on the horizon and the people going up and down in the Space Needle elevator.

Random acts of meanness had been my specialty lately. I needed a therapist. And probably so would everyone I interacted with. Once the little family headed toward their silver Audi, I opened the moo shu pork container and rested the email on my knee. Aunt Madeleine had good timing. I could use a dose of her encouragement.

Aunt Madeleine was also Sister Madeleine. Well, ex-sister. Six years ago she headed out on a short-term mission exchange and experienced life in a small Croatian village. Aunt Maddie experienced a spiritual and personal awakening. The day she was supposed to return to New York her legs wouldn't cooperate. She said it was as if they were frozen, and she knew she had to stay. Her order didn't exactly have an employee transfer benefit, so she quit. The next day her legs were good as new, and she said she kept hearing the sweet sound of chimes.

The people in her small town still called her Sister Madeline, but they stopped treating her as a fragile icon. In one of our cherished phone conversations, Aunt Maddie said she felt as though she had crossed over into a life surrounded by humanity. "This must be what Jesus felt like." She laughed at this comparison, but I understood—she was finding the sacred in the ordinary. It was a lesson she had been trying to teach me all my life, and here it was fully dimensional and it took her by surprise. But for me, it was the example I needed to begin my own awakening. I saw how faith could play out in a woman's life.

My mom had been appalled that her sister chose to use inheritance money for this lifestyle. Their father had worked hard to build his synthetic roofing business, and when he died, Mom and Aunt Maddie each received a substantial sum. Mom didn't ever blatantly express her disappointment with Maddie's choice of investment—people—but whatever Mom said at the time disturbed my romantic view of Aunt Maddie's courage. I envisioned the movie where Mary Tyler Moore is a nun who must decide whether to leave the church for the cute doctor, Elvis Presley. At the closing, the camera jump cuts between a crucifix and Elvis strumming a guitar. You just knew she was going to choose Elvis. Sorry, God.

Of course, my aunt didn't get Elvis. But she did get her legs (and heart) back.

Today's email was a response to my most recent rant about life. Mind you, even a week ago when I had a career crawling in the right direction I wasn't all that happy with my lack of purpose.

Dearest Libby,

Your grumblings do not sound like a whiny, spoiled brat, as you put it, but rather the growing pains of a young woman who realizes life is more. Not "more than" anything. But MORE. Always MORE. Be watching for it! It can happen right where you are. Your life does not have to drastically change like mine did. You might not want to hear this, but the position you are in at work could be right where you should be. You've wanted to read more about faith. I think a perfect book for you right now would be *The Practice of the Presence of God* by Brother Lawrence. It speaks about this very thing...finding God where you are at, even in the simplest of tasks. Brother Lawrence shares a simple yet profound understanding of God and faith and everyday meditation through the work we do, the life we lead. He was a kitchen helper for his monastery. He did not have worldly wisdom, but he understood what it meant to seek God completely. You will tell me what you think?

Somehow they have put me in charge of a humanitarian conference in Rome (look at me, world traveler). This consortium could really help create a better structure for the ongoing needs of orphaned children. Wish me luck.

One day you will meet up with me somewhere in the world. I see it happening.

Aunt Maddie

"Libby, it's time to find your purpose," I whispered, sending my earlier epiphany into a mess of cooling noodles.

Could it be that this well-timed email from Aunt Maddie was something fated? Her encouragement to be watching for something special felt orchestrated...divine. Was it arrogant to assume such a thing could take place in my life? I felt giddy for the first time in months.

Giddy juxtaposed against a demotional breakdown meant one thing: I needed an "Ariel view," my term for the sanity my best friend brought to my life. She leveled my anxious highs and phobic lows to a place of near balance.

Ariel Keller is the most like-me friend I have ever had. Perhaps she is actually the most like-I-want-to-think-I-am friend because she is naturally cool. I have to work at it and then still catch myself in the middle of the most uncool conversations or predicaments.

Had she not dropped out of the high finance world to enjoy the life of a barista at Elliott Bay Book Company, Ariel and I would probably never have met. With her newly pierced nose, she served me soy vanilla lattes with cinnamon every day when I moved to Seattle five years ago. I basically camped out among the walls of books and the creaky hardwood floors at the bookstore. Eventually I mustered the courage to initiate a conversation with the sarcastic, lively, dark-haired gypsy behind the café register.

Finding a good friend when recess is no longer a part of life is harder than dating. But soon I was sharing my load (a bad habit of mine) and treating her like a long-lost friend. One rainy Friday afternoon after I had asked for a refill, she pulled up a worn stool to my table, and I told her the story of my homelessness (blatant uncoolness).

I tossed out the line I used when casting for empathy from strangers. Only Ariel remained seated for any words that followed. "While I was in Paris for my final semester at Northwestern University, my family not only changed the locks but changed the address of my home."

I vividly recalled hearing the news.

It was the day I broke down on the phone with my mother. It took a lot of courage and desperation for me to blubber my loneliness over the long-distance connection. As I spit out the words, "I just want to be home again. I...I want to be speaking English, and...and...reading in our window seat facing the garden. I..."

She interrupted me at that point to inform me those things would never happen again. "Well, except speaking English," she offered as my weeping turned to animal moans.

Mom had accepted the psychology department chair at UCLA. Dad had agreed to relocate if she agreed to return to the Midwest after retirement. He was a self-employed life strategist. Ironically, he helped people work through life transitions...while his wife reported the loss of the family home with the warmth of a stock update to their lonely daughter curled in a fetal position thousands of miles away.

Welcome to my life.

My crying did not seem to affect my mother in the slightest. Well, other than it made her uncomfortable. She closed with a really memorable line.

I knew this to be true, because I remembered it.

Clearly.

Verbatim.

"I gave up plenty of offers during the course of your childhood for the sake of the work...the work of parenting. I would think that your pending graduation from college would lend itself to new freedom...for both of us. Bye, dear."

Click.

From then on I watched the Paris rain without warm thoughts of home to push me through the isolation. At that point I became a foreigner to those around me and to myself. Even the faith I had found during my early college years, which usually kept me afloat after a mother storm, seemed flat and thin...stretched too far away from its point of origin—a small, musty, brick church with orange carpet in Evanston, Illinois.

Paris transformed into a vast playground for a once-shy young woman who found herself untethered to anything familiar. When people asked where my home was, I listed a city close to wherever they were from. Why not? This should be the privilege of the homeless. The world was my home. This autobiographical revision led to interesting encounters and many party invitations.

I spent a good portion of the remaining three months living it up with New York neighbors, Colorado comrades, and fellow Floridians over red wine, Brie, and Gauloise cigarettes. I was everyone's little bit of home away from home. I still had a collection of phone numbers and email addresses from all over the United States. But I would never contact any of them. After all, I wasn't myself at the time. They wouldn't even recognize the uptight person I was back in the States, back in the land of cubicles and panty hose and time clocks.

After graduation, I leapfrogged several jobs in the Chicago area, but the lack of a personal support system and few chances for advancement threw me into a depression. When the market continued to offer nothing more than hyped-up assistant positions (how ironic), my little sister convinced me to come and live in the Seattle area. She and her husband, Nate, had moved to the Northwest after their prom/wedding ceremony. One of those odd cases of true, young love, it seemed.

I was longing to be a part of a family again...or for once. And the thought of being near my nieces Helen and Libby (my namesake, poor gal), was enticing. An offer for me to actually live with them was never extended, and I decided that was too much for me, anyway. A single woman should enjoy the chance to live downtown instead of in the affluent suburbs.

I relocated to the wetlands of Washington and chose to room with the only Seattle transplant I knew from Northwestern days—Ferris Franklin. We got along swimmingly because Ferris was like a brother. In fact, we looked of the same gene pool with reddish-brown hair and fair skin.

As it turns out, almost-siblings have a definite honeymoon period.

Within a month the buddy-fun started to wear off. I realized my mood swings were not really mine—they were reactions to Ferris' bizarre, almost menstrual-like cycles of grumpiness. I started to wonder if his real name wasn't Ferrina. But on his good days we were in sync. We both liked to have our space, which was difficult in his one-bedroom apartment. We liked a bit of a mess so that we could have our belongings near us at all times. And we both had a strong penchant for cheese-and-tomato pizza at midnight. But after a few months I needed more space, had heartburn, and was sore from sleeping on the "futon mattress," which looked suspiciously like two dog beds pushed together.

It was at this pathetic point in time that my coffee server turned into my real estate agent. Ariel hooked me up with her cheap-cigar smoking uncle who ran an apartment search service with such clever ads as "Your Place or Mine?" They were actually chartreuse flyers that filled the metro wastebaskets. One had stuck to my foot during my first week in town. It looked scary, like a ploy to round up ladies of the evening. Ariel promised me that Uncle Clay was indeed scary but legit. I was so eager to get off of the pet mattress that I accepted her offer to accompany me to his office.

For several weeks we followed Clay's Pig Pen shroud of smoke as he showed us a fine selection of upscale drug houses. I suspected he listened to the police scanners to find his next property. Just as I was about to beg Cass for a place to stay, Clay actually earned his fee. It was a one-bedroom located in the Queen Anne area. The rent was just over the max I had set for myself. Brick building, warm honey-colored wood floors, built-in bookcases, and a real breakfast nook. I even liked the ambience of the worn rugs, thin cracks in the ceiling that resembled a topographic map of the Mississippi water system, and chipped high gloss paint around the doorway. It looked like maturity at a very adult price.

I justified the splurge because it had a window seat, and I was now a window-seatless orphan who deserved to reclaim childhood comforts. I was also banking on the then recent promises for quick advancement Cecilia had made when I entered the Reed and Dunson program.

If only I had known I would *never* be able to afford that window seat.

As I took in the awesome Seattle cityscape against a baby blanket pink-and-blue sky backdrop, I had to admit, even if things were not turning out as planned, I was very lucky to be here. I wondered what a Croatian sunset looked like. Would I ever see the life Aunt Maddie made for herself?

Would I ever see a life that was truly made for me?

The next best thing to a date with a personal oracle was a fortune cookie. I pried open the golden, mouth-shaped cookie that was ready to spew deep wisdom.

"Life is an uphill journey. Don't lose your footing."

What a cheap-shot fortune for any Seattle dweller. I shook my numb legs back to life and began the trek back to my apartment. The Chinese food expanding, I unhooked the top of my pants and loosened the strap of my shoes (Convenience Advantage: mugger) and got out my cell phone (911 Advantage: me). But my breathing was so ragged I figured I would have a heart attack before anyone good or evil got to me, so I used the first number on my speed dial and left a message for Ariel.

"I ate two adult portions of Chin Chin's without you. And I got demoted. I have a week to learn how to be an assistant. Oh, yeah…I have been faking life. Call me."

The red flag did not fly in my consciousness until the middle of the night. Wide awake, tossing and turning, I realized I had used my in-the-moment call on Ariel instead of Angus, my boyfriend. If after four months Angus was still not my in-the-moment call, he would certainly never become my one-and-only anything.

My mind made a shocking confession. I had chosen Angus to distract me from my life. He was never meant to become a part of it.

I stared at the ceiling and listened to my stomach churn.

A lethal dose of MSG in Chin Chin's? Or a side dish of reality?

Four

I awoke to rain rushing over my window on Saturday morning. Sometimes I felt as though I lived in a 400-square-foot vehicle going through one gargantuan car wash. Yet I didn't find the fickle Seattle weather depressing. Somehow rainy days and Mondays never got me down. Though I'm not morose necessarily, I finally lived in a city where the weather patterns seemed to reflect my persona.

While lounging in my pajamas, I munched on toast with crunchy peanut butter and sipped my last can of Diet Coke. I had finished off my Tully's ground espresso the day before, and I couldn't deal with walking the five yards to one of the countless conveniently located coffee shops in my neighborhood. So I sipped cool caffeine and watched cartoons, pouting because Ariel hadn't called me back after my obvious SOS message.

I sucked peanut butter away from the peanut chunks and then spit the chunks into my empty can. Nothing against peanuts. It was totally for entertainment purposes and the challenge. This is what the real me did.

"Stelllllaaaaaa!" Angus' familiar routine started up like a oil-deficient lawn mower. My forehead tightened and my hands molded into fists. My body was telling me something, but I was too perturbed to listen.

"It's open!" I yelled, immediately bothered by my own tone. I remembered my midnight thoughts about our relationship and felt bad. "Come on in." I called out with an effort at cheer.

"Geez. Whatsa matter with you?" Angus came bounding in with his usual black T-shirt and black jeans—both with strategic holes I helped him make by dragging bricks over them as soon as they were released from the Old Navy shopping bag. The hole-thing was part of his rocker image. An image dated by about twenty years to the rest of the world, but a look still passable for normal in Seattle. When I asked him why he didn't just buy used black T-shirts and jeans for an authentic look, he rolled his eyes. His "you so don't get my scene" look. I wanted to point out that few did because his band, Mistaken, struggled to get any kind of play time in this music club-loaded town.

"Sorry. Really." I was. He had puppy dog eyes. But, sometimes, when he opened his mouth...

"Is this one of your designated lazy days? I kinda wish I had stayed in bed longer. I'm wiped after our long rehearsal." He went into my kitchen and, surprised to find no coffee brewing, returned with a box of Frosted Mini-Wheats.

I neglected to mention that I saw red ants near the box yesterday.

"I have some bad news." I said, inhaling a big breath and preparing my story of woe.

"You don't want me to move in?" He kept mentioning this. It made me very nervous. I liked having a significant other, but one complete with their own significant-other dwelling. I ignored him and forged on with my important news.

"I got a demotion."

"I second that demotion...." he sang out a variation of the old Smoky Robinson song. This was the way we conversed. I said things, and then he played off of them to veer toward tangents relating *nothing whatsoever* with the concern, dream, sorrow I had just expressed. He was a strange mix of a handsome, dark, almost-philosopher and a pull-up-the-girls-dresses sixth grade dork.

With clarity that comes from understanding you've been pretending your way through life, I wondered whether I was attracted to the frosted or wheat side of Angus.

"It was a huge disappointment. I had plans. I was supposed to make my big move by now." I weighted my words, hoping to communicate the severity of the situation.

"Do you want to go to Pike Place Market?" While this could have seemed like one of those aforementioned tangents, it wasn't really. He knew I enjoyed the market when I hit depression mode. I took it as a gesture of love (he hated the tourist element unless they were paying a $10 cover charge to hear him).

I kissed his cheek and then bent over to look beneath the couch for a pair of jeans I wore last weekend. I owned two pairs, Fat and Fatter, and rotated them according to my cycle of water retention. Today required Fatter.

"Dang, I cannot find them." I continued to strain forward, rummaging.

"Nice view though," Angus says with an annoying chuckle. The geek side of him was coming out like acne.

"Found 'em!" I overlooked his last comment (this was a pattern) and focused on the previous one—the one indicating *sensitivity* to my sad state of being.

Holding hands, we strolled down Pine Street toward the market. His soft, nearly delicate hands had caught my attention in the beginning. He had been reading *Hamlet* at Elliott Bay when my eyes gravitated toward his slim fingers and followed his silver thumb ring as it turned pages, brushed hair from his eyes, scratched his nose, and knocked his coffee mug off the table.

Seeing the incident taking place before he was even aware of what he had done, I quickly crossed the room to help him clean up. At first he thought I worked there, so he apologized but left me to do the work, but when he realized I was just another customer he got on his knees to help. This is when I noticed those intriguing eyes—a hint of green blended with the almost cocoa hue, highlighted by dark, long lashes. His voice was a nice medium tenor with pleasant inflection. A voice that I swear he manipulated into a fake English accent that day.

Angus and I initially hit it off on a very innocent conversational level. I was curiously attracted to details about the artistic underbelly of the city, and he was curiously attracted to my interest in him. The question-and-answer sessions soon fell flat and were replaced by kisses and small talk. It felt so good to do something apart from the corporate culture that consumed me during the week that I bought into a cubic zirconium version of "like"—it wouldn't pass for real under scrutiny, but it sure sparkled.

Even while it was happening, I knew I was playing dress up in my personal life only because my professional life plan was falling so short of "the dream." If I could not be defined by an adequate professional title, then I would improve my social title.

And "girlfriend" sounded just fine.

Hanging with Angus' crowd did have its benefits. I was no longer shocked by bus-riding Goths or dog-collared clerks at the 7-Eleven. And I was proud of my enlightened, liberal state. Enlightened without substances, that is. I didn't get into the drugs that made the rounds of this social group, so after about an hour with some of his friends who did indulge, I felt superhuman. Exceedingly smart, clever, fast-thinking, and overflowing with active brain cells. Brilliant.

Perceived genius, it turns out, is addictive.

The market bustled beneath a late morning rainbow. Everything shimmered as visitors and regulars melded into a unified group of shoppers taking in the colorful produce, infamous fish market, and treasures sold by artists and vendors. After a few minutes of wandering and sneaking grins at each other, Angus and I stopped at a display of jewelry. I used to feel badly if I didn't buy. But a Seattle native once told me that expressing appreciation for an artisan's work was part of the market exchange.

"Look at these. Do you think they'd look cool on my guitar strap? They match your eyes." Angus kissed me and picked up several crystals with thin silver hooks.

Well? They were pretty, but I didn't see how they fit his man-in-black image. And I said so with a "you'll look prissy" add-on. (I imagine this part playing in slow motion before Judgment Day officers. "Did you know this would start an argument?" they would ask from behind clipboards. "Maybe...Okay! I knew it would start something.")

Angus appreciated the candor.

And then he bought them.

"Why do you do that?" I asked. Surprised to be looking for a fight in place of my morning coffee...though I had known deep down...

"What? Not follow your commands?"

"I didn't command anything. I did, however, provide you with some valid input. Input you *asked* for and totally disregarded."

"No. I regarded it and disagreed. There's a big difference. You're one of those people who thinks your opinion is the rule. You'll be shocked to know that when other people express their opinion, they also actually believe that opinion to be true."

The petite Asian man on the other side of the table handed Angus his change and began arranging his jewelry in color-coordinated piles while looking off into the crowd surrounding the nearby $5.99 bouquet display. He acted interested in the bounty of six-dollar floral bunches, but he was turning red anticipating my response.

This was how we worked. Angus and I started as one fine-looking couple, but we became a two-headed monster in the public arena. And neither of us had been the diffuser in past relationships. We were fire starters, the both of us. He was nicer on a day-to-day basis than I, but I'd found someone with my temper.

Turns out, I didn't love dating me.

I wasn't about to say it aloud, but Angus was right about me. When it came to basic issues or questions of taste, I did think my opinion represented the moral majority. I was the first to admit I didn't have my act together, but somehow the little decisions that created my act shined a bit too perfectly in my mind's eye.

He knew he was right, and he knew I knew it because he dropped the argument, not as a peacemaker but as a fighter who had no need to throw a final punch when his contender was already maimed enough to concede. The difference between us—I always liked to throw that final punch. (This next part would also be shown in slow motion.) "Don't come crying to me," I paused for effect as I faced him, "when club bouncers call you Nancy and ask you out. You say I don't 'get you,' but *really*...pastel crystals on your guitar strap...do you even get yourself?" I had to shout the end of this, because he was already ten paces ahead...and counting.

A woman reinforced her child's fleece earmuffs with her hands and looked at me with disdain.

I stink. There's nothing worse than realizing you stink, except figuring this out the day after you've decided to figure out who you really are.

I didn't even try to follow Angus. Instead, I pretended my boyfriend and I hadn't just argued. I walked away with my head up and a "do-de-do" sort of whistle in my step. And just like an intoxicated person whose crawl pace fooled no one—my la-di-da stroll read like guilt. Kids would point and say, "Mommy, that mean lady can't hold her words."

I made my way across the brick street to the original Starbucks, tossed a five-dollar bill into a guitarist's case a few yards from the entry, and went into the cozy stall with a long, old-fashioned bar.

The first sip of hot, fresh coffee lifted my spirits enough for me to consider the pleasure of having the day to myself, but I was still angry at my behavior...and his. On my way out, I stepped into a picture being taken by some tourists of the front awning. "Who's that angry lady?" their friends would later ask while perusing digital slide shows.

The guitarist pulled at my sweater with his mittened hand and said five bucks paid for a special request.

"Um...let's see. How about 'Brown Eyed Girl.'"

"Ah. A Van Morrison fan. My pleasure." He started to strum.

"Wait, let me ask you something." I glanced at his guitar case and saw "Property of Albert" written with whiteout along the lid. "Albert, as a musician who wears black and has a certain image, would you pin blue crystals to your guitar strap?"

Albert scratched his head under his Mariners baseball cap. "I would."

"Oh."

"If I was forced at gun point to play at the Ice Capades."

He started laughing. I started laughing. It was as though he knew about the disaster that had taken place. He was my soul mate. He was at least thirty years my senior and missing four front teeth, but here he was. Before I could ask for his phone number, I carried my little victory with me as I maneuvered through the weekend crowd. I could not get any more pathetic.

What on earth was up with Ariel? Why hadn't she called?

Five

On Sunday morning I walked along Pine avoiding the requests for handouts by staring straight ahead and ignoring the ruddy-faced men and women who watched the trickle of pedestrians with sleepy eyes. A couple of the regulars I greeted with a shake of the head and a smile. Some people barked unkind remarks at those requesting money.

I don't mind that they exist.

With horror I realized what I had just thought. Who am I to grant them approval to exist? Who am I to "not mind"? I was just like everyone else holding my latte tightly against the wind. I was also sidestepping these human beings who had once been first graders with large-print books, thick crayons, and reams of butcher paper dreams.

Wait! I pulled a Fred Flinstone foot stop.

I could evolve. I backtracked to one of my regulars. Occasionally I had given him my pocket change but never a personal exchange.

With eyes and a hairline that indicated he was my peer, my regular slumped against the brick wall of the Luster Spa—an image that would send Ariel into a tirade about the contrast of affluence and poverty in this city.

"Hey. Hi. Um, hi."

"Whoa." He looked up at me blankly.

Yes. Whoa. The breath. But, upon observation...the eyes...under drooping lids...the eyes were bright blue and kind.

"I'm Libby. Libby Hawthorne." Oh, great. My full name. At least I hadn't given him my address.

"Hey."

"I nod to you on my way to work a lot. I smile at you...?" This was going as well as my attempts at cocktail hour banter.

He continued a dialogue happening in his head. "Then my parents and sister died in an air balloon accident. Now I'm alone."

My body recoiled. There was no proper response for this strange announcement. I didn't believe it for a second. Maybe a split second. But he said it with a rote tone. Just when I was trying to become a better person, I was being had.

I could look past this. He *was* alone. It shouldn't matter how he ended up that way.

"What's your name?" The personal approach might pull him from his routine.

He seemed to think about this for some time. As though the question involved a formula, "Darrell?" he looked for affirmation.

"I just wanted to say hi, Darrell. I come by here every day. Well, every weekday that is. I work at..." I stopped myself before I could reveal everything about myself. "Just down the street. That's sad about your family."

He didn't care about empathy. I think I saw his bright blue eyes drop to my chest and then to my purse. I pulled back. "Sorry you're alone, Darrell. See you next time," I said, defeated.

"Poof, like that." His eyes faded and he looked past me to a better mark.

I didn't change the world. But I shook up my routine.

While waiting in line for a bagel at my favorite bakery, I stared at the faded orange tiles and tried to envision all of the empty cubicles and offices I would face on Monday. I vowed to call a few of the pink-slipped employees next week to see how they were coping. Underneath this planned gesture of goodwill lurked a little bit of envy.

Forced change *can* be a good thing.

Forced change had, after all, brought me to Seattle. My family moved, scattered, and I followed the sane limb of our family tree.

Forced change redirected my major from business to literature. Well, okay...a seriously demented business advisor, Dirk Atkins, started pursuing me, so I chose to pursue world literature and it had turned out to be a good direction.

Forced change sent me to Paris for my last semester of college study.

Well, okay...my former advisor's misplaced interest turned to obsession, and I had to run away to Paris. I changed my required senior thesis from Nineteenth Century Midwestern Literature of the Plains to Eighteenth Century Paris Literature Along the Seine. I flew to the city of romance...alone. And Dirk promised to destroy the fictional notes he had placed in my business file about *me* stalking him in case he ever got in trouble.

I've never trusted that he eliminated this fantasy file. Prior to all job interviews I'm nauseated, certain the lies will appear and mar my otherwise decent school record. "Ms. Hawthorne, it says here that you stalked your advisor. How does this past incident prepare you for a future at (fill in the blank) corporation?"

Upon reflection, forced change was about the only way I ever made a decision to alter my life's course. How sad to think I couldn't muster the courage to make good choices on purpose or in accordance with a higher calling.

Mr. Diddle pointed at the folded piece of paper I had under my arm. "What is on that paper?"

"Okay. This visit I have an agenda. I received an email from my Aunt Maddie. You know the one?"

"Yes, you've mentioned her. She sounds fascinating."

"She is, and she suggested that I read a particular book. It's probably not something you'd get in, but...well, here." I was embarrassed to show him. This man knew better than anyone where I spent my Sundays. He would think I was a hypocrite when he saw the title. I watched his face as he read the highlighted portion of Aunt Maddie's email. He nodded, paused, and nodded again.

"Good book. I think I have several copies in several editions."

"Multiple copies? You've only got one copy of *Tuesdays with Morrie*, for Pete's sake. Most *individuals* own more than one copy of that book.

There's the one you buy yourself and then the one you get for Christmas from a relative and then the used copy some friend gets for you because they can't remember if you've read it…"

"I'm getting your point." Mr. Diddle motioned for me to follow him. Nomad got in line and we made our way to the small religion section. I had browsed there a few times when Mr. Diddle was back in his office. He pointed to the bottom shelf and then rubbed his lower back, indicating that he would not be the one to retrieve the volume. I sat on the floor and brushed Nomad's ears with the back of my hand while skimming the untidy row of spines. Two copies of a small white book with blue lettering caught my attention. I pulled gently from the top of the spine to bring the book out of its narrow home. A motion as familiar to a reader as it is to a slot machine enthusiast.

"I expected it to be much bigger, the way Aunt Maddie talked about it." I looked up. Mr. Diddle was back at his counter. Nomad stayed with me as I began to read.

On Monday Cecilia's manic mode provided a morning's worth of entertainment. She buzzed around the office in what seemed to be some bizarre nesting ritual. Consensus by the coffee machine was that she was actually marking her territory before Blaine arrived.

He would be my boss. I cringed at the thought of saying "Blaine" twenty-four times a day. "Any more memos, Blaine?" "Milk with your coffee, Blaine?" "Can I schedule a tee time for you, Blaine?" "Does your stapler need a refill, Blaine?" What if he asked me to call him Mr. Slater? I dumped my decaf coffee and filled up with a double of the hard stuff. Sometimes caffeine gave me a better outlook.

I organized my desk in mock unity with Cecilia. I'd promised to have a better attitude if I got to stay on. Of course, I figured staying on would involve a promotion. Nevertheless, I'm still here, and the attitude should be adjusted. In one of her loops through my part of the hallway, Cecilia stalled. Her thin loon neck craned to see me through the crack in the door. I was unwinding paper clips to clean out croissant crumbs from my keyboard.

"Oh, good," she yelled, too strung out on adrenaline to adjust her volume.

"Pretty resourceful, huh?" I replied, feeling casual with her. Like two people who have faced tragedy together, we were oddly linked. We were chums. That, and I still had a "whatcha gonna do to me now" mind-set. Oh, silly Libby...I would find out.

"I will have maintenance take care of the little things, Libby. Your time would be better spent packing your personal belongings."

"Excuse me?" Hey, amnesia woman! If you'll recall, I'm one who remained after the corporate rapture. Remember?

"Well, the computer and work files will stay for your replacement. You need only move your personal things to the cubicle across from Blaine's office. I guess I should've mentioned that last week. But then, how long could it take to set up a cubicle? Like a minute?" Cecilia snorted her condescension.

"Cubicle?" I wasn't really asking. And I didn't want the word to be spoken again, so I filled the vacuum created by the force of bad news with words. Any words. "Oh, yes. Cubicle. Thought you said *cuticle* and I could not figure out what you meant. I thought you were confusing me with your manicurist again. Like my first day here...remember that? That sure was fun back then. Five years ago when I started the account executive training program and thought (shrill laughter) that it led to actually *being* an account executive." I held my belly in a faux Santa laughter pose.

She was already down the hall. I lost her somewhere around cuticle. I hadn't even insulted her.

A total waste of courage.

I sat back down and surveyed my wonderful, little office. Sure, "small, dark" office in previous descriptions, but suddenly it had the charm and potential of a Soho loft. I could put up mirrors along the south wall reflecting a potted plant garden on the north side. That mural of Marilyn Monroe I have always wanted would be painted in the far east corner and bleed onto the ceiling for a three-dimensional look.

And...dang.

I used the paper clip to carve Cecilia's home number and direct line to her suite at the Desert Rehab Center into my small, dark desk with smooth, self-locking wooden drawers complemented by charming pewter deco handles and matching slender metal legs, and...dang.

My personal belongings consisted of a PalmPilot, which I didn't know how to use, a piece of red licorice, a special pen I'd bought for my one-year-on-the-job anniversary gift (I thought it'd be used to endorse my first check reflecting a big raise. Instead, its first usage was to write Cecilia's cell phone number in the men's bathroom at the King metro station), and a photo of me and Ariel sitting on the coffee bar at Elliott Bay. Ariel had written "Girls with a latte to offer" on the blackboard-finish frame.

It did not escape my attention that there was no photo of Angus to gather and transport. My mind rewound to "I second that demotion" and I shivered. Photo placement of a guy in a business setting was unthinkable unless one was very serious.

Or very desperate.

Marsha Whitefield, now a mere cubicle over, placed a photo on her desk after one kiss...or even before. The shot was always taken by surprise attack (just like the kiss, I presumed) on a first date; you could tell, because the guy was...well, still with her. Mystery date of the month was usually framed within the doorway to Marsha's apartment, upon arrival, and looking very surprised or angry to be greeted by the flash of a Minolta.

Here I had a willing guy. A decent guy who looked good in his uni-hue, death-of-a-Garanimal outfit. But I would never pin snapshots of our good times on my bulletin board. With that sobering assessment of my lackluster love life, I grabbed my roller chair and trundled down the hall to the professional equivalent of a permanent time-out corner.

Would my future ever involve a strategic, intentional forward move?

Six

Ariel sat crouched on my stoop. Her long blue-black hair draped her face as she leaned over to paint her toenails. When she looked up and saw me, she let out a "Whoop! Whoop!" and raised a grocery bag containing ingredients for her Fiesta Night Spéciale.

She gave me a quick hug and we headed up to my apartment, where she patiently listened to my confessions of suckiness. I curled up in my papasan chair, positioned in the doorway of the kitchen so I could watch her cook enchiladas.

"Extra peppers?" I whimpered between contemplation and confession.

"Sure, hon, sure." Somehow she never sounded condescending.

"Maybe...maybe extra lime and cilantro too?" I was reverting to sick days home from grade school when I could request any television show and exactly how much chocolate I wanted in my glass of cold milk. Of course, it was our beloved nanny, Charlotte, who squeezed in that extra shot of Hershey's. I smacked my lips recalling the childhood beverage bliss and anticipating the adult version. The blender finished grinding a special concoction, and then Ariel topped off our drinks with lime wedges and swizzle sticks.

For the next couple of hours we gorged ourselves, laughed, and tossed around the rubber ball I used to exercise my wrists to avoid carpal tunnel at the ripe ol' age of thirty. I recounted my week over and over, partly because I forgot what I'd told her and partly because she kept asking the same questions over and over. Even in the fog of gluttony, I questioned myself. I wanted to be free desperately, but from what?

"It's not too much to ask is it?" I asked vaguely.

"What was the question?"

"I worked hard and followed their rules for five years. That should be honored, right? A plus B equals C. We all learned that equation. Shouldn't they follow it?"

"They?"

"The big corporate, own the world, run our peon lives 'they.'"

"Ah, yes. I vote yes. But do they take votes?"

I pointed to her. "You have just pinpointed the cause of the problem. No, they don't take votes or ask for opinions."

"So in the past twenty-four hours you lost a job, were assigned a new one, and had a major blow out with Angus. You realized that you have been faking your way through life and that you are kept from your purpose because other people won't follow the formula. Does that cover it?" Ariel had her feet up in the air cycling. She said it would help her body process her food and drink more quickly, thus easing her bulging belly. I sensed she was getting more sick with each push of the pedal.

"Yes. That about...oh, and I scared a little boy. Not entirely intentional, which should count for something." I said this from my upright position on my Pier 1 settee.

"Right. You scared an innocent. And your summation...you suck. That is a bit harsh. You did have quite a blow, did you not? All of the bad behavioral issues relate to that one important fact. It really cancels out the evil behavior. Let's just focus on the positive. You go first." She had slowed her pedaling while talking. At one point, she lost her rhythm and was pedaling both feet in the same direction.

"This could be happening to shake me out of my routine. I was beyond bored with the job I had."

"Right. Right. Good. Keep going."

"Well, with a demotion I won't have a more responsible, stressful job."

"Bravo. Bravo."

"Or the extra money that goes with such responsibility and stress."

"Positive only, please."

"I decided to start figuring out who I am and what life I'm supposed to lead." I braided the fringe on my afghan—a gift from my grandmother for my college graduation. It was brown and orange and quite horrific, but under certain circumstances the wavy lines were like a Diaper Dan dress up doll. I tied bows with the yarn. I followed the squiggles with my finger. I poked my thumb through the stitches. It was comforting.

"And..."

"Um...and...my friend Ariel came over to take care of me."

"And..."

"Stop resorting to the expensive psychiatrist response. Or what I affectionately call 'a dialogue with Mother.' So that is it. That is enough information for now. Besides, it is almost time for the *Dick Van Dyke Show*. I'm still getting my neighbor's cable for some reason."

"Can't we watch something intended for our generation?"

"I love old television shows on cable. They're timeless. Please tell me you plan to stay over tonight?"

"I plan to stay over tonight." Ariel reeled in her long slender legs and hugged them momentarily before lying on the floor straight out, like a child preparing to do snow angels. Then she started snoring.

I tossed the afghan on her and put a sweatshirt under her head. I read my aunt's email one more time and tried to focus on the positive aspect of the last twenty-four hours. Aunt Maddie would call this heartache "growing pains." And I could almost hear her throaty Lauren Bacall-ish voice telling me that everything was going to be okay. "Life always hurts when it's about to become something more." This imagined conversation made me feel better.

I didn't make it till the *Dick Van Dyke Show*. But I did dream that Cecilia and Angus tried to strangle me with an afghan, and Albert strummed his guitar in the background while Dick Van Dyke, Mary Tyler Moore, and Elvis crooned, "Don't fence me in...."

Dressed in my favorite black linen pantsuit, I devoured scrambled eggs with Tabasco as my "meet the new boss" breakfast on Friday. Protein firepower.

In past years I downed a shot of Nyquil fifteen minutes before a review session to calm my nerves, but ended up drooling and unable to accurately write down Cecilia's bizarre comments. Accuracy would be vital for either a harassment lawsuit or a tell-all memoir. But that didn't matter now. I ran out of Nyquil, and I got demoted. Saved by bad luck all around.

My foot up the corporate ladder had turned to a shove down the "thanks for playing" slide. My only hope was to dictate my role in this new work relationship. I would not be seduced by anyone's casting couch invitation for an empty-headed gofer. I wouldn't be intimidated by Mave, Cecilia, and most definitely not by Blaine.

I created even bigger hair with extra-hold spray, I tightened my bra strap by an extra notch for lift and hold, and I forced high heels onto my wide feet accustomed to the roaming luxury of flats. Even though this revved-up version of me seemed entirely right for the aforementioned couch on the way to the aforementioned role…it was my attempt to be larger than life. The look had to be very, very intentional.

As I stepped over Ariel's crumpled body on my floor she awakened with a snort. "What's wrong? What? This bed hurts." She propped herself up on her elbows.

"You slept on my floor last night. I'm heading into work early. I left some coffee in the pot for you."

"Holy cow, it's *you*." She shook her head to catch up with the moment. "You look like you just stepped out of *Working Girl*, Libby. Pre-corporate makeover, in case you thought that was a compliment. All you need are tennis shoes." Sitting up and instantly perky, she said, "Don't you try for a good first impression when meeting a new boss?"

"What are you saying, exactly?"

"What *exactly* are you overcompensating for?"

I pointed to the coffeepot one more time and headed for the door. Without turning around I yelled, "I'm being intentional."

Sure, my efforts *could* be misconstrued as overcompensating for a lack of confidence, yet it was the opposite. I had confidence. Confidence that I would fail miserably when in the presence of strong personalities. And this was sure to be such a gathering. I could hold my own with intelligent, on task, focused people. I fancied I was one of them. But when my opposition included beings who transformed into super antiheroes with underworld powers too horrible to imagine, I became the damsel in distress without a caped savior in sight.

It never failed in these scenarios. The "others" plotted morale ruin via the exchange of disturbing tirades and opinions warped by too many "I love myself" weekend encounters, while my mind filled with sarcastic comebacks. But my lips stayed tightly pressed, refusing to voice my views. I was silent except in important, personal matters, like placing crystals on guitar straps.

The 7:00 AM bus placed me at the office nice and early. Maybe if I took my time getting my coffee, organizing my cubicle, and practicing my breathing, I would come across as sharp and centered. But I wasn't really sure how to prepare for a meeting in which I would be discussed in third person.

In the light of early morning, my clean, fresh-start cubicle was almost pleasant. A new beginning was a new beginning, right? I didn't need to keep harping on the fact that I was moving backward. I didn't even let myself get upset when I walked by my former small, dark office and saw several members of the janitorial staff scrubbing it down like a scene from *Silkwood*.

That could have been offensive.

But in this moment of possibility I felt great. I think a new beginning gives off a certain exciting energy. And this beginning read like *more*.

I was so busy fantasizing about what my new life might look like that I barely noticed the other employees filing into their assigned stalls. Marsha Whitefield peered over the cubicle wall. She was now one very thin half-wall away. Lord, help me. We were of…the same status.

Ouch.

So what if at one silly point in time my path intersected with Marsha's. I'd be moving on. "Hey, Marsha." I squinted up at her. The fluorescent lights were atrocious. I'd used a desk lamp back when I had an…ah, well.

"Welcome. Hope you like the neighborhood. It's not really so bad. Rachel and I have a pretty good time here on death row."

Well, that was kinda funny. Rachel was on the other side of me. I knew she was smart and sarcastic. Maybe this would be fun. I'd been secluded in my…you know what…and said I liked it that way, but this was starting to feel fine.

"Morning, all." Cecilia's falsetto cheer rang out in the hallway. Her office was the length of three cubicles. Thank goodness her windows ended at Rachel's space. It was dangerous to be in her line of vision when her eyes began to roam anxiously, ready to hone in on someone to torture, humiliate, or toy with while her nails dried.

Surprisingly I felt my face blush as Cecilia glanced my direction on her way to greet Mave at the front desk. She looked startled to see me in a cubicle, and then an "ah…yes" purr escaped her throat. "Meet us in the conference room in an hour, Libby."

My reaction sickened me. It was as if I were embarrassed by my demotion. As if I had let *her* down.

I finished straightening my few items and practiced reaching for the intercom—a feature and action that came with assistantdom. It reminded me of playing library with my childhood friend Kim…calling one another with her little brother's Fisher Price phone and marking the inside pages of books with my parents' inked address stamps and commenting, "This one is due in two weeks. You may return it during library hours or use our outside box after hours." *Then* we happened to do this with actual library books of my mother's.

As Mother wrote a check to purchase the $200 worth of books she was referencing to teach Psych 420 "Psychosis and You," we sat with our backs straight, our feet dangling over the crimson red, cobalt blue, and yellow gold Turkish rug in our family study. She tapped her foot and kept shaking her head with disappointment as she gave a one-hour lecture on respecting the property of others and about how as women (we were eight) we should aspire to owning libraries or to creating scientific data and great literature to fill them…we did not have to assume the role of a mere librarian.

I had nodded, understanding my mother was a snob. Or at best, misinformed.

She concluded her sermon and the silence filled us with hope that we were about to be freed. Grinning, she scribbled out IOUs on our behalf. We each owed her $100 before we reached age twelve. That was the most time she could give us. My practical young mind noted that this was the most time Mother had given me in weeks. Her going rate for interaction with a daughter was apparently $100 an hour. For months after, Kim and I played office instead of library—we were corporate executives discussing plots to take over each other's cosmetic empires (nanny Charlotte watched daytime soaps). We'd close our scenarios by exchanging IOUs and saying, "Due at the end of the month! That's all the time I can give you." We laughed hysterically.

The walk down Mommy Dearest lane made my left eye twitch. I massaged the outer corner gently. It was then that the intercom came to life with an unnatural buzz. I reached for the button and used my best corporate executive voice to communicate with Philip, the receptionist. "Yes?"

"Libby, there's a delivery here for you, sent over via messenger." His elf-like voice sounded as though it traveled via tin-can-on-a-string technology.

"Something for Blaine already? Guess it had to start sometime." I would trot right on over there. I would walk the corridor of assistant-like duties. So it began.

"Uh, no. It's for you actually."

I walked down the hallway and turned left into the alcove. Philip sat at attention on a bar stool on the other side of the reception desk, his birdish appearance making his perch all the more comical. He jutted his headset-covered chin forward with each new call. I cocked my head sideways to take in this strange creature for a moment.

It was then that I saw Cecilia from the corner of my eye. She was laughing—mouth wide open. A hearty horsy laugh—the kind that accidentally comes out when one is in the presence of a handsome man who cripples one's composure.

Cecilia and Mave were a giggling, matronly pair of bookends wedging in a wondrous display of Armani-covered shoulders. Crisp white cuffs appeared as a tan hand smoothed black, slightly curly hair. A gesture, I noted, done seemingly out of discomfort rather than vanity. The elevator opened and they stepped in and turned around. Just as I was about to see his face, Mavis stepped in front of Mr. X and pushed the button for the twentieth floor, the top of the building and the last of the five floors controlled by Reed and Dunson. The door closed and my mouth opened.

"Who...who exactly..."

"Blaine..."

"Geez, where?" I ducked slightly and stepped to the side looking down the hall.

"*That* was Mr. Slater going up to the conference room. They asked me to remind you to join them in about 50 minutes," he said. And then he added, "Nicely put together."

"You can say that again." I was thinking about how a broad-shouldered man seemed so secure, so solid, when I noticed Philip's look of disgust. He was commenting on the package. Was it obvious that I hadn't been?

"Er...I mean, indeed it is." I looked down at the little box wrapped with yellow and pink paper and tied with spring green ribbon. A piece of parchment paper was scrolled up and looped through the bow. I unfolded the tiny sheet and was jolted a bit by the handwriting I knew so well. *You were right. But so was I...the blue matches your eyes. Good luck with the job. —A.* Lying in tissue were the crystals Angus had purchased at the market. He had affixed earring loops to the hooks. They really were beautiful. Little prisms of color shot across the wall and ceiling as I lifted them to eye level.

For the second time this morning my face blushed out of shame. My boyfriend sends me a gift, and I'd been caught pondering another man, and not just any man, but the one who'd be my boss, the one who'd never know that I was a bright, promising executive-in-training with a future. Clients had raved about my job performance, my instinct, my creativity. But rumors of my past would not fall upon his perfect ears. This man would only know me as the assistant with a sharp tongue and a chip on her shoulder.

And the man who sent me this gift would never know my future. Angus and I had reached a fork in the rocky road of dating. The arrow toward dissolution flashed in neon.

I returned to my desk, pinned the crystal earrings to my bulletin board as a substitute for the happy photos, and wrote a goal on my calendar: "Libby accepts her new position with grace and shines as a stellar assistant." My mother would wish herself dead and then turn in her grave if she knew how low my goals could go.

Seven

Philip tweeted into the intercom. "They want you upstairs."

Amazing-suit man wanted me.

"Could you inform them that I'm on my way, Philip?" I was already stepping into a role. My mental pendulum swung from paranoid flunky to arrogant sophisticate.

"They didn't request a summary report of your activity, as fascinating as it is." he responded, so very aware of my demotional status.

As I swung by the main desk and awaited the elevator I casually sauntered over to his laminate receptionist bar. "Philip, the only reason I wanted you to call them again was so you could show how efficient you are. I'm headed up there as part of the In-House Efficiency Task Force, and there are five more positions to be...well, taken care of. But who knows? Some of the remaining employees might decide to step down on their own. There might not even be a need for force...er...task force." I whipped around as the ding of the elevator marked my words.

Stepping into the elevator, reliving that dreadful day and the subsequent in-elevator revelation just a mere week ago, I focused my mind on my personal mission to be the real me. I had to go into this potentially threatening meeting with a mental list of what I wanted to get out of it. And I had four floors to figure it out.

More. I thought of the key word and saw it pop over my head like a Sesame Street lesson. But what does More look like? I quickly pulled a photo of Aunt Maddie out of my day planner. She was smiling—glowing, really—beneath a baseball cap and held a young boy on her slim hip as her other hand rested on the shoulder of the boy's mother. They stood in front of a makeshift medical clinic. On the back she'd written, "I can't believe God gave me a second chance to live such a life. My love to you, dear Libby."

There was real joy in this image. How many photos were taken every day where forced smiles feigned joy for a captured moment?

Captured. That is how I felt. But how does one break free from captivity? Whatever happened in this meeting, I needed to resist rocking the boat. Until I figured out an alternative plan, this job was my lifeline. Sure, there were plenty of other PR agencies in Seattle, but there were now more than fifteen very qualified PR people from Reed and Dunson out hitting the pavement. The idea of searching for a job instead of searching for my purpose seemed not only daunting but counterproductive.

"More. More. More." I sang as the elevator door opened and my eyes linked with those of Blaine.

"I'm afraid you've run out of floors." He reached to block the elevator doors from shutting in on me, as I had not moved a muscle. His sudden movement scared me and I nearly fell off of my high heels.

He pulled back, startled. The doors closed. I couldn't recall the steps involved to open elevator doors. I started to go back down.

God, help me. Really. This is not a great start.

This time the doors opened to Philip. And *he* looked embarrassed. "I just called to say you were on your way like you requested. Cecilia said...to send you back up."

My smile was meek. I looked like a buffoon, and in front of Philip. "Dang elevator!" To emphasize my nonpoint, I hit the steel doors with my flat hand. When one is in the midst of extreme humility, it is best to pass blame to inanimate objects.

Philip returned the meek smile. He looked scared of me, but no longer because of my charade of power, but because of my display of abnormal behavior. He pushed the up button for me and waved. "B-bye" he faltered, flapping to the moron.

I waited. Flustered.

Ding.

Blaine appeared once again before my very eyes. He sort of crouched down low and leaned slightly away from me, like a fireman coaxing a frightened woolly ram from a rocky, dangerous cliff. I had seen this on *Real Animal Rescues*. I stepped forward on shaky legs. I could be heading into the slaughterhouse at this point, but at my pathetic level of function, I went ahead and followed my Armani-caped savior.

"Libby, I hope we didn't inconvenience you," Cecilia said snidely.

I decided not to comment. My eyes scanned for strategic seating. If I sat by Cecilia, she could dig her nails into my arm and say things like, "Be a doll and get me some more coffee." I headed for the seat by Blaine. He stood to pull a chair out for me.

I didn't know where it came from, but a lie emerged from my mouth. "I returned to Philip's desk because I left my pen downstairs. You know, Cecilia, this pen you gave me when I made assistant account executive is still my favorite after all these years."

The comment worked. Cecilia had no recollection of *not* giving me the pen, so she looked at me fondly and glowed with false admission of a sweet gesture. And in a quick comment, I'd made it clear to Blaine that I wasn't a secretary. From the corner of my eye, I saw him nodding respectfully. Was he holding back a smile?

I kept my glance on him too long and Cecilia noticed. "Stick with us, Libby. You don't want Mave to rethink her decision to keep you on board, do you?"

Blaine sat up and looked startled by such a comment, causing Cecilia to rescind her meanness. "I meant that I don't want Mave to rethink it. I believe you are a fine choice to serve under Blaine. I'm glad we kept you."

If she was waiting for a thank-you from me, it wasn't happenin'.

Mave opened a folder loudly to command our wandering attention. "Shall we?"

"Yes, Mave. Please. Please." Cecilia motioned her approval with her coffee cup saluted toward the professionally acceptable hit woman.

"Libby, your new position as assistant to the account executive vice president will be considerably different than your previous position. You had a lot of autonomy before. More than your post should have allowed for." Mave offered up a bit of a reprimand to Cecilia, who was staring at Blaine unabashedly.

"In short, your freedoms will be reduced, but your job expectations and requirements will increase. You might hear the word 'assistant' and think it is below your level, when in fact it will be more work and more accountability without many of the perks you enjoyed in the past."

"It's a good thing you don't write our promotional copy," I said before I could censor myself. My hand flew to my mouth, too little too late. Blaine laughed quietly. Mave did not.

"I'm sorry," I explained, "but the description sounds so serious."

"This is serious, Libby. I'm not here to sell you on this job. I'm here to paint the picture, the real picture, of what your responsibilities will be at Reed and Dunson from now on. Don't consider this job change to be your ticket to easy street around here."

"Believe me, that's as far away from my interpretation as one could get. What past perks are you talking about, exactly?" Try as I might, I couldn't imagine what they considered a perk. Free toilet paper all day? My "buy 10, get 1 free" coffee card did get extra punches because I bought Cecilia two lattes a day. I'd be sad to lose that.

Mave tapped her fingernails on the table and searched lower on the piece of paper in front of her. "It says here you received two weeks of vacation. Of course, with the job change you won't have that."

"That much, you mean," I said, correcting the ending of her sentence.

"No. You won't have that benefit. Not for two years."

"No vacation for two years? How..."

"You'll be required to practice a new skill set, or perhaps an old one that will need polishing and perfecting. Are you prepared for what this means?"

"I do," I said without thinking.

Cecilia stifled her laugh and Mave furrowed her brow.

"What does this mean exactly?" I asked.

Mave returned her gaze to the folder. "Your areas of weakness will be evaluated by Blaine Slater." She paused, nodded to Blaine, and continued.

"And a plan of action will be created. Job seminars, course work, job shadowing, perhaps."

"Job shadowing?" I envisioned myself walking five paces behind Philip, taking notes, while he gloated with a grin that pulled his red cheeks to his elfin ears.

"We may have another assistant within the corporation mentor you so that you can see how Reed and Dunson prefers its assistants to be and to work," she explained.

"Broken and without compensation" my mind hollered. It's not enough to be demoted, I have to be demoted and told I'm not qualified for the post.

Mave interpreted my expression perfectly. "Maybe we should be asking Ms. Hawthorne if she accepts this position. I'd assumed Cecilia discussed the implications fully and asked you this important question."

With my stomach churning and my hands shaking, I said, "I accept this position." I could turn this in to a positive. The worse the job is, the more motivated I will be to make a change for the better.

Blaine cleared his throat. "If I might comment?"

Both women purred.

"I have looked at your file, Libby." Blaine turned in his chair toward me. "And you are quite qualified, more than qualified, for this position. We will discuss your skill set at greater length later. Today I have meetings back to back, but I'll spend time with you on Monday first thing."

"I'll bet she can't hem pants," Cecilia sneered.

Mave turned to her cohort and shook her head.

I looked over at Cecilia with awe. Even she usually knew when to keep her true nature to herself. Something Mave said was flashing in my mind. She called Blaine the new account executive vice president. That was Cecilia's position.

"May I ask...what is Cecilia's title?"

Everybody raised their eyebrows at this question. I wanted to take it back.

Mave responded, "The announcement has not been made, so of course you must keep this confidential, but later this week Cecilia will be honored with the position of Executive Director of Accounts."

Cecilia stared at the large diamond-and-emerald ring on her right hand.

I wasn't the only one affected by the corporate shift.

"Congratulations, Cecilia," I said softly.

She nodded, still mesmerized by her jewelry and the soon-to-be past life it represented. Everyone in the room knew that the "director of" title could be translated as "a short jump to figurehead" in the language of real life. It was just a matter of time before Cecilia would be asked to represent the company only at corporate anniversary parties and when a low-level client that nobody could be bothered with needed a companion for dinner or a ride to the airport.

With a little relief and a surprising amount of compassion I realized that the shame I'd been feeling earlier wasn't truly mine, but was Cecilia's.

Eight

On Saturday Ariel called around noon to be sure I wasn't wearing the purple silk shirt we both had purchased at Nordstrom's anniversary sale. I assured her I only saved it for nights out in nonsmoking environments. We, along with Ferris and our friend Oliver Weston, were going to the Below-Zone club to watch Angus perform. They were attending out of politeness, and I was attending out of girlfriend responsibility. However, as the day wore on, I knew there was another purpose for tonight.

Angus and I had barely spoken all week. On Friday I'd thanked him for the earrings and we filled silences with talk of weather, schedules, and my new job. It was almost as if...as if it were our recap conversation.

The inevitable recap takes place about the time you are no longer waking up with the solitary thought *I'm single again*. It happens just as you forget how his voice oddly dips at the end of a question. It happens when you cannot quite recall how his features fill his face and your mind recalls only a blurry flesh canvas of Picasso lips, brow, and eye. And it always occurs in some unexpected place like the noodle aisle at an Asian market or by the crosstown map at the bus station. Simultaneously you look up and overlap each other to say, "I didn't know you liked squid ramen/rode the number 35 too."

Once the irony of your bizarre crossing of paths is diffused, the illegitimate recap begins. Illegitimate because he says nothing of the nineteen-year-old Gap assistant manager he kissed in the dressing room (they hit it off so much that it *seemed* like a real date) and, of course, you forget to mention that his DVD collection was sold at your apartment's swap meet to pay for your new leather jacket.

And as you walk away from the always-a-letdown recap, either relieved it is over or freshly brokenhearted, you realize afresh that you are indeed single. How is it that life happens that way?

I pulled myself out of this melancholy scene. I didn't shake it completely, though. I had seen the future, and I knew it. I began scouring my closet for a good breakup dress. I couldn't spend time searching for my life truth *and* striving for significance in a relationship that had been doomed from the start. We argued so much about whether we were too alike or too different that we forgot to discuss who we actually were.

The one photo I had of Angus and myself rested on my dresser. Angus' friend Johann took the photo at a street fair last year. I was wearing a summer dress that resembled maternity wear, and we were eating from the same spindle of cotton candy. I selected the same dress for tonight. I could say goodbye to the dress and to Angus in one shot. I slipped the dress over my head and was horrified when the tentlike frock had to be maneuvered carefully to fit over my hips. Lesson learned: Never make fun of how plump you looked in an older photo until you have evaluated your current size and look.

I put on a black cardigan sweater and the Pike Market crystal earrings as I went down the stairs of my apartment to the cab waiting on the street. I didn't know if the earring thing was a cruel gesture or a sentimental one. That is how little I knew myself. Sentimental or sadistic? I had them on and off about four times on my way to the club.

Angus had been trying to set up a gig for months at this bar in Belltown. Then out of the blue he got a call for his band to stand in for some LA band that got the lucky call to stand in for the band replacing The Cure at some major environmentalist shindig. For the past week Angus mentioned this three degrees of separation from The Cure about every other conversation. No doubt, they were bragging it up as well.

Below-Zone was starting to fill up with confused music fans. Some had misunderstood Angus and thought he was opening for The Cure. Others were die-hard fans of the punk band that was originally slated. But they were warm bodies, albeit dressed in hip-hugging leather and sporting pink spiky hair, and with a couple beers their discerning tastes only required loud music. Angus was good at loud—on stage lamenting rage and failure or at home with me expressing angst. He was in a constant state of regret. Once when I gently confronted him about it, he thought for quite a long time, and then loudly said it gave him edge. Not "an edge" but *edge,* as though he meant adrenaline. He'd been pleased with his response all evening while I daydreamed of showing him the edge of the ledge.

Ariel was waving frantically from a tall bistro table toward the far back corner right behind a big speaker. Ferris and Oliver were with her already. They had probably selected the seating arrangement...we would vibrate all evening but we'd be able to hear each other talk. I was surprisingly calm about my plan for tonight as I walked over to my friends. The breakup seemed out of my control yet fully in it. I rarely had this kind of feeling and was afraid I'd never have it again unless I honored it.

"I see the fan club positioned itself well away from the stage." I greeted Oliver with a real kiss on the cheek and Ferris with a simulation.

"We're here for you, aren't we?" Ferris pushed my chair in behind me. "And why is it that Oliver always gets a real kiss and I get blown off?"

"Because she has seen you scrub a toilet. There is no romance potential anymore," Ariel matter-of-factly stated, hailing a bald waitress.

"Exactly." I choked on my gum, laughing. Getting out tonight was what I needed.

"What'll it be?" The waitress-and-charm-school dropout hollered from two tables away. A table overflowing with grunge-ites blocked her path to us.

"Just Coke please. With lime," I said to a round of strange looks from my friends.

"Since when?"

"Can't a woman change the way she lives?"

"Cokes all around. And the appetizer platter," Oliver yelled to the unenthused waitress, who saw her potential tips for the evening take a sharp, carbonated dive.

Ariel drummed the table along with the opening band's beat. I hoped my pals would not bash Angus the entire time. They liked him as a person but accused his music of being high decibel without a cause.

"Before the big show begins, I have good news to share," Oliver announced, pushing his bangs away from his dark brown rimmed glasses. "I've been invited to be a part of an exhibit and fund-raiser event for the Seattle Art Museum. They are highlighting local talent. A good public relations move for them and a great opportunity for me."

"We'll be there. How great, Oliver," Ariel said, cheering on our friend.

"It's about time they thought of you," I added.

Ariel nudged Ferris. He looked up slowly. "Their shows are probably too commercial for your latest work."

"I'll be showing my photographs. Those seem tame enough for the after-5:00 office crowd," Oliver conceded.

"Never mind Ferris, Oliver. He is still mourning Tanya," Ariel said.

Our waitress arrived with a platter of greasy food in various forms and four large Cokes, all with sections of lime and red straws.

"It's officially over?" I asked. "When did this happen?"

Ferris held the ice cubes under the surface of his Coke with his finger, squinted his eyes, and thought for a moment before responding. "No talking for a month. Is that official enough? She sent her Neanderthal brother to pick up some books I borrowed from her. Is that official enough?"

"Tanya owned books?" I asked. Everyone but Ferris laughed.

Ferris was a cynic on any given day, but when you add on broken-hearted, he was a complete downer. I was curious how Tanya broke the news and the heart, but I didn't figure he'd appreciate my impromptu research survey right then.

"Hey, where is Pandora 'Princess of the Pack' these days?" Oliver asked, noticing that our third femme fatale was missing. Pandora Garrett was a former high school pal of Ariel's, who entered our motley circle a couple years ago when she returned from New York to produce for a Seattle documentary company. Her "princess of the pack" identity emerged when she became the designated yuppy-puppy dumping ground among our network of friends and acquaintances. She took in the dogs that couples adopted to practice their parenting skills and then ditched when either a baby or an animal services representative arrived. The marriage counselors who suggested this great plan seemed to forget that they were talking to workaholic urbanites with tiny, expensive apartments and no time to spend with each other, let alone a dependent dog.

Pan was the only person anyone knew who owned a house (thanks to a kind, dead uncle) with a real backyard. She started by taking Baxter, an adorable hound dog, after our friends Milton and Katrina got pregnant. Then came Wendell, the Dalmatian my sister adored when she first decorated her house in art deco. He was the first color-coordinated accessory to go when the kids arrived. Last count, Pandora was up to five dogs and three cats, and she was in a constant state of pandemonium keeping up with vet appointments and dog walking.

"You reminded her about it, right?" I asked Ariel.

"One of the dogs was sick with worms or something. Or a fungus. Something unsuitable for table discussion," she muttered.

I looked over at her. She and Pan had had a big fight recently, but nobody would fill me in. Neither one was a game player, so I knew it was a serious dispute. Ariel asked me about my work meeting. She was ending any further discussion about Pan. "I think I held my own," I responded, letting her off the hook for the time being.

"Are you still in your I-stink mode?" Ariel asked.

"Basically, yes." I pondered my agenda for tonight. "Angus will soon think so."

"Uh-oh. I wondered why you were wearing the *Little House on the Prairie* number. It had to be full-blown depression or a breakup tactic. Hmm?" Ariel looked me over. I laughed. She had pegged the style exactly.

"You're breaking up tonight?" asked Ferris with obvious anger, apparently ready to draw a sword in haste to keep yet another wench from destroying a good man.

I shrugged off his bitterness.

Oliver leaned in. "Okay, lass, tell us the story."

"We aren't headed anywhere. We barely get along. I mean, we appreciate one another, but we're starting to tear one another down on a regular basis. It isn't healthy."

"It isn't healthy? Meaning you are bored or you have found someone more interesting." Ferris was ready for a fight.

My mind flashed to Blaine. I shook my head like an Etch-a-Sketch to clear it. "Ferris, this isn't a good conversation to be entering into with you right now."

"I find it utterly disgusting that women think the end of a relationship does not warrant an advance conversation with a guy." He made the motion of washing his hands. "The end is just something to take care of. Broke a heart. Done." He motioned as if crossing off a shopping list item. "Women have blamed guys for this same nonchalant demeanor. It is a total double standard. Women are two-faced." In silence we awaited his next mime interpretation, but he gave no further performances.

"We still don't like guys who do that," Ariel countered, strong chin out.

I gave her a disapproving look. "Thanks for the help."

Ferris looked away, disgusted. I knew he thought Angus and I made a bad match, but his wounds were so raw he wanted an argument more than he wanted to be right. I left it alone, glad to hear the band announced. I hadn't even noticed the opening act, though they definitely were strong competition for the loud portion of tonight's affair.

"What's this?" Ariel said with disgust as she pulled a patch of fuzz from the weave of my sweater.

Ferris and Oliver both said, "Eww."

I thought for a moment. "I think I last wore this at Pan's house. That looks like..." I paused to examine the feline fur. "Rafael. He's the long-haired one, right?"

"I assure you I have no idea." Ariel took a deep breath and exhaled slowly. "Libby, even secondhand cat hair can kill a girl's dating life."

"Better stick with Angus," Ferris said with a grunt.

My headache was in full swing. I excused myself to the restroom. The swinging door to the women's bathroom opened to a black-and-purple interior with a slanted ceiling. Rummaging through my purse for my travel pack of aspirin, I barely gave notice to the leggy blonde in fishnet stockings leaning over the sink until I felt her stare in my direction.

I stopped digging and looked up. She had blond hair on one side of her part and black on the other. It was rather stunning, so I stared back.

"Aren't you Angus'?"

"His?"

"Girl."

I nodded, even though I wanted to argue that Angus didn't own me.

"I'm Karina. I was his before you. Well, a couple before you, actually." She leaned in closer to the fogged up mirror and applied black eye liner—around her mouth. She had to stop for a second as she let out a short laugh. "Does he still talk with an English accent when he makes love?"

"He only speaks in ancient Chinese proverbs," I said and turned to leave. The truth was, I had no idea. I kept Angus at a distance. Some self-protective part of me knew I was kidding myself by trying out this alternative life. I may have walked into the bathroom uncertain, but I was full of resolve when I returned to the table as Angus and his band started in on their playlist. I would follow through.

Oliver headed out prior to the encore, saying he had some matting to do for the upcoming show. That was being gracious. The guy who frequented jazz clubs would rather pick his nose with a shoehorn than listen to this music longer than necessary.

Ferris stood quickly at the finish, saying he didn't want to stick around for the postgame show…meaning my postshow agenda. Ariel leaned down to my ear and said, "He'll get over it before I host your fabulous birthday party. Just a couple weeks away, right? I'll call you tomorrow to see how this all goes. Be strong." She then headed out with Ferris.

I waited at the end of the bar and watched as women of various shapes and ages approached the band members. The power of a guitar and a torn T-shirt was fascinating to watch. To these women, Angus was an artist filled with deep dark places and sensitivity that only the right woman could understand. If only the swooning multipierced girls knew he had a poster of *Knight Rider* on his wall and collected Goofy paraphernalia (not as in that is my opinion of it…but as in Disney).

Angus broke away after he noticed me waiting. "You got a nice pair there, lady…" He pointed to my earrings. I didn't offer up a comeback.

"Hey, great show," I said instead, hugging him tightly.

"Thanks for coming, Libby. You look nice. I haven't seen that dress in a while."

He noticed.

"Hey, babe, I know I had talked about us heading out together, but…"

I would not miss "babe" at all.

"I'm really beat…and still kinda hyped at the same time." He was trying to get out of our date tonight. This was the end. "I know you hate it when I'm revved like this. A few of us are just going to stay here in the bar and down a few to come off of the performance high. One of the managers said I reminded him of Jude Shea tonight. Isn't that the most awesome comment?"

"You do sort of look like him." I said this out of generosity and not out of knowledge. I knew very little about the group Torrid's lead singer and guitarist other than what I'd read in the paper a year ago when he disappeared from the public eye. Angus had that in common with the star…he was definitely out of the public eye.

"No, dude. He meant I was playing like Shea. There are not many guys out there I'd ever want my artistic persona compared to. But that one I'll take."

I slapped him on the back in fine dude fashion. "Way to go then. You guys should celebrate." The bartender took away the shot glass I was spinning for a diversion. "Angus, I've been thinking about the state of our relationship."

"Washington?" He pointed a finger in a "got ya" kind of way, but there wasn't any punch behind the joke. "I'm sorry about the other day at the market. That was my fault. I guess I've been thinking quite a bit about us too. What have you been thinking?"

"That we're sort of….at the end of whatever this was." I looked down at the sticky cement floor. This bird's eye view of my floral tent dress depressed me all the more. It actually would have been better to look really hot. I knew that rule. Look fabulous when you break up with a guy. I cannot do anything right.

"Wow." I thought maybe he was shocked…maybe it had not occurred to him. But then he nodded. He wasn't surprised, but he did surprise me with his next move.

A perfect movie exit kiss. I was pressed against the bar and he knocked the breath out of me. Was this an expression of thankfulness or regret? *Just enjoy it, Libby,* I told myself. I gave myself over to our finale.

If Pan had been there, she would have zoomed in for a close up.

Libby, I thought, *this could be your last kiss for a very long time.*

Nine

After loitering on the corner outside the church for fifteen minutes trying to muster up the courage to go in and then also deciding to bypass my usual Sunday at 80 Days with Mr. Diddle, I returned to my apartment determined to use my Sunday honoring this new stage of life with an exciting, totally out of character ritual. I called it the "Little House on the Prairie cocktail," and it required the following ingredients:

> lighter fluid
> frumpy dress
> one bathtub
> a match

In the movies they do such things on a whim and in a tiny, black wire, hotel wastebasket that rages with dangerous flames. My Ms. Safety version: I mixed my bonfire in the bathtub with my trusty extinguisher by my side and my swim goggles wedged against my forehead should the flames threaten to singe my eyelashes. I was stripped down to my underwear and wore a robe in case a neighbor called the Seattle fire department. I took all the fun out of being radical. And nobody was there to witness my bravery. I would have to recount this (without mentioning the extinguisher and the two buckets of water...and the eyewear) for anyone to know I was cool.

So what if the water I had first put in the bathtub made it a short-lived thrill? There was enough flame action for me to feel rebellious. My ceiling fan did nothing to clear the air, so I threw on my sweats and climbed out on the fire escape.

I took in the significance of last night's decision. I was alone. I'd dumped my boyfriend...though that was just a technicality; we dumped each other. My head pounded and my body ached. Turned out that post-breakup pain was the physical equivalent to forty-eight hours after the Kick Boxing IV class, as though it takes every muscle you have to dislodge a person from your life. It should be painful, I reminded myself. It should matter.

The phone rang. Angus? Ariel? I really didn't want to talk to either right now. I stumbled back in to my apartment to check Caller ID. Mom. Ah, so much better. I knew she wanted to discuss my birthday gathering. Sweetly, Mom and Dad were flying up to ring in my thirty-first year.

"Hello, Mom." I knew my quick identification would bug her. A fire starter.

"I hate those caller ID things. Too much information, if you ask me. They completely take away the caller's privacy."

"Usually when a person calls another party, they're not trying to be anonymous. Unless you had planned to whisper obscenities or ask me if my refrigerator is running?"

"Why would I ask about an appliance?"

"If it's running, you'd better chase after it." I gave her the punch line from a sixth grade crank call joke. Why did I start these tangents?

"Well, at least you picked up this time."

That would be true. "So what are you up to today?"

"We were just discussing what dessert you might want for your birthday. Dad suggested parfaits. I was thinking something more like mousse. But we'll figure it out."

No "what would you like, Libby?" was offered up. I reminded myself that it was nice they were helping to plan the gathering from afar. Maybe I could use some family support right now.

"We want you to come a bit earlier than planned. Could you get to Cassie's by three on Saturday?" She was going to say something else but stopped. I wondered if she was deciding whether to ask if I planned on bringing Angus. I knew she didn't want to say his name. That could be misinterpreted as an invitation.

"Mom...um...three sounds fine. And it will just be me. Angus..."

I stopped there. I didn't know whether I should tell her about the breakup.

"Great!" She said with glee. Too much glee.

Maybe it'd make her mad—me choosing to be single. "I...broke up with him yesterday."

Pause.

I heard muffled talking. Maybe it was their poodle, Freud, choking on his nongender-specific doll.

"Mom?"

"Yes, dear. I heard you. Angus broke up with you yesterday. I'm very sorry. I was just telling..."

"*I* broke up with him, Mother."

"Right. You girls of today have learned a few things in the area of relationships." Her voice trailed.

Fine. When I'm eight I'm called a woman. Now that I'm well into child-bearing years, I get "girls." She sounded like a homemaker all of a sudden.

"But you've learned nothing in terms of asserting yourself in academia, corporate life, politics, decisions."

Ah, there was the mother I knew and failed.

"Just letting you know." This conversation was over its civil word limit.

I could hear my dad's voice in the background. More silence.

"Hey, dear." Dad's voice filled the receiver. "Your mother just wants your day to be special. And with Cass a bit preoccupied and not up to it..."

"Is she sick?" What a bad sister I am. I lived here and didn't know she was sick.

"Oh, no. No." He was flustered. "I mean...with the kids and all, she's very busy."

"I'm fine to do the whole belated birthday thing when you guys come up for Christmas."

"No deal. We're needed up there and we want to be available."

Good grief. How much trouble did they think hosting my birthday party would be for Cass? I could grab a cake and candles at a mini-mart on my way over, for Pete's sake. We said goodbye and I hung up wondering if I'd ever have a normal conversation with members of my family. "Will I ever understand any of them? Ever?" I yelled.

I felt dirty. Grungy. Time to rinse away the film of last night, this morning, and this entire past year, if possible.

"Holy cow!" I yelled when I went back to the bathroom to assess the damage of my rebellion. The once peach ceramic wall tiles were black with soot. The room still reeked. My shower curtain was shriveled up to the hooks, melted. My bar of Dial looked like rubber cement dripping down the wall.

Cleaning this would make a great Monday night activity. Today, I'd take a nap.

Ten

"Good news," Rachel said, beaming at me as I came down the hall. "Cecilia's gone for the week. An emergency with Stone and Rawlings. Seems one of their lawyers had a bizarre connection with former Enron bigwigs. She flew to Texas last night."

"I guess I won't ask how your weekend went." I imagined what it must be like to be on Cecilia's speed dial.

"Ya know...as I sent her off with a list of her top Texas media contacts and her refill of Xanax. I was a tad elated."

"You had to *take* her to the airport?" I wanted to hug her. She made my Monday that much better because *she* served Cecilia. Blaine had to be better than that. Or maybe everyone who earned more than the United States president expected such service.

"Well, she doesn't drive and she doesn't trust cabs at night. But it was so worth it to wake up this morning and know that I could deal with her via email and emergency phone calls this week. I can handle anything from a distance." Rachel looked exuberant.

"Well then, we should celebrate. Let's break for real coffee at ten. My treat..." As I was removing my coat and wondering what cubicle inhabitants did with things like coats and hats, I noticed a small present by my keyboard. Uh-oh. An Angus apology already. I looked around cautiously and buzzed Philip.

"Yes, Libby?" He was annoyingly chipper for 7:50 AM.

"Um…was there another messenger delivery for me early this morning?"

"No. Only employees can enter the front doors before eight. Should I be watching for something?" He was watching his Ps and Qs…unsure about the validity of my task force authority. I would ride that for some time.

"No, nevermind."

"Nevermind." Marsha did a Gilda Radner impersonation from the other side of the fabric-covered divider. She obviously also watched late night cable.

Okay, forget the new beginning high. Forget the good attitude. I wanted a door with a lock…a dead bolt. I waited for her to pop her head over the wall again, but apparently that was it, a one-word joke, and a one-word reminder to watch my decibel level from now on. I gave a fake laugh, not sure of the cubicle camaraderie protocol. Rachel popped up on the other side. She looked down on me and rolled her eyes with a "this is what I put up with around here" look. My real laugh presented itself.

I casually tore open the lavender paper covering the square flat box. A scarf? A wallet? An early birthday present from one of my accounts? Former accounts. I lifted the black lid to find a beautiful silver Montblanc pen with my initials engraved on it. I opened the card quickly. It seemed like such a personal, impersonal gift and certainly not something Angus would think of. My eyes skimmed to the bottom of the note.

Blaine.

My face turned red.

I surfed back to the start of the note.

> *Since I discovered how meaningful pens are to you, I thought I should at least match Cecilia's past generosity. Consider this my advance thank-you for all of the extra work that goes into working with the "new guy." I'll try to get up to speed quickly, for your sake. Sincerely, Blaine*

Nice touches. Humor. Self-deprecating. Work "with" the new guy instead of "for." He had everything just right. I rolled the pen up and down my palm. I loved it. This guy was smooth. Either he was quite kind and generous or he was buying my loyalty.

He had it. For now, anyway.

The intercom lit up, but it was a different light than Philip's.

Blaine! I put the pen back in the box and then in my drawer. I would be casual about the gift. Professionally casual. "Yes, Mr. Slater, can I help you?" I figured that was a correct response.

"Good morning, Libby. Could you come in to my office for a bit of a meeting? Just us. Bring a notepad or your PalmPilot. Whatever you use for notes."

"Yes, Mr. Slater."

PalmPilot? Did he expect me to use such tools for work purposes? I grabbed it out of my drawer and placed it on top of a clean steno pad I had nabbed from the highly guarded material resource room (supply closet to normal people). I hoped I didn't need to know shorthand. Or math? What if he asked me a math question?

His office door was open slightly, so I knocked as I went in. He was just finishing up on the phone. I looked at him while he spoke. Generous lips and eyelids, a wide but not large nose, and deep eyes. Brown? Green? It was hard to tell. I caught myself squinting and reminded myself to be respectable, so I sat down and looked intently out the window. Elliott Bay glistened in the morning sun and shadows. I shifted my glance back to the office. Rows of books—real literature, I noted—were placed on the granite shelves along the brick walls. Nicely matted black-and-white photographs of everyday things like a shoe, an umbrella, a flower in a vase were leaning against the walls awaiting a work order to be hung according to corporate code. A box of family pictures was opened and just a foot away from me. Another box held framed degrees...an MBA from somewhere, it was covered up, and a PhD in Public Policy from Chicago University. No wonder Cecilia was setting boundaries for her territory. I don't know if the Desert Rehab clinic gave out degrees, but I guessed it was the only postgraduate facility she'd attended.

When Blaine got off the phone, I pointed to his photographs. "Those are nice. I like everyday images in black-and-white."

"I'm just beginning. I started taking photographs instead of therapy."

"That's your work? It's really good. My friend Oliver will be showing his work at the Seattle Art Museum soon. You should check it out."

"Is that an invitation?"

"Absolutely. I'll send you an email about it. Oliver would love the support."

"That would be great. About now...sorry to keep you waiting. Adam isn't too excited about this move. His mom and I are trying to brainwash him about how cool Seattle is and what a great place it could be for him to hang out in the summer."

Summer? I was about to ask if he was sending Adam away to boarding school, but he continued. "Every kid struggles with change. Heck, I'm struggling with it, and I made the decision." Blaine look directly at me. I was smiling, I'm pretty sure. But he immediately shifted into a business mode while tightening his tie. "Libby, let's start with some basic communication goals and go from there."

"Sure." Sure. Now that was intelligent. "Let us, shall we?" Oh, my.

"What would be your first goal?"

Oh. I have to participate. I thought I'd be taking notes. "Well, I guess I want it...the communication." I was about to backpedal, and he could tell by my raised hand, so he interrupted.

"No, don't. That isn't too rudimentary at all. I agree. First there has to be communication. So often that is not the case in a business partnership." Partnership. I liked the sound of that lingo. Maybe what I liked was the way his eyebrow furrowed in earnestness as he said it. Maybe...

"Absolutely. It's easy to create a noncommunicative relationship without even realizing it. I should know..." I stopped there. This wasn't a therapy session.

"I agree. What do you need to feel good about communication with a team member?" He leaned forward and folded his hands together. Was there a correct answer? Now I was feeling self-conscious.

Just answer. What do I need? How often do I get asked that? Never. "I need respect. I need reasonable demands. I need room to be challenged, so I like goals but not a list of how-tos, necessarily. And...I don't want to run personal errands for you." I don't know what the equivalent to buying

Midol would be for Blaine, but I wouldn't let myself become anyone's personal shopper.

"Excellent. I guess I should be the one ready to take notes. I agree with all of those. And I expect the same in return, Libby. I've had coworkers use me before. I didn't run personal errands for them, but somehow I did end up providing corporate favors, thinking it was a matter of loyalty, and it was really about someone looking for a free ride along a path of promotion. People on my team earn their position, but they also start out with respect from day one. Only negative actions take away from it."

I was about to tell him that I was good at getting demotions without any help, but decided not to demean myself right off the bat. I liked the fact that he started out with respect as a foundation. He came across as an ethical, up-front kind of guy. He and Cecilia were going to clash bigtime. She would assume she could toy with him because he was handsome and...a man. I sensed he could hold his own.

"We are definitely on the same page then, Mr. Slater."

"Blaine. Please."

"Blaine." There. I said his name. It fell from my lips with more pleasure than I had expected. Maybe I would want to say it twenty-four times a day. Should I mention the pen yet? I wanted to thank him. He still seemed very businesslike, though.

"I suppose you heard Cecilia is in Texas. Most unfortunate timing since she and I had planned to meet for most of the week. But after thinking on it, I'm glad to have a chance to study some of the client files and get used to the flow around here. Maybe you could show me around today in place of Cecilia."

"Of course." I said the words, but then I thought about it. I wasn't Cecilia...I wasn't a partner showing another partner around. I would be a secretary showing her boss around. And I would, for the first time, have to face people in every department as an assistant. I would deal with the looks of "Oh, right...poor Libby" and have to avoid any dialogue about my change.

It was my job though. There wasn't anything wrong with his request.

He studied my face during my internal digression.

"You know what? Ken Dunson will be back in town tomorrow and is meeting me for lunch. He'll want to do the tour thing to show me the scope of his company, I'm sure. Sorry. Wasn't thinking."

I looked at my savior for a second time. He knew exactly what I was thinking. I felt very vulnerable all of a sudden. I glanced down to see if my slip was showing. He made me want to be professional. Cecilia was demanding, but only in a scary, dysfunctional way. She really didn't command excellence as much as she demanded service.

Blaine flipped through a file on his desk and raised it in front of his face. "First thing I like to do is review personnel files. The only reason I even tell you this is because your file is strong. Your reviews are excellent. Your attendance is impressive. Your extra hours reflect a strong team player...putting out when the company needs you."

Putting out. Strange wording on his part. He paused for a second...realizing something didn't sound right but not sure what.

"However, there is something in the file that I feel must have gone unnoticed in the past. And that concerns me. The information from your business program..."

Oh, no. Could Dirk's comments really be on my business file?

"I can explain that. Totally. I'm not a freak," I blurted before I could think about it. My outburst actually negated the sentence I just said.

"Wait." He held up his hand. "Though I'm curious as to what would follow that opener, I'm about to share a good thing." He laughed.

Great. My stupidity amused him. I became a bit defensive.

"I thought you were referring to...well, switching majors at such a late date in my program. That could look like I didn't know what I wanted, but I assure you that I did." That was a 9.5 recovery, at least.

"I was referring to your change, but in a good way. It seems that when you were hired, the business course work was emphasized more." He seemed almost apologetic as he tapped his fingers on the glass surface of his desk. "The fact that you switched to a more creative major tells me that maybe Reed and Dunson has been missing out on some of your strengths."

Oh.

"I don't see any mention of you serving on any of the creative teams, even though it seems you were the right-hand person on several accounts involving creative tactics."

"Yes, that's true." Cecilia liked to do all of the event planning and publicity brainstorming. It gave her an excuse to shop for inspiration or take all-day lunches for her brainstorming sessions.

"Did you prefer it this way? Maybe I spoke out of turn."

"No, I wanted the opportunity." How could I say this tactfully? "She...

Cecilia, loves a good party. I mean...she has celebration in her blood. That aspect of the overall strategy suits her."

"Well, as much as I like a good party," he said sounding more like Walter Cronkite than a true partygoer, "I like a team that uses the strengths of its members. You'll be working with me on my accounts and no longer for Cecilia's client list. And I'm bringing some accounts with me that could use some fresh perspective. Are you interested?"

"Yes." I was very excited about the idea of investing time in the creative aspects of a PR campaign instead of filling spread sheets with demographic research and strategy forecasts. And this meant that my file was clean of any Dirk mentions, or surely Blaine would have caught it.

"As I set up my schedules, I will keep your interest in mind." He handed me a printout of clients. "Could you pull these files for me today? I want to take them home with me tonight to start reviewing them. Some are reassigned from Cecilia's group, so you'll recognize them. Others are accounts that will need new files set up. They are the companies or individuals who agreed to wait on signing their previous contracts in order to join me at Reed and Dunson."

"That has to be flattering. Nobody has ever waited for me." I said that last part? Nice pathetic touch.

Blaine smiled. "I find that hard to believe."

"No, it's true." I almost started crying. What was the matter with me? Breakup blues? It couldn't be the demotion because this meeting felt better than anything I had experienced here in five years. I was actually hopeful about my career for once. Missing out on a pink slip and my golden chance to have a real job and a real vacation didn't even seem like such a bad trade-off.

I stood up to avoid showing any further emotion. The poor man was just trying to do his job, and he had to walk on eggshells around me. I decided to change the subject. "I will get right on this. Say, when will your family be joining you?"

"They were here this last weekend, actually. I wanted to ease Adam into the transition and make him part of the apartment search and all those big things. Hey, let me show you a picture of him."

Of him, but what about the little woman?

He went to the photo box and pulled out a picture of the three of them at a baseball game. At first my eyes only focused on Blaine. He was in the middle and he wore a white T-shirt that showed off a summer tan. His sunglasses were pushed up on his forehead and he had an arm around Adam. Adam. Man, he looked just like...who? Something about the baseball cap...

Dang.

My heart started beating quickly. It was the kid I frightened at the park. If not for the distraction of those binoculars, Adam would have pointed me out to Blaine and his wife! My lip quivered at the thought.

I barely glanced at his wife. She was model beautiful and perfectly tanned and toned. It only took a glance to take all that in.

"Cute!" I exclaimed with false enthusiasm.

"Thanks. He's nine. Do you have kids?"

Great. I look like someone with kids. Somehow that felt like an insult. Either because I was so very single and without any chance of getting pregnant or just because it made me feel plain old. "No. No. Definitely have been spared that."

That sounded rude. I tried again. "I mean, I just haven't gotten lucky."

Not so good. One more time.

"I mean...not lucky enough to find *the guy*, yet. You know."

"I understand." He didn't even laugh at my faux pas. "It is so cliché, but Adam really is the joy of my life. I would hate to think who I would be without him. He helped me define myself at a time when I really needed it."

I understood that. Until recently, I was waiting for something to define me. Now I was trying to define myself.

Instead I said, "By the way, thanks for the pen, Blaine. It's fantastic."

He paused and rocked back and forth, heel to toe a few times. I thought I lost him for sure, but then he uploaded again. "You're welcome. I wanted to thank you for the work involved in starting a new job, especially when you're joined with someone totally new. And also, I wanted to apologize in advance in case the life stuff gets mixed up with my work for a while."

"Life stuff?"

He motioned toward the photo. "My apartment hunt, settling into the city, that stuff. What I mean is, if this gets too..." he paused and seemed at a loss.

I tried to help him. "If this gets personal, you mean?"

His bright eyes returned and he nodded. "Exactly. We wouldn't want that."

It almost seemed as though he was asking a question.

Eleven

I stepped out into the hallway with the list of impressive clients. I could do creative PR campaigns for the likes of Winfield Galleries, the Chicago Center for Artistic Endeavor, The Seattle Film Center, Crest Ridge Vineyards, and on and on. This demotion, truly, was the only way I could have gotten out from under Cecilia's thumb. I'd never really thought that through before. Sure, I had plotted takeover tactics to implement during her next trip to the spa, but I had not planned for a day when I would not directly answer to her. Maybe all the women on death row understood this land of untapped opportunity. Maybe assistant land was the faster route to shareholding and paid parking. I already knew that if I had landed a job assisting someone like Blaine five years ago, I'd be a lot further along.

I was still mulling over the benefits of grunt work when Marsha asked if I was headed for coffee break. I told her I was reviewing budget details with Rachel. Entirely made up, but I didn't want Marsha to join us for our off-site extended coffee break.

"Very well." She twirled her dyed blond hair with a startling red nail. It was chipped and she had been picking at it. That's what that annoying sound had been.

From another cubicle came Tara. She bounded actually. Tara was in her early twenties and assisted the assistant to Ken Dunson. She handled a lot of the corporate travel details for the bigwigs and occasionally sought out my advice for trips. The trips I planned meticulously except for the part of how I'd actually take them.

Tara smelled like Love's Baby Soft from my grade school days. I'm sure it was something more hip than that. Tara had always come across calm and quite professional for someone hired based on a one-sentence résumé: "Ken's daughter-in-law." Although she was educated, she only entered the inner circle because of her selection of husbands. Ken's son was an engineer with Boeing, and they were trying to save up to buy a house, which in Seattle takes a lot of money. And I imagined that they wanted a lot of house too.

"Welcome, Libby!" Tara hugged me. So far everyone had treated my job change as a positive thing. Nobody mentioned the "D" word...but I guess after so many people lost their jobs entirely, it was understood how great it was just to stay on board.

"Thanks, Tara. How goes it in the head office?"

"So far, so good. Though we're supposed to add a corporate executive in a couple weeks...without an extra assistant, so I will have my hands full. It's sort of a figurehead position but was part of the merger arrangement. I think Ken is beginning to regret signing off on that part of the deal." Her hand went to her mouth and she looked around. "That wasn't just spoken. I'm sorry. It slipped. I'm usually so careful."

"Don't worry," I said. "I would think Ken had to do a lot of compromising to get the merger through." *Like, Cecilia is still here,* I wanted to joke. Instead, I added, "Sacrifice is part of growth sometimes."

Marsha was still twirling her hair and biting the morbid nail. Her eyes brightened as a thought entered her head, "Hey, that reminds me. Libby, you should join our book club. You're a reader, right? We meet this Thursday at the Elliott Bay Book Company. Downstairs." I wanted to ask who the "we" was first, but I got my answer.

"Yes! That would be great," Tara added. "We" must be some of the assistants.

"When is your first meeting?" I asked innocently.

"Oh, we've been meeting for two years. It was a larger group, but now it is just Tara, Sasha from design, and myself. I've taken the lead." Marsha said, not catching on that this information led to a different question...why wasn't I invited before? I didn't have to ask it, though. I was starting to understand that this company was divided into a caste system. Seemed like a pretty self-imposed one, though. It could be good for me to feel a part of an office group. Before, I was in no-man's-land between management and the secretarial staff. Somewhere in the back of my mind, I wondered if getting too involved at this level could keep me here, but I let that concern go. It resembled something my mother would think.

"Oh, right. I believe I have heard of it." I cleared the air. "I love to read. Maybe a reading group would be fun. What are you reading?"

"Temptation in Tuscany." Marsha's eyes grew bigger and she winked.

I laughed, but she didn't. Her eyes stayed big and she kept winking. Did I just sign my Thursday night over to discussing a romance novel with some long-haired hero on the cover?

Tara looked at me and nodded knowingly. "Not our typical selection...but it was Marsha's month to choose, so we decided to go for it. It actually is a pretty great read!"

"All right. Well, I'll go get a copy of it and join you guys on Thursday. Thanks."

"Come on, Tara...our break is almost over." Marsha started to head out. Rachel looked over her cubicle wall as they were leaving and motioned with her head for us to exit the other way.

"One sec." I buzzed Blaine quickly. It was going to be hard to get used to checking in and out with someone. It had not occurred to me to ask first.

"Hey, Libby."

"Uh...Blaine...I'm headed out for real coffee. I mean, if that's okay. Can I bring you anything?"

"You mean a frappacino doesn't count as a personal errand? I'm in luck."

I blushed slightly. I was starting something with this offer, but I didn't mind things like this.

"I will take a venti mocha brownie frappacino with whip...without...no, with...thanks."

"So you aren't a real coffee drinker, I take it."

"Are you judging my order?"

"Yes. But I will go get your melted down candy bar with a straw."

I could hear Blaine laugh before I hung up.

Rachel whispered, "So it's 'Blaine' already, is it?"

"He asked me to use his first name. And thank goodness. The guy is maybe three years older than me. How humiliating to have to use a proper salutation all the time."

"Let's go."

We took the elevator to the ground floor headed out the main doors to a surprisingly warm morning. The wind was calm, and we made our way to the closest Starbucks without having to hold our hair or dresses in place. The line was quite long, so we kept walking. There is always another a few feet away.

Rachel said, "I didn't want Marsha and Tara to know I was in earshot...but I almost interrupted when I heard them mention the reading group."

"Why don't you go?" I asked as we entered the next location and placed our orders.

She gave me a "you're kidding" look.

"I thought it was sort of..." I wasn't sure if I was about to insult her.

"An assistant thing?" she said without taking offense. "It is. Which is fine...but sorry, hanging around these people all day and then joining them for an entire evening is not what I want to be doing."

"I hadn't thought about that." I grabbed my drinks from the counter. We wandered over to a free table in the corner and cleared off sections of the *Seattle Times*.

"I probably sound like a total snob, but if I were you, I'd be a bit careful. Maybe sign on for this book and then have something come up later that conflicts with the time. Something like a regular manicure appointment. This group would consider that valid."

"Do you think it's bad to hang out with them?" I valued Rachel's opinion. Maybe I had jumped into the secretarial pool without a life jacket.

"I could be totally wrong, but..."

"Rachel...tell me!" I was starting to worry.

"They're eager to have you be one of them. You know, welcoming a demoted assistant AE into the fold makes them feel good. Sorry, but I had to say it."

"You have to come with me, then," I said before I could think. I didn't want to feel like the welcomed failure.

"Look, I might be wrong. Either way, they gossip incessantly, mentioning information about their bosses that I know is confidential. I despise Cecilia as much as the next person, but I wouldn't talk about her with them. I've watched them undermine each other several times."

I felt so naïve. That was exactly Marsha's style. But Tara seemed normal. I said this to Rachel as we drained our lattes.

"Tara is smart and clever, so that makes me more leery of her."

"Wait. If they are obvious gossips, you don't trust them. I get that. But if someone is smart, you don't trust her either? Isn't that extreme?"

"Truth is, you're the only person I'd trust with information around here. I know you wouldn't use it later just to get ahead."

"Oh, sure. The demoted chick is safe," I said, twisting her words intentionally to lighten the mood. "I do appreciate the heads up. I've worked here for five years, and yet I feel like the newbie. I always kept to myself before. Maybe that wasn't such a good tactic."

"It doesn't mean that they aren't nice. They can be great coworkers. Just avoid the loose talk part."

"So how about the reading group? Please? Now I will feel like a lamb going to the slaughter."

"It might be totally fine."

"And you're saying this so that you don't have to go with me?"

"Yes," she said, laughing as we headed back out to the street. "I really would consider going, just to help you out, except that I have already established myself as the secretarial loner."

"What have I done?" I shook my head and promised myself to be more careful. I was so eager to be accepted by anyone that I was pretty gullible. I looked down at the frappacino in my hand...what if I was misreading Blaine? Could his talk about creative work and using my skills really be about earning loyalty in a new setting? Would I really see anything come of his big talk? Suddenly I was extremely skeptical of Blaine's motivation. Yet I'm a pretty darn good judge of character.

Or am I?

Twelve

"Will she make a good dog parent?" I asked Pan while petting two of her canine children and throwing a gym sock for another.

Sandy, one of my former coworkers, had just left Pan's house after spending quality time with a couple of the dogs. I was curious about Pan's evaluation system. Sandy was looking into adopting a dog because she and her husband had just hit their three-year anniversary and had "the child talk." They were undecided but did agree to read up on parenting and ask their individual therapists, who were quick to suggest Plan Dog.

"Well, the fact that she's even considering taking in one of these dogs is a plus in my book." Pan was in her cool, retro kitchen making macaroni and cheese from scratch. It was logical that macaroni and cheese existed before the blue-and-yellow box, but I was impressed.

"Why? What's wrong with these dogs?" I tried to tie the ears of the cocker spaniel together, but he wouldn't get into the fun of it.

"Nothing. Couples only want to adopt a pup so that they are dealing with the same issues that come along with a baby. I just had one adoption fall through because the wife convinced the husband that these dogs would be too trained. The poor guy loved Hershey, my brown lab, but his wife was sure their experience would be tainted. So annoying, especially when you consider that within a year, the pup they choose will probably just end up at the humane society." Pan stirred her pasta with excessive force.

"You know what we should do? Well, first you should open a restaurant because you're an amazing cook. But then you and I should start an animal adoption business for people who don't want one of those messed up dogs."

Pan's forehead rippled and she shook her head.

"And our promise would be: No relationship was tested on this animal."

Pan started to laugh so hard that she closed her eyes long enough for me to dip my finger in to the cheese sauce. "This is a totally different subject...but did Ariel invite you to Angus' concert last weekend? I'm curious. I had asked her to tell you about it."

She paused mid-stir and looked over at me. "It's not as different as you might think."

"Excuse me?"

"The subject is not so different. To answer your question, Ariel did mention the concert but only after a heated discussion. It wasn't exactly a warm invitation, so I thought it best to stay away. Sorry I wasn't there to support you and Angus."

"I broke up with him that night."

Pan raised her eyebrows. "I always figured it was a passing time thing for you. But...wow. How'd he take it?"

"He took it well. Too well for a girl's ego to remain intact."

"Someone new in the picture for you or for him?"

"I don't think so. Angus felt like one suitcase over the baggage limit, you know?"

"I understand." She laughed. "I get these dogs because people are deciding all that life stuff. And really, I'm probably doing the same. I keep taking them in to help me decide if I could face the commitment of marriage or kids. More and more, I'm not sure.

"Either that or they're ensuring that you won't have to face that decision. They are a protective barrier between you and guys."

"Watching afternoon counseling television, are we?"

"We all create our own barriers when it comes to relationships. I do it too."

"With sarcasm," she said without any of her own.

"That was a mighty quick response."

"Am I right?"

"Beside the point," I pouted. "When is that 'cheeses of the world' pasta dish going to be finished, anyway?"

Pan served up the delicious main course in two green-and-blue striped bowls.

"Can I say grace?" she asked. Pan had grown up with sort of a schizophrenic version of Christianity, but as an adult, she'd developed a healthy faith. She started to pray and the dogs settled at our feet beneath the table. It was comforting. "Lord, thank you for the gift of friendship. Bless this food, this time, and our lives with your goodness and guidance. Amen."

"I've been trying to go to church for a while," I blurted.

Pan paused while salting her pasta but didn't look up. She seemed to be giving this news serious consideration. The saltshaker was set down beside her bowl. "How does one try to go to church exactly? And I'm not being sarcastic."

I fumbled with my fork and stabbed at the noodles nervously. It isn't every day that you out yourself as a person of faith. Pan would be the easy one, the understanding one. Ariel would be accepting but not understanding. "You know. I walk to the corner, I watch people go inside, I stand there and consider how I'd feel being in the church, and then I get nervous, and so I go get coffee and pastries and visit with Mr. Diddle."

"Your thing with that old guy and his bookstore baffles me."

I looked at her pleadingly for more than judgment.

"I wasn't finished. I do understand the church thing. You can find me walking my dogs most Sunday mornings. There's something so intimidating about entering those doors. Will they like you? Will you understand what's going on? How do they take communion? Are they teaching something you believe in?"

I realized I was nodding fiercely. "Yes. All those things. And I wonder whether I'm at the right place in life or, I don't know, worthy to go through the doors."

Pan shook her head in protest but smiled. "If we had to wait until we were worthy of grace, we'd *never* make it into a church. Isn't that the entire point of grace?"

"True. This is exactly what I need...a new way of seeing faith." I'm not so weird after all. A huge forkful of cheesy goodness filled my mouth. "Aunt Maddie had me get the book *The Practice of the Presence of God*. I've just started it. There isn't much to it, page count-wise, but I think that's part of the message as well. The most difficult and the simplest thing are the same...seeking God's presence in all that you do." My eyes stared at the formation of noodles for a moment.

"This one?" Pan reached over to her bookshelf by the dining table and held up a copy with the same cover as mine.

"That's it."

"This totally helped me decide to move from New York. All my friends there said I was crazy to leave authentic film Mecca, but through months of prayer and asking for direction I felt this huge burden lifted. It took me a while, but I got it."

I motioned with my fork for her to explain further.

"I understood that the ideal place for me to be wasn't related to where others said I had the greatest career advantage. If I went where I was supposed to go, then I'd be closer to my purpose."

"Are you?"

"I believe so. I hope so. There are days and nights when my thoughts get the best of me. And those endless hours alone in the editing suites can make even the most sane person stir-crazy. But every week there is some point when I realize, yet again, that I'm where I'm supposed to be. And even though there are things I hope will be a part of my life or that will change, I'm also very content. I never had contentment in New York. There were too many ads, skinny models, or limo-encased tycoons to make you feel as though you should want a different life."

"I'm glad you're content, Pan. You're a good example for me right now."

"So you'll go in next Sunday?" she asked, eyebrows raised.

"Maybe. I'll probably get closer, at least."

"I'm sure it's a good Christian practice to play hard to get with God," she added.

"Welcome to my church of sarcasm, Sister Pan." We laughed and continued to indulge in the glorious carbs before us. Only the sound of the dogs licking their chops in anticipation of cleaning the bowls could be heard.

Then she turned to me with a serious look. "Do you want to know what Ariel and I are arguing about?"

"Yes. I mean, whatever you can tell me."

She paused for a moment. "I won't go into details, but our argument relates to what we were discussing before…the dog adoption thing."

"Ariel wants a dog?" I was shocked. She was such a free spirit and not exactly good at nurturing anything that required routine and consistency. The girl changes her hair style monthly.

"Not exactly," Pan said with her eyes downcast. I could tell I was losing her. I'd given her too much time to think about the sin of gossip. She was fading.

"Tell me…" I begged. So unbecoming of me, but I absolutely hated the fact that Ariel was keeping something from me, even if it was a dog. "What?" I almost grabbed her shoulders, but she pulled away. My erratic behavior wasn't helping.

"No. I can't. If Ariel wants to tell you, she can."

"Tell me what?" I asked, thinking I could trip her up. She'd had two glasses of wine, after all. I had the advantage.

She wagged her finger at me. "Nice try. Talk to Ariel. In fact, I think you should. Just don't tell her I told you to."

The window for gossip had been slammed shut on my fingers. Wounded, I filled my bowl with another round of dinner, much to the disappointment of the waiting canines. I would approach Ariel. We shared everything. What could she possibly want to keep from me? I was her best friend. Or used to be.

Thirteen

I slogged home. The assistant tasks I was forced to master were taxing my nerves. Keeping up the good attitude was taxing my soul. A herd of stray cats chased my lethargic body up the stairs from the street to my apartment entry. I was a big fat human joke to these quick-footed nomads. I shooed them away like old Scrooge. "Get away, you nasty, lazy chillin'"

The hallway smelled like old socks and oil. I breathed it in, refreshed. At least the sulfur smell from my fried bathroom had cleared out. I would not take responsibility for oily sock smells. There was a flyer taped to my door. I'd received these before. A neighbor down the hall hosted Bible studies and periodically invited other tenants to join. You'd think walking down the hall would sound easier and more enticing than entering a strange church. But both actions were equidistant from my comfort zone.

I pulled the memo off and the tape made a snap sound. My back was bent like an old woman's under the weight of my leather case and Prada bag. Not that they were heavy. I'd just assumed this position lately. As soon as I was in the apartment, the bags were released, free to follow gravity to my dusty floor.

My message light blinked out its SOS pattern. Ariel had rigged that for me. Maybe it was her. We hadn't spoken much since my breakup night. She'd emailed me a few times to check in. Nothing seemed different except for the gap in our connection that she and I both knew existed but could not discuss for whatever reason.

I had three messages. A Wednesday night record for me. Everyone communicated with me via email during the days, and I hardly ever had need of a phone after 5:00. I should never confess that fact to anyone. If that isn't the mark of a nondater, I don't know what is.

Message 1: Mother asking if I could come at 3:00 instead of at 5:00 on Saturday.

What? Did our conversations make that little of an impression? Good grief.

Message 2: Dad telling me that Mom meant only to remind me to come at 3:00, oh, and Mom would be making berry cobbler as my special birthday dessert.

I guess my throwing up Mom's blueberry muffins every Christmas and her blackberry jam pancakes every New Year's wasn't consistent enough to warrant a deduction. Berry. Puke. Berry. Puke. Does anyone know who I am?

Message 3: This one had to be played a few times. My pulse quickened at the sound of that voice.

Libby? Libby? It's Cecilia. Are you there? I cannot reach Rachel...it's 5:15. Is the office falling to pieces? Does the work ethic turn to absolute crap when I leave? Anyway...call me as soon as you get in. This is an emergency. You owe me, Libby.

She left no number. I was just about to pick up the phone to check my last incoming call when the phone rang again. I reluctantly picked up. "Hello?" I answered in a near-Irish accent, hoping it could allow for a "sorry, wrong number," if necessary.

"Thank goodness you're there."

Okay. The woman who once asked when I stopped wearing my hair in a blond shag (what?) had no problem recognizing me through my Lucky Charms spokesperson impersonation. "Yes, Cecilia. I just got home and played your message. I'm sure Rachel was in the copier room. She has been staying late every evening."

Pause. "And you would know this how? It is only 5:40 your time."

I needed to get this over with. The cliff was right there; I had to jump. "You said I owed you something, Cecilia?"

"Libby, I'm furious. Furious. Here I'm dealing with a major corporate crisis on behalf of the company...and I get a call, out of the blue, from Crest Ridge Vineyards, the biggest vineyard account on the West Coast, telling me that they are sad to no longer be working with me but are excited about what Blaine Slater can bring to their PR efforts. They wished me well, Libby. A corporate kiss off."

"I...I..." She didn't know about losing some clients? I was confused. Was Blaine here to replace Cecilia completely? Had I been a part of an immediate purging of all things Cecilia without even knowing it?

"Do you know when one person wishes another person well?" Cecilia said "well" as though it were a swear word.

"There are all sorts of occasions where that sentiment can be..."

"Either someone is in remission or getting fired."

"Now wait, Cecilia. I don't know everything that is going on, but I do think I would have heard rumors by now. And there has been nothing like that. In fact, people are eager to have you back in the office next week." Okay, I lied. But she was scaring me. And I felt a wee bit sorry for her. I hoped she didn't know I was the one to call Mr. Fattello of the vineyard to arrange the conference call with Blaine.

"Really? What about the account? You work for Blaine. Surely this rings a bell?"

"Well...yes. I received a list...the name...of this account and was told it was going to be one of Blaine's from now on."

"List? What else do you know, Libby?"

Dang, she heard that. I wasn't the one who should be conveying this to her.

"Blaine brought some clients with him. I got that list of names and then was told Crest Ridge was an add-on. After all, I'll bet Ken Dunson wants to be sure Blaine has more than a full load of work. Good grief, you are in Texas putting out fires. You shouldn't have to handle every stinkin' account too!" I thought that was a nice touch. There was silence. I pulled it off.

"Point." She said that instead of "good point," which made you aware that she was tracking the score to some game nobody else was playing. Willingly, that is.

Cecilia sighed heavily. "This conversation is just between us. I'm sure there is an explanation similar to the one you described. There is probably an email all about it in my in-box. I couldn't get online from the center."

"The center?"

Another sigh. "Business center…at the hotel. The places I stay do not have vending machines, game rooms, or parking lots. They have spas, penthouse suites, five-star restaurants, private lounges, valet parking, and full-service business centers."

"Got it. No Motel 6 for you. And I'm sure the details are in that email. Mums the word on my end."

Then she hung up. No goodbye. No thanks. Just gone. I was thrilled. Now I needed to track down Rachel and find out what she knew. From the list I'd been working with, Crest Ridge wasn't the only large account that was going to be wishing Cecilia well. I tried information…unlisted. I tried the office again, but no answer. Philip was still there, but he wouldn't release a home number for Rachel. He took his job way too seriously. I tried the "in-house task force" threat indirectly again, but he probably thought I was testing him.

There was no way to reach Rachel.

Except.

Ugh.

I unfolded the piece of paper with Marsha's number on it. She had drawn a ring of flowers around her M. I would have to use the reading group as an excuse to get Rachel's number.

I started pacing as I dialed. The things I did to keep my demotion.

"Hello?" her voice was falsely light but the nasal quality could not be disguised.

"Marsha?"

"Libby?"

How does everyone recognize my voice so easily? "Yes. Hi!"

"I'm so glad you called. What are you up to? Wasn't today at work just a bore?"

Great. Small talk.

"Oh, hey…look, I'm actually headed to a manicure appointment, you know how hard it is to get in sometimes!" I used Rachel's suggestion early. "I wanted to call Rachel and ask her to go to the reading group with me tomorrow. Do you have her number?"

"Oh," she said, obviously disappointed.

Swell. She wasn't going to make this easy. "That's okay, isn't it?"

"Oh, sure," she said with a sarcastic tone. "Just don't hold your breath. Rachel decided a long time ago that she was too good for us. But give it a shot. Of course, *we* would love to have her join. We adore Rachel. Absolutely adore her."

Abhor her. It was obvious.

"So you do have her number?"

"Let me grab my cell. I have it listed, though it really is just using up space." She gave me the number and then took in a big breath. "Now, where is your manicurist? Do you go to Latisha at Samson's Salon? She's the best but she has quite the little attitude for a manicurist. She said she did Courtney Love's nails for years. Spare me…"

"Oh my gosh, thanks for reminding me. I have got to go. See you tomorrow…and at the group!" I hung up quickly and dialed Rachel immediately.

One ring. Two rings. Three rings. Should I leave a message? Four rings.

"Hey, I'm on my way, already!" Rachel's voice blasted my eardrum.

"Rachel?"

"Libby?"

Good thing I wasn't into prank calls. Everyone seemed to know my voice.

"Yes, it's me. I have a bit of a situation. Guess who just called?"

"Dang it. The only night I leave the office before seven. What did she need? Dinner reservations for some swanky singles bar in Dallas? Or did she have a hangnail?"

"No. It's big. Well, interesting at least. Rachel, do you know if there has been any communication with Cecilia about the transferring of some of her accounts to Blaine? Remember that group of files I snagged? Apparently Cecilia knows nothing about this."

"I'm not surprised."

"She got a call from Crest Ridge saying they were sorry to not be working with her anymore. She had no idea. But she said her email wasn't working and so maybe there's an email from Ken about all of this. Do you have any idea?"

"I think Ken was sending something out to Cecilia via Tara. I'm out of the loop on the big stuff."

"Well, this won't help her response to this news, but at least she'll be informed."

"I'm so glad you're the one that Cecilia called."

"One more thing...I need you to come to the reading group. I told Marsha that was why I called for your number. I was afraid she'd get snoopy." I was milking this.

"Swell. Just what I want to do, bond over trash lit."

"I didn't know how else to..."

"How does it feel to be a part of Cecilia's tangled web?"

"Exhausting. Absolutely exhausting. You didn't say yes to the reading group."

Rachel sighed and said, "I guess the good part is that they can't talk about me if I'm there, right?"

Fourteen

Rachel picked me up shortly before 7:00 to head to Elliott Bay Book Company. She had a large Americano in hand, and I could tell it was at least her second since she left work ninety minutes earlier.

"Too bad they don't meet at a bar. That sure would help my mood."

"And they wouldn't pollute my sacred bookstore with this trash. Here, look at this." I tossed her my copy. "Good thing I didn't try the 'couldn't find it anywhere' excuse. I stepped into Barnes and Noble and nearly tripped over a huge promo display. They even enter your name in a drawing for a trip to Tuscany when you buy the book."

Rachel glanced at the cover and rolled her eyes. "Unbelievable. Though wouldn't it be something if you won?"

"I used Marsha's name in case they were using the drawing as a way to gather email addresses for the marketing of other similar reading material."

"You overthink things, don't you."

I shrugged. There was no way to discount the truth.

By the time we parked the car, Rachel had lined up a friend to call her by 8:15 so she could fake an excuse to exit. I made her promise to take me with her.

"Girls. Over here!" Marsha waved excitedly and shouted as soon as Rachel and I made our way to the downstairs area of the bookstore.

Keeping *Temptation in Tuscany* tucked inside my sweater, I looked around to note who else in this city would be witness to my cheap reading material.

"Yoo-hoo. Let's get this party started." Marsha raised her voice to an ear-piercing shrill.

Rachel grabbed my elbow and steered me toward the center table where the three other women were seated. "This won't end unless it begins," she muttered.

"We never thought we'd see you here, Rachel. You are so mysterious. We were starting to think you had some fabulous, secret love life on the side."

"Just good taste."

Marsha didn't seem to understand Rachel's jab, so she smiled and reached for her copy of the book. "I'll start the discussion. Steamy, definitely. Too hot to read when you have no one to share it with. Right, Libby?"

I opened my mouth to argue, but why bother.

"Sasha, now you."

Sasha fanned her short auburn hair several times with thick hands, a pensive expression on her face. I wondered if she was thinking of another word for steamy so she would not look like a reading group copycat. "I found it to be..."

"Don't look now, but a very hot guy is checking me out. He's coming over here. If he asks to sit down, the rest of you have to vamoose. Got it?" Marsha spoke through barely parted lips that were spread in a welcoming smile.

I didn't turn around to look. Instead, I skimmed the back cover of *Temptation* so I could come up with my own borrowed adjective.

"Join us?" Marsha asked, leaning forward, her chest grazing the top of her cappuccino foam.

All of a sudden the cheesy descriptions disappeared as a pair of hands covered my eyes. Startled, I dropped the book, and I heard Marsha drop back down into her chair with a thud. My hands flew up to the jokester's hands. They were smooth and strong on the outside, but I could feel the roughness of calluses against my eyelids. I could hear the creak of a leather jacket.

Angus.

"Hey, you," I said calmly. The hands left my eyes and Angus stepped to my side so that I could see him.

He gave me an endearing look. "I saw you come in and didn't want to sneak by."

"Thanks, Angus. Good to see you."

Sasha shifted her chair closer to Angus and Marsha raised her eyebrows at me. I wasn't about to introduce Angus to this gathering.

He liked the spotlight. He looked at each of the women and placed his hand on my shoulder. "Ladies, this is where Libby and I first met. Remember, Libbs?" He leaned down with dramatic flair and kissed my cheek. "You look good, Stella," he whispered into my hair. I nodded and waved to give him his cue. He smiled at me, nodded to the ladies, and turned to leave. Female stares followed his black jeans up the stairs.

"Rachel doesn't have the secret life, you do! Color me jealous," said Marsha.

I changed the subject quickly. "Rachel, what do you like about the book cover?"

Rachel glared at me but took her cue nonetheless. "I was surprised to see pink and orange paired up with such a great piece of literature."

Sasha waved her hand in front of my face. "Tell us who that was, girlfriend."

I cringed, but as Rachel said, this wouldn't end unless it began. "It was Angus. We are friends."

"What's with the leather look?" Marsha hummed.

I shrugged. "He's a rock musician. Black is his thing."

Marsha and Sasha nodded knowingly. "Uh-huh," they crooned.

"What are your top ten favorite romance novels?" I asked, dangling a carrot.

"Way to take our reading group to a deeper level, Libby," Marsha said, applauding.

As they started their individual lists, I turned to check the clock above the café counter. I could have turned the other way and not noticed what I noticed. But I didn't. And I did.

Ariel was coming from the narrow hallway between the coffee bar and the bathrooms. I knew she hadn't been working, or we would have seen her. Maybe she was in to check her schedule. My first thought was that Ariel could be my chance for an easy exit. I waved, but she was looking toward a small alcove by the stairs. I scooted my chair out and stood to see past the banister. And I saw him.

Ferris. My Ferris.

He was wearing his dark gray sweater with a white T-shirt underneath. I happened to know that when combined with his perfectly worn Levis he considered himself date ready. I sat down. Ariel waved to her coworkers and walked over to Ferris. They headed up the wooden stairs, laughing together over something. Something their crazy friend-in-common said the other day? Or maybe laughing because they were doing something behind the back of their crazy friend-in-common? Could Ariel be hiding a relationship with Ferris?

Confusion and jealousy flooded my brain. The good thing was that now I couldn't care less how I handled my exit. I had to get out of there. I turned to the others and interrupted Sasha's number seven pick with, "Look at the time. I have to go, but it was great. Thanks. See you guys tomorrow." I stood up to leave.

"Don't go, Libby. We're just getting started," Tara said.

"I'm bummed, but I gotta go."

Rachel, still waiting for her emergency call, turned to me with a "don't you dare leave" look on her face.

"I'm afraid Rachel's my ride." My coworker's face lit up and she stood immediately to follow me out. Her phone rang just as we reached the night air.

"I think I want to walk home."

Rachel just rolled her eyes. This wasn't a good area for an evening stroll. We both knew it. I sulked in her passenger seat while she went off on Marsha's warped view of love, sex, and relationships. I think she was on such a high from leaving on time (and twelve shots of espresso) that she didn't notice my silence. My eyes were trained on the road ahead as my mind scurried past my recent encounters with Ariel and Ferris.

There wasn't anything in their actions toward one another that suggested it was a romantic get-together. Except for the date attire. It wasn't as though I caught them kissing. But they were together in some capacity. Was I so narcissistic (read: insecure) that I didn't think my friends would choose to do things together and without me?

Yes.

When it came to Ariel and Ferris, I was the common denominator. And I always figured they got along mainly out of devotion to me. Every group of friends was made up of at least two other subgroups. And there were certain subgroups that were perfectly acceptable to see outside of the primary group. Like me and Ariel. Me and Ferris. Or Ariel and Oliver...who had been friends before. But Ariel and Ferris together made a very improbable subgroup. Maybe they had called me to join them, but Rachel and I had left already. Maybe...maybe.

Rachel, high on caffeine and the thrill of getting out alive, sang show tunes at the top of her lungs and barely slowed down to let me out. I dropped my keys on the street and then the sidewalk in my frantic rush to get to my door and to the logical explanation that surely was waiting for me. But when I made it inside my dark apartment...and my eyes went to the phone on the breakfast bar counter...the red light was steady. No SOS signal cast repeated shadows across my wall.

Did I know the people in my life? Here I was seeking knowledge about who I really was, and instead of happening upon some strong truths that would move me forward in life, I was discovering the secret lives of others.

"Eureka!" I stopped mid Sonic Care brushing. Toothpaste sprayed across the bathroom mirror. My party. That was it. Ferris was merely helping Ariel with my birthday dinner. Planning a party is the one perfectly good reason to organize a subgroup of any formation at any time and with any mix of primary group members. Once again, when I paid attention to my life, all the pieces fit together.

Fifteen

I finished creating the last of the new files for Blaine. Surprisingly, I felt a sense of accomplishment with such a small task. My old job was ongoing without points along the way to say "job well done" or to cross something permanently off the list.

"You missed a great conversation last night," Marsha said through the crack between our cubicles where computer cords fed down to the outlets on the floor. I could see her nostrils and a section of her lips.

I didn't respond. If I didn't want to catch the original conversation, I certainly didn't want to hear her replay version.

"Yo! Libby."

"I'm glad you had a good conversation."

"You should be sorry you missed it."

"Uh-huh." I slammed the edges of the file folders down on the desk several times to align the edges. Startled, she pulled back momentarily, but soon her eye returned.

"Tara thinks Cecilia is on her way out. Not by choice, mind you."

"I don't put too much stock in gossip."

"This isn't gossip. Libby, haven't you figured out by now that the assistants know more than anyone else in this company? We all knew about the merger months before the middle management did."

"Everyone knew before it was announced," I said to take away her thunder.

"But I knew about your downsized career days before you did," Marsha volleyed back.

I stopped shuffling papers. She knew she hit a cord and continued at a rapid pace. "Maybe it was a week before. Margaret from human resources left a list of all the people who would be, how should I put this, exiting the 401(k) program and insurance plan by the coffee machine. I saw it all."

"I still have those benefits," I said indignantly.

"There was also a list of those who were being moved to a lower tier of benefits. You were number four. Then, when I was told to move my extra boxes of envelopes and letterhead out of this cubicle, I already knew it was for you."

"What's your point, Marsha?"

"Cecilia is on her way out. She hasn't even responded to the email that was sent to her about some of her accounts being shifted to your Mr. Slater. And if Cecilia is out soon, that means Rachel dear should be job hunting."

"You sound a little paranoid."

"Hey, I'm on the safe side of the fence. I'm just letting you know. Besides, you should be happy. Do you realize that if your Blaine is made head honcho, you step up with him. Congratulations, Libby. You could end up saving face, after all."

"Blaine is not taking over," I said without much conviction.

"Why do you think we are having an impromptu departmental meeting this morning?" Marsha asked but didn't really ask. "They want us to bond with Blaine before Cecilia gets back from Texas and starts causing problems, that's why."

I didn't ask "what departmental meeting?" because I didn't want to give her the satisfaction. I smiled and acted in the know. "If you'll excuse me, I have to get this information to Blaine for the meeting. He requested it days ago."

I watched the thin eyebrow raise and I knew a minor victory had been won. As I pushed backward in my roller chair, I hoped she was wrong, for Rachel's sake, and maybe a little for Cecilia's sake.

"How is the house hunt going?" I asked, poking my nose into Blaine's office.

He looked up from the computer screen and seemed relieved for the distraction. "Good. The search is over. In fact, it looks like we will be neighbors."

"You're kidding!" I said a bit loudly. I would have pegged him as a house on Lake Washington kind of guy.

"I'm not a stalker, really." He beamed unlike a stalker would.

I laughed. "I wasn't worried. Honest." I couldn't help thinking: *I wish. I wish.* "I just figured you'd go for a different area."

"Queen Anne is perfect. I walked around this past weekend, and everything I need is right there—great grocery stores, restaurants, retailers, coffee shops..."

"You don't mind sounding like a girl, do you?" I said, forgetting about those corporate boundaries I was going to work on.

He smiled and shook his head with disbelief. There was an awkward pause, so I started to back out the door until I remembered that I had the files in my hand. "I have your accounts. Do you want them here or back in the file cabinets?"

"Here is good." Blaine reached for the stack and bit his lower lip nervously as I walked toward him. "I saw you," he blurted. "While I was walking around looking for girl things."

"Why didn't you say hi?" I quickly scanned memories of the weekend. I could only hope he didn't see me wearing the *Little House on the Prairie* dress.

"I didn't want you to think I was following you. I mean, who wants to deal with coworkers on the weekend, right?"

"Right." I said, but I didn't mean it. Not in this case.

"And you seemed really focused. I think you were waiting to go into the church. At least it looked that way. The little brick one on the corner?" He was fumbling with some papers and seemed worried that I might be offended. "Maybe it wasn't even you. I was dizzy from walking up and down the hill looking for a breakfast place a friend had suggested. So..." His voice trailed off.

My face grew hot. "That was me." I thought about how stupid I must have looked standing there, debating about whether this would be the Sunday I'd go inside.

Blaine seemed to misunderstand the reason for my embarrassment. "You were probably waiting for the bus, now that I think about it."

"No, it was me…and I was waiting to go into the church."

He nodded, relieved. "I'm thinking about trying that one myself. That is, if you wouldn't mind?"

Oh, great. One more reason to be nervous about going. "Why would I mind? In fact, I'm trying out churches, so it isn't mine or anything. Free country and all that."

Blaine stood up and rolled up his sleeves, trying not to make eye contact. "Maybe we could both try it this next weekend?"

Just when I thought there wasn't anything more awkward than attending church as a single, I saw myself walking in to the church with Blaine, his wife, and Adam. A "bring a spinster to worship" ministry for the Slater family.

"Maybe we'll see each other there sometime," I offered.

His face fell slightly and he looked at his desk as if looking for something to throw at me. Or maybe he wanted to jot down notes in my file. "Exhibits unhelpful and antisocial behavior."

"I'm sorry. I was imposing," he said softly.

"I just need to do some things on my own."

"I understand completely." Blaine's supervisor mode kicked in as he tapped a pen on the desk. "By the way, we're having a departmental meeting in about fifteen minutes. Ken thought I should address the team now since we aren't sure when Cecilia will return."

"Do you need anything for the meeting?"

"Confidence. Any advice?"

He had to be the most honest, vulnerable guy I had ever met in my life. My heart quickened and I couldn't hold back my smile. "I used to think that when people said 'just be yourself' they were highly misinformed. But I'm starting to believe that is what works. In your case, I really believe it."

"Good last-minute advice. Thanks."

"Told ya." Marsha mumbled from behind her steno pad as we waited for the rest of the department to file into the conference room.

"It's a meeting to introduce Blaine. That's all."

Marsha patted me on the shoulder and then looked past me to Rachel and shook her head. "It's a shame. Just when Rachel was starting to become friendlier."

Ken Dunson stood at the head of the oval table. He held the Reed and Dunson snack bowl and ceremoniously passed it to the first person seated to his right. This was a tradition the employees appreciated. As the vessel made its way around, bags of chips and cookies and gummy creatures were selected.

When most people had their preference, Ken cleared his throat. "I'm headed to the airport in a few minutes, but I wanted to be here to introduce our newest Reed and Dunson member. He is new to us, but Blaine Slater is not new to the public relations industry. For more than ten years, Blaine has earned a reputation for clever campaigns, lasting relationships with clients, and intuitive, successful decisions in an ever-changing market. We are lucky to have him, and in Cecilia's absence, I'm pleased to welcome Blaine Slater to the head of this table today."

Everyone clapped, but Marsha kicked me under the table and winked. It reminded me of her response to Angus, and I cringed yet again. It must have reminded her of the same thing because she jotted a note down on the back of her steno pad and held it up: *If I were you, I wouldn't keep a hot boyfriend like your rocker a secret!*

I slapped the pad down onto the table with a loud whack. All eyes were turned our direction, and Blaine stopped his introductory speech to address the commotion—us. "Oh no, I've inspired note passing already! I'm in trouble."

Everyone laughed. I felt bad for disturbing Blaine, especially since he had confessed to being nervous. "I'm sorry," I said directly to him. He nodded graciously and continued. I was so embarrassed that I stared straight ahead the entire time and barely took in a word. I did notice how well the group was responding to him. They laughed. Nodded. Clapped. And seemed totally engaged. When Cecilia addressed the team, she would start talking about last night's date or the fabulous oatmeal-and-mango massage therapy treatment she tried. Nobody paid attention. People actually read and wrote emails on their BlackBerries. Once, a woman even used the intercom phone in the center of the conference table to order a spinach salad and rye sandwich for lunch.

Blaine concluded the meeting with praise for everyone on the staff, and he promised to learn his way around Reed and Dunson and become useful as soon as possible. The group loved that. More clapping. On the way out I kept my eyes trained on Rachel. I didn't want to talk to or look at Marsha.

But unfortunately, I had to hear her. "I'm sooo sorry, Mr. Slater. That was bad of me and Libby. It had nothing to do with you, I swear." Her big, flirty laugh made my jaw go tight.

"As long as you weren't rating my speaking skills, I will forgive you and Libby."

I held my breath at the mention of my name by Blaine. I'd never find my day in the sun—my chance for promotion and my dream trip to Italy—if I was labeled a troublemaker. I turned to apologize again, and instead watched with horror as Marsha turned the steno pad around to show Blaine.

"You see. It wasn't about you at all. Libby has a delicious, leather-wearing, rocker boyfriend she has been keeping to herself. That's all."

Blaine appeared to skim the note. "You are forgiven then," he said flatly, with a forced smile. I tried to catch his attention—to say what, I don't know—but he was already shaking hands with Brad Wendell, the account executive for Salt Lick Potato Chips.

The hallways were cleared by 6:00. Only the diehard workaholics who had offices and decent pay stayed any later on a Friday night. The glow from Blaine's desk lamp was the sole illumination in the hallway as I paced back and forth. Unable to make a decision about what I would say to him other than one more round of apologies, I grabbed my purse that was draped over the back of my chair and started to walk in the direction opposite his office.

"Libby?"

I froze.

Blaine's voice became louder as he approached my back. I turned quickly, getting my dangling purse strap tangled in my legs. "Hey," I said cheerily, stepping sharply to the side to regain my balance.

"I thought everyone was gone by now."

"I'm sorry about the meeting. Marsha's note just triggered a reaction. A wrong, bad, unprofessional reaction..." I berated myself and was prepared to keep going until Blaine held up his hand to stop me.

"It actually broke the tension. I should thank you." Blaine's tan and manicured hand cupped his chin, as if he needed help to hold his head up. It was an endearing gesture. Too endearing. I looked away.

He continued with a slightly slower cadence. "Honestly, I'm the one to apologize. Here I was asking you about going to church together and you are dating. How awkward for you. Not that our church thing would be a date-date, but you don't want to have me tag along with you and your boyfriend. I didn't think...I mean, of course you'd be dating...but the way you said that you hadn't found the right guy before, I just assumed..."

It was my turn to hold up my hand and stop him. "I'm not dating anyone. I did date the quote-unquote hot rocker, but that was a very short phase and it ended recently. I came to my senses, thank goodness."

Blaine tried to hide a smile behind a momentarily raised folder, but I saw a glimpse of his white teeth before he said, "So you said no to the church thing because...well, you just didn't want to."

And hello...you're married.

"The truth? I've been trying to get back into the church scene after quite a few years away from it. I didn't want to add to my nervousness by combining the stress of hanging out with my boss and his family. Or I didn't want the commitment of saving a pew for everyone and being a more conspicuous newcomer."

He laughed. "If I go, I won't require a whole pew. My family all lives in Chicago."

"Until they move," I said to finish his sentence.

"Nobody else is moving."

I stared blankly at the man whose shirt matched his eyes.

Blaine leaned his head slightly to the right, looking as puzzled as I felt.

I interrupted the silence. "Are we talking about that family?" I pointed to the photograph featuring Blaine with the toothpaste model and the child I scared.

"Yes. My sister and Adam live in Chicago. They're not relocating. I'm just hoping Adam will spend some summers with me in the future."

"Sister? You're not..."

Blaine's puzzled look returned and then his eyes grew wide with understanding. "No. No. Regina is my sister and Adam's my nephew, though I think of him as my son."

"That's great," I said softly.

"Do you have any siblings?" Blaine asked.

In fact, I think he repeated the question, and I don't recall responding that time, either.

I couldn't tell you how I made it out of the building with my purse and my composure. I'm not really sure how I managed to get on the number 15 bus, let alone get off at the Mercer Street stop. I'm not sure how I walked the several blocks to my building and hiked up the worn carpeted stairs to my apartment. I don't recall any of this. I do know that I was really, really happy Blaine had a sister.

Sixteen

Some women dress for men. Some women dress for other women. I, however, dress for my parents. After much consideration and checkbook analysis, I purchased a new happy-birthday-to-me outfit to wear to my birthday party at Cass's house. A long suede skirt with cute fringe at the bottom and a cream-colored blouse with beading at the cuffs. Deep brown, high-heeled, sophisticated boots finished off the look. It was the new me. The me trying to become something else. I wasn't sure what the look was exactly, but I thought it would at least reflect that effort had been made.

I had not seen my folks in several months. In a single woman's life, that is the equivalent of oh, say, five years. You could have the "I'm not dating" conversation with a parent on Saturday and then have your ring finger scrutinized by them the following Wednesday just in case your status had changed. Just in case you had forgotten to mention bumping into *the* one while waiting for your single serving of pasta at the local romantic restaurant.

Since mother knew Angus was no longer in the picture, I would receive the usual interrogation. Had I been making myself available? Was I giving the wrong message to academic-oriented men by hanging out with my circle of arty friends? Could it be I had made the choice to be single and wasn't woman enough to own up to it? (Because they would support me should I make that choice.)

But I had a decoy up my stylish sleeve for this encounter. I have been demoted, deported to a cubicle, and de-vacationed. Surely these disasters would satiate my problem-solving parents. And the fact that my recent failings could probably equal the number of candles on my berry cobbler made this an even more ideal case study in Pathetic Living 101.

Nate had originally offered to pick me up, but Cass called last-minute to request that I take a cab to and from my own party. "No problem," I had said stoically. That actually meant I would have more freedom to plot my departure time.

I sidled out of the backseat of the Yellow Cab and thanked Harley the driver. He wished me happy birthday and sped off, leaving me standing at the foot of a very pristine hill, known in these neighborhoods as a mere lawn. I don't think I'd ever feel at home in these mini-mansions. There was something so disturbing about the giant, angled roofs and disproportionate gables. It was like a huge scary pop-up book with tales of suburban royalty and knights of conference room tables.

There wasn't anything more depressing than being envious of a life you didn't even want.

I rang the doorbell and noticed a new hangnail. I quickly pulled back my hand and placed it at my side. It would remain in hiding for the next three hours.

Cass opened the door and hugged me tightly.

I patted her head and wondered when we started being a family that touched?

From over her shoulder, I purveyed the posh living room, which had received another recent, expensive makeover. Some new pieces of framed art to the right of the fireplace featured meadows of what appeared to be metal sunflowers. Weren't real sunflowers a prettier image? Was this some sort of statement about industry and nature coexisting? My mind went deeper into minutia and the hug continued.

"Hey, your place looks great," I mumbled and awkwardly stepped back into my personal space.

"Really? You like it? I'm going for something different to reflect another side of me." She said this with a look that pleaded for validation.

I responded as a good guest. "It's beautiful. And it's totally you. Now I see it." I said this jokingly, but she took it as sincere and I left it at that. Five minutes here and I was already out of sync.

"Goodness, are the Dixie Chicks in town?" Mom asked, motioning up and down to showcase my outfit as she approached me for a quick hug.

"You look wonderful, Libby," Dad said, but only after chuckling over Mom's comment.

Mom did a twirl about the entryway to show me her travel-friendly, flowy, wild-colored print skirt. It was everything my outfit wasn't, and that was all the statement she wanted to make. She ushered us all into the living room with the clap of her hands above her head, like the dancing waitresses at the Greek restaurant on Ariel's block.

I turned to roll my eyes at Cass, but she was staring off into space. No fair. She could go to her happy place, and I was still present with the Simon Cowell of mothers.

"Hey! Where are the nieces I love to pieces!" I said this loudly enough to bring the girls out from their rooms.

"Nate has them," Cass said slowly, as though she had been sucking on ice for too long.

I waited for more information, but none followed. I looked around at everyone's diverted glances. Mom sat down in an overstuffed green chair and slapped the arms with her large, ring-covered hands. "We might as well have the conversation now, Cass."

I watched my sister bow her head down. Her hair fell forward and she left it there, defeated.

"What…?"

Ever so quietly Cass spoke her secret to me. "They are with Nate…" Her silence took the last bit of breath from my lungs. "At his apartment."

Whatever blanching is…I did it. Right there on the new crimson carpet. "What do you mean, Cass?" I reached for her hand instinctively. Moments before I had tried to let go of her, and now I wanted to pull her over to my lap and hold her like a child. My mind scanned the many recent messages from her scrawled down by Philip on pink and yellow memo sheets. Sometimes she was asking to get together for lunch. Sometimes for a shopping day. I swallowed hard when I thought of a most recent one that was merely "Want to get together and talk?" In my haste to improve my life, I had not wanted to be around Cass and her utopia. I had forgotten that becoming a better person required being a better person.

"Uh..." Cass looked to my parents for emotional support. I ignored this extreme misjudgment and looked her in the eyes. She continued. "Nate moved out three months ago. We are...you know," she laughed self-consciously, "we are separated. Oh my, such a cliché, isn't it, Mother?" She turned to Mom, who was skimming the edges of a Dale Chihuly glass sculpture on the end table with her index finger. The high-pitched squeal that resulted from this action was Mom's controlling way to interrupt without speaking. It might as well have been a gong.

We all stared at her. Me out of frustration and annoyance, Dad out of pure curiosity, and Cass out of hunger for answers to her big life questions.

After what seemed like an entire concert performance, Mom nodded as if giving permission. For what, though? For Cass to share her pain or her problems?

"Cass. I'm so sorry. I didn't know..." Admitting this last part was difficult. If I had only known, right? Isn't that what we always say...freeing ourselves from ultimate responsibility. If only I had known...then what?

"Cobbler time!" Mom shifted the focus to dessert. I gave her a stony stare and asked Cass if she was okay.

"The hardest part is on the weekends when Nate has the girls. You know...I've never lived alone."

"Living alone teaches independence," Mother Superior chimed in on her way to the kitchen. Her perfume, a sort of musky scent of grass and lemons, wafted in her wake. My eyes watered.

"Mom. Really!" I used a tone I never dared before. But she was wrong to say such a thing. "Cass, you are an independent spirit. You always have been. You'll be okay. Besides, you two are meant for each other. It will work out." Not knowing the circumstances, *that* might have been a careless thing to say, but I meant it. I really did believe they were meant for each other. Maybe I had resented it just a tad in the past, but really I was more amazed by it. I held on to their example when I became too cynical about romance and dating and the quest for finding someone who loved me enough to sacrifice for me and who wanted to know why I liked to wear gym socks and skate around my apartment on Saturday afternoons, and why I chose relish as my only condiment for hot dogs at Seahawks games.

"I sure could go for something sweet and tasty." Dad rubbed his stomach to remind us of Mom's badly timed suggestion. Cass and I looked at one another with mirrored half-winces, half-smiles. Even in this difficult moment, the workings of my parents' finely tuned coercion teamwork almost made us laugh. I placed my arm around her small shoulders as we walked to the dining room.

Normally I would have been ticked that no mention of my birthday had been made up to this point and on through the dishing out and eating of the cobbler. But I was now glad for the lack of attention. We all ate in silence. Each miniscule bite I placed in my mouth rested there for about three minutes before I could force it down. I would be toasting my birthday at the midnight hour with Pepto-Bismol. Oh, joy. And I couldn't breathe well. At first I thought it was the tightness of my new skirt. But it was the uptightness of my old family patterns.

Cass was the one most willing to try conversation. She discussed what the girls were up to in school, what they thought of their teachers, and how much they had grown. "They think it's fun to have a sleepover with their daddy at his play home. That's what they call it..." she choked on the girls' sweet interpretation of a family in trouble.

"How about we retire with our coffee to the lovely living room?" Dad suggested, rubbing his hands together to warm the moment.

I offered to clear the dishes and start the coffee, eager to get rid of this perfectly unsuitable treat for my birthday—Ariel wasn't going to believe this fiasco. I let my mind wander to happier possibilities. I'll bet she and Ferris are hard at work planning my party...where to buy the freshest lobster, what scent of candles to burn in the entry of Ariel's apartment, where on earth they will find a screenplay of *Out of Sight* autographed by George Clooney, etc. That would be my real birthday celebration. It'd be my belated gathering, but it'd be the one worth waiting for.

I stared out the window above the sink as I slowly rinsed the Mikasa china plates. I could see the neon colors of little Libby's sand pail and shovel half hidden by the purple hydrangea bush. What would happen to my precious nieces? All those times I didn't return Cass's call or accept her invitation to come over to watch a video, I was also saying no to those adorable munchkins. I had missed opportunities to be a good sister and a good aunt. Conviction set with my stomach about as well as the berries did.

I braced my elbows on the sink's edge and rested for a moment, both hands remained beneath the rushing warm water. If I confessed my recent failings, it could take the pressure off Cass. Mom and Dad would spend the rest of the evening giving me ten steps to a new and improved professional me. On the other hand, it could sound as though I'm a totally insensitive whiner who is self-absorbed during her sister's most difficult hour. I was never a good judge of such things. I have almost swallowed my size seven foot many a time among family and friends.

When the timer buzzed on the Krups coffeemaker, Cass returned to the kitchen to help me. While our parents debated the negative effects of using artificial sweeteners in the living room, Cass whispered, "I baked you a chocolate marble cake to take home. Hopefully you will get a real celebration. I should have told you straight out on the phone. I certainly didn't want to tell Mom and Dad this soon, but they really wanted to visit and the timing with your birthday seemed good otherwise." Cass reached up to open one of the kitchen cupboards. There beneath the opaque, Tupperware covering, I could see the outline and magnificence of my cake.

I gave her a sideways hug and pretended to reach for the frosting for a quick taste. She slapped my hand down. "I know they are totally disappointed in me." She looked down at her hands. They were frozen in tight fists.

"No, don't do that, Cass. They have no reason to be disappointed. Why? You are being brave in the middle of a hard time. You love your girls, and..." once again I was stepping into an area I knew nothing about. Did she love Nate? Had she asked him to leave?

Reading my thoughts, she reached for my arm. "I do love Nate. And he loves me. This isn't probably a typical separation. We just...got lost. Us. We were Mommy and Daddy twenty-four hours a day. I can't remember the last time Nate called me by my name. Now we point to the other spouse and say, 'Let Daddy tie your shoe.' 'Show Mommy your painting.'" She hugged herself against an imagined cold wind. "We realized we hadn't had a real conversation in months. And sadly, that isn't an exaggeration."

"But a breakup? I mean, how does this...how does being apart help that?"

"We are both desperate to become the individuals we were when we fell in love. And we needed space to do that. I want to rediscover him as Nate, the great guy with kindness in his smile and patience that never runs out. And he wants to see a bit of the Cass who could laugh at spilled milk, enjoy pointless television once in a while, and who lived for a long solo bike ride down by the waterfront. "

I nodded. I remembered her like that. "Which Cass do I thank for the cake?" I teased to lighten the moment.

"Funny. Now get back out there," she turned her narrow, pretty face in the direction of the living room, "so you can spend your birthday hearing how they plan to fix my life."

I smiled an evil grin. "Don't worry, sis. You made me this fabulous cake, and now I have a gift for you. Shall we?"

Cass had a sly, curious smile on her face as she loaded up a tray with the coffee carafe and china cups and followed me back out to the den of persnickety parents. She placed the selection on the center table and then joined me on the yellow satin couch closest to the kitchen. Mom and Dad sat across from us on its twin.

"It's like we're on *Family Feud*," I said. There is that big toe of mine... pressing against my back molar again. Cass giggled and our parents looked baffled. They were not television junkies like their children.

"I have an announcement," I said boldly. Mom's back arched as did her eyebrows. Dad nodded and leaned forward, resting his palms on his shins.

"Yes, dear?" he asked.

"I've had a change recently..."

"Aldus broke up with her," Mom interrupted and looked so completely bored and informed that I swear she was about to stifle a yawn. Instead, she reached up and rubbed the turquoise turtle necklace at her throat.

A huge sigh escaped my lips. "I broke up with Angus. And that is not my news."

"The guy who looks like that beautiful lead singer of Torrid...Jude Shea?"

"Please," I crooned. "Angus had good eyes, but overall he is not nearly as ethereal-looking."

Cass thought about this for a moment and then jabbed a thin finger into my meaty upper arm. It was as though we were in high school for a moment. "Jude has those amazing lashes and such a bad boy reputation."

"Bad boy is putting it lightly. Isn't he a total druggie?"

Cass pulled an overstuffed jade pillow from behind her head and hugged it in front of her. "Maybe he's misunderstood."

"He forced a night security guard to take him to the top of the Space Needle last year so that he could bungee off the top...while high...and without a bungee cord."

"I read that he passed out before he could try."

Dad coughed a couple times to halt our tangent. "Cass mentioned you were nearing a promotion. That's quite admirable."

Mom interrupted with her enlightening question. "You've been with that company for how long now?"

"Well, I have a funny story about that promotion." Deep breath. "The company went through a major merger. Which is exciting from a corporate growth perspective, but a lot of people lost their jobs. And I didn't. Not exactly." I was a lousy joke teller and an even worse bad news/good news/bad news revealer. "I got a bit of a demotion. But it is a good situation, and I have a fantastic new boss."

"A bit of a demotion. What does that make you then, dear?" Mom took on the posture and tone of Barbara Walters when she goes in for a friendly comment about a celebrity's biggest secret or shame. Her eyes shifted to the left for a moment. She was doing the math. If one executive trainee without a future is given notice that she has even less of a future, how many failures is that in total?

"What does that make you?" she repeated with a brief smile at the close.

The phrasing of the question made me want to respond "a loser," but I knew what she was really asking. "Well, instead of an assistant account executive, I'm an assistant to an account executive. Blaine Slater. He's one of the best AE's in the business. Just moved from Chicago..." I paused to take in the visual that name resurrected. The image of him looking over my file and commenting on my creative potential put me at ease. "He is new to the company and already is making heads turn." Mine especially. "He is a good guy, a family man, and also really into team playing. I'm glad to be a part of his team." I fell deeply into my interview persona, a tragic consequence of too many mock interviews with my mother every year since seventh grade.

Cass gave me a sideways glance and in her eyes I saw not only appreciation for derailing any talk of her separation but an entire thesis on "going overboard when a few words would suffice."

"We'll Google him, dear. Go on."

All of a sudden, I felt fat and dumpy in my suede skirt. My boots felt tight, my big toes were numb and tingly. I wanted nothing more than to be home in my sweats. "That's it. I got a demotion. My career could look brighter..." I stopped there. I didn't want to betray the private truth that was forming for me. I was grateful for my new situation, and I didn't want to see it completely destroyed tonight. Not even for the sake of a diversion for Cass.

"Working for a man," Mom stated and sighed. She liked men as colleagues, but she would never want one immediately above her in status. She always said this was one simple rule that kept her career thriving from day one.

Dad stepped into his professional role. "I see that this could be a good move. Perhaps it's a case of one step back and two steps forward?" He turned to Mother and said softly and sternly, "You know, dear, not all men are placed in companies to keep women down."

Mom shrugged her shoulders in unconvincing acquiescence and adjusted her Southwestern attire. I knew she had never seen a cactus up close.

"And I don't want everyone thinking Nate is the bad guy." Cass responded to a nonexistent conversation. But I followed her tangent. And she was right to announce this. It was easy to see the spouse in the apartment across town as the bad one. The Leaver. He was, I'm sure, actually trying to keep life as normal for Cass and the girls as possible.

"No, dear. We have great respect for Nate. In fact, we had a good talk with him about the situation right before we came here," Mom said.

Cass clenched the pillow more tightly. "You didn't tell me that. What did you say? You didn't guilt him, did you?"

Dad added some cream to his coffee to lighten the moment. "We wanted to approach him with the plan we are about to share with you."

Uh-oh. I glanced around looking for charts and a telltale overhead projector.

"P-plan? Like your retirement?" Cass asked hopefully.

"We are moving in."

Cass and I both sucked in our breath at the same time, speed, and velocity. The flame of the silver block candle on the coffee table leaned toward us and then went out.

"We'll help with the girls. We can certainly help you increase order in the home. And, of course, we'll be here to solve this family issue."

"That cobbler was so good. Should we have more?" I chimed in to create a diversion so Cass could jump ship. Instead, she jumped right into the current of control.

"This is not a family issue. Well, it is, but it isn't our family issue. It is *my* family issue. Nate and I are not a puzzle to solve. We are a couple in need of space."

Ah, space. That final frontier that distanced us from our parents had just been annihilated.

"You think you need space, but what you really need is us. We're moving in." Once again Mom clapped her hands above her head. This time apparently to signify that, for all pretense and purposes, a contract had been negotiated. The hemp fabric of her loose blouse slid from her bracelet-clad wrist to her shoulders. I noticed her biceps were more toned than mine and tried to recall where I had placed my gym card, gym bag, workout clothes, and motivation for such things.

I looked to Cass and raised my eyebrows in our nonspeak for, "Do what the lady says and nobody gets hurt."

While poor, frustrated Cass bit her tongue and turned blue in the face, my tongue located a last bit of blueberry in my upper left wisdom tooth.

It was now officially, unequivocally, my worst birthday ever.

Seventeen

I stared down at my blue clogs. Drops of rain buoyed on the surface and formed a sloping smiley face. The rain was winking at me, prodding me like a school yard taunter to step forward.

This would be the perfect day for me to go in those double doors. A new year of my life and a chance to begin again with the elements I wanted to take with me into this decade. What would those be exactly? I interrogated myself instead of moving. Faith, happiness, contentment…purpose. Direction.

I checked my watch. The service would start in five minutes. I could hear the first welcoming chords of the organ. Families and individuals reached for those doors, opened them, and went in. If I shuffled in behind the next group, I could appear to be connected and then slip into a pew in the back. I always imagined that my initial venture would be on a rainy day. There were so many distractions to hide behind when the weather was wet—umbrellas opening and closing, brightly colored boots being wedged from children's feet and lined up under the coat rack, people shaking their heads to unsuccessfully rid locks of moisture.

I could write Aunt Maddie about my experience. She would love to have a peek at an American church these days. The bus doors opened and shut behind me. A man in rainbow-striped suspenders walked past me to wait for the next bus. If a grown man can wear suspenders and short pants with boots, surely I could enter a house of worship.

I shook my head to unsuccessfully rid my locks of moisture and walked toward the back. The final aisle was my destination. I walked toward it, glad to be breathing in the history, the meaning, the sacred air.

"Any closer?" came a familiar voice.

I turned slightly to my left and gave Mr. Diddle a sly look. Nomad awakened to the sound of his master's voice and trotted over to us, slow with sleep and age.

"Closer to what?" I asked innocently.

"Did you bring me a Danish?" He smirked, looking a lot like the winking raindrops on my clogs.

I reached into my Columbia jacket and my fingers located the inner pocket and the small white bag containing a glaze-drizzled strudel. Mr. Diddle leaned forward but the rules of appropriate personal space boundaries kept his nose too far from his pastry. He licked his lips with anticipation. I handed him the bag and reached into the pocket again, this time for Nomad's treat.

"The other place even offers free dog biscuits to customers. Wouldn't that be a cool way to serve your loyal customers and feed the hungry canines of Seattle?" I turned our attention to his areas of weakness and not my own.

"Publicity propaganda!" Mr. Diddle hollered with lazy lips that allowed a flake from a sugary layer to tumble onto his horizontal-striped knit sweater woven in the shades of a carnival.

"Good business," I corrected.

"You seem to believe in your little business tactics."

"They are proven methods of customer service." I pointed back out toward the front of the store. Someone had drawn graffiti symbols in the dirt of the window. "Putting up a sign and cleaning a window are not business tactics. They are common sense."

Mr. Diddle turned his back to walk with wide steps toward his checkout counter. I'd never noticed how he and Nomad walked the same cadence. "I'm just saying, you show a great deal of *faith* in what you believe in." He said this quietly, but I saw his sides expand and contract with laughter.

I got the point but would not give him the satisfaction of further discussion. I decided to go immediately to the religion section. Let him see that I was serious about learning more and growing in my faith. I'd already admitted to myself that I was a person of faith. There was no changing that...except in growth. I had told Pan. I had even told Blaine in so many words. So now I could be open about wanting to deepen my walk in front of Mr. Diddle.

While I was sitting down on a red, white, and blue rag rug and skimming all the titles, Nomad leaned against me with his full weight. I liked the feeling of his body rising and falling with each deep breath as he began to sleep. The rhythm soon made me tired and my eyes became heavy. Every few minutes Nomad's back right leg would kick and jolt me back to awareness.

"Oh, I have something for you," Mr. Diddle said casually.

"More travel books?"

"No."

"Are you finally going to let me write up a travel itinerary for you? I think you should take a vacation. It's not right for someone to work so many years without some kind of break or change of scenery."

"Who would run this crazy busy hub?" he asked teasingly.

"Well, it would have to be someone who could handle the high stress and demands of this kind of establishment."

"Exactly. Me. I hired me in the beginning, and I have no intention of firing myself. But I do take your advice to heart. Some day, my dear, I will surprise you and ask for one of those brilliant itineraries. Now wake that drooling dog and come on over here."

I tapped the top of Nomad's head until his eyes opened halfway. He yawned and repositioned himself so that he was stretched out on the rug and not on me. I stood and did my own stretching before walking over to the counter.

Mr. Diddle's glasses were on the edge of his nose. He was totaling his inventory. I stood in front of him patiently and impatiently, like a student awaiting her grade. "Almost done here," Mr. Diddle said, and then he started to whistle. "Ah, found the error. I hate it when I'm off by just a few pennies."

I almost asked what it could possibly matter, but it was clear by his meticulous focus that he and I approached life with different standards of preciseness. When I was about to excuse myself, Mr. Diddle looked at me, smiled, and reached below the counter, where he retrieved a present wrapped in white sketch paper and red string.

"How'd you know?" I stammered.

"A little bird told me."

"We don't know any of the same birds."

He smiled a knowing smile. "We do now. This little bird lives in a far-off land and she loves you very much."

"Aunt Maddie? How..." I remained baffled but was enjoying the mystery surrounding this gift on the counter.

"You left that printed email here a while back, and on a whim I wrote to your aunt just to tell her that we'd found a copy of the book she suggested for you and to let her know what a wonderful niece she had."

"And so she told you when my birthday was?"

"She mentioned earlier this week that she wished she could be here with you."

"This week? So what? Now you're pen pals?"

He pushed his lips together and grinned, obviously pleased.

"This is very interesting."

"It is indeed. I kind of like this email correspondence. I get why your generation has embraced it. It makes me more of a man of the world, don't you think?"

"A man of the world would understand the concept of advertising."

Mr. Diddle pushed the small package toward me. "Aren't you curious?"

I nodded and began to undo the loose knot of string in the center of the gift. The paper unfolded when the string was removed, and I could see a bit of dark brown leather. Pushing aside the wrapping, I saw a slim, elegant leather-bound book with a delicate attached gold ribbon bookmark draped in the layers of thin pages. The gold-edged pages had worn places, which gave them the rich look of copper.

"It's beautiful, Mr. Diddle. I love it. Is it poetry?"

"Look and see. You're a browser, remember?"

I laughed and picked up the slim book. I opened to where the page marker was set and it was the book of Psalms. Surprisingly, the print on the fine pages was easy to read. "You bought me a Bible?"

"Not just a Bible...but a travel Bible. Do you like it?"

I held it close to my chest. "I love it." I stood on tiptoe and leaned over the counter to kiss my old, dear friend on the cheek. "I absolutely love it. You just made my birthday, Mr. Diddle."

Eighteen

Other than the rumor mill about Cecilia being AWOL, there wasn't much excitement to welcome me on Monday morning. The only personal call I had was from the doctor's office confirming my annual exam. I always scheduled it for the week of my birthday so I wouldn't forget. I read that trick in some fitness magazine, but it was rather a depressing ritual. From now on I would schedule my womanly exam every Flag Day or something. Who needs such an experience on her birthday?

Why is it that at twenty-six I felt strongly independent and near a finish line of some sort, and now I feel tired, behind schedule, and far from "in the running"? Where was the in-between where you live out your fantasy of being young, vibrant, and on track for fulfilling the American woman dream?

My fellow Emerson High School graduates had three kids and two husbands by now. They probably saw thirty-one as their procreation finish line. The end of a strong showing in the baby-and-life category. Me...I was just hoping for a beginning of some kind. Not the kid thing necessarily, but a different kind of birth. Mine.

While I wasn't thrilled to be forced to wear nylons and sit upright, I was relieved to be at work. The weekend had been quite emotional. To have projects in front of me and tasks at hand felt controlled and safe. Blaine was back from a weekend trip somewhere and feeling a bit haggard. He kept popping out to ask me questions rather than using the intercom. I think he was watching for Cecilia to get in. He kept adjusting his tie and going to the watercooler.

"I can let you know when she gets here," I said on his fourth time by my cubicle.

He seemed startled and then looked a bit shamed. "Yes, actually, that'd be helpful." He smiled sheepishly and took a swig of water. Man, he was adorable. I'm not a woman who fawns over men easily or frequently, but he was so endearing sometimes. Maybe it was because he looked embarrassed just then and didn't try to cover it up. As he headed back to his office, he said, "Just don't be obvious about it."

Funny too.

An email from Rachel came through with a little "ping." The Pavlov effect kicked in and I clicked on the envelope.

> To: Company
> From: Rachel for Cecilia
> Re: Cecilia's schedule
>
> It has come to my attention that there has been some confusion about Cecilia's schedule. She is not slated to return from the Texas situation until later this month. Please route any questions or communications through me. I'm sorry for any inconvenience the earlier lack of information has caused.

"Ping." Two immediate emails from Blaine came through. He was eager to distribute more memos and to schedule more conference calls with some of Cecilia's previous clients. This time I walked the short distance to Blaine's doorway and stood there until he noticed.

"Yes, Libby?"

"I'm glad you figured out just how efficient technology can be," I said.

He returned in kind. "Amazing stuff, this email, but may I remind you that I won't always be the new guy to make fun of."

"I guess I had better enjoy it while I can. Anything else on the docket for Cecilia's accounts. I mean...our new accounts?"

"About that, Libby. I probably shouldn't hesitate about this because Ken has given me the go-ahead, but I'd rather we not refer to these folks as anything other than Cecilia's clients. I'm not clear yet how much she knows. In fact, I was going to feel her out today if she came in. I really hate working on anything that is not on the up-and-up with everyone involved."

"Cecilia's accounts. Got it. I appreciate your stand on that."

"You're pretty loyal to her, aren't you?"

I swallowed hard. "What is that called when the kidnapped person becomes supportive of their captor?"

Blaine laughed and looked genuinely relaxed for the first time in a couple weeks.

I surprised myself by saying, "For some reason, I want to protect her."

He nodded. "I can see that. I don't blame you. She is good at what she does and has a big reputation in the industry."

"Oh, I'll bet."

"Her competitors do respect her...and fear her a little too. That's why I really want this transition to be done properly. And once we get these accounts on our shoulders, she'll have more time to bring in the bigger clients. It's what she is good at. I'm sure that's part of Ken's vision."

I liked his version of Cecilia's future, but I thought he was being a bit too optimistic about her fate. I smiled as I realized Blaine had been nervous about Cecilia all this time out of niceness and not corporate pettiness. He was a rare breed.

Rachel walked behind me and whispered in passing, "Code Blue."

"I will get those letters out for you to sign this afternoon," I said hurriedly and turned from Blaine's doorway so that I could follow Rachel to our secret meeting place. When we reached the main floor lobby, she went right and I went left. After turning several corners we reached the night janitor's closet just seconds apart. I tapped twice on the door and she opened it from the inside.

"How obvious is it that we both liked *Harriet the Spy* as grade-schoolers?"

"Very," she said, barely cracking a smile. "Truth is, I haven't heard from her, Libby. I sent that email around saying she was detained in Texas completely as a cover. I'm really worried about her."

"You really are worried about her."

"I just said that."

"I know. But you are really worried about her. What brought this on?"

"Look, I know she treats me terribly, but this is about more than Cecilia." Rachel whispered but became impassioned by her line of reasoning. "What are we all striving for in this company? To get promotions. To be respected. To be professional women who have it all...only to have it taken from us because we have passed age fifty? I mean, this is ticking me off a little. What does Blaine have that Cecilia doesn't?"

"Well, this is a first impression, but integrity, work ethic, scruples..."

"Okay, so he isn't the bad guy. But you know what I mean about Cecilia. There is just something worth protecting in her."

Rachel was stating everything I had wanted to express to Blaine minutes before. Yet hearing it from her made me want to play devil's advocate. "Are you forgetting about ironing the drapes? What about when she had you hem her pants during that conference...you were under that table for two hours before they took a break."

"I know," Rachel shook her head with disbelief. "Crazy. But Cecilia is in trouble, and I don't know what she's going to do. I'm afraid she'll respond irrationally. I wish the lunatic would at least check in."

"She hasn't called at all?"

"I don't know how much you should know. You are Blaine's assistant. I don't want you to feel obligated or morally bound to tell him."

"If it sounds like something I would need to divulge, I will stop you."

"I called the hotel in Dallas to confirm that their wireless Internet service was working." Rachel looked at me and paused.

"Nothing I need to run and tell Blaine yet. Go on," I coaxed her from my perch on an upside down gray bucket that featured the poison symbol.

"They said Cecilia never checked in. They had the reservation I booked, but she never showed."

"But she called me from there when she was tracking you down..."

"She could have called from the center of the universe. We'd never know."

Something stuck in my head and my thoughts couldn't quite get around it or through it. "Cecilia mentioned the word 'center' during our conversation, and when I questioned what she meant, she rephrased it, saying the hotel had a business center."

Rachel's face went pale, which was startling to see on this tan-skinned beauty. "Oh, no. Are you thinking what I'm thinking?"

"Well, we both know what Cecilia was up to when she disappeared in the past. It wasn't for management training or racial sensitivity seminars."

"Go on," Rachel encouraged me along. Neither of us wanted to actually say it.

"Rehab."

Rachel slapped her forehead with her hand, causing her entire head to slam against the door. The clash of body and metal echoed, and we held our breath until we were sure nobody was going to open the door and expose our clandestine conference.

I continued, this time standing to pace back and forth in the confines of our closet. "How long. What is typical?"

Rachel looked upward to count off the past times Cecilia disappeared. "If she goes somewhere for plastic surgery procedures, she usually reappears in four weeks. Her rounds at the Center for Sustenance Over Substance, aka SOS camp, are for three weeks."

"Okay, so we at least have three weeks."

"To what?"

"Stall for her. This is no time for her to disappear. She'll lose her job for sure."

"I sent that email." Rachel grabbed a set of rubber gloves and tried them on.

"It was too vague. We need to imply that there is more going on. We need to buy her time and make her look good."

Rachel looked up from her rubberized, yellow hands. "I cannot negate an entire reign of terror. Don't set the bar too high."

"We can make her absence logical rather than suspicious. Build up the Texas story or imply she is working on something of a classified nature."

"That last part would be true."

"Exactly. So classified it is downright secretive." I nodded, pleased with our progress. We could pull this off without having to make up elaborate stories. Nobody would have to know that Cecilia took random vacations whenever she needed to. "Does she really have a drug problem?"

"Back in the sixties and seventies, yes. Now she returns more to stabilize..."

"And harmonize." I finished the phrase. I had heard Cecilia use this mantra numerous times while berating an employee or a customer service agent. "Remember that week she demanded we all go vegetarian during her detox food purge..."

Rachel's eyes lit up and she finished the story, "And then one day after lunch we found her in the men's room with Philip in a headlock, and she was yelling, 'You reek of leg of lamb, you traitor.'"

"Good times."

Only Rachel could understand this twisted sentiment. "It ain't over till the mean lady swings. These industrial cleaners are going straight to my head. Give me a ten-second lead before you exit."

I gave her a full minute. Unlike my sensitive friend, I was enjoying the scents of pine and ammonia. A nice reminder not to judge Cecilia's past too harshly. While I sat in the closet, on a bucket, I had an overpowering urge to go tell Blaine everything—not as his employee, but as a confidant. I shook off the thought as I stood up to leave. Blaine's intoxicating smile was obviously going straight to my head.

The empty apartment greeted me—the front door moaned, the fridge hummed, and the floorboards creaked. Not ready to face only mechanical conversation, I picked up the phone and put it back down several times. I wanted to call Ariel to see if she'd mention her outing with Ferris, but I was afraid she wouldn't and then what would I do? Bring it up? Or fall into the tunnel of distorted questioning and self-loathing? Probably the latter. I hung up again.

Tired of the pressure of my pants' waistline against my nonexistent waistline, I decided to change into shorts and a T-shirt. Why pretend I was going to go anywhere else this evening? I looked around at my bedroom, which was in complete disarray. Cleaning could be my redemption tonight, but I knew it wouldn't be. I felt very alone these days. Being single had never actually bothered me before, not the way it seemed to trigger dark fears in women like Marsha and even Ariel, to some extent.

Ariel. I walked over to the phone again and hesitated. Then it rang, startling me. Maybe I was in sync with Ariel. Surely it'd be her. I picked up.

"Are you alone?" A muffled voice croaked on the other end of the phone.

A strange pervert or a funny friend? While I was deciding whether to respond to the voice, it rose up again with more command.

"Either you are or you aren't! Don't go moronic on me when I need you most."

I was afraid to say the name, but my mind was already thinking it. *Cecilia.* My voice surprised me with its attitude. "There is a place you can reach me during normal business hours. You might remember that place with desks and cubicles and paper shredders." I wasn't going to let her push me around on my own time.

"That place is all I can think of."

She sounded sad. I cut the woman some slack. "I'm alone. What's going on, Cecilia?" I walked over to the cupboard and reached for my last brown sugar toaster pastry and plopped down on the couch. I needed comfort food to face her.

"First, I need to ask you for a favor. This conversation must be completely off the record. Completely. Can you agree to that?"

I seemed to be having a lot of secret conversations lately. This one scared me the most. Cecilia did stretch her limited understanding of common courtesy by asking rather than commanding the favor. I continued to give her undeserved slack. "You are calling me as a...um, a friend, right? So why should it be considered anything other than off the record."

"Blah, blah, blah. So we're in agreement, yes?"

"Yes." I kicked my coffee table out of frustration, but the pain just made me more mad.

"I know what my future looks like at Reed and Dunson. I've witnessed countless colleagues go through the exact same process of elimination. Pretty soon I will be asked to head up the humanitarian committee. That is the kiss of professional death."

"We have a humanitarian committee?" I found this fascinating.

"A board actually. It gives the company major tax write-offs each year. But it is also a way to appease the employees they are writing off."

I took another bite of pastry. "Who's on this committee?"

"Did I not just say?" She sighed loudly. "Former high-powered executives who were willing to settle for figurehead roles on a pathetic board. You wouldn't have heard of them…which was my original point."

I heard some hollering in the background and apparently Cecilia did too.

"I have seven minutes left. Look at the stinkin' clock, would you!"

"Watch it!" My ear throbbed, my patience waned.

"Libby. Listen to me. I've found my ticket back to the top. Not only do I have a knack for sniffing out opportunity, but I'm a genius. Normally I wouldn't give you the chance to work with a project of this caliber, but I'm desperate."

I don't need to take this. "Feel free to exclude me, Cecilia. Come back to the office and deal with your own genius idea." *Rachel and I are running out of time and desire to cover for you anyway.*

"What I'm about to tell you cannot involve anyone, Libby. Not Rachel, not Blaine—especially not Blaine—and certainly not Tara. This is a one-shot deal. A master plan to save my arse and to redeem your sorry state of career, I might add."

A loud thud reverberated through the phone. Cecilia yelled, "If you throw the other shoe at me, I'm no longer selling cigarettes to you and your idiot friends. Got it?"

I tried to remember if I had any more aspirin in the bathroom cabinet. "I have a condition of my own, Cecilia. I'll help you if you are up front with me. Where are you calling from?"

"I'm at the SOS again," she said, quickly adding, "but on the urgent self-care wing, not the rehab unit."

"Thank you. Now go on."

"Well, just for old time's sake, I decided to attend one of the circles."

"Circles?" I reached for a blanket to cover my bare legs and hoped that somebody truly was timing this call.

"Purity circles. You talk about what you want your life to look like on the outside without drugs or alcohol. I got there a bit late, so I sat in the back row on one of those horrible blue plastic chairs next to this scruffy young man. Well, the meeting was a total mistake...totally touchy-feely and without any direction, so I started digging through my purse for my iPod."

I laughed. "I don't take you for an iPod person."

She ignored this comment and forged ahead, her minutes quickly dwindling. "This scruffy guy looked over my shoulder as I scanned my artist list. I was about to berate the rude ragamuffin when I noticed his beautiful, sensitive eyes under the disgraceful mop of hair."

"Cecilia, so help me...if you called to tell me about your latest love conquest, I will not be a part of any plan. So stop right there."

"Normally, I would have considered that direction as well. But when I saw those eyes, that smile, those very white, slightly crooked adorable teeth, I knew I had more than a good time sitting to my right. I had my ticket to the top. This is my genius, Libby. While most ordinaries would be tripping over their tongues and struggling to find a dull writing utensil and a piece of paper to mooch an autograph and thereby build their 'guess who I met' party repertoire, I understood exactly what I could offer this celebrity and what he could offer me in return."

She had my attention. My mind scanned the many magazine covers I had seen on the newsstand in front of the Thriftway the other day. Who was recently busted for drugs or thrown from a multimillion dollar film project? "Who? Who?"

"They're sending mean Rodney to force me off the phone. I'll call you tomorrow at the office to outline my plan."

"Why aren't you using your cell phone?"

"The night guards confiscated it," she said and then raised her voice for the benefit of those near her, "some blond brat from Orange County turned me in for talking after midnight. Wait until I write an article about this for *Vanity Fair*. This will be as hot a spot for recovery as Detroit in winter."

"Who is it, Cecilia?"

"We have to act quickly. Don't make any plans for the weekend."

"Who is your ticket back to power, Cecilia?"

"Jude Shea," she whispered with what I assumed were tightly pressed lips.

"My sister and I were just talking..."

The dial tone interrupted me, but I barely noticed. My hand went limp and the phone fell between the couch cushions. I could feel the rush of power transfer from Cecilia's petty mind to my own. Seattle's biggest hometown music hero-turned national superstar wasn't stiffing his music company billions of dollars in record deals and concert revenues to live the high life in Belize...he was at the SOS attending purity circles and sitting on plastic chairs.

And only Cecilia and I knew it.

Nineteen

"You look like the cat that got the canary," Cass stated as she refilled her water glass from the carafe at our linen-covered table. "Did something good happen at work this morning? Or maybe an encounter with that new boss you mentioned? I got the sense you liked him."

I shook my head severely. No. No. "Blaine? No, he's just a great boss. Besides, I'm keeping some really big secrets from him."

"Maybe he has potential."

I shook my head again. "I'm trying to be more realistic about my life, more intentional about my purpose. I don't want to fill my head with false romance possibilities. That kind of thinking made me go out with a guy like Angus."

"What is a guy like Angus?"

I spread butter over a slab of beautiful foccacia bread, took a bite, and shrugged as though I didn't know, but I wanted to be honest with my sister. These moments of reflective conversation were rare for us. "A guy like Angus has some nice qualities, or at least comfortable qualities. But his life was so different from mine. I'm always on the outside looking in at societal groups. I've never fit in anywhere, so I make myself conform, try a new way of living, and hope that one day I will look around and realize that I belong."

"How soon before you knew Angus wasn't more?"

"The first week." I looked up repentantly from a forkful of romaine lettuce.

"Why'd you keep dating him?"

"To avoid dating."

"Makes sense."

"You were protected from the whole single scene. Basically you feel compelled to date and date and date, and you experience buyer's regret on a regular basis. So when I felt uneasy about Angus by the first Saturday, I figured it was just part of that lamenting. It'd be like buying that house we always liked in the old neighborhood because it had a great porch. Remember? Well, it had a great porch but the roof was caving in and the siding was sliding off...and the door frames looked like they were borrowed from a different-sized house. For a few weeks you'd focus on the porch because that was the selling point and somehow it made your life richer and better. But after that the weather would get cold and you'd be forced to spend time inside, and pretty soon you'd notice the cracks in the walls and the gaps in the floorboards."

Cass stared at me with her lips slightly parted and her eyes squinting with disbelief. "You're such an overanalyzer. No wonder relationships end. You probably wrap the tentacles of tangents around them and choke them to death."

I started laughing and so did she. "You're so right."

"Is Blaine a guy like Angus?"

"Not at all. Honestly, I don't know what kind of guy Blaine is." I paused with my fork in the air. This was an interesting revelation. Normally, I would have mentally written Blaine off as purely a superior being. Therefore, I would have done anything to appease him, as in saying yes to his church self-invite. I hadn't really placed him in any category. He was just Blaine...a nice, respectable guy who was trying to do his best job possible.

"Earth to Libby."

"My problem is that I had a crazy, inappropriate supervisor before, so now that I'm in the presence of a normal, functional, and kind leader, his kind actions feel personal. But I can step back and appreciate Blaine for who he is and what he's trying to accomplish."

"Hearing your description makes me think about how I felt when I met Nate." Cass smiled tenderly. "After our strange family, Nate seemed so normal he was exotic. At such a young age he wanted to work toward a real relationship, a family, a house, a commitment. In some ways, he was offering to accompany me on a journey to a shared destination." She pressed her lips together as though refreshing a coat of gloss. "The destination we had."

"Have, Cass. You have those things." I reached across the restaurant table and touched her hand. The move surprised her, but she seemed grateful.

"Yes. We do."

When our orders of linguini were placed in front of us, we ate much of our meal in silence. We looked at one another frequently and smiled. After eating half a loaf of bread, I broke the silence. "I always figured our family seemed normal to you. You got along with Mom and Dad. You followed a logical path in life. They never give you grief. I assumed we lived these opposite lives in the context of the same family. Good daughter life. Messed-up daughter life."

"They don't give me grief? Mom and Dad are staying in my guest room, three yards away from my room. They are at the breakfast table before I even get up. They are combing my daughters' hair and selecting their outfits while I'm still looking for my favorite coffee mug, which is nowhere to be found because apparently the shade of pink was offensive to Mom so she got rid of it. This is big grief."

She was right, of course, but I was determined to win my argument. "You haven't had worthless relationship after worthless relationship. You haven't worked for a company for five years just to get demoted. You might have this season of misery, but you are still the daughter Mom can talk about at university fundraisers."

Cass's eyes were wide with disbelief. "You've got to be kidding."

"What?" I eyed a pat of butter wrapped in gold foil and considered whether eating it without bread would be a regrettable choice.

Cass started talking a mile a minute. I put my foil-encased temptation down. I couldn't believe what I was hearing. "You are the college graduate who can do 'anything you put your mind to' and will surely someday be a powerful executive. Libby, you are her pride and joy. And if you say you don't know this, I will scream in the middle of this restaurant. I will."

I was tempted to look around for the *Candid Camera* crew. Had she not witnessed the conflicted conversations between Mom and me for the past twenty years? From the moment I could utter a word, my mother was correcting me, coercing me, and chiding me. So much so that when Cass was born five years later, I prayed to God that she would foot the bill as the perfect daughter because I sure wasn't going to. Not ever. And until now, I thought that prayer had been answered.

"Unbelievable." Cass shook her head silently back and forth. "Libby, you have some huge blind spots. I don't know how you make it through life sometimes."

"You know, I'm starting to get that about me. But, Cass, all I hear from Mom is what a great home you have created, and how you finished high school focused on what you wanted and you went for it. Do you know how many times she has thrown your perfect family in my face...?" I stopped there. In proving my point, I was hurting her. Her perfect family was struggling.

She seemed to sense the reason for my silence. "Mom has never told me she is proud of that, and now I've not lived up to that one area I had going for me. But, ya know, Libby, I don't think any family is perfect. I do know that I love Nate, and I love my girls, and each day I tell those girls that they are wonderful. That I'm proud of them. And that I love them no matter what." Her voice was strong but quiet and controlled.

I felt ashamed for the times I belittled her choices and her strengths with "Oh, what a perfect life" comments to her. I did to her what Mom did. We finished our tiramisu in silence. It was a lot to take in for a lunch hour. I had to get back to the office, so Cass headed back with me. She veered off toward Crate & Barrel.

True to form, earthquake central seemed to have developed a new fault line. Me. When I walked on to the Reed and Dunson main floor, Philip looked at me directly and then down at his *GQ* magazine cleverly tucked into the latest stock reports.

"Blaine's been looking for you," he said, clearly pleased with the idea of me being reprimanded.

I acted indifferent and kept walking. I could tell that Philip wasn't really reading about Armani's new line of faux crocodile jackets. He was watching me walk toward Blaine's office. The hair on my neck stood at attention. Maybe it was just because I was late. He was waiting for me to get in trouble.

I received similar responses as I walked past coworkers I did not know by name, only by descriptions. Short Skirt Sally, Bluebeard Bob, Tuna Fish Sandwich Tim, Watercooler Walt….they all turned away just as I looked in their directions. There was a certain rush about this. I felt as though I were in the middle of *The Firm*. Could I make it to the staircase before they caught me? Who betrayed me? If only I had worn sensible shoes, I could escape. But I was wearing my birthday boots today. I left the fringe at home, but the power of the boots was with me.

My movie fantasy momentum crashed when I saw Blaine standing by my cubicle. He was definitely waiting and watching, and not for Cecilia this time. My hips seemed to lose their grip on my legs and I wobbled toward him.

"Wh…what is wrong?" I should have acted as though I hadn't noticed the mood shift in the office. I qualified my question. "Do you need me to schedule another conference call this afternoon?" I looked at him, doe-eyed. Was my lip quivering? Breathe. Wait. Hear what it is before jumping in to the confessional.

He looked down. Bad sign. "Could I talk with you in my office?" He motioned toward his open door and then ran his hand through his dark waves. He'd never spoken to me in a boss tone before.

I didn't like it.

I wanted him to know my value as an employee, to be proud of me, to be my champion should the chance for promotion ever enter my life again. Now that a pink slip was in reach, I didn't want it anymore. I wanted to prove my worth.

"Have a seat. Want a Pepsi?" He headed toward the little fridge by his bistro table with mosaic tile inlays.

"I'll have what you're having." Why was I speaking in the dialogue of a date scene?

Blaine extended a can in my direction. My hands were shaking, betraying my anxiousness, as I reached to receive the beverage. "Thanks. Tell me what is going on, Blaine. I want the bad news. I want to get it over with…" When I opened the can, a spray of foam went everywhere. Floor, table, wall, me.

Blaine's scramble to help me clean became a stay in my professional execution. Here we were, on our hands and knees, mopping up sticky soda with bar napkins and random sheets of copy paper from his recycle bin. I was trying to keep my boots out of the drying sap. These babies had to last through my birthday dinner at Ariel's house.

Blaine pressed down on a particularly soaked spot with both hands and a fist of pink memos. I reached for his tan hand. I wasn't trying to be forward, I was trying to calm the situation so that I could be read my rights and start calling headhunters. He looked at me. Now he had the deer eyes. I removed my hand.

"Blaine, please be up front."

He sat back on his heels, tossed the brown, wet memos into the garbage, and looked at me, somewhat defeated. He straightened his tie and stood up, motioning to the dry chair across from him. "Maybe we should use the furniture for this conversation." He was clearly uncomfortable.

Why did I touch him?

"I'll get you started. 'Libby, you are fired because...'"

He laughed. "Libby, you're not fired. The news is not about you, though it will affect you." He sighed then and said, "Ken called our accounts in Dallas. Cecilia is not and has not been there."

My look of worry eased the pressure to feign surprise. "Really?"

"Furthermore, we suspect that she might be up to something."

I snorted. "I'm sorry, but that is not news. It is Cecilia you're talking about, the woman who hired a private company to show up at midnight and repaint the names on the parking places so that she could get a spot closer to the elevator."

He smiled and nodded. "I suppose it isn't such startling news."

"Might I add that she's disappeared for short stints in the past? Sometimes it's work related; sometimes it's more of an impromptu vacation. But as strange and overbearing as Cecilia is, I can honestly say she's one of the most dedicated people in this company. She has moments of genius." I stuttered over the word "genius" and hoped Blaine didn't notice.

"Your loyalty is admirable, Libby."

"Thank you."

"This is why it's possible Cecilia will try to contact you."

"Me?" Dang. "Oh, that's hard to believe. We aren't exactly close."

"Don't worry. Cecilia is responsible for Cecilia ultimately. Ken just wanted you to be informed. He told Rachel as well. Needless to say, if you hear anything from her, please let us know. It's for her safety."

Blaine sounded like an FBI agent trying to convince a fugitive's wife to help bring her husband in. I caught myself before I could laugh. Blaine would take that response as insubordination, but I was wise enough not to respond with affirmation. The last thing I needed in my quest to become authentic was another lie on my plate. Instead, I stood, formally shook his hand, and returned to my desk, where I stared at my calendar entries with doubt.

My phone rang. The screen showed Philip's extension. Mr. Nosey was probably eager to find out how my meeting with Blaine went.

"Yes?" I said sweetly.

Philip sighed, "So you're back at your desk finally."

I remained silent.

"Your cousin is on the line again."

"Cousin?"

"Yes. She's been calling every fifteen minutes, driving me insane and filling up the lines. You know personal calls are discouraged. Especially from neurotic relatives."

"Can I take that call now?"

"Here she is."

I heard the click and then someone clearing her throat.

"Hello?" I said tentatively.

"Libby, it's me." Cecilia's barely disguised voice filled my head.

I looked around and cupped the mouthpiece to be discreet. "This is not a good idea," I said through clenched teeth.

"The plan is in motion. Further instruction will follow later today."

"Don't call me here. Everyone knows you're not in Dallas."

"Speak up. You're such a mumbler."

Simultaneously I coughed and said, "They know you're missing."

She piped back a bit indignantly, "When the key person is gone, they should notice!"

No comment.

She continued, sounding a bit irritated, "Further instruction. Be on the lookout. And if my plan is ruined by your incompetence, I will see to it that my last act as an executive is to throw you out on your ear or other body part."

"Such sweet talk. Might I remind you that I'm your only hope?"

Cecilia grunted. "My career is resting on the shoulders of a terminal assistant. This must be what they call 'hitting bottom' in the purity circles. I may have just had a breakthrough moment. Now I won't have to make up something during my counseling session."

"You know, while you're there, you might take advantage of professional help."

A shadow crossed the opposite wall of my cubicle and I swiveled around in my chair to see Blaine waiting outside of my nondoor. I nodded to him so he knew I saw him. "I have to go."

I hung up, interrupting Cecilia's rant involving profanity.

"Sorry," I said to Blaine. "It was a personal call. My cousin Gertie is at a slim-down camp. She had a Ho-Ho in her hand, and I was trying to talk her out of it. It won't happen again."

"I Ho-hope not." Blaine handed me an account folder with some handwritten notes for me to add to the client's computer file.

I hated that I just lied to a good man. This could not possibly be the way my life was supposed to be going.

Twenty

"Isn't this your stop?" A cute, older gentleman seated next to me on the bus nudged me. I looked out the dirty window to the street sign.

"Yes, it is. Thank you." I smiled and got up to leave.

He stood and followed me down the narrow, metal grid steps to the sidewalk. "I knew because we always get off at the same time. I go downtown for yoga classes on Tuesdays and Thursdays. I thought I needed new hips, but it turns out I only needed to stretch and exercise."

"That's great. You live around here?"

"We're neighbors. I live in 310C. I'm Levi."

"Did you just move in?"

He scratched his bristly five o'clock shadow and looked up. Deep hazel eyes rested between red-rimmed eyelids. "Twenty-some years ago."

"I'm sorry. I haven't been very aware of my surroundings in recent years."

"You always look a little preoccupied, now that you mention it."

We walked up the street steps to the apartment entrance. His ascent was at the pace of a much younger man. I tried to keep up. Our manager, Newton, was fiddling with the radiator. The man was a sad namesake for Isaac Newton. He couldn't figure out how to work anything mechanical.

From what I could tell, he got the position of manager because his father owns the building and he's an only child.

"I occasionally leave notes about a Bible study on your door," Levi said.

"Oh...you're the one. Thank you. I may take you up on that sometime."

"No pressure. It's a standing invitation. I also welcome anyone to join me for church on Sundays, but a lot of folks shy away from that initially."

"I have a church. Well, sort of. But thanks."

"Oh, yeah? Is it near here?" He asked the question but was smiling as though he understood that I didn't really attend *any* church.

"Pretty close," I said with a hint of pride in my voice. Levi headed for the stairs and I walked toward the elevator. "Guess I'll have to take yoga," I said.

Levi smiled and said, "I highly recommend it."

"I'm Libby, by the way," I called out as he started up the red carpeted stairs with pale patches worn by decades of ascending and descending feet.

"I know. Good to meet you, Libby."

"Libby?" Newton coughed my name.

"Yes?" I looked over my shoulder at the man still bent over the radiator. I noticed he had a fork in his hand instead of any logical tool.

"You got a couple packages. Over there on the counter. I signed for them. I didn't peek at what's inside them, I swear." He made his scary statement without looking up or turning around.

"Well, that's appreciated, Newton." I walked over to the small stack of packages and FedEx envelopes by an old, mahogany desk he used as a lobby counter. I sifted through various-sized items trying to recall what I'd ordered from Amazon last. My eyes fell on foreign stamps that lined the upper-right corner of a small flat box wrapped in brown paper. It was from Aunt Maddie. I clutched the package to my chest, excited about what it might contain. With her, I never knew, and that was the fun of having her in my life. One time a plastic wind-up bird arrived wrapped in a tin box. She had seen the toy in the local market and thought the expression on its face looked like me. I took it as a compliment...until I started to think of Philip as a bird.

I kept sifting through the pile but didn't see any other pieces addressed to me. "Did you say packages? I only see the one."

Newton turned around to see what I was holding up. He seemed baffled by my question for a minute. Then his droopy lids rose slightly with recall. "Over there." He motioned toward the other side of the cramped lobby. On the floor, next to a chaise lounge chair with faded blue fabric was a computer box. I walked over to it expecting to see Aunt Maddie's return address somewhere. There was only a regular shipping order folded in the plastic pouch glued to the top. Sure enough, the label was addressed to me.

"Can I keep it in the office overnight? I'll probably have to cab it in to work tomorrow and have our shipping department send it back to Apple."

"Surprised you'd get a Mac in Microsoft city."

"It isn't mine. I didn't order it."

"Well, either way, it cannot stay here or in the office. If somethin' happened to it, I'd never hear the end of it. If it has your name on it, it goes up to your place."

"One night in the office. Nothing will happen. Please?"

Newton ignored me by continuing a different conversation. "Sure, it's a bit awkward. But if you slide it, it ain't so bad." He was obviously not planning to assist me.

I leaned over and pushed the side of the box toward the elevator door, which shut as soon as I came near. While I waited for the archaic mechanism to return from the fourth floor, I watched Newton jab the fork between the radiator and the wall.

"Wouldn't a screwdriver work better?"

He looked at me as though I were an idiot. "How's a screwdriver going to help me get my chocolate Donut Gem out from behind this thing?"

The elevator returned with a reluctant beep and the doors opened, stalling every couple of inches. I raised my hands to concede to Newton's reasoning and shoved my mystery box into the elevator.

As curious as I was about the computer box, I first wanted to see whatever it was Aunt Maddie had sent. I sat in my window seat and leaned against two African print pillows I had discovered at an estate sale in the University district. In those days, Oliver used to drag Ariel and me out every Saturday to help him in his quest for vintage silverware. The pillows had been my consolation prize after a particularly long Saturday involving Oliver's type A shopping strategy and very few snacks or bathroom breaks.

I opened the gift, taking time to appreciate that my aunt had touched this very paper. A homemade box was filled with a folded-up handkerchief, Maddie's version of practical tissue paper and not the actual present—although with her initials monogrammed in pale lavender thread it was a treasure to me. In the center of the white linen lay a beautiful silver necklace cross with an intricate pattern of vines woven around it on both sides. I draped the long chain around two fingers and lifted it up to the light. The etched silver sparkled in the late day sun.

The handkerchief smelled of fresh air and saltwater. I pressed my nose to it several times to take in the scent of life by the sea. A folded piece of stationery remained in the thin cradle of cardboard. I quickly opened and read the note.

> *Dearest Libby,*
>
> *Think of me thinking of you as you open this small gift filled with big love for your birthday. I cherish our relationship and think of you fondly and often during my days at the orphanage. I'm watching the sunset now and wondering what life is like for you these days. Your mom told me of Cass and Nate's trial, and my prayers are with them (especially while Cass is hosting your folks, ha!). I know you will be an encouragement to your sister. You doubt yourself, but truly you are the strong one in your family. Don't forget that I know this about you.*
>
> *A young woman who volunteers with me at the community center sells these beautiful necklaces during Easter season. I saved this special one for the right time, and your birthday seems to be it. I love God's perfect timing.*
>
> *I hope you're enjoying Brother Lawrence and his wisdom. I know you hesitate, waiting to be at the right place in life, career, and mind-set to embrace faith, but I also sense that*

time is now. You don't have to have all the answers to believe completely in God's direction for you. If that were the case, I'd still be in the same old place I was years ago, and not nearly as fulfilled. Read it several times and reflect on it and allow the subsequent lessons to lead you.

    Like the vines that embrace this silver cross, God's love intertwines with your life in beautiful ways. Watch for it, Libby. It is a gift. And so are you.

Love,
Maddie

    P.S. I'm delighted to have communication with your bookstore friend. Is he as charming as he sounds in his emails? He has a very big heart and quite an appreciation for you, my dear.

The phone rang and startled me. My nerves were so on edge since Cecilia involved me in her huge news. As I said, hello, I realized this could be Cecilia. My stomach knotted up, and I wished I'd let the machine do my screening.

"I'm used to being stood up by the male population of Seattle, but not by my girlfriends. Did you forget about our movie date?"

"Pan! No. I mean, yes. I forgot only because I got this great package from my aunt and I lost track of time." I looked at the clock. We had planned to start a monthly movie night with Ariel. I had even picked the movie for our first outing. "Is Ariel there?"

"She called and said she had to work."

"That's good she called, right? You two have been kind of estranged lately."

"She left me a message during the day so she wouldn't have to talk to me."

"I'll be there in no time. Get my ticket and the grub. I'll pay you back."

"Darn right you will. And you'll pay for my ticket if this movie is anything like I think it will be."

"Deal."

I hung up and rushed to my closet. I put on a baseball cap, baggy jeans, and a black turtleneck. I egotistically thought that maybe by total dressing down, I actually would make people curious about the girl who obviously did not want to be recognized. Good thing I kept such thoughts to myself. I'd be committed by my friends otherwise.

Pan greeted me with popcorn, a box of Goobers, and a preshow commentary. "You know, this actress has more romances in one movie than I've had in five years. And I'm supposed to pay nine dollars to support this blatant inequity?"

She was a bit down on romance lately. Her last significant boyfriend worked at a drive-in and ended up dating the woman who wore a red-sequined leotard while roller-skating figure eights around customers' cars at the top of every hour.

"Yes," I said strongly. "And do you know why?"

"Please explain."

"We will support this film because that actress happens to be over thirty. And from now on, I'm going to support women over thirty any and every way I can. I think you should join me in this important cause." The word "cause" happens to be one of Pan's trigger words, and I knew she liked the idea of a woman over thirty getting work in film these days. She understood the politics that played on both sides of the camera.

"Is she still single in real life?"

"Very. In the break room at work there was a magazine cover story all about her tragic parting with that guy from the cops show on Thursdays." To build the empathy I added, "And she was devastated."

Pan rolled her eyes, but I could tell her heart wasn't mocking me.

"These seats okay?" I pointed to the center section about three-quarters of the way up the stadium seating theater.

"Yes, this is good."

"I read a review that says they filmed some scenes without her wearing any makeup. When she is going through her rehab in the movie, she insisted they make it authentic. I understand she even shows some cellulite in a shower scene."

"This is a romantic comedy? Rehab and cellulite? If I stick with filming documentaries, I might have material for Hollywood after all."

We both liked to be on the end seat, so once the movie started, Pan slipped down to the row in front of me. It worked great. We passed the popcorn and treats back and forth with ease. It turned out to be an entertaining movie. I actually was rooting for the inevitable coupling. Sometimes, that is not the case. Bitter and yet so young...that's me. Though the "so" might have to go within the next few years.

I missed the cellulite scene because I was preoccupied about my birthday party. Pan hadn't mentioned attending yet, and I was starting to question whether she had made Ariel's updated guest list. Would I ever get a straight answer out of Ariel or Pan?

"Wait until I tell you about a project I'm trying for. It's finally something I want to do, and it could be my ticket to producing my own work," Pan whispered during a scene where our makeupless and still flawless heroine steals a car to chase after the love of her life.

When the final credits rolled to the sound of a new sure-to-be-a-hit song, I turned to Pan and inquired about the project. She faced me with a broad smile.

"Well, it's for the Experience Music Project at Seattle Center. They're sponsoring the production of a music documentary by a local director. You have to be invited to compete, and I received approval to submit."

"Pan, that is great. I haven't seen you this excited in so long."

"Exactly. This is the first project that has really struck a chord with me. No pun intended." She gripped my arm and gave a slight scream of joy.

"What kind of project will you do?"

Her expression became more subdued, and she reached for the box of Goobers in my lap. She held it up and let the last few fall into her mouth. The crowd dissipated while she slowly chewed her chocolate-covered raisins. I waited patiently, fingering the new cross at my neck.

"It's a lot of work. I have to submit a documentary proposal involving some aspect of the local music scene while also tying it to a more universal theme. It's tricky. They'll get a lot of 'Seattle then and now' submissions."

"Oh, and 'Seattle today and tomorrow,'" I said, laughing. Even though our industries were different, Pan and I still ran across a lot of the same celebrated clichés that made us scratch our heads and wonder why we ever tried to be in a creative field.

"Exactly. I really want to wow them with a strong theme and a strong list of interviews and shot possibilities that would floor them. I don't quite have the concept yet." She licked her fingers to rid them of popcorn salt while she thought about her possibilities. With a laugh she said, "The other day when I walked over to get an application for this competition, I passed by the International Fountain. And you know how they play music while the water sprays from that center globe?"

"It's cheesy, but I like it."

"Me too. Well, they were playing one of Torrid's last songs. No wait, one of their last good songs, before they did that messed up CD."

"Point?" I encouraged the ending to her tale.

"All I could think about was how great it would be to find out what really happened to Jude Shea. I could do an entire documentary related to the mysteries of music or the stories behind the stories. Something like that."

"Jude Shea?"

"You do know he's been missing for more than a year, right? Poof. Gone. And they were at the top of the charts for three years."

I acted as casual as I could, given my predicament. "Sure. But don't you think the whole Jude disappearance thing would fall in the cliché category?"

Pan looked hurt by my comment. I'd only meant to deter her. She pursed her lips for a moment. "Maybe. But the thing is, Jude isn't a cliché unless he's treated as such. The guy truly contributed a lot to the local, national, and, I would say, the international music scene. His disappearance might have been selfish or about publicity, but his contribution cannot be ignored."

"When is it due?" I had to keep her away from the Jude line of thought.

"Shall we?" Pan motioned for us to head for the exit. "In a couple of weeks I have to submit a proposal and a film short. Then the committee will announce the winner at a big EMP event coming up. Life is crazier than ever, but I have let competitions and grant applications come and go before. I don't want to let that happen with this one. It would mean so much to my career. Did I mention that the winner gets an unheard of budget to complete their project *and* their documentary will be aired on national television and be made a regular feature at the EMP? Constant exposure."

"National? No, you left that part out." As we walked behind a slow-moving couple with arms linked, I wondered if I should tell her what I knew about Jude. It was incredible information, and it could be her ticket to this competition and beyond. On the other hand, there wasn't much Pan could do even if she did know about him. We couldn't allow him to be interviewed yet. And Jude was Cecilia's ticket out of trouble...so I'd be sacrificing her master plan, whatever that might turn out to be.

Pan finished her thoughts about the application process as we stepped out into the night air. "That would show them I could back this thing with integrity."

Integrity. There was a word I was longing to live out. And yet here I was remaining silent about a topic of importance to my dear friend so that I could help an executive on the run while working behind the back of a boss who seemed to exhibit true integrity.

Before we parted company, I decided to feel out the situation for the weekend's party. "Pan, what are you doing this weekend? Do you want to go get coffee?"

"Oh, I would, but I have to walk the dogs. I have six now. Can you believe it? But that guy...remember the one who fell in love with Hershey? He has decided to ignore his wife and get him. I'm so glad. And I think it's a perfect match. She'll warm up to him. I mean, who couldn't, with those warm, brown, sweet eyes." She looked so wistful and romantic that I thought maybe the dogs were becoming her relationship killer.

"Is that it? Walk the dogs?"

"Pretty much. I do need to work on my film log for last week. Did I tell you I'm doing a documentary on teaching English as a second language in public schools?"

Okay. I had to face it. Pan had not been invited.

We reached the top of Pine and headed for the bus station. Pan's bus came first but parked way down the line. She took off for it and then stopped midway, "Hey, see you Saturday night!"

Would I ever learn how not to worry?

I headed home feeling much better about my friend-given birthday party. Who doesn't love the idea of a night all about them? If only thoughts of Jude Shea weren't crowding out my visions of an ideal birthday soiree. Why did Cecilia confide in me instead of Rachel? And why was I so willing to be faithful to someone who cared so little about my career and so much about her own? I didn't even know what my former boss had up her sleeve, but my gut told me it wasn't going to be simple.

I touched the cross at my neck once again as I rode the bus home. Aunt Maddie was right. I'd been waiting to become something or someone different before I stepped toward faith. Carrying a heart burdened with confusion and concern, I realized how desperately I needed faith here and now.

Twenty-One

When I stepped out of the wind and into my apartment lobby, Newton barely glanced up from his gossip magazine. He had either retrieved his old Donut Gem or purchased a new package because he had chocolate embedded in the corners of his mouth. When he smiled at something he read on the magazine cover, he looked like a deranged clown.

Inspired by Levi, I decided to take the stairs. My life had been filled with plenty of other humiliations; I didn't want an old man to be more limber and fleet footed than I.

I turned on the television as soon as I walked into my apartment. This was a habit I had broken about a year ago when I realized I had the television on from the time I got home until I went to bed. Today I gave myself grace and scanned the channels eagerly. The laugh track to the latest not-funny sitcom offered a slight distraction from the thoughts rattling around in my head.

After changing into my pajamas, I made some hot cocoa and topped it off in a mug with lots of whipped cream from a can. Pity party, table for one. Maybe I was a bit more like Pan than I cared to admit—the romantic comedy seemed to turn my view of my single life toward the dramatic. The apartment seemed lonely. My pajamas were old and frayed, and it didn't matter because nobody would ever see them unless the cubicle clique reading group did slumber parties too. From my same old spot on the couch I could see at least a dozen things that needed the attention of a willing man with a hammer, a flair for spackle, or at least a sturdy tool belt. The image of Newton holding up a fork over the radiator made me grimace.

If I had a heroic landlord, he would have carried this computer to my apartment for me and then down to a cab tomorrow morning. Maybe the shipping company would come and pick it up for me. It was their mistake. Somebody named Libby Howard or Liberace Hawthorne was desperately in need of their computer. I sipped on my cocoa and casually walked over to the box to examine the photos on the side. It was a nice-looking, expensive computer with an endless list of features. I'd bet Lydia Hayward didn't get demoted; *she* probably advanced in her chosen profession and received a bonus. She needed a computer to match how fabulous and successful she was in her life.

I opened the shipping form and read the information. My name was on the slip, but it hadn't been sent directly from the computer warehouse. At the top of the paperwork was the name of a private company, The Mail Station. Only a PO Box address and a toll-free number were listed. No matter where they were, they were closed by this hour.

My eyes were glued to the pretty photos of a nicely dressed woman and a very stylish man enjoying their new computer at a cool-looking coffee shop. I didn't know if it was because the woman in the photo wore a suit that resembled one I almost bought the day I invested in my fringe skirt, or because the stylish guy reminded me a bit of Blaine, but something possessed me to break into the box. I would call the shipping company tomorrow and tell them I thought my parents had sent me a computer for my birthday but then realized my mistake after I'd already spent the evening experimenting with it.

Satisfied with this warped scenario, I pressed the flaps of the box lid to the sides and my nose took in the scent of fresh plastic bubble wrap. I placed two sheets of it on my kitchen table to play with later.

A slim silver laptop was nestled midway through the box's innards. The promotional description said the thing weighed only 5.5 pounds. I had to hold it to disprove that bunch of malarkey. As I lifted the cold-to-the-touch piece of equipment and placed it on the floor in front of me,

I was surprised how accurate they were. It clearly weighed less than my library bag on checkout day.

A narrow package remained in the box. On the outside were more photos of happy people showcasing how fun the accessories alone could be, given the right circumstances. Wow, a battery. Look at me, I have a power cord. Fantastic...an external mouse, should I need one. Get out of here! A refrigerator magnet in the shape of my new computer would remind me that the reason there was no food in the fridge was because I was paying off my brand-new, high-tech laptop.

I released the contents of that second box onto my floor. With a series of lies to myself, I had emptied the carton of its treasured possessions and now faced something I coveted. Even though I'd never before pined away for a laptop, I would be brokenhearted tomorrow when I resealed everything and returned this so that Lizzie Haworth could write a bestselling novel from her newly leased penthouse apartment with a swimming pool on the roof.

I held my breath and lifted the screen of the computer. No sirens went off. Only the very faint alarm of conviction sounded in my spirit, but the television's volume muffled that adequately. Before I went any further, I refilled my mug with lots of whipped cream and a little cocoa and returned to face the consequences of my actions. As soon as I hit the power button, the screen lit up and icons zoomed into place across the top, side, and bottom panels. It was then that a most interesting feature appeared—a "Welcome, Libby Hawthorne" cartoon banner was flown across the sky of the monitor by a little yellow plane containing an exuberant, waving pilot with old-fashioned goggles. Lyndon Horne was going to resent the company for messing up his welcome page.

The tiny plane buzzed around and around while a puffy cloud formed in the center of the screen. The happy, but not brilliant, pilot flew his plane into the cloud and did not come out the other side. Instead, the cloud morphed into the shape of an envelope addressed to me. A "read me" link was placed in the stamp corner. This was wild. Why hadn't I purchased one for myself? I looked over my shoulder at my decent television that had been a hand-me-down when Cass and Nate went flat screen. What once evoked feelings of pleasure and contentment now inspired nothing. My heart was hardened toward my old companion.

Click.

The envelope morphed once again, this time into the shape of a piece of paper. Words began to type out onto the page:

> L-i-b-b-y,
>
> You had better be alone when you read this. Turns out the annoying blonde from OC is a top-notch computer consultant and programming genius. Thankfully, the pressure to run her Fortune 500 company caused her to crack and end up just a couple doors down in my wing.

I placed my mug down on a magazine and rubbed my eyes with the back of my clenched fists. This couldn't be happening. Cecilia came up with this? Maybe Rachel and I had underestimated her power to function without an assistant within yelling distance. The letters kept appearing onto the snow white page, so I started to follow along.

> All communication will come to you via email. Calls are too dangerous. I think that twerp Philip wasn't buying my cousin impersonation. I suppose even pretending I'm related to you in any way was an absurd tactic. A cable company will set you up with wireless tomorrow. You have a nice laptop well beyond your means in front of you for a reason. You are expected to check for communication before you go in to work, during lunch, and all evening up until midnight. Stop whining.
>
> From now on our special person will be referred to as "Hudson Young." Hudson has come under my influence and has agreed to return to the public eye with me at the helm of his official unveiling. He seems to think this place has changed him, so he does not want to reemerge as he was. He is leaving the newer, improved image up to me. As you know, molding the identities of young men has been a favorite pastime of mine for years. Piece of cake. Beefcake, that is. From now on, the event of his outing will be referred to as "the grand opening." Got it?

> Hudson will arrive Saturday afternoon on American
> flight 253 direct from here. You will hold up a sign with his
> cover name on it. He will come to you. He has a partial
> disguise, but you must come up with something to last a
> couple weeks. I will not return until things are in motion.
> Until then, you must keep Hudson completely hidden from
> the limelight. You are the most unsocial person I know.
> If he stays with you and models your deadbeat life, he
> should easily stay away from anyone who is anybody. Don't
> blow it.

"For five years you worked me into the ground under the premise that I would some day be an account executive. *That* is why I have no social life!" I raged against the machine for a few seconds. How was I going to hide the most-wanted rock star in the town where he became famous? Girls and women had photos of his face emblazoned on their tight T-shirts, appliquéd on jeans, and tattooed on various body parts. I stood up to pace the length of my living room. Each round by the computer, I stepped on a piece of the bubble wrap to appease myself.

Heart racing, I looked around at my unkempt apartment. Even my precious window seat looked poor and deadbeat. I couldn't host a rock star here. I had no desire to have a man living in my apartment. Sure, I fantasized about a handyman to fix crooked floorboards and de-wedge stuck windows, but this was something completely different. I could feel my face turn red. I saw stars and needed to lie down and close my eyes. A few moments later the room stopped spinning, but I still felt as though I were out at sea.

Saturday.

That gave me a couple days to fake a sense of composure, clean my apartment, create my own plan to hide Hudson, come up with an excuse for having a man around me 24/7, and lose ten pounds. This would be the first time in my history that losing ten pounds in a matter of hours was the most reasonable item on my to-do list.

Saturday!

That was the night of my birthday party. I wasn't about to miss my own gathering with friends because of my high-profile houseguest. I looked at the phone book placed beneath the left front leg of my couch to keep it level. A celebrity day care listing was probably out of the question. I was mad that Cecilia didn't check with me at least to see if this was okay.

But what upset me the most was that Cecilia was right. Stepping into my life was probably the best way Jude Shea could be guaranteed complete solitude and anonymity. It had worked for me for more than thirty years. Why not for him?

Late at night, the ping of the computer announced the arrival of a new email. I rolled over and placed a pillow on top of my exposed ear.

Twenty-Two

"Isn't that your friend Ariel?" Rachel pointed across the street toward the Nordstrom Rack.

The sun's reflection on the bay was bright. I shielded my eyes with my hand and saw a woman who was clearly Ariel standing on the sidewalk. Her weight rested back on her right leg and her left leg crossed in front. She turned her head side to side watching the pedestrian crowd for someone.

"We have a few minutes left of break. Do you want to go over and say hi?"

"Yes. Ariel left me a message with the party's start time, but I wanted to ask if I could bring anything."

"I wish I could come, but I have to go to the symphony."

"You don't sound thrilled about that."

"It's a blind date."

"Enough said."

As we waited for the signal to change, the morning's wind blew a large gust. Bags swirled about shoppers like runaway kites. The light changed just as a child's hat flew off and Rachel started to chase it alongside an office building. The frazzled mother was holding a tiny infant in her arms and trying to grab the little girl's hand.

Other pedestrians started to cross the street, but I waited for Rachel.

Ariel was still watching for someone. I waved several times to get her attention. Her eyes lit up and she nodded her head in recognition, but she remained standing. Rachel was clear down the block but holding up the captured fleece hat with a victorious smile. I decided to start across the street and let Rachel catch up, but as I looked over at the Rack I saw Ariel and the person she had actually nodded to.

It was her friend, all right, but it wasn't me. It was her new best buddy, Ferris.

He stopped just a few inches away from her and they began talking with serious expressions. Ariel glanced down at the cement or then out to the bay. Ferris motioned with his hands in the air several times.

I stepped into the street when the light changed again. The mother with the two kids reached her arm across me and kept me from walking any farther. I shook my head to clear it and thanked her. My gaze remained steady on my two friends. I'd always assumed Ferris and Ariel had spoken to one another mainly out of respect for me. When they walked two doors down and stepped inside a doorway protected from the Seattle wind by a pale green awning, Ferris placed his hand along the small of Ariel's back. This was clearly not about me.

Breathless, Rachel came back alongside me, her red cheeks practically neon.

"All is well. Child's head is saved from the cold. Let's go." She reached for my arm to lead me across. My feet stammered the first few steps.

"Ariel's gone. I didn't see which way she went."

"Well, I want to check out that very cute shirt dress in the window anyway." My friend's leading was now a tugging motion. Eventually we came to stand in the spot Ariel had been moments before.

"Isn't that adorable? I wish I didn't have these good birthing hips. You could wear that."

"Uh-huh." I offered, but my eyes were not on the dress but on that pale green awning, which also had cream script font running along the front and side.

While Rachel examined the striped clutch that went with the shirt dress, I moved a few feet over and strained my neck to read the writing. "Psychic Readings by Viola Light." When did Ariel start buying into psychics? And why would she choose Ferris to go with her rather than me?

Rachel looked at me as though I were in need of medication.

I snapped back to reality, whatever that was, and rejoined Rachel in the present conversation. "It's for the best. I'd hate to get back late. Blaine has a ton of work right now. We're setting up his travel schedule to meet a lot of the clients face-to-face."

"I cannot believe Cecilia would let this happen without a fight. Just when you think you have someone figured out…" She shook her head and hugged herself against the wind.

"You find out that you don't know them at all." I finished her sentence with thoughts of Ariel.

"Exactly."

"So are you in cahoots with Cecilia?" Tara said from behind me at the coffee station.

I turned around to look her in the eyes and started laughing. "The mere thought of such a thing makes me laugh. Coffee?" I held up the freshly brewed pot. She stepped back as if afraid I was about to throw hot liquid on her head. When she saw that I was I sincere, she raised the pink mug in her hand to proper pouring level.

"Sure."

"What's that crazy woman up to? Do you know?"

"Good coffee." Tara's perky little lips hovered over the ceramic edge. She was trying not to smear her lipstick. "Well, Ken knows she isn't where she's supposed to be."

"So, when the clients from Dallas called, the cat was pretty much out of the bag?" I made small talk, realizing that the closer Tara and I were, the less suspect I would be when Cecilia's plan exploded one way or the other.

Tara's eyes grew wide; the perky lips formed a perfect O. "Oh, no. Ken called those clients to follow up after accounting figured out what was going on."

Uh-oh. "Did…did they track her purchases on the company card and realize she was, um…someplace other than Dallas?" Beads of sweat formed on my palms and along my spine.

Tara shook her head, allowing celebrity-looking curls to brush by her bright eyes and serious expression. "The exact opposite. Cecilia's company spending is so ridiculous that when her recent statement showed little activity for the past two weeks, red flags went up all over the place."

"I hope that doesn't mean something bad happened to her." I offered up a different scenario and breathed a sigh of relief—they had not traced any recent purchases to Cecilia. She had planned well.

"They don't suspect foul play or anything like that. There were some charges, but nothing compared to her usual travel expenses, like open bar tabs, and that favorite spa she goes to in Dallas didn't appear once."

"Cecilia doesn't go a day without charging a manicure or bikini wax to the company, right?"

"Precisely. So accounting called Ken and notified him that something was up."

I continued my bit. "Good call on their part. If Cecilia doesn't charge something every few hours the woman goes mad, I tell you, absolutely mad. No purchases means she's been locked up in the center..." I stopped myself before I looped this conversation back around to the truth, "...the center of the pit of despair. Total despair."

"There was some activity. Cecilia purchased a very expensive laptop."

I spit out my coffee. A little stream shot toward Tara, who stepped back in horror.

"Sorry. Heat-sensitive teeth." I tried to wipe off the spray of brown dots from her suit lapel. She removed the napkin from my hand to do it herself.

"They can trace things like that, right? They'll know where she received it?" Would I get any sort of severance package if I was fired rather than let go? I remembered my last bank statement and my heart began to race again. My resume would be such a clear picture of my professional decline by the time all of this was played out. I waited nervously for Tara's response.

"She did it online and with a company that could not trace where the computer was shipped. Other than verification that she is still alive, that was a dead end."

"Thank goodness!" I yelled in celebration.

Tara stopped wiping her lapel and gave me a look of disapproval.

"I mean, thank goodness the woman is alive. She might be a pain in our necks, but the woman deserves to live, right? Yes!" I raised my fist and shook it a couple times.

"Of course." To avoid eye contact with me, the older but less mature, more crazy coworker, Tara looked at the clock on the wall between us. "Well, we'd best get back to woman our posts."

"That's funny, Tara. See ya." I gave her a baby wave with my fingers motioning.

This secrecy business was exhausting. It was only 11:00, and I wanted to curl up and take a nap in the patch of sun on the office carpet, in my car, in the elevator, anywhere I could get away with it. Instead, I went back to my cubicle and started typing boring letters that gave my mind too much freedom to roam around the land of "worst case scenario" while my hands followed their work routine.

Blaine came out of his office and watched me type for a few words.

"Yes?" I asked.

"I'm looking forward to tonight. I haven't had much time for outings, and you know what my upcoming travel schedule looks like."

"Tonight?" I asked. I looked up at Blaine and realized how relieved I was that he was heading out on his trip. I wouldn't have to lie to him about Jude or Cecilia. Maybe God was working this all out for me. I sighed with relief. Blaine was still talking about something and then stopped when he heard my sigh.

"Sorry, what were you saying?" I said, returning my attention to him.

"Is tonight not going to work out?"

"Tonight?"

Blaine laughed and scratched his chin. "Have you considered becoming a counselor? You're quite a listener."

I glanced down at my calendar. "Tonight is the art exhibit! I've been thinking it was Thursday today instead of Friday. I'm so sorry. You must wonder how I get work done."

"You do seem preoccupied lately. I see you look off in the distance and your thoughts seem to follow."

"My neighbor Levi said I seemed preoccupied too. And not just lately, apparently—I hadn't noticed he lived in my building for five years."

"Pretty social, are you?"

"I seem to have quite a reputation for living a solitary life." I wagged my finger at him. "But tonight I'm going to the museum with you. Well, we're going together. You are going with me, actually. To get out. To experience Seattle. All that good stuff."

"Should we grab something to eat before heading over there?"

"I don't know. I'd like to be there when it starts, to support Oliver."

"I could order Chinese to be delivered to the office."

"Don't you mean your assistant could order in Chinese?"

Blaine took a couple steps back, tapped a file folder against his leg a couple times, and said, "This is not official business. I'd better take care of it." With that, he turned and walked off. I watched his broad shoulders make their way down the corridor. In two days he'd be heading across the country for one long series of preoccupying meetings. In two days, Blaine would no longer stand between me and whatever crazy scheme Cecilia had to get her job back and my reputation restored.

"I'll be free," I said quietly.

My stomach did a little half-flip with a twist. It must have been nerves.

Twenty-Three

"Dinner for Blaine is here," Philip said via intercom.

"Don't you announce yourself anymore?" I scolded.

"After-hours protocol requires that an employee escort visitors back out. I'm off the clock. May I presume that you will see to it that Shawn gets out of the building?"

"You may. Send him over."

I buzzed Blaine to let him know his order had arrived.

"I told Philip to notify me, not you, when it got here."

"Don't worry. I'll still let you pay."

He laughed. Seconds later he was standing in his office doorway waiting for Shawn with his billfold wide open.

I could smell the aroma of lemon chicken. While Blaine took care of receiving the order, I quickly logged onto my personal computer to check for any recent emails from Cecilia. I had hoped there would be a note indicating that she had come to her senses about sending Jude to be in my care. Instead, there was one message with subject line: "Plan for grand opening in motion." I looked around to be sure nobody would be walking by my cubicle. Blaine was checking the order while Shawn waited patiently. I read the contents of the email:

> Libby, 4:26 arrival tomorrow. Have a placard ready with appropriate name. Don't be late.

I would have to clean my entire apartment tonight after the exhibit. Now I wished I could head straight home.

"Shawn is ready," Blaine said.

I clicked off the computer and stood up quickly. "No problem."

I escorted Shawn back through our main lobby and to the elevators. Philip was still there, tidying his desk for the next morning. "I thought you were leaving," I said through slit eyes.

Philip raised his pointer finger in the air. "No, actually I said I was off the clock. I give this company ten minutes of my personal time every morning and every evening because maintaining a clean workspace is my responsibility and contribution."

"So you contribute to the company for twenty minutes a day?" I said sarcastically.

Shawn laughed but Philip raised his eyebrows so high they disappeared into his blunt-cut bangs. "You know what I meant."

"Well, if your contribution is finished for this evening, do you want to leave with Shawn so that I can lock the door behind you both?"

"I happen to be done."

I sent Philip and our delivery man out in to the sunshine and headed back upstairs. The elevator door opened, and I followed the scent of dinner to Blaine's door. Some evenings I waited so long to eat that I ended up on the couch munching on chips and salsa in front of late night television. This meal would give me energy to be social at the exhibit and still clean my bathroom later.

Blaine was seated cross-legged on the floor. All the take-out boxes were opened and placed between two sturdy paper plates and plastic forks. A can of Diet Coke with a straw was by my spot.

"I see you opened the soda for me," I said, smiling.

"I figured that was safest. We both have to appear in public in an hour."

"Good call. This is quite the spread. You know how to order takeout."

"Believe me, for many years all I ever did was order takeout at home. Which is a terrible crime, considering I grew up in a cooking home. How about you. Any cooking?"

I sat down across from Blaine, thankful I had worn slacks today.

"I don't cook. I grew up with a nanny who was pretty inept at the household chores, but she was a very strong person when it came to emotional sustenance. And she could play gin rummy like a pro."

"That will sound more exciting should you ever write a memoir." Blaine reached over to the white box in front of me and retrieved a fork full of cashew shrimp.

For a long time we ate in silence. We were both hungry and shy, it seemed. Then I made the mistake of looking up. Our eyes met and stayed focused on one another for a moment while my mind played the term "locked" over and over. "Their gazes locked" was the kind of description used in romance novels, not in my life. Yet tonight it happened.

"I also learned to play five-card stud. You don't know what you've got until it's gone. Right?" I continued the earlier conversation.

Blaine's head bobbed side to side with uncertainty. "I hope that isn't true." Again his eyes seemed to peer right through to my thoughts, my insecurities, my hope.

I looked at the noodles on my plate.

"Want a fortune?" Blaine extended a small soup lid piled high with fortune cookies.

"Don't mind if I do." I took a moment to decide which cookie should be mine. Finally I chose two cookies from opposite sides of the arrangement.

Enthusiastically, I cracked open each one and read them aloud. "You will achieve contentment if you believe. Telling the truth is the key to success."

"I believe. Do you?" Blaine asked with piercing sincerity.

The phone rang and saved me the embarrassment of commenting on the wisdom of these two fortunes. My belief these days was underrated. And truth seemed a distant goal as my life appeared to be shrouded in white lies. What would Blaine think if he knew the truth about my deception?

While on the phone, Blaine mouthed to me that this conversation would be long. I took my cue and began to clean up the dinner remnants. As I headed to the hallway with a plastic bag full of leftovers, Blaine motioned for me to come over to the desk. He wrote something down on a memo pad. "It's Ken. Meet you there."

An industrious staff from a promotions company was bustling about the museum along the gallery wing. They were all dressed in black and looked a bit more like bank robbers pulling a heist than professional display artisans. Tables were being covered with black linen and champagne glasses clinked as they were set up in a three-dimensional pyramid by the bar.

"Libby?"

Surprised to hear my name, I turned quickly and nearly fell over my own feet.

"It's me, Heidi. I used to work with you at Reed and Dunson, right? We entered the program together." A tall, attractive woman with short brown hair and a long, graceful neck approached me with her hand outstretched.

It took me a moment to recognize this professional-looking woman as the same girl who had helped me carry bags of sand to Cecilia's office. Our first official assignment wasn't for the sake of public relations or account management or client development. It was to fill Cecilia's new Zen garden.

"That's right. I didn't blame you for moving on. Remember when they discovered that the floor beneath the Zen garden wasn't reinforced up to code?"

Her mouth opened wide and she yelled, "Yes! I had to start seeing a chiropractor after shoveling all that stinking sand back into bags and hauling it down to the truck." She paused to survey the workers bustling about her.

"Are you helping with this event?"

"The museum hired my firm to execute the function. I gave them a great break, though, since we want to be known as local artist friendly."

"Your own firm? I guess moving on was a good decision for you." I tried to look genuinely happy for her.

"Well, I could tell right away that there was only room for one golden girl to make it to AE...and that was you. You were the trainee star. Are you still with them?"

"Yes, yes...I'm still there." Now it was my turn to look around the room.

"They probably have you running the show."

Well, I do seem to be in charge of a three-ring circus lately. "We just went through a big merger. A lot of people lost their jobs, but the company is doing well. I'm thinking about going international." Of course, I meant that I wanted to travel in the near future. She would assume I meant international offices for Reed and Dunson.

"Fab for you, Libby. Too bad, really. We're so in need of a fireball. This is not the first time I've thought of you for our firm." She was digging in her small leather fanny pack, discreetly tucked beside her nonexistent waist. "Here's my card. Call me if you decide you want to stay in the good ol' U.S. of A."

I took the card and examined the very respectable address.

"Andres, that sign is backward...backward!" She yelled out to an underling across the room. He was caught up in the mesh of a computer-generated image of a camera. She checked her watch. "We are behind in our setup schedule."

"Go save your sign. Good to see you."

"You too, Libby." Heidi walked toward the near disaster with amazing speed, considering she was wearing four-inch heels and a black pencil skirt.

Never before had someone offered me a job or complimented me about my work. And Heidi and I'd been rivals. She was my number one competitor through all the stages of testing and training. When she left, I'd been thrilled. A few weeks later I found out she was given a great PR coordinator position with one of the other top firms. Even so, grand visions of my rapid climb up the ladder kept my jealousy to a minimum.

Now Heidi ran her own company, and I was running an underground railroad for spoiled rock stars who liked to leap from tall buildings while high and then wanted to change their image.

What did it matter? I was going international. Someday this wouldn't be a misleading statement but would be an on-target plan. A moment of faith calmed my nerves as I headed toward Heidi to offer help with the final touches.

The first after-work guests arrived and were ushered into a more intimate area where sculptures and hanging black-and-white images created sound barriers for this crowd that usually worked the Seattle nightlife after hours. Chardonnay and Pinot Noir were poured in generous glasses as Seattle's twenty and thirtysomething elite toasted one another and the museum's latest effort. Their purchasing power shone in the whites of their eyes and the whites of their perfect teeth.

"Libby!" Oliver called out to me and came over to where I was gathering stray helium balloons. After a quick, friendly hug, he escorted me to his corner display, which had a strong visual advantage. Everyone entering from the main door would walk to this corner and most likely stop. His work was phenomenal. Scenes of the bay, the skyline, people in the park, faces of locals, fishermen, tourists. Already a small group had gathered to view his work. Everything he did focused on the heart of Seattle...the people, the moods, the eccentricity, and the intelligence.

I noticed a few people lingering behind Oliver, so I motioned for him to do his thing and I headed for a less crowded area. I had about made it there when several of the balloon strings interlaced. I looked up to figure out how to detangle my only contribution to this party's setup when someone bumped into me. Peering through my silver strings I saw a gentleman holding two champagne filled flutes above his head to keep his balance.

It was Angus.

"We've got to stop meeting like this," he said, offering me an air kiss.

I smiled and looked back toward the front door, hoping that Blaine would be making his entrance soon. I'd wanted Angus to see me with Blaine by my side—not alone in a corner with a balloon bouquet.

"Want one?" Angus extended one of the flutes to me.

"Aren't you taking that over to someone?"

He shrugged. "Yeah, but I can give her mine."

"No, thanks. I'm not indulging much these days."

"Drinking never was your thing. You were the first girl I ever dated who could be herself in my crowd. I liked that about you."

I was touched. I'd always felt as though I were a chameleon, but I appreciated his compliment. "You're a good guy, Angus." I leaned in to give him a real kiss on his cheek.

Angus looked me in the eye for a moment, his face a bit flushed.

"And I noticed that you have on a bit of color. You rebel, you." I pointed to his black jacket's breast pocket, where the hint of a dark red handkerchief was visible.

He looked down at it and laughed. "Danielle talked me into it."

"I like her already. You should get the bubbly to her before the bubbles are gone."

"Right." He awkwardly leaned in to kiss my cheek this time.

I watched him walk through the growing group of guests. He nodded to a few folks here and there. This wasn't necessarily his crowd, but Angus had lived in Seattle long enough to know quite a lot of people. Everyone who met him became fond of him, even if he wanted to present a bad boy image. I wondered if people liked Jude Shea when they met him. Angus would flip if he knew I was going to the airport tomorrow to pick up one of his idols.

"Who was that?" Blaine's voice inquired from inches away.

I turned around and smiled but was greeted with a rather serious look. I pointed over my shoulder. "That was my...ex."

"The hot rocker guy?" He asked, shifting his weight from foot to foot.

"You have to take into account that the description came from Marsha. But, yes. That was him."

"It doesn't look over."

Still holding the balloons, I turned my wrist to check my watch. "That's because you aren't that late. The party has barely started."

Blaine looked down at the floor for a few seconds. I was afraid he was sick from his last plate refill of kung pao chicken. "I meant you and him."

"What?" I never expected Blaine to be the one who was jealous. I didn't know whether to be offended or flattered.

He self-corrected. "I'm sorry. I believe you."

I went the way of flattered. "There are more interesting social lives to track."

"I've worked with people who are not always on the up and up."

I felt my face grow red and my palms began to sweat. He knew something.

Applause filled the foyer as the mayor and several other local officials discussed the importance of celebrating local artists. They got their votes, but what did Blaine say? I couldn't hear a thing. His lips were moving but I couldn't stop staring at his eyes.

"What did you say?" I asked, though I wasn't sure I wanted to know.

He shook his head as if recounting his thoughts would take too much out of him. "I want to be honest with you. I believe you are the kind of person who wants and deserves to be treated that way."

Had he spoken to Tara? Or worse, had he read my email from Cecilia over my shoulder?

"I won't play games, but I also have to hold back on an impulse I have because there is too much going on right now. My move here. Your transition in job duties. The overall settling in of the company. And then there is this strange situation with Cecilia."

"What are you trying to say?" I was sincerely baffled.

"I appreciate your allowing me to join you for this event. I practically forced the invite with my pathetic new-guy-in-town story, but you were very gracious about it. And then I show up late."

I relaxed and allowed myself to breathe again. "No problem. I had a chance to catch up with an old friend, so it worked out perfectly."

Blaine raised his eyebrows.

"Not him. Someone who worked with me at Reed and Dunson years ago."

Blaine continued his end of his conversation. "I appreciate tonight, but I also appreciate you. I have an idea what your years at Reed and Dunson have been like."

I saw Heidi shake hands with the mayor. She looked really happy. "My steno pad and cubicle are a pretty good clue," I said.

"They've missed out by not noticing you."

"Thank you," I responded shyly.

"I don't plan to make that mistake." Blaine reached for the balloons, which I released to his care. He could throw emotional curve balls at me more than anyone I had ever met. But all confusion aside, I had received two compliments from two people in one night. This was a personal best, and for the rest of the night I would walk on air.

That is, until hours later when the gravity of tomorrow's quest resurfaced in my subconscious.

Amid dreams of running from groupies and riding in limousines wearing a floppy hat and a prosthetic nose, my eyes flew open with panic. "Pajamas!" I yelled into the lonely abyss that was my apartment.

Twenty-Four

The only reason I was excited to follow the airport parking signs was that it meant I got away from the busy late afternoon traffic on I-5. Otherwise, I was dreading each step which brought me closer to facing Jude Shea.

I snagged a parking ticket from the machine and the striped metal arm lifted for me to pass. I stalled Pan's car; my stick shift skills were rusty. When I asked to borrow it, I told her I was working late and wanted to get over to the party without worrying about the bus schedule.

Lurch. Saved by the instinct of my feet, which recalled many driving lessons in business complex parking lots on the weekends during my sophomore year of high school. My dad had carried a clipboard so that I would not be startled by the procedure of the proctor on the day of the test. Mom had worn and used a whistle when she drove with me so that I could get used to driving under the duress of traffic distractions. I was probably the only teenager to ever welcome the actual testing day. It was a meditation retreat compared to my parent-guided practices.

Once safely in a numbered parking space, I slanted the rearview mirror to check my lightly applied lipstick. Still there. I pinched my cheeks to add color to my skin, which was the pale shade of trauma.

Cecilia's last email at noon reinforced the code names and procedures.

Her only instruction for now was to take him directly home and to sit tight until she gave further instructions on Sunday. I didn't even bother telling her about my birthday party. I'd decided that I would bring Hudson with me and think of some excuse for having a handsome, never-before-mentioned man accompanying me.

How sad that I would need an excuse, a story, a tall tale for this advent.

Hurrying along the retail area of the airport toward the main terminal, I checked my watch. Only then did I realize I had left the sign with his name on it in the car. I looked around the mini food court for something to serve as paper. Two young boys walked by with white pizza boxes. I quickly headed for the counter they just left.

"I'd like one of the to-go boxes. To go."

Blank stare.

"I'll pay you a dollar for one."

"You want the box, but no pizza?" The young freckled girl asked with a slight accusatory tone.

"Yes, thank you so much." I decided to keep the conversation positive.

She shook her head rigidly. "You have to order pizza to get the box."

I wasn't going to win this argument. "Okay, give me whatever is ready." I shoved money at the girl, and she entered numbers into her register with her blue nails. She looked over her shoulder at the mini pies resting below the red glow of food warmer lights. "That would be pepperoni. Would you like cheese bread with that?"

"I don't even want the pizza. What do you think?"

"Oh, right," she said, as if our box discussion had been hours beforehand.

With practiced moves she folded up a pristine slab of cardboard and then placed a pizza shiny with meat and cheese juice in the center.

I started to salivate.

"Did you want a drink with that?"

My look said it all. She turned her attention to the next customer in line. I rushed off toward the gates for American Airlines. While walking by the departure and arrival monitors I slowed enough to skim the list. His flight was ten minutes late. Just enough time for me to whip out my lipstick and write "HUDSON" on the front of the box above the label for Pal's Pizza. I was too anxious to recall the fake last name Cecilia had assigned our celebrity-in-hiding.

I scanned the gathering of people waiting outside of the metal detectors. A young man held a bouquet of flowers. A tall older woman clutched a small terrier dog to her chest and watched the corridor beyond the security forces with anxious eyes. A cluster of teen girls exchanged lip gloss and mascara wands and shook long strands of hair away from their shoulders in unison. Strategic placement was important. If Hudson looked at all like Jude, those girls might recognize him. I figured the safest place to stand was between the terrier lady and a family of two little girls, a baby boy, and a father holding a sign reading, "We love our military mom."

The passengers of Hudson's flight started to round the corner and walk in our direction. Strangers who had become acquaintances while in flight said their goodbyes and their well-wishes for whatever was discussed in the close quarters of an airplane row of seats. Unless Cecilia was a master makeup artist, nobody coming along the pike was a possible Hudson. Maybe I should have referred to some magazines or online tabloids so that his face was fresh in my mind. I knew of the guy, of course, but I was far from a groupie or up-to-date fan. Just when I was ready to call Cecilia on the cell phone, I saw him. Everyone did. He had on cowboy boots, a ten-gallon hat, and a shock of straw blond hair beneath the monstrous head topper. In fact, it may have been straw. Cecilia had turned him into the farmer in the dell.

Quickly, I positioned the pizza box so he would see it as soon as he lifted his Stetson. He was talking to an elderly gentleman with few teeth and a big smile. They were lost in conversation and were within a couple feet of me. I rattled the pizza box for effect. They kept walking and talking. I caught a little bit of the conversation, and it involved fly fishing and salmon. Hudson had apparently thrown himself into the role of outdoorsman with great abandon.

I turned on my short heels and started after the two gentlemen. Their pace was surprisingly fast. If I didn't catch him, Hudson would disappear into the crowd and I would completely ruin this chance for Cecilia and for myself and for him.

"Hudson!" I yelled toward the crowd ahead of me.

The cowboy stopped in his tracks while his fishing buddy continued on a few paces. Hudson looked at me, at the pizza box in front of my chest, and back at my face. I nodded long and hard as though we were both in on the same big punch line. I was the obvious bad actor here. He nodded back at me with a very charming smile and turned to catch up with his friend. He tugged on the gentleman's flannel shirt to get his attention, extended his hand for a firm shake, and the two said their goodbyes.

"Libby." He stated this but his eyes questioned it. I followed his gaze down to my shirt and saw the scene I was creating. Pepperoni grease was dripping out of the box and onto my blouse. Appalled, I pulled the box away from me, only to reveal a much more startling scene. My blouse was absorbing the grease and rapidly become a very orange, very transparent top.

"Oh!" The air left my lungs and I looked around frantically. I'd have to hold the pizza box to my chest for the rest of the journey home. The rayon fabric stuck to my skin and a trickle of grease was making its way from my bra down to my belly button. I didn't even get my few minutes of professionalism. I went straight to loser. At least Hudson would not have to figure this out. I was up front. Boy, was I up front.

Hudson responded to my cry with heroic practiced flair. He grabbed the box, stripped off his denim jacket, tossed the pizza in a nearby trash bin, and draped the jacket around my shoulders in one swift motion.

"Oh!" I said, this time out of thanksgiving.

"Shall we?" He said with a tip of his hat and a flat palm on my back. We headed for the baggage area and retrieved his one duffle bag in silence. Not another word was spoken until I pointed out where my car was parked.

"This is me." I opened up the hatchback of the sea-green Honda Accord and Hudson tossed in his belongings. "You packed light," I commented.

"They don't recommend that you bring much from your past life—it tends to cause problems, if you know what I mean. Besides, I was leading a much simpler life by the time I decided to go to the center."

When we settled into our seats, I pulled the denim jacket tightly around me and sat for a few moments, my hand with key hovering near the ignition. "Was it hard to make that choice?"

"May I?" Hudson motioned to remove his hat and I nodded. "It was difficult the first few times I went in. I have a track record with certain facilities, and it isn't filled with gold stars. I was a jerk, basically."

"Drugs probably change who you are."

"They do. But I'd be lying if I said I was nice before I got heavily into the meds. Fame entered my veins long before any numbing agent, and believe me, celebrity can be far more mind and personality altering. I started in music because I loved to play and I thought I had important things to express."

"So what changed?"

"The deals came, the tours, the fans, the groupies, the tension in the band, the money, the fights about money...I became out of control and completely careless in attitude and actions. I'm sure you've read about a few things."

I shrugged, giving the guy some grace. "Does fame have to corrupt?"

"It doesn't. I met some decent guys—and women—who never lost a sense of themselves in all the chaos. But for me, I never felt worthy of the fame, so I fought it. Then, when I was so low, Libby, that nothing numbed my anger and fear anymore...I didn't feel worthy of being saved. You know?"

I rubbed my lips together and swallowed around the lump in my throat. "Believe it or not, I do know what you mean. I haven't been that low...or high, but I've certainly struggled with not feeling worthy of...certain things."

"Ah, the human condition," Hudson said as he adjusted his seat and stretched his legs. "Sorry to get so deep so soon, but ya gotta understand that I've been talking about this stuff for days on end. Now it's just flowing out of me."

I smiled. "I completely understand. Let's get home so you can rest."

"That'd be good. I could sleep for a week straight."

I reached toward the ignition and paused. "Could you start that week tomorrow?"

A half-raised eyebrow was his response.

Waving the keys in the air I explained. "I sort of have an...engagement tonight. And Cecilia—well...you met Cecilia. She'd kill me if I left you unsupervised the first night." Before he could respond to my choice of words I clarified, "I mean, I shouldn't leave you alone."

"What's the engagement?"

I felt my face grow warm. "My friends are throwing me a birthday party."

He sat up in the gray upholstery. "Happy birthday," he said warmly.

"Thanks."

Pushing up the sleeves of his flannel shirt, he considered the outing. "Won't your friends and your boyfriend think it is a little lame to bring a stranger?"

I fake laughed with dramatic flair. "Oh, no boyfriend to worry about. But my friends will be a bit surprised that I'm bringing a guest." A very handsome guest who resembles a rock star.

The tapping of Hudson's fingers filled a few seconds of silence. For a minute I was afraid he had heard my add-on thought. "So do you have a story for me?"

I must have looked surprised or taken aback by the question because he quickly said, "You are the PR professional."

I nodded. "Good point. Give me the drive time to come up with something."

I started the car with a lighter spirit and much more confidence about how tonight and the days ahead would play out.

"Go, Grease Lightning."

I gave him a sideways stare. "I had almost forgotten about my pathetic mishap."

"You actually forgot that you're sitting in a pool of pepperoni juice?" He teased.

"And you actually forgot I'm keeping a very big secret for you?" I bounced back.

Hudson feigned fear and raised his hands in submission. "You are going to enjoy this aren't you...me being at your mercy?"

I started laughing and didn't answer. He was right. Maybe not in the way he was implying, but I, Libby Hawthorne, was already enjoying the encounter I'd been dreading. I knew there was a lesson to be learned about trust and faith in this moment, but I had to focus on shifting gears and making up more lies to share with my friends and others.

I circled my neighborhood blocks in search of a parking place for nearly fifteen minutes. For the first time in my recent life I was able to see the benefit of my purse full of seemingly pathetic bus tokens. A spot on the corner opened up.

Hudson used his pinkies to drumroll on the dashboard. "And the story is...?"

Truth was, all I'd been able to think about was how the grease was transforming into a layer of lard on my torso. "The story is..." I stopped the car and stalled the conversation. "The story is simple but realistic..."

"I'm fascinated to hear it," he said with more than a hint of a smile in his voice.

"Me too. Ba-dum-dum." I gave myself a drum emphasis, again to stall. Hudson folded his arms and turned to lean partially on his door so he could look my direction. I took a deep breath and let it flow out of me. "You are a client from Texas. No, no. Wait. I don't want to tie you to work. That would be too close to the truth."

Did I hear myself? I was afraid to be in the vicinity of truth. This wasn't good.

I continued at a pace of lies that could only be achieved by someone who had labored in Cecilia's shadow for five years. "You are my cousin from Texas. You came to Seattle for a convention of some kind at the fairgrounds. And you have decided to stay in town longer to check out the Pacific Northwest. What should the convention be for? It should be something you know a little bit about or something you could at least..."

"Sheep."

"Excuse me?"

He grimaced and then nodded. "Okay, so I was a 4-H'er in middle school. There are dozens of blue ribbons stashed in a shoebox in my childhood home—unless Mom sold them on eBay." He looked away. Our false story was bringing up the real one.

"You were a 4-H nerd. Maybe we should say we're very distant cousins."

His humor returned. "Hey, I did not say nerd. Let's be kind to my heritage. Besides, I might have to draw on my teen work experience to start a new career."

"Do you remember enough to pull off this part of the story?"

"How much do your friends know about sheep?" He asked sincerely while replacing the mop of yellow with the Stetson on his head.

"Good point. You're pretty sharp for..." I stopped myself from saying "someone who bungeed off the Space Needle."

"For someone who did drugs?" He attempted to finish the sentence for me.

"No. I wasn't going to say that." I unlocked my door and continued. "I was going to say for a guy who only had sheep for friends. Geez, I need to shower," I lamented, afraid to look down at my oil slick.

Simultaneously, we stepped out onto the street and looked at each other over the top of the car. "You might need a squeegee," he said.

"Big, big secret," I reminded.

The neighborhood was bustling with weekend activity. A string of solo coffee goers sat in the Adirondack chairs outside Caffee Ladro, faces shrouded by the newspaper or yellow paper cups. Hudson seemed cautious but also very excited to be experiencing the sights and sounds of life around him. A cluster of teens approached us. Individually, they barely glanced up, too in tune with a conversation or lost in their playlists pounding through headphones. As a group they split like an amoeba to go around the two superfluous adults and then melded back into one being on the other side.

I reached for Hudson's elbow. "That was a good sign."

He nodded, but his face showed the shock of being treated like a regular, unimportant person by a pack of CD-buying, song-downloading individuals.

I motioned toward the stoop of a five-story apartment building. "This is me."

Hudson raised his hand to half-mast, a curious look shadowing his face. He turned to look back at the block we had traveled, then back at the stoop, and up at the building's awning. Pointing as he went, he counted the number of brick entrances and shook his head with pure disbelief.

"What?"

"I lived here in the late eighties. Room 204."

I shook my head before my lips started moving. "I don't think that is possible. The Regal Queen was an apartment building way back, but in the eighties it was a hotel. They only switched it back to apartments ten years ago."

"I'm tellin' ya."

"The eighties? How old *are* you?"

"Don't start adding up the years. I was fifteen when I ran away from my home in the suburbs. I lived on the street for a few months before I hooked up with two other guys." Hudson's eyes focused on nothing but his past. His posture went loose like a teen boy with limbs too long to keep track of. "We all worked shifts at the mini-mart and the bowling alley...and we lived here. They allowed people to live here month-to-month."

"You were so young."

"I grew up quickly in those three years." He kept shaking his head.

"And those other two guys? Were they...?"

"Yep. Ray Stricter and Trevor Lawson." He spoke the names of his other band members with a bit of reverence.

"Maybe we had best not say those names out on the street. Come on." I grabbed the melancholy man and pulled him by his shirt into the lobby.

Hudson's wide eyes scanned the room from wall to wall, from floor to ceiling. He looked a little disoriented as his head rocked on the axis of his tan neck.

Against all odds, Newton looked up to see who had entered the doors and let the breeze disturb the dusty fringe on the worn oriental rugs. Never mind that he generally refused to look up from his magazines to acknowledge me or any of the other tenants or visitors who graced this lobby. Today he was aware of his domain.

I turned Hudson toward me to keep his face from Newton's line of sight.

"Order pizza?" Newton questioned with lips that barely moved.

"No."

"Smells like pizza to me. I could really go for some pizza."

"Maybe there's a piece lodged behind the radiator," I offered as consolation and criticism.

The elevator was open, so I ushered Hudson into the narrow space quickly. "Wow, this is exactly the same," he declared.

As the doors closed I saw Newton's eyes narrow with curiosity.

"Newton is not the swiftest guy, but I don't want to give him reason to notice you." I leaned against the wall of the elevator. This was too strange. What're the odds that I would live a floor away from where Jude and friends spent their formative years?

"You have to admit…" Hudson peered over at me.

"Yes, I do." I laughed nervously.

"Weird." We said at the same time.

"But not as weird as it would have seemed a year ago." Hudson said as though thinking out loud.

"I know what you mean."

The elevator door opened to my floor, and we walked down the hall. From several yards away, I noticed a sticky note. Now it was my turn to count doors. Sure enough, it was a sticky note with my name on it, on my door. I reached for it quickly and shoved it in the pocket of Hudson's denim jacket in case it was an embarrassing note from Newton. The last time he left me a note it was to ask that I not wear so much perfume because it "irritated his eyes and nose membranes as only cheap and tawdry perfume can do."

Aunt Maddie's necklace gave me confidence. I felt so put together with my classic long skirt, white blouse, brown boots, and a tasteful but ornate single piece of jewelry. I wished I could pull this off all the time. I had a knack for disheveled. I put my hair up with a silver-and-amber clip I had bought at the downtown market.

"You look nice," Hudson said.

I turned around from the mirror to take in the full view of Hudson after his exhilarating shower and without the ridiculous blond acrylic hair. His dark, wet hair draped over his forehead in a very unkempt, attractive way. He wore a black V-neck sweater and dark, loose-fitting jeans. He didn't look like a rock star—he looked like a model.

"What are we going to do with you looking like this?" I waved my hands up and down.

He looked down at his clothes a bit remiss. "I thought I was dressing up to escort a kind, pretty lady to her birthday dinner." He said this without coming across like a complete liar. "Should I change?"

I felt my face flush. "No, you look great. Really great. But you also look like Jude. We can't go back to the straw hair…"

"But the hat could work, ma'am." Hudson tried out an accent. It wasn't bad. It wasn't good, either.

"Don't try to fake the accent. Let's say you were born elsewhere and relocated to Texas in middle school."

He dipped the hat lower to cover his forehead and the famous thick eyebrows that set off his brilliant eyes. "So just the hat and the sheep story?"

"Yes," I said, hoping that we could both pull this off long enough for Cecilia to return with a plan and for everything to get back on track.

Twenty-Five

The singer Sade's smooth and seductive voice filled the narrow hallway outside Ariel's apartment. I rang the doorbell and racked my brain to consider any last-minute instructions for Hudson. His time around Pan was my main concern. With her documentary project in the works, music and musicians would be on her mind.

We waited and waited. Finally the door opened. Ferris stepped out of our way and ushered us in with the wave of his hand. He wore a false greeter's grin on his flushed and sweaty face. Either he had just left a heated argument or a one-on-one basketball tournament. I looked him in the eyes, but he would tell me nothing.

"Ferris, this is Hudson. He's my cousin from Texas...which explains the hat."

"Though originally from Illinois. Me, not the hat," Hudson added. We sounded sadly rehearsed, but Ferris seemed unfazed by my guest's presence.

"Where's Ariel?" I asked.

"Freshening up, I guess." Our greeter mumbled his ambivalent response.

"Well, cousin Hudson, I'll leave you in Ferris' care while I go search for the newly freshened Ariel. Is that okay?"

"Sure."

"Drinks are over this way." Ferris pointed to his right at the small dining room where a makeshift bar was formed out of a bookshelf topped with a large rectangular mirror. It was loaded with an ice bucket, sodas, mineral water, champagne, and Oliver's favorite Irish beer. As Ferris turned toward the beverages, I gave Hudson a look of concern. The guy is out of a detox center for a day, and I'm parading alcohol in front of him. This wasn't good. Hudson leaned in as far as his hat would allow him and whispered, "Don't worry. Those sodas have my name on them."

Loud enough for Ferris to hear, I added, "Hudson, remember you promised to be my fellow Coke drinker tonight."

"I did indeed. Got any lime, Ferris?" Hudson followed my friend. My friend and now Ariel's...what? Psychic buddy? Boyfriend?

"Libby?" Ariel's faltering voice emanated from her bedroom down the hall.

"Coming," I answered. My mind went straight to a prayer for Ariel and for our friendship. *Let me be a friend she can confide in. Help us be honest with one another.*

I ventured into the living room, where the gentle glow of candlelight cast cartoonlike shadows of the furniture against the pale yellow walls. Lit tapers and votives were placed on the mantel, side tables, and book-shelves. Mirrors recast the glow to more mirrors. Tea lights in small, translucent purple bags lined the perimeter of the room and continued into the hallway.

"Beautiful," I sighed. "Ariel?"

"Hey, birthday girl!" Ariel cheered from the bathroom. I sensed an undercurrent of unhappiness in her voice. Her throat always got raspy when she cried. I knew this well from years of phone call recaps following many bad dates. Ariel opened the door slowly and turned off the light quickly. Even as she did this, I saw her red nose and her eyes. The girl with the creamiest skin tone was also the biggest blotcher.

"Ariel, what is it?" I grabbed the hem of her shimmery maroon shirt as she tried to make her escape to the kitchen. She wouldn't look at me. It did not take a genius to figure out what was going on. My best friend—the person who took me in like family when I moved here, the woman who talked me through my emotions when I signed my apartment lease—was hiding her relationship with Ferris from me. And the two had obviously had a quarrel.

Had they fought over whether to tell me?

We stood in the hallway, a cloud of silence covering us for several moments. My fingers nervously twisted the cross at my neck while her fingers, delicate and ringed, slipped into the back pockets of her cuffed jeans. Ariel finally looked at me and softly said, "This night is about you, Libby. I don't want to..."

"Ariel, I hate that there is this big secret between us. You have your reasons for not talking to me about it, but enough is enough. You had to know that sooner or later the rest of the group would figure out that you and Ferris..."

"Some things are too personal, ya know? I'm sorry, Libby." She turned yet another shade of pale and reached out to grab the blue-and-green striped wall behind her for stability, but she continued. "I thought you'd freak out. You and I agree on a lot of things, but let's face it, you are strong in your values and worldview. I mean, other than dating Angus, you've stuck to a pretty straight road map for life."

My heart leapt in my chest and I laughed nervously...not because Ariel was about to tell me the obvious truth, but because Ariel spoke a truth about me that I had not yet embraced. I was a person of faith. I had never confessed to standing outside the church every Sunday to her, yet she knew me this well.

She looked at me, baffled by my laughter.

"I'm surprised you see me that way," I explained.

My friend's face softened. "Honestly, it was out of respect that I kept quiet."

It was too fast to sift through all the emotions, but now that we were on the edge of outing Ariel and Ferris as a subgroup, I felt much more comfortable about it. I didn't see them as a couple, but that didn't mean it wasn't a good match.

"Ariel, I must admit that the first time my radar even picked up on your relationship, I was upset and felt left out and hurt. And I was more than a little afraid of losing you as my best friend." I shrugged. "But you know how neurotic I can be."

"Relationship?"

The sound of the doorbell rang out from a small speaker box above our heads. Ariel turned and walked toward the main room. I began to follow her when she stopped suddenly. My face was inches away from the back of her neck. Without turning to look at me, she whispered, "Relationship? There is no relationship and that is the problem." With that confusing pronouncement, she continued on to greet Oliver and Pan, who were already being introduced to Hudson.

So Ariel liked Ferris but he did not like her? Is that what she was saying? Ferris would be lucky to be with Ariel. My protective nature kicked in.

Pan looked away as Ariel entered the dining area. Her line of vision seemed a bit fixated on Hudson. The reality of my situation returned to me. I would need to intervene before any of my secrets could be uncovered. I half-skipped over to Hudson's side so that I could help play out our charade.

Oliver, who does not miss anything, gave me a stare. "That was a peppy trot."

I was about to respond with a "ha, ha" when Hudson spoke. "She reminds me of the fillies in Texas."

"Fillies in Texas?" Pan and Oliver responded in unison. They also shared a look of borderline mockery but were still in their polite social behavior mode, so the look didn't turn into sarcastic commentary. Not yet, anyway.

"Hudson, my cousin, is from Texas. He's just a farm boy."

"Born and raised." Hudson said, standing tall on his heels, looking proud of establishing the lie so early in the evening.

"You don't have an accent," Pan stated.

I waved my hand in a dismissive manner. "Hudson exaggerates. He was actually born in the Midwest and then moved to Texas as a teenager."

"Yes, that's it," Hudson reinforced, returning to his humble, flat-footed position.

Pan was scrutinizing the two of us. I chewed the inside of my cheek nervously.

"Welcome, Hudson. I'm glad you could join us for Libby's birthday night. I'm Ariel. Sorry that I didn't greet you." Ariel seemed more than ready to play the role of hostess for the stranger in the room.

Hudson extended his hand and the two shook slowly and several times.

Ferris and I both cleared our throats, and Hudson dropped Ariel's hand so quickly he actually flung it down.

"What takes you away from the farm?" Pan asked, slightly amused by the scene and, it seemed, slightly interested in Hudson.

"It's my birthday!" I said and clapped my palms together in a prayer position. My effort at distraction was met by looks of disapproval from everyone except Hudson. His slight smile made me laugh. My friends all assumed the laugh was part of my self-celebratory mood.

Ariel patted me on the shoulder as though I were a slightly dangerous but mostly pathetic character. "Yes, Libby's right. This is her birthday. I'll go check on dinner." She glanced at her watch. "Lasagna should be done soon." She turned and headed to the kitchen. "Ferris, help me?"

"Lasagna!" Oliver clapped his hands together, mocking my move from seconds before. I couldn't help but laugh. We all did except for Ferris, who followed Ariel with a look of determination on his face. Pan gave a parade princess wave in their direction and then shrugged in my direction. She pointed discreetly to the hallway.

I took the cue. "Can we get refills here? Pan and I need to talk about something important."

While Pan and I added ice to our drinks, Oliver opened his ale and extended one to Hudson. "Secretive bunch. You get used to it. And after some time and counseling you can believe that they don't go off and talk about what a daft loser you are."

"Good thing I've just finished extensive, advanced counseling then. No thanks on the ale. That's sort of a been there, done that thing for me."

"Sorry, man. AA is sort of retro...back in style."

Pan shook her head, still negating Oliver's earlier comment. "We don't really go and talk about one another. I just want to ask Libby for advice on my documentary submission for the Experience Music Project."

Hudson raised his eyebrows with interest at Pan's words.

"Hudson, Oliver is into photography. Maybe you can ask him about that," I said, encouraging their interaction.

"And what are you into?" Oliver asked of Hudson as Pan and I walked away.

"Um...sheep," I heard Hudson reply a bit apologetically.

"Sheep?"

I giggled as Pan and I disappeared to the little library Ariel had made out of a walk-in closet. Gold paint on the walls, deep red shelves loaded with great books, a border of mirrors between the walls and the ceiling for added light and a cozier feel, and two estate sale treasures—chaise lounge chairs facing each other. One a royal red and the other ochre yellow. I would never leave this room if I were Ariel.

"Don't even," Pan said before I sat down on the red one.

"What?"

"You two talked," she accused more than stated as she plopped down on the yellow chair, exhausted.

"And?"

"I cannot believe that you of all people can back this choice."

I sat back on the red chaise and stretched my legs out before me. My head rested against the velvet fabric. My thoughts sifted through images of Blaine for some reason. I blinked myself back to the present conversation. "Maybe my view of what love looks like has changed. Why would I be opposed to Ariel finding the one? I might be a tad cynical, as you are, but since when are we against love?"

"Love!" she bellowed. "What does love have to do with it?"

"Well, if Ferris can work through his issues, maybe love is where this will lead?"

I scanned the row of books just above my shoulder. Ariel's alternative, contemporary taste in furniture and clothing did not translate into her choice of reading material. The first three rows were all Victorian romance novels. I reached for one with a peach-and-black spine and an elaborate script title: *Tender May Desire.*

"Neither of them uses the word love. It's about convenience fear," Pan insisted.

"Can I let you in on a little secret?" I leaned in toward Pan.

"What?"

"I don't think they're too sure about the relationship."

"Relationship?"

"That's exactly how Ariel said it."

Pan pursed her lips for a moment, rolled her eyes to the top, sighed, and said, "Why do you think that?"

"I saw them head into an office for a psychic. I was a bit surprised.

I don't see Ferris agreeing to that sort of guidance. I'm kind of disappointed."

"Where did you see them?"

"Down by the Nordstrom Rack. Rachel and I were on an extended break, and while Rachel spotted an interesting outfit in the display window, I saw them head to the psychic office."

Pan laid flat on her back and stared at the ceiling. She closed her eyes for a moment. I thought I had bored her to sleep. Then her eyes flew open, but she stayed in the same physical position. I wanted to tell her she looked as though she were in a coffin, but thought better of it. She raised her knees to settle into the cushion of the chaise. Her hand went to her temple and her eyebrows scrunched together. She looked like Oscar the grouch, but I kept this to myself too.

"Green awning?"

My mouth dropped. Now she was psychic. "How..."

Pan turned on her side and looked me straight in the eye. "They weren't there to see Viola Light, if that is what you think."

"But I swear they went in."

"I'm sure they did go into the other office housed there: Dr. Sheila Winters, MD. Fertility specialist. Pregnancy consultant."

"Who?"

"CIA meetings are canceled until further notice." Oliver's voice bellowed down the hall as though he spoke through a megaphone. "It's lasagna-for-Libby time."

Pan sat up. I couldn't move. She said, "I was just clarifying what you saw. Talk to Ariel."

"But?" My unspecific question faded as really bad singing became louder.

"Happy birthday to you. Happy birthday to you. Happy birthday, dear Libby."

Pan and I stood up simultaneously, nearly bumping knees, and walked the short distance to the closet door. Pan stepped behind me so that I could face the choir first.

Gathered in a cluster, clogging the hallway, were my very secretive friends and my secret rock star...all singing to me. It seemed that as the secrets shared space and oxygen, they somehow canceled one another out.

This belief was short-term, but long enough for me to enjoy a moment of being celebrated by people I cared about.

"Hey, Hudson. You have a nice singing voice," Pan said when they were finished.

"He sings to his sheep," I joked and gave Hudson a stern look. He shrugged and smiled. I wondered if he even wanted to be kept undercover.

Twenty-Six

Friends seated around a table sharing a meal always feels more like family than family ever could. Usually. Tonight I sat with the same sense of emotional distance that family dinner had evoked. Did I know anyone here? My thoughts narrowed and went deep while candlelight flickered and my fork shoveled delicious lasagna to my otherwise closed mouth.

Words flitted about me. Topics changed as though someone with a well-timed sense of dialogue controlled the conversation via a remote from a nearby corner. Pan and Ariel exchanged a few words about the food. Pan politely complimented Ariel's garlic bread, and Ariel complimented Pan's salad. And, like most exchanges this evening, talk went back to Hudson for one reason or another.

"Isn't Feta from sheep, Hudson? Or goats? Isn't it better for you than cow cheese? Does cheese raise cholesterol?" Ariel inquired, as though asking a panel of scientists.

"Cow cheese. That's a lovely phrase," Ferris muttered. I looked over at him and could see he was disturbed about Ariel's interest in my guest.

"Oh my gosh!" Pan yelled suddenly. We all looked at our friend, who proceeded to slap her hand down on the table several times while her eyes darted back and forth as one does when scanning their mind for forgotten or repressed information.

"Stevie Wonder? We are playing celebrity charades, right?" Oliver joked.

We all groaned. Pan snapped her fingers and pointed to Hudson. "You..."

I stopped chewing and braced myself for Hudson's outing and the dissolution of my career.

"You should meet my friend Max!" She looked around the table at all of us, waiting for affirmation. When she only received blank stares, she said, "That guy I featured in my alternative art documentary short a couple years ago. Remember? You remember," she whined to jar our memories. "I came back to Washington to film the story. And then I made the huge decision to return to Seattle. Does anyone pay attention to my life?" She lead her pathetic life witnesses back to these significant facts.

"Ah, yes. Max," Oliver spoke first. "You two dated, right? That didn't last long."

"Beside the point," Pan said, blushing.

The name Max was familiar. An image emerged of a guy in black silk overalls with a coil of barbed wire for a necklace and a tattoo on his chin.

Hudson looked around at everyone and then at Pan with focused attention. "Why should we meet?"

"He's an artist."

"I'm afraid I don't know much about art," Hudson said with actual disappointment.

"Don't worry," Oliver commented. "Max doesn't do real art." With that snide remark he and Ferris both broke out in laughter.

Ariel waved a piece of espresso cake on her fork and challenged the boys. "Hey, art comes in all forms. Max is an ideal example of how creative energy can inspire dialogue and controversy. That *is* art, my friends."

Oh, no. It was all coming back to me. The tattoo on Max's chin was of a ewe. I put my head in my hands for a brief moment and then looked up and shook my head at Hudson—my warning to enter this conversation carefully. Or, better yet, not at all.

"Well, now I'm beyond curious. What does Max do?"

Pan sat up straight, eager to represent her former crush with the utmost respect. "Max was...is...on the cutting edge of live art. He orchestrates these fabulous displays of animals in their natural habitat..."

"And takes a picture?" Hudson interrupted, genuinely intrigued.

"No."

"Paints them?"

"Good try, my man." Ferris was coming out of his dark mood and becoming quite lively. We all were catching this turn of mood and riding the wave of one long, drawn-out, but nonetheless funny punch line. I found myself looking forward to Hudson's response. The night was looking up.

Pan reached for the salt-and-pepper shakers and a butter knife. She arranged these utensil stand-ins for roaming quadrupeds in a triangle beside her plate. "He creates a moving picture with live animals." She made the pepper shaker "baa baa" in the direction of the butter knife.

Hudson leaned in, his chest nearly touching the whipped topping on the slice of cake before him. All of his being was intent on solving this mystery. "Are they puppets?"

Ferris, with his mouth still full of dessert, chimed in, too close to hysterics to hold in his opinion. "The guy choreographs living, breathing barn animals, for Pete's sake!"

Pan's face fell as we all snorted with laughter. Hudson smiled but remained calm, seemingly to counter our rudeness. "Who watches?"

"Brilliant question and the point of bafflement for us all. Nobody watches except for the artist himself and, of course, any starving documentary producer looking for a bizarre story," Oliver responded. "However, speaking as an artist, I would like to offer up the dilemma, 'If a so-called piece of art is ever-changing and nobody is there to see it…does the art still exist?'"

Hudson immediately answered, "Yes, it does. Or else we'd have to conclude that art is only done for the end viewer and not for the sake of creation or expression. And that'd be a loss." He paused and thought about this for a long moment, cleared his throat, and repeated, "It'd be a great loss."

I sat back in my chair and sighed the sigh of comfort, happiness, and satisfaction as the evening with a near-disastrous beginning came to a most uplifting close. Warmth rushed over me, and I wondered, only a little, if it was the second helping of double-caffeinated cake or Hudson's surprising likability and his perfect answer.

When friends morph into their "other" selves before your eyes, it is a fascinating process to witness. By the time Hudson and I were saying our goodbyes, I had watched Ariel and Pan both step into their Dating Barbie personas in response to Hudson's charm, which seemed to multiply like yeast in the warmth of their glowing response.

So avid was their desire to connect, I almost shut Ariel's waving hand in the door. Pan was even more aggressive and had placed herself between Hudson and me until we stood at her car.

With a whisper of nerves, she had rambled, "I forgot I will need my car for that thing tomorrow, Libby. Do you mind if I drop you off at your place? And, of course, I'm more than happy to drop Hudson at his hotel..." she left her eyes as wide open as her offer.

I thanked her for her kindness and told her that there would just be one stop.

"Are you two distant cousins?" Pan seemed perplexed and a tad possessive as she maneuvered the streets of Seattle with one eye on the traffic lights and another on the slice of Hudson she could take in from the driver's rearview mirror.

"Yes and no," Hudson cooed the last part and we both watched Pan's eyebrows flare with curiosity. Her typical cover of indifference was blown completely.

"I don't think a guy who hangs out with sheep for a living should add to his confusing reputation by indicating a too-close-for-comfort relationship with his cousin," I said.

This got Pan to laugh at us and herself. "Yes. Just because you look like a rock star does not mean you cannot end up imprisoned by a pathetic reputation."

"I look like a rock star?" Hudson asked with farm boy innocence.

From the passenger seat, I turned to scowl at him. His face seemed to float in and out of being as random rays from passing headlights turned intermittent spotlights on him. He was smiling.

"Well, a little. You have a Bon Jovi forehead and a Rick Springfield mouth, and maybe a bit of Jude Shea in the nose." Pan explained her flirty statement with bold strokes of matter-of-fact information. She was turning back into the former Pan.

As we pulled up to the Regal Queen, I unsnapped my seat belt and said, "Funny you should mention Rick Springfield. I think Hudson resembles him most of all."

"He isn't a real rock star. He is a persona. A has-been persona," Hudson muttered as he climbed out of the backseat.

"I'll call you if I locate Max, Hudson." Pan yelled out the window. "Happy birthday, Libby," she said as an afterthought. It didn't dampen my good mood at all.

Twenty-Seven

I fumbled with my key long enough that Hudson...Jude...considered trying out a credit card break-in tactic. But just when he removed a Chevron card from his wallet, I managed to unlock and open my front door.

"Thank goodness," he said. "The last thing I need is a breaking and entering charge on my record."

"Oh, yeah. *That* would ruin your reputation." I laughed nervously like the disposable girl in the movies—the one who gets dumped or killed by scene 3, depending on the genre.

We entered my apartment like a couple. Like synchronized acrobats, we dropped our belongings, shed unnecessary clothing, and headed to our assigned place. Me in the living room near the hide-a-bed love seat and he in the bedroom. I'd decided that it would be easier to hide evidence of a quest if I let Jude have the bedroom. Ten minutes of silence had passed when I blurted, "Are you going to bed?"

"Just changing clothes. What'd you have in mind?"

"A recap."

"I can't do a nightcap, but I wouldn't mind watching a movie."

Nightcap? "My cable...my illegal cable is out again, but I have tapes."

"Capes? Are you one of those Goth chicks?"

The conversation quickly deteriorated. Jude reemerged from the bedroom with my bathrobe draped around his shoulders.

"What superhero are you supposed to be?" I asked, laughing. His antics caused me to miscount the scoops of fresh ground coffee I was adding to my filter.

"I thought you said to wear a cape. Let's see...well, I'm Protector of Sheep," he said, and then he raised his eyebrows at my late night caffeine effort.

"Hey, superheroes don't judge. I happen to like coffee at night. It helps my dreams be productive."

"Just think. You could get paid hourly at night."

I pointed to my nose. "Sounds like...oldest profession in the world."

"Not what I meant," he said seriously and then laughed.

I started my coffeemaker and turned to him. "You mock, but I do resolve inner conflicts. I come up with solutions for work issues. I sometimes solve world problems...but I rarely remember those upon waking."

"That sounds like a cop-out."

I shrugged. "I suppose. But I believe I really do tap into genius now and then."

"Or you think you do," he said while taking my robe off his shoulders and hanging it on the coat stand.

With his attitude, I wasn't sure if I wanted to share my brain power serum. So I zinged him. "Like when you bungeed off of the Space Needle? That was genius?"

Jude folded his hands over his heart. "That hurts."

"Sorry," I said, meaning it.

"Quite all right. I'll take a cup of genius when it's ready." He settled into my couch as though he had done that a thousand times.

And I kinda liked it. A couple minutes later I went to the coffeemaker and poured two cups of coffee.

"Hey, interesting reading material." Hudson saw the book from Aunt Maddie and picked it up. He read the back cover copy and then opened it up.

I winced, not because I was embarrassed, but because I didn't really want to explain my strange state of faith. I handed him his coffee. "I just got that, so I can't tell you anything about it. My aunt suggested I read it." I said that last part as though that would explain it all. It was my disclaimer as if to say: *Don't ask me about God...I read* Vanity Fair. *That is just to please religious relative.* But, of course, I didn't feel that way.

My cell phone rang and I jumped up from my chair across from Hudson and scrambled to locate the miniscule equipment. I knew it was Cecilia, so I took the phone and headed for my fire escape.

"Hello?" I grunted as I opened the reluctant window and then exhaled as I tried to close it behind me. A two-inch gap remained. "Hold on," I barked at Cecilia before she could say anything.

I leaned down to speak through the gap. "Turn on the television, would you?"

Hudson looked at me. He understood that I wanted privacy, but instead of turning on the television, he nodded to me, took the book, and headed to the bedroom.

I wasn't sure how I felt about him reading my special gift from Aunt Maddie. But what was I sure about in my life right now?

"Anyone frickin' there?" Cecilia hollered into her phone and startled me. I fell hard onto my rear on the metal grate.

"Ow!"

"Considering that one of your few job responsibilities at Reed and Dunson has been to answer phones for the past five years, you're really quite bad at it."

I checked my watch. "It's after midnight, Cecilia. If you want professional phone etiquette, call during business hours."

"Honey, you're on the clock 24/7 for this project." She coughed into the phone. "You haven't reported in about the package. If I hadn't just had a cut and color by Giavanni at the spa this afternoon, I'd be pulling my hair out. Why haven't you checked in with the computer? Or did you think that was just an extremely generous donation to the almost-out-of-work secretaries' fund?"

Without thinking, I spoke the truth. "I got back late from my birthday party. I was going to log in before I went to bed. All has gone well. The package was at the airport..."

"Hold on, little miss bad judgment. You left the package alone on its first night in the city? What part of 'mess up and...' don't you understand?"

"I didn't leave it." Dang. She wouldn't like that, either.

There was a long, long silence. I pulled the phone from my ear to check to see how many bars I had. The battery was fully charged. After a few more seconds, Cecilia let out a shrill, haunted house laugh. I was about to ask what it looked like on the other side of the deep end when she stopped laughing and spoke in the acerbic voice she used to train anyone new to the ways of the corporate food chain.

"I'm the one risking the most by placing this vital project in your hands. If it was your birthday, you should have ordered in cupcakes from the Dandelion bakery. And then you should've sat with the package in your dismal apartment with the shades drawn until the delivery boy knocked on the door. And then you should've opened the door just wide enough to retrieve your one "celebrate me" cupcake so you could then sing to yourself and pretend to blow out a candle, because a real candle might be seen from outside your thin, cheap shades. Do you see where I'm going with this alternative plan?"

Crazy land? "You don't want Hudson to leave the apartment. Got it. My friends had planned this party for weeks, and I wasn't..."

"Libby, don't say anything that would indicate subpar loyalty or performance. I can't handle it. I'm on the brink, as they say on the D ward."

"What is the plan? I have to go to work on Monday. He'll be alone then."

More silence. I could see her examining her nails one by one the way she usually did when anyone wanted a direct answer. She was buying time.

"This needs to be carried out before Blaine returns. I can't lie to..."

"Mm-hmm," she said knowingly, as if she expected this comment. "I want this resolved as much as you do. I need to get back there; my maid quit on me. I can only imagine what she did to the place."

"Then come back. We can communicate in person." Did I say that? I envisioned Cecilia dragging me into her office throughout the day for plot updates. Scratch that. "No, you're right. You get the plan in motion before you return. I promise to check emails every few hours."

"Good." She seemed surprised and relieved by my on-board attitude. I was about to hang up when she added, "He is quite nice on the eyes, isn't he." She did not inflect for a question—it was a statement. "I'd worry about you and him and this time alone if you were anyone else. Normal, I mean."

"Please save further insults for email."

"Lib-by," she said sternly and with two distinct syllables, "you cannot risk Hudson being in public again. What if one of your friends lives in the real world? They'd know in a heartbeat that the pursuit of Jude is only heating up thanks to Paulo Carrera."

"Who?"

She sighed heavily. "This ignorance eases my worries only slightly. He's a big-time lawyer, but that doesn't matter. Forget I mentioned it."

"Is Hudson suing? Is the label suing?" For some reason I whispered this. "Shouldn't Hudson know if there is a suit?"

"I'll inform you on a need-to-know basis. If you don't screw up, Hudson will be unveiled and back in talks with FreeTime in no time. Suit or no suit. Gotta go. It's late."

I flipped my phone to the off position. My heart was racing. I was no longer worried about messing up my status at Reed and Dunson. Hudson's entire career and probably life were dependent upon this plan succeeding. I prayed that whatever came out of Cecilia's head would be phenomenal. The woman had several star moments in her career. Sadly, I'd witnessed mainly the sadistic ones.

Like when she figured out that college interns often work for free.

She signed up for two dozen with a local university, but instead of exposing them to the world of public relations, she had them paint her apartment. Then she bused them out to her cabin in the San Juan Islands and had them fill the huge holes in the winding five-mile stretch of gravel driveway. She made them camp alongside that road with limited provisions and no form of communication for four days until they finished. That was the end of our intern program.

I climbed back into my apartment and shook out my leg cramp. There was complete silence in the bedroom. I tiptoed over to the doorway. Hudson had fallen asleep propped up on a stack of pillows, the book loosely grasped in his left hand. I walked over to him and removed the book gently. I noticed the calluses on his fingers from years of guitar playing. Just like Angus. I examined his face now that I could without embarrassment. His features were perfect. His cheeks, forehead, and brow were wide, open, and accepting...unlike the gaunt, angry look I'd seen in photos. Maybe this is what rehab had done for him. Maybe this is why even Pan hadn't recognized him. He was a new person. There was a half-smile playing on his lips. I found myself mimicking it with my own lips for a split second. Then I turned off the nightstand lamp and walked out backward.

My coffee was wearing off already. It had been quite a day. Quite an enjoyable day, even. I kicked my shoes off and lay down on the couch fully clothed. I never did get a new pair of pajamas.

A stream of moonlight illuminated the cowboy hat resting on the floor by my bookshelf. I always thought I'd be one of those women who might never be able to get married and co-habit with someone else. By the time I moved out of Ferris' place I had written a list of more than a thousand great reasons to live alone.

That cowboy hat lassoed by the God's night-light seemed to override every one of them.

Twenty-Eight

I held a paper bag of bagels and cream cheese with my teeth while I maneuvered the door of Caffe Ladro and two cups of coffee. Under my arm was another bag with a cheese Danish in it for Mr. Diddle.

Hudson stood on the corner looking around at his old neighborhood. The cowboy hat rested on his head as it did yesterday, but looked much more natural in the morning light. This tall, nicely built man seemed more at ease today. When he shifted his weight and turned toward me, he smiled warmly. I wondered if I was just a convenient, new groupie to him.

He took the bag from my mouth and one of the coffees. "I have missed Seattle's world of coffee. Did you know there are parts of the U.S. that do not have three coffee shops on every block?"

"Get out of here. That cannot be!" I pretended to be shocked. "While you're enjoying being back in your old territory, you have to promise me that you'll keep a very low profile. I got chewed out by the queen of mean last night for taking you to Ariel's house. I should probably chain you to the sofa, but instead I'm going to trust you."

He bowed his head slightly. "I will be good. I feel bad enough that I'm invading your life. What's your motive for all this? Is it purely out of love for Cecilia?" He let a little laugh escape his lips.

"Motive sounds a bit sinister."

Hudson gave me a look that pulled the truth out of me.

"Maybe I'll have a chance to redeem a sidetracked PR career. I wasted a lot of time believing that if I just kept my head down and did the work, I would receive the proper recognition."

All he said was, "Recognition?"

"Well, advancement."

"How'd that work for you?"

I laughed. "I have paper cuts on paper cuts from filing. What do you think?"

"I hope this plan helps in some way. Actually, I really just hope it isn't a disaster. Can I trust Cecilia?"

I thought about this for a minute and sipped my hot Americano before saying, "I think you can. She makes life harder than it needs to be for herself and for others, but the woman knows PR, and she is better networked than Bill Gates."

"Well, I'll trust the process. That's a therapy motto, by the way."

"I thought it was the slogan for the Department of Motor Vehicles."

"Meanwhile, act like I'm not here. I'd love it if you did exactly what you do every Sunday morning. You buy coffee and pastries and then you...what?"

"I...we will go to my favorite weekend hiding place. You're a reader, right?"

"Yes, but that doesn't matter because I'm not here."

"Right. Well, I take the bus to a wonderful bookstore. You'll love it. Walk this way." I started off around the corner.

"Isn't this a bus stop right here?" He pointed to the obvious bus sign a few feet away.

"You said you wanted to see what my Sunday was like. I go this way."

"Say no more."

We walked and sipped in unison around the block. I checked my watch. It was five minutes before the church service. Right on time to not go in, yet again. This time I had an excuse. I glanced past the doors propped open as we walked by. I saw a couple of young women who looked around my age. They were passing out bulletins and laughing.

"Do you ever go there?" Hudson asked.

"You aren't here," I said and kept walking.

"So you don't. Because you kind of looked like you were curious. And then you had that book. That gift from someone."

"You are the most persistent nonexistent shadow a girl could have."

He shrugged and sipped his coffee.

We stopped and waited for the bus. He avoided eye contact with me, so I decided to tell him a little bit. Only enough to make amends. "I've considered it. I actually consider it almost every Sunday, but I never go. There, happy?"

Hudson's eyes returned to mine. "I hated religion. I was angry at my parents, and my parents represented everything society wanted to push at me or on me, including religion, which is stupid, really, because my folks were about as far from faith as you could get. But they owned this huge old Bible, so I figured that the authority that whipped my brother and me with a thick leather belt was the same authority in that book."

"Tough home life."

He barely nodded, and then he looked away. I caught him squinting as though shielding his eyes from the sun on this overcast day.

"Did you figure out that your parents weren't the same as God?"

"I did, Libby. I'm no zealot, but I'm starting to get a more personal picture of what faith means. That's why I'm willing to step back into life. I want things to look and feel differently than before. I'm ready for a life with meaning and a life on my own terms. I'm like you, in a way."

The bus pulled up.

We boarded in silence and remained quiet until I nudged for him to get off. I was dying for the conversation to continue, and I hoped he didn't forget what he was about to tell me. "How are we alike?" I wanted the answer desperately. Maybe it would help me solve a few of my own questions.

He hadn't forgotten. "I also thought that if I kept my head down and did the work, I'd eventually have the status or recognition I would need to do things my own way rather than serve someone else's vision. But other than our first six months as an opening act for Seattle's B-list bands, I never had freedom. We got more and more indebted to people who were telling us what music we could or couldn't create while they took us to the cleaners, basically."

"That had to be heartbreaking," I said gently.

Hudson smiled and gave me a puzzled expression.

"What's that look for?"

"You're interesting. Most people would listen to my story and think 'Boo-hoo, you rich, spoiled rocker. You had it all and you threw it away because it came with a price.'"

"No, I get it. Maybe I wouldn't have handled it the way you did..."

"Drugs? Women? Wild antics?"

"Right. Those ways," I said, rolling my eyes for emphasis, "but I can understand the extreme disappointment of reaching the top and realizing you still didn't have the dream or the freedom or the...the what? Fulfillment you had hoped for?"

"Not just that. I probably could have found fulfillment if I had my head on straight from the beginning. But I started off as a boy who was already disappointed, hurt, and angry. I wanted one of two things from the music, and they were both impossible."

"This is it," I said pointing to the familiar door of my Sunday hangout. "What were the two things?"

"Revenge or salvation."

I grimaced with empathy and nodded. I couldn't believe I was standing here having a heart-to-heart with Jude Shea and realizing I was luckier than one of the most famous guitarists of this century.

"I promise to keep this in mind, Jude...Hudson." I looked around and mouthed *Sorry*. "This isn't just a PR strategy...it is your life." *And it is even more serious than you know*. "Let's go in. This is a great escape, I'm telling ya."

The tiny bell sounded as I opened the door. I whistled to alert Nomad to my arrival. I heard the click of his nails on the floor and then the sound of Mr. Diddle's steps overhead. There was a very small attic he used for occasional inventory overflow. I also suspected that he lived in the somewhat dismal space but was too proud to admit it, so I never inquired.

"You're late. Did you bring an offering?" Mr. Diddle's cheery voice rang out above our heads through a heater vent. It startled Hudson, who nearly dropped his seeded bagel.

"I did. And I brought a new customer. This is your lucky day."

The footsteps quickened as they neared the hatch in the ceiling at the far end of the bookstore. I motioned for Hudson to watch. I knew he would find Mr. Diddle to be a curious, likeable man.

Chewing on our bagels, we both kept our eyes on the hatch. Mr. Diddle was our morning matinee and he did not disappoint. He had on black galoshes that appeared to be about three sizes too big. They squished and squeaked the way rubber does as he stepped down the ladder. The gap between the galoshes and the folded up hem of his overalls revealed freckled legs. By the time we saw he was wearing an elf-green flannel shirt and matching cap, Hudson was smiling ear to ear.

"He belongs in a fairy tale," he whispered.

"I love guests!" Mr. Diddle cried as he dismounted the ladder like a gymnast. He turned around and clapped his hands together while walking toward us. "Welcome. Welcome! Any friend of Libby's is a friend of ours."

I handed over the Danish. Mr. Diddle opened his eyes with delight. "Ooh. This one's a beauty...good for a free pass to browse, I'd say."

"Whew. Good thing I brought it. Mr. Diddle, please meet my friend Hudson." I decided not to get into the cousin story.

I didn't like lying to Mr. Diddle. I was, however, pleased that the "friend" part of the statement felt true already. Hudson leaned over to shake Mr. Diddle's hand and they looked at one another for several seconds.

"I have good news for you, young man," Mr. Diddle said, rising up on the pads of his feet to get closer to Hudson's face. "I just got in a lovely volume of Bob Dylan's lyrics."

I could feel the blood drain from my face. "Why do you think he'd want that?" I asked with more force than intended. Hudson looked taken aback by my response, but Mr. Diddle wasn't fazed.

"Am I right, Hudson?"

"Yeah. I'd love that."

Mr. Diddle turned his shiny face toward me. "See, my dear. I'm not useless."

"I know that." I softened my face and let my hunched shoulders return to a normal position. I had overreacted. I was still curious as to how Mr. Diddle pegged Hudson for a musician. It was one more piece of evidence to support my theory that he held special powers of discernment and insight. "I'll be over in travel. Hey, how is *my* aunt?"

"*My* good friend Maddie is charming." He laughed. "Your throw rug is waiting for you." Mr. Diddle seemed very pleased with Hudson's presence.

I wondered if he thought we were dating. I'd have to let him know that this wasn't the case. "Are you from Seattle originally, Hudson?"

I could feel my throat tighten. Unfortunately, I was in mid-swallow of coffee. I coughed and nearly choked. The two men looked at me. Hudson from above me at his 6' 2" height and Mr. Diddle from below at his 5' level. I felt like part of a comedy act. "I'm fine," I said.

"I'm originally from this area," Hudson answered. "I've been gone for too long and now hope to resettle back here. That is, if I can find a job."

I gave Hudson a "don't push your luck" look.

Mr. Diddle watched our exchange. "Hudson, you must go to the Experience Music Project. The Bob Dylan special exhibit is only in town a bit longer. It's wonderful."

"Oh, we will," I said enthusiastically. I was just glad Mr. Diddle hadn't asked Hudson what kind of work he was looking for.

The two men looked at me again. I was intruding on their private conversation at this point.

"Weren't you going to the travel section?" Hudson asked with slight amusement in his voice.

"Yes, dear. Run along. I'll take care of your friend," Mr. Diddle said.

Before Hudson followed his little book guru into the belly of the used book section he turned to me and said quietly, "You can chill out a dash, Libby."

"Sorry. But I swear he has a sixth sense about people. I was afraid..."

Hudson shushed me by putting his finger to my lips. He opened up his jacket a bit wider to reveal a black concert shirt promoting the Wallflowers, the band with lead singer Jakob Dylan, Bob Dylan's son.

"Oh," I said sheepishly.

"Yeah. Now go plan a trip. I think you could use a vacation."

I acted insulted, but I couldn't help grinning when I turned around.

Twenty-Nine

Now that I had kept a very huge secret for two days running, I was empowered. I knew I was cocky about returning to work only because I didn't have to face Blaine yet. I wore a classic gray skirt with a black turtleneck instead of my usual Monday wool trousers, and I waxed my hair back in what Ariel and I call a *Victor/Victoria* slick. I walked quickly and proudly along the avenues on my way into the office. The air lately had turned crisp and cool. It made me think of pressed white shirts, plaid skirts, and Mary Janes. I never went to parochial school, but I'd always been jealous of the girls who did. It was like being jealous of the girls with braces. Both groups would deny there was anything remotely good about their circumstances, but from the very boring sidelines that represented my slightly crooked but normal teeth and my public school education, I considered their denial of happiness a certain assurance of their coolness. But Mom said my teeth and my school would give me better character in the end. Recent choices in my life would prove her wrong. That could be the up side to all this.

My attitude outfit and hair received a few looks, double takes even. I walked taller as I went by Philip's bar-desk. He looked at me with an extra dose of suspicion. I nonchalantly asked, "The task force has been keeping me so busy I'm behind on calls...do I have any more messages?" Implying power was as effective as having it.

"You do have a message already. But it's personal."

I placed my elbows on Philip's work station, an act I knew that drove him crazy. "Personal? You mean from you, Philip?"

His face grew red and so did his neck. "Not on your life. It's from Pan."

"Where's the message?" I asked, looking at his alpha-ordered pink slips.

"I threw out the initial two written messages and then put her through to your voice mail on the third call. I told her that I reserve voice mail for work-appropriate messages, but she became rather terse with me."

"I'll go give it a listen. Sorry if she was...terse, did you say?" I started toward my cubicle when a great idea struck me. I looked back at Philip, who was already using Windex to wipe my elbow prints from his glass.

Rachel walked toward me in the hallway. "Nice look, Hawthorne. Very urban chic. Are you interviewing for the executive training program?"

This was one of our most frequently used running jokes. We cracked up. As she passed me, she whispered, "Special meeting at 11:00. Be there?"

I nodded and my stomach flipped. Had she found out something?

At my desk the voice mail light blinked at me. I pressed play and heard Pan's voice rambling. It was more like a strained version of Pan's voice...not one I had heard before. I pressed repeat because I couldn't understand her the first round.

"Hey, Libby. Got the word on Max. Max...you remember my whole story at your party. I know you guys didn't like him. Anyway, I found him and I'd love to take Hudson. Hudson...dang, Libby, I cannot stop thinking about the guy and that is so not like me. Tell me something awful about him so I can forget him and move on. No, wait. Don't tell me anything bad before I take him to see Max. Let me hang with him before I decide whether I want to be deterred. Listen to me rambling. I'm pathetic. Call me."

I could only imagine the messages poor Philip had taken and then tossed. This wasn't like Pan at all, but Hudson was unlike most guys. He'd been charming and generous and patient the entire evening at Ariel's house. Wait until she finds out about his identity later. She'd flip. In the meantime, how could I let my friend down nicely?

I logged on to my computer, deciding that I would talk to Pan later, once she had sifted through her hormones and came out the other side a bit more rational. Pan was the one I could always count on to be logical and on my side of the love equation...the side of skepticism.

One new email from Cecilia appeared in my personal folder. I opened it and kept my curser on the screen reduction icon in case someone walked by.

> No more outings. This isn't your chance to get a life; there are high stakes. Am planning a return in a week and a half. Have heard Hudson's former pals are in the city for some event. Be careful. I need some things from apartment ASAP. Find a reason to go with Rachel...I'm having her do my cleaning. Smuggle out the following items and mail overnight tomorrow.

Philip buzzed me and emphasized that I had a *personal* visitor. I quit reading the email and printed the page.

A shiver went up and down my spine. Hudson wouldn't show up here, would he?

"Who is it?"

"Someone who should not be visiting during business hours, I can guarantee it. But she does have a strong fashion sense."

"Didn't you notice my outfit today? Pretty sharp. Come on, Philip, admit it."

"I appreciate your effort," he said, as if the effort had been for him.

"But?"

"Your hair looks like the feathers of a seagull after the Exxon Valdez tanker spill. I think your slacks were nice. I'll send her to you."

I stood up and watched over the cubicle wall. As I had suspected, my friend with fashion sense was Ariel. She stepped into the small lobby, looked around without a hint of concern for being out of place in her red-plaid miniskirt and black leather wrap shirt. I waved her over.

"Hey, this is a great surprise," I said. "Are you on your way to work?"

"Finished. I opened." She looked around with non-seeing eyes. "I haven't seen your new set up. It's nice."

"You didn't come by to see my cubicle."

She toyed with the leather tie at her waist. "You're right. I came to apologize for my mood at your birthday gathering. I wasn't the best hostess..." she paused and looked up to search my face for a reaction.

"Don't apologize. It was a great birthday. I had such a good time. And your place was so pretty. I appreciated every touch."

Ariel sat on the edge of my desk, stretching her fishnet stockings and knee-high black leather boots into the hallway. "I wasn't in the best place mentally. But the party actually opened my eyes to what was wrong."

"Really? How so?"

"Lately I've become so focused on myself, I lost my lifelines—you, most importantly. My self-absorption alone should have told me I'm not ready for parenthood, right...?" her voice trailed as she saw my expression of confusion. Her eyes opened to the size of silver dollars. "That slipped out. I came by to ask you to dinner so that I could discuss the p-word with you in depth. Can we try for tonight at Lacey's Grill?" She stood up to leave.

"Oh, no...you don't get to leave. That word does not even belong in sentences we exchange. I'm not waiting until tonight, Ariel." I thought of Cecilia's email. "Besides, I have to work late. Pan sort of eluded to the p-word, but I didn't believe it. Are you?"

She looked around and pulled a spare roller chair from the next cubicle over so she could sit knee to knee with me. She clasped her hands together and said, "Let me ease your mind here. I'm not pregnant, but I want a baby."

I said nothing. My face was still frozen in the perfectly appropriate "Does not compute" expression.

"I wanted a baby. Did want. Past tense. For about six months I've considered going it alone. Well, the raising a child part. After some careful consideration, I realized the only guy I could possibly ask is Ferris. He is kind, somewhat normal, mostly balanced, and responsible."

My mouth was still open.

"Come on, Libby. This isn't all a complete surprise, right? I'm sure Pan gave you an earful of her whole take on this."

I shook my head. "I'm trying to get my mind around this. How could you be thinking these big life thoughts and keeping them to yourself? And why'd you tell Pan and not me?"

"Pan saw me head in to Dr. Winter's office downtown a few times. She's a..."

I held up my hand and nodded. "I know who she is. But you and Ferris?"

Ariel waved her hands in the air to erase any further thoughts I might have about her and Ferris, "First, I wanted him to be the father through artificial means, if that helps your reaction any. Second, there is no need to worry...Ferris is responsible, too responsible to get sucked into my madness. He's sweet, though. He said maybe there was a possibility for love between us, but I didn't see it...so then I started freaking out about him wanting a relationship. How messed up can I get?"

"Can you blame him? A fantastic woman says she wants to have a baby with him. I'd be gravely disappointed in him if he wasn't thinking long-term."

"As in...you're disappointed in me?" She asked nervously.

I shrugged and then shook my head. "I'm not. I'm sad you didn't confide in me, but I get that you have a desire and it became all-consuming. I'm not there yet personally, but I can understand it. Just look at me and the quest for the perfect microwave pizza. Sometimes it's hard to shake an important focus."

Ariel laughed. "Well, thankfully it all became clear at your party."

"How so?" I asked.

"One glimpse of real love, and I knew Ferris was right—I wasn't prepared to enter into parenthood without having it all, including love."

"So what did Ferris say to you that changed how you felt?"

"Not Ferris, Libby. Hudson."

My heart sank. "What do you mean, Ariel?" I reached for the pen Blaine had given me. It seemed to offer some support.

"Hudson and I chatted almost the entire time you and Pan were in my study. After our first exchange I felt the butterflies and I just knew..."

"You knew?" Oh, great. Both my friends were in love with him. Jude had this effect on women even when he was only Hudson. Good thing I didn't crush easily, or I would have my own feelings thrown into this mess. "You like him?"

"I know he's your cousin...is this weird? This is weird, right?"

I decided to take advantage of this angle. "Yes. I'm a bit uncomfortable talking about family like this."

"Don't worry. I'm not after him. I won't become the stalker girl your family laughs about over Thanksgiving pumpkin pie. My point is that I felt something. Attraction. Hope. Potential. I didn't see that I was almost settling for half of my dream until that evening. Love could still come my way in an unexpected moment."

"Hallelujah," I said with great relief.

"Hey, it wouldn't be that bad to have me in your family tree."

I reached for her hand and held it. "You already are my family, Ariel. I'm just glad you have your whole dream back."

"Me too."

At 10:50 I grabbed some empty folders and started my trek to the main floor's janitor's closet. I didn't see Rachel on the way, so when I reached the door, I tapped twice. Sure enough, my cohort was there.

"What? No snacks? I'm insulted."

Rachel reached behind a bucket and removed two Hershey bars. "With almonds or without."

"With." I perked up at the sight of chocolate. My morning had been so packed with confessions of unrequited love that I hadn't had a moment to get coffee. This was the next best thing. I took a bite and then held up the bar to examine the teeth marks. Mom was wrong...I should have had braces.

"I'm doing it, Libby."

I looked up from my dental impression to see what she was doing. Nothing.

"I thought I'd get a bit more of reaction," Rachel said, clearly disappointed.

"Sorry. What are you doing, exactly?"

"Going to Europe. My brother is in Barcelonia as we speak. I plan to meet up with him whenever I can wrap up a few details here. I have a call in to Ken."

"I...I don't know what to say. Why now?"

Rachel looked at me with shock. "I thought you of all people would understand. Don't we share the same dream of leaving all of this behind to travel?" She waved her arms around as though the 4 x 4 closet represented our entire existence.

She was right, but I didn't want to acknowledge it openly. She and I had discussed our pretend itineraries ever since she started a couple years ago. But now she was going to make those real, at least one of them, and I was still going to be here, telling lies, and trying to maneuver my way back into a career that never existed. "I thought you were saving to go this summer," I said instead of crying.

"I figured that if an advanced degree isn't going to take me anywhere right away, then my passport will. You could join me, Libby."

"I couldn't leave Blaine." We each heard that with a different perspective.

"You're right. He'll lead you to a better professional situation than Cecilia ever would. You might have had the luckiest demotion in the history of corporate America."

"Could be." Yet as I said that, I wondered if I kept my job but lost a chance to travel, would I be settling for half a dream the way Ariel almost did? What would or could stop me from joining Rachel or Maddie? Or maybe the question was *who?*

My pulse quickened.

Blaine.

"I really believe that," Rachel said with sincerity.

"What?" I asked defensively, as though she had read my tangent thoughts.

"Little distracted, are we? Your demotion. I think it's a good thing in a way."

"I do too. But I'm worried that I don't know what I'm after anymore," I said aloud, though I hadn't really intended to confess that to anyone.

It seemed that Rachel didn't hear me. I stood up from my leaning pose against the wall of the small closet and stepped toward the door.

"Happiness," she said clearly and loudly.

"Hmm?"

"You're after happiness, Libby. We all are. You just need to figure out what that is from within rather than from other people's definitions. Who cares about titles if finding your purpose is part of the process?"

"My purpose is to file," I said jokingly, but I understood what she was saying. I had never given Rachel credit for spiritual insight, yet here she was telling me exactly what Aunt Maddie had been trying to tell me forever. I thought of Brother Lawrence finding complete fulfillment and purpose while doing his mundane kitchen duties. Could I find my way to personal, intended happiness while serving in a very unglamorous assistant position?

Rachel seemed to interpret my silence. "Libby, what I'm doing might be what you want to pursue, but it needs to be the right timing. You of all people should know this."

"Of all people?" I asked, bewildered.

"Isn't God's timing a big part of your faith?"

"It is. I mean, at least I consider that to be part of faith. I'm still figuring that stuff out, to be honest."

"That's what makes you so darn likeable. I've never been a big fan of organized religion, but I've witnessed your quest, Libby, and I find it admirable. And, honestly, it's even part of why I've taken this leap. I have settled for a really long time. Not in the scheme of my entire lifeline, but in terms of my goals and desires."

"But aren't I settling by staying?" I implored.

Rachel shook her head adamantly. "No. Libby, I believe in what you might end up doing if you stay. There is nothing wrong with holding out or holding on. But for me, it's so clear that this is over." To reinforce her point, she spelled it, "O-V-E-R. But you have a chance to grow here finally. Blaine is a godsend, don't you think?"

"Yeah," I said. But we each heard that with a different perspective.

Thirty

"Double residency requires additional monthly fees," Newton said without looking up from his magazine when I entered the lobby.

I kept walking and avoided looking over at him. I didn't plan to acknowledge his comment or existence.

"I saw him go up and never leave. And I've already had a complaint about the loud music coming from your apartment."

I waved as I headed up the stairs as though Newton had merely given me a cordial greeting the way most apartment lobby managers would. The loud music he referenced greeted me midway up the stairs. It wasn't Torrid music, but it was a similar genre…lots of bass and drums. Hudson and I would need to have a little talk about his guest etiquette.

I didn't need to bother unlocking the door, it was ajar with a Nike shoe wedged in the opening. *Cecilia had better return soon*. I pushed the door fully open using my grocery sack from Larry's Market. I had planned on making spaghetti and garlic bread for my guest so we wouldn't have reason to leave the apartment tonight. The idea of being alone with Hudson every evening caused me more than a little discomfort and embarrassment.

The scene playing out in front of me caused me to look back at my door to verify the number. My recent acquaintance, Levi, was jamming to music that was blaring from my stereo. I went over to turn down the sound. The silence seemed more violent than the drums on the CD had. I looked past the older man, who now stood looking guilty, and saw Hudson lying on the back edge of my couch singing into a spatula.

"What are you thinking...Hudson! Hudson!" I yelled to vent my panic.

Levi reached across the couch to pull the spatula from Hudson's hands. He handed it over to me as a symbolic gesture of power transference. I took it and stood there looking even more like a housewife shrew as I waved it in the air and chastised my guest.

"This is not acceptable," I said, mimicking the nanny from a popular reality show.

"You said you never cook. I didn't figure it'd be a problem," Hudson said, flipping his body down to the couch cushions and then propping himself up to a seated position. Levi joined Hudson on the couch. They sat there, old man and young man, awaiting their punishment.

"First of all, I have cooked. Well, I've engaged in cookish behavior and used this very spatula to scoop out double fudge frosting from a can. Second, Newton told me the music was too loud. What if he'd broken his ten-year record by leaving the front desk and coming upstairs? Did you think of that while you were...what? What was that? My eyes cannot convey to my brain something logical, so you'll have to explain it. Levi, what on earth are you doing here?"

At first their faces were stern and frozen as they took in my rant. But once I had finished they both broke out laughing. They laughed so hard for so long that I turned the music back on and stormed into the bedroom. The bed was made and the room was clean. Maybe Hudson had a few principles of polite refuge behavior. I sat on the edge of the bed and tapped my toe to the still-loud music. As I weighed the decision to either go back out to the living room or to hold my sulky ground here in the bedroom, the music was turned down and I heard a knock on the door. It was Hudson. I looked up at him and shrugged. It was my way of apologizing.

"Cookish?" He said, laughing.

I smiled and shrugged again.

He came over and sat beside me. "Sorry."

I whispered, "Is Levi still out there?"

"No. I sent him home."

I shook my head several times. "How do you turn 'be on your best hermit behavior' into an opportunity to invite a stranger into the apartment for a private rave?"

"I have an explanation. I'm a person of reason despite tabloid headlines of the past. I found this in my jacket, from that first day." Hudson reached over to the bookcase and retrieved the wadded up Post-it Note I had grabbed off my door.

"The note from Newton?"

"No. It's a note from Levi." He handed it to me. The message was in tiny, precise handwriting: *Don't forget, the Bible study is every Thursday at 7:00 p.m. Join us if you are ever interested. We serve brownies. Levi, 310C.*

I looked over at Hudson for further explanation. I prompted him for real answers instead of decoy sticky notes. "So you found this note in your jacket, read it, and had a hankerin' for brownies?"

"Levi lived here back when I did. He was sort of a father figure for the three of us. I went to a few of those Bible studies back then too. The guy witnessed to me often. Not always with words, but in how he would treat me."

"That's amazing," I said with sincerity. "Such a small world. Did you guys play air guitar during those Bible studies?" I was teasing him, but my spirit stirred with excitement over this unfolding faith story. Hudson was full of surprises.

He moved to the floor, where he sat cross-legged with his back against the wall. "Levi was one of the local music scene pioneers. He was in a couple bands that never caught national attention, but he was known as *the* guy for any music connection you needed...musicians, clubs, agents, labels, whatever. He was basically a legend."

"And he was a Christian? Talk about living a double life."

"Actually, he stepped out of the scene when he became a Christian. When I first got some band play, there was already a buzz about him 'going Jesus.' The up-and-comers kinda steered away from him, and he initially stepped away from them. But lots of the big names still sought him out."

"Like who?" I was fascinated by this story.

"Probably anyone you heard of who went national still worked with Levi."

"Did he have to step away from it like that?"

"Ya gotta understand the drugs and recklessness that were part of everything then. He made the choice. And then after about six months, he started being more of a presence again, but his mission was more to be a mentor and share his faith along the way."

"I'm surprised the little guy didn't get beat up."

Hudson laughed. "There were probably some who would've. But mostly, there was reverence for the guy. He was a gifted musician and everybody respected that, so they let him do his thing."

"You met in the building?"

"Yeah. Levi was getting together that weekly Bible study, mostly for interested musicians, and a friend of his who knew me from a couple gigs mentioned that I lived in his building. Between work shifts and playing clubs, we were hardly around this place, but Levi watched for us one night and told us to come to the study sometime."

"Did you go?"

He shook his head. "Not initially. I pulled a Libby, you could say. I started up those stairs on several Thursday nights, but as soon as I heard someone else coming up, I'd take off down the hall and pretend to be looking for my keys."

"Pulled a Libby," I snarled, feigning complete indignation.

"Back to *my* story...finally I went. It freaked me out because going to that meeting and possibly running into other musicians would be worse than joining AA."

"But if other musicians are there, wouldn't that make it acceptable?"

"No. But Levi knew what he was doing. He told everyone who went there that it was totally about exploring faith. 'No obligation to buy' he would say. And we all made a covenant agreement to not 'out' anyone until they were comfortable with it."

"I want to be more honest with myself and everyone about my deepest beliefs," I said. I was about to tell him about the time Cecilia saw my Bible on my desk when I noticed his raised eyebrows. "Oh, sorry. Back to *your* story. How long did you go?"

"For the better part of a year. Then Torrid started getting serious attention, and I stepped away. After that I felt bad and would avoid Levi. He was a good man and the mentor I needed, and I let him down."

"The man joined you for a session with cooking utensils. He's forgiven you."

"Libby, you should have seen his face when he opened the door and saw me today." Hudson closed his eyes and shook his head.

He was emotional. I got choked up too. I could imagine what a great reunion that was. After wiping his nose, Hudson said, "The guy looked at me for three seconds and then just grabbed me and hugged me."

I had to laugh when I thought of little Levi hugging Hudson. He probably came up to Hudson's chest.

"We talked for a long time and then I invited him back here. I didn't want to be gone in case you called me or returned early. I knew you'd freak."

"Good decision after all."

"This is all too weird to take in."

"We both needed to see some reason for this entire clandestine situation," I said.

"I definitely did. The strangest part for me is how someone like Cecilia is actually responsible for me reconnecting to my faith and music mentor right now. That has to be God. Cecilia was nice enough to me, but the woman had a guy give her a pedicure during our chapel service at the center. She's not exactly spiritual."

"Cecilia! Dang. I need to leave again," I said, jumping up off the bed. I had forgotten about meeting Rachel at Cecilia's apartment. "I'll be back as soon as I can. I'll bring you dinner after I run this errand. Any requests?" I looked around for my backpack. I would need a way to load up the items on Cecilia's list.

"After I told Levi about our hiding out, he offered to bring us some of his homemade fried chicken tonight. I'll save you some."

"Levi wouldn't say anything, would he? In his former circles, this news would be more than a big deal."

"He's the most discreet guy I know. He did warn me about the manager here. I guess he's nosey. I'll stick with the cousin bit if he comes around, although—"

"What?"

"I have this strong nudge to get the ball rolling on revealing my identity. I need to step up, take the flack for my absence, and move on."

"Cecilia has a plan in motion," I reassured my private rocker instead of following the strong nudge in my own heart to inform him of the pending lawsuit. I sure hoped Cecilia was doing the right thing.

"Do you think there's a way to pull off my return to the spotlight that also showcases the band and doesn't tick off the fans?" Hudson asked passionately. "If nobody sees my sincerity now, I'm doomed. Maybe I should talk to Cecilia about this. One bad move and the band might think I'm trying to steal their thunder."

"Believe me. Whatever Cecilia is doing…she is focused on succeeding. This is her return to the spotlight too."

Gong. A warning signal went off somewhere in my mind.

Thirty-One

Rachel stood on the corner of Cecilia's street underneath a decorative outdoor light that cast more shadows than radiance. A couple sat on a nearby bench and spoke in the hushed tones of romance. I walked by them, stealing a long enough glance to know that I had never experienced that kind of love.

I greeted my friend. "It's chilly out here. I could've met you upstairs."

She shook her head and jangled several keys from a platinum key ring. "There are many security doors in the building. You wouldn't have gotten past the night watchman." Light from the lamppost reflected off the ring.

"Are those diamonds?" I asked, trying to get a closer look.

"Can you believe it? We could hock this and both go to Europe. Come on, what do ya say?" Rachel laughed, but I could see the glint of sincerity in her eyes.

"Don't tempt me after the great 'your purpose could be here' speech. Did Ken call you back?"

"Yes. It's official. He wants me to give him two weeks' notice so he can get back and start the hiring process. I must warn you, he mentioned that maybe you could cover for a few weeks if they don't fill my position right away. If that doesn't tempt you to cash in this key chain and head for the airport, nothing will."

We walked through archways laced with roses and ivy before arriving at the brick-and-steel entry. A tall, broad-shouldered man in a dark gray uniform stood at attention beside the double glass doors with an etched design of a heron.

"Evening, ladies." The man nodded in a cordial fashion but did not change position until Rachel held up a security pass card. He passed a scanner attached to his wrist over the card until it beeped and then opened the door for us.

"I couldn't believe it when you buzzed me and said you wanted to help me clean."

"My curiosity about Cecilia's dwelling could not be denied."

We walked about eight yards through an intricate indoor garden with waterfalls and exotic plants with fan-shaped leaves and vivid colors, the bright ones you rarely use from the crayon box because they don't seem real, and reached another set of doors. Rachel swiped the card again. The sound of a chime welcomed us into the urban castle.

"I suppose saying I'm speechless is...what? An oxymoron or something."

Rachel whispered, "A person we know and interact with daily lives this way." She used a key on the lock beside the elevator; the door opened and we stepped into luxury space. I promptly sat on the deep green couch and looked up at the mirrored ceiling. "Do you think they have video cameras up there?" I asked, making faces.

"I know they do. And it's mic'd too."

"Good to know." I stopped making the faces and stood up in silence. But I had to let out a giggle as the elevator's mechanical voice announced, "You have arrived."

"Condo 1201," Rachel said, motioning to the right in the autumn-toned corridor with amber lighting resembling a Woody Allen movie.

I waited for her to walk ahead so I could reference the crib notes written on a small sheet of paper. Cecilia's list of required items were arranged in order of logical room placement.

> *collagen shots*
> *Hermès scarf*
> *Chanel sunglasses*

> *Dolce & Gabanna belt*
> *Gucci stilettos—black*
> *Mail from Paulo Carrera*
> *Baccarat crystal bottle*

I was reading them over when my head rammed into a mosaic design wind chime hanging at eye level. "Ouch!"

Rachel, who was standing in the modern yet serene living room, looked over her shoulder. "I should've warned you. I still have a cut behind my ear from a few days ago."

"Any other danger zones to watch for?"

"There's a tricky step up into the bathroom. Her designers had to make room for the heated subflooring."

"That has a sane purpose," I said and then casually added, "Why don't I start there?"

"Sure. I'll sacrifice bathroom duty. Thanks again for helping. I need to get home soon to start packing and making arrangements for the trip."

"I need to get back to…" My voice trailed off when I thought of Hudson eating Levi's fried chicken. I did want to be there with him. The past few days of conversations with him had been helping me process my own life questions.

"To what? You have a hot guy waiting for you?"

Yes, I do. "Actually, I need to get home so I can pack for my imaginary trips."

"Libby, I'm so excited I can barely stand it."

I looked over at my friend and coworker. "I'm happy for you, Rachel."

From a supply closet, she removed a duster for herself and a bucket and rubber gloves for me. "Thanks for saying and meaning that. Your day will come."

I shrugged and accepted my tools of the trade.

"You create the best itineraries I've ever seen. You're destined for adventure. I know it." She paused and smiled. "Now go scrub the toilet."

I walked down the coffee-colored hallway, passing several pretty framed images of Seattle gardens before stepping up to the marble bath area the size of my living room. Cecilia's bathroom had a large jetted tub, a double sink, armoire, antique vanity, and a huge glass-enclosed shower.

I saw everything except for the mini-fridge Cecilia mentioned in the voice mail message that followed her email instructions.

"Do you mind if I turn on some music?" Rachel yelled.

"No, not at all."

"Thank goodness she has a killer sound system. But can you believe the woman doesn't have an RV?"

"No way," I called back. "She's always so up on celebrity news."

"True," Rachel called out.

"And she always is up on the latest edition of *Seattle's Rich and Famous.*"

"Only to look for her next bachelor victim."

"And the most recent episode of *America's Most Wanted.*"

"That's her cross-reference media resource...in case the bachelor is actually the father of five from Wisconsin who robbed a Dairy Queen."

I laughed and considered how nice it was to bond over Cecilia's quirky behavior. Too bad the woman behind that behavior was calling the shots in my life currently. When some jazz music started up, I quietly shut the bathroom door and began my secret search. In the vanity drawers the scarf, belt, and the sunglasses were found easily enough. Quickly these were stashed in my backpack. I opened the armoire and took in the scent of fresh Provence lavender. I reached in and felt below the stacks of towels for a button or something suspicious. Nothing. Next, I opened the cabinet below which opened like a drawer. It was lined with white ceramic and was filled with bottles of Perrier, club soda, and cranberry juice. To the far right was a small silver container that looked like an eyeglass case. It was very cold to the touch when I verified the contents—three full syringes. I removed the small Mariner's soda can ice sleeve I had purchased three years ago at a game. It fit perfectly.

I sprayed Windex on the mirror and covered my reflection with cleansing foam. This was me. My head in the white cloud of delusion and confusion. Shouldn't life and faith make a lot more sense at this age and at this point in my noncareer? I wiped away the streaks and a moment of mental clarity followed.

Blaine. All this focus on Hudson and Cecilia and now even Rachel's decision had kept my thinking patterns from circling in on Blaine. He was part of my answer, but I wasn't even sure what I was asking anymore. A few weeks ago my only concern was whether or not I would get the promotion, and let's face it—the life—I thought I deserved. Now there were so many question marks in my life I felt like the Riddler's troubled sister.

A small crystal clock on the vanity sounded off the hour with a polite bell. I'd overstayed my time in the bathroom, so I rejoined Rachel in the living room. She was fluffing pillows and staring at a framed photo of Cecilia over the fireplace.

"Haven't you seen enough of this woman?" I asked in jest.

She remained mesmerized by the image. I walked over to stand beside her and discovered why she could not turn away. It wasn't a photo. If you stood directly in front of it, the image of a young, stylish and decadent Cecilia became a hologram.

When I regained my ability to think and speak, I said, "Wow. The picture of Dorian Gray has taken on a new dimension. This is amazing and slightly..."

"Narcissistic," Rachel said, finishing my sentence. "How did I not notice this before?"

"It looks like it should be moving."

All of a sudden Rachel started looking around the room.

"I said that. Not the hologram," I teased.

"Aha!" Rachel leaned over and grabbed a remote from the arm of the swivel chair. "I thought this was just a spare for the Bose stereo, but I think I figured out something. Watch." She pressed play and the hologram started to move. It was Cecilia waving and walking forward. She looked about thirty and was dressed in a dark, fitted, and elegant shift. That image faded and a new one popped up. This one was of her in the next decade. She had on a single strapped, very chic, and very short dress in front of a brightly lit club sign. A bit of the Seattle skyline was visible behind her. Rachel skipped forward to the next image. It was of Cecilia and a handsome Latin man. She had on a full-length gown that shimmered as the image moved. Cecilia leaned in toward the handsome man and looked up at him like a schoolgirl in love.

The next several images were of Cecilia in her office, in a conference room, and several with her shaking hands with well-known national business tycoons.

"Ya gotta give the woman some credit," I said.

"She has lived more than both of us combined. Even if we never adopt her sense for the corporate kill..."

"Or manic behavior," I added.

"Maybe we'll get an ounce of her ability to be herself at all times. She's consistently being Cecilia."

"She can be full of surprises," I said, thinking of how focused she was on turning things around for Hudson. It was to her benefit, but still she had found a way to help someone needing her expertise and she was stepping up.

Rachel thought about this for a moment and then shook her head. "Not really. She's wild or reckless at times, but her behavior is always self-centered."

After the series of moving pictures, a grid of countless channels emerged in the large framed area. "Ooh," we said simultaneously.

"All the times I've been here to run errands, water plants, and clean her windows; I could've been watching cable!" Rachel plopped down on the couch and flipped through highlighted show titles with trembling hands.

"I can see you got a bit of her addictive personality, if that helps any."

"Funny," Rachel said, but her eyes stayed glued to the screen.

I decided not to distract my friend any further. This was my perfect chance to finish gathering items on my shopping list. I stared at my wrist and continued with my search and seizure. While I sifted through piles of envelopes in Cecilia's office, I realized that I was depending on a woman with holograms of herself in her living room to deliver a happy ending for me and now for Hudson.

I noticed Paulo's name on the return address of two cream envelopes.

Mission accomplished.

A strange chill went up and down my spine. I shook it off and went in search of the Baccarat bottle, whatever that was.

Thirty-Two

"Do you need help moving?" Philip asked when I entered the building the next day. He was sipping his morning Starbucks out of a mug sized somewhere between a demitasse and a six-year-old girl's tea set cup.

"Moving?" Panic struck. Had I received another demotion without knowing it?

"Since this is where all your personal calls are being routed, I just assumed you're moving in."

I wouldn't give him the satisfaction of a response. In fact, I walked quickly by him so that he could not inquire about the contents of the Macy's bag I had draped around my wrist. On the way to my desk, I wondered and worried why I had so many calls. It was probably Cecilia pretending to be a relative again. The woman had my cell phone number but still risked everything by calling in here. This wasn't building my confidence in her abilities at a time when I needed desperately to believe she was going to redeem us all.

My phone light flashed.

It's Pan. Are you completely avoiding me? Do you not want me near your cousin? I want to connect him with Max this week, and I want to be sure you can come to the EMP event next week. Have you heard the news? Ray Stricter and Trevor Lawson are going to be there to help judge the finalists for the documentary. I can barely contain myself. Even if I don't win the grant, the idea of having them view my work is enough. Call me, ya lousy friend. And connect me with Hudson. Does the guy like dogs? Okay, sorry to use up your work phone time. Call me. And fix your stupid cell phone.

Delete. Next. I dug through my purse and found my cell phone. The battery was low again. I wasn't good at maintaining electronics or household plants. I plugged the phone into the universal charger in my cubicle wall.

It's me. What is wrong with your cell phone? Am I supposed to trust you with anything if you can't keep your cell phone service up and running? You took the wrong items. I said Hermès scarf and Chanel sunglasses. You grabbed the Hermès sunglasses and the Chanel scarf. Call me on my cell phone at 11:33 and not a second before or after.

I glanced into the shopping bag but did not bother to verify this accusation. After all these years, I was only slightly surprised that she knew.

Delete. Next.

It's Ariel. I hope I didn't upset you by coming to your office. I feel like I've messed up our friendship. Let's go out soon. I want to apologize again and again and get us back to normal. I miss you. Don't hate me.

Delete. Next.

Libby, it's Marsha. It's late at night and I found out something delicious. I know your bedtime is like 9:00 or something. And I didn't want to talk about this at work in case little ears were listening, so listen up. Rachel is leaving. That's right, you heard it here first. I'm planning a going away party for late next week. It's all hush-hush, so call me on my cell phone tonight.

Delete. I'd have to warn Rachel about the party so she could exit early that day.

Tap, tap.

I looked up toward the sound, and Marsha's face was hovering above the fabric wall. She gave me a thumbs-up. Then she pointed to the phone in my hand in case I wasn't making the connection. I thumbed back and listened to the next message.

Libby, help me. You think you remember how hard it was to live under the same roof with Mom and Dad, but you don't really remember. Save me. Mom and Dad are taking me and Nate to lunch. It's a badly veiled intervention. Please come and run interference. We'll be at the Ginger

Teahouse at noon. If you can't make it to lunch, then maybe we can all come over to your place tonight. Remember, I'm your only sister. At some point in your life, you'll be glad you saved me. Gotta go.

Delete. Another message remained. Philip wasn't kidding. Did I know anyone else?

Libby, it's Blaine. I'm sorry I've only been emailing instructions from the road rather than calling. This business trip has been all-consuming. Turns out there's a lot to learn about coddling these clients. Maybe I should've job-shadowed Cecilia for a few years! Anyway, I miss you...your input. I should be home soon...back in the office, that is. Maybe even tomorrow. I need to come home and do laundry and catch up with life. I'll email through some follow-up letters that should go out right away. Can you fake my signature? I'll owe you coffee for making you resort to petty crime. I hope things are going okay for you. Thanks for everything.

Replay. Replay. Save.

He misses me. He tried to cover it, but the nice man with the great suits and fabulous personality and actual morals misses me. He felt bad about having me sign his name and Cecilia didn't bat a false eyelash asking me to harbor a fugitive. I was probably interpreting the niceness as something more. As much as I hated to think that I was remotely close to a Marsha-type woman, the truth was that as soon as I discovered Blaine was single, I was attracted *to him*. Was it the single woman assessment process: nearby handsome single man, must pursue, must achieve happily ever after destiny? Or was there more to it?

After all, Hudson and I completely hit it off. We had such a strong, real connection that any other girl might consider that a potential romance. Ariel and Pan both responded to him like that. But I saw him and our conversations as well-timed, much-needed blessings. Maybe Blaine's niceness was only meant to be that too. I needed to wise up and shape up before Blaine returned. He'd think I was a complete dolt if he knew what I almost let myself believe.

Rachel's voice startled me. "You don't usually look like this until, oh, say, eleven. Rough night?" She winked and handed me one of the cups of coffee she was holding.

I saw the top of Marsha's fluffy bangs rise above the edge of the cubicle. I decided to play it up. "You know how it is. Juggling several boyfriends and this job has turned out to be so huge. I mean, I do all the secretarial work during the day, and those special management projects at night. It's too much."

Rachel caught on quickly. "Woman, they've got you working too hard. Do you think it is worth it? All this to get Cecilia's position? Do you even want it?"

I had to stifle a laugh. "I haven't decided, but I definitely want the option."

"I cracked under the pressure. Good thing Barcelona has fabulous sanitariums."

"And to think you could have had Ken's position."

We both giggled at that. I watched the hair fluff disappear. Surely that last bit was more than even gossipmonger Marsha could believe.

After Rachel returned to her space, I picked up the phone and dialed Cass' cell. I got her voice mail. "Tonight won't work. Don't bring Mom and Dad over to my place. I'll be at the Ginger Teahouse to intervene during the intervention."

With my perfect cup of coffee and a lighter spirit, I retrieved my emails and opened up the drafts of letters from Blaine and started to rewrite them. Only when I heard the sound of the squeaky mail cart did I remember the bag of items that needed to be shipped to Cecilia. I reached for yesterday's *Seattle Times* that lay under a stack of folders. Quickly I wrapped each item in a sheet or two of the paper. Usually I'd have the warehouse prep and package items before mailing them, but I knew better than to have anyone other than me see these contents. Thankfully, Cecilia had a PO Box set up so I didn't have an incriminating address with a line referencing "Recovery Ward No. 7" in it. Roger was passing by my cubicle doorway with the cart. I flagged him down.

"Catch me before you head up another flight?"

"We coulda wrapped that."

"It's last minute. You know how bosses can be."

Roger shrugged with indifference. "Suit yourself."

"Five minutes. That's all I need."

The squeak started up again. I looked around for something to use as the mailer. I reached for a few large bubble wrap envelopes but the crystal perfume bottle would never survive. Then my foot bumped against the

Nike box under my desk. I started keeping a pair of walking shoes there after I noticed none of my pants were fitting well around the waist anymore. I bent over and felt the roll of stomach edge over the belt of my slacks, and I noticed how pristine these shoes looked. I grunted over the direct correlation and dumped the clean contents out to make room for Cecilia's odd list of possessions.

I kept my ears alert for the sound of unoiled wheels. Everything fit into the box, and I placed the envelopes on top and closed the lid. A couple rounds of clear packaging tape secured it and a quick handwritten label slapped on top would do. It looked like graffiti mail. I stood up and looked around for Roger, who was nowhere to be seen.

"Where's Roger?" I asked. Something I was starting to like about cubicle land was the fact that you could toss out most any comment and get an answer.

Rachel responded to me this time. "Roger went upstairs."

"Geez. Am I so unforgettable?" Then I was reminded why cubicle land was so annoying.

"Your hot rocker sure didn't forget you. What a hotty!" Marsha interjected.

I called up to Leila, one of the few human resources people from the days of old who survived the merger, and asked her to send Roger back down. I returned to the letters. I was getting close to the end of the list and was glad for it. An entire morning had been spent spewing cordial corporate blah blah. All the names and letters were about the same. My eyes were crossing.

And then I saw a name I knew. And I didn't know it from the white label on a manila folder—Paulo Carrera. On the email message for this letter, Blaine wrote: *You'll have to research this address information. Get a file started on Paulo and send him a letter of introduction from me. Cecilia had some info on him, and it seems as though he is a serious candidate as a client.*

No research was required. I had Paulo's address at my fingertips. Well, and taped in a Nike box. The hair on the back of my neck stood at attention. Dare I open these envelopes and find out more? It was a bit bizarre that while Blaine was considering pursuing Mr. Carrera, Cecilia was receiving mail at her home address from the same man. Now I heard the edgy groan of hard plastic wheels stretching their circumference over the wood floor planks and the occasional runner secured with double-backed tape. Tape! I grabbed my scissors, edged along the box lid, and removed the letters. I couldn't mail these to her until I knew more about this strange connection.

Roger stood outside my cubicle leaning against the cart and sighing heavily.

"Sorry," I said as I quickly retaped the box. When I handed it over to him, there were ribbons of tape stuck to itself and winging out around the edges. I tried to push them down while he held the box, but I gave up when he looked up at me from beneath the bill of his baseball cap and closed his eyes with exasperation.

"Done. I'm done. Thanks, Roger."

He gave me a slight wave and tossed the box in the bottom of an empty metal bin. I cringed and hoped the perfume bottle survived the journey.

One aspect of my faith I was no longer denying was that most coincidences were really much more. Why would Blaine be courting Paulo as a possible client? I hated to do this, but it seemed to be my only choice.

I cleared my throat. "Marsha?"

Silence.

"Marsha?"

I saw the fluff of bangs followed by the entire round face of Marsha above the cubicle wall. Her face was flushed and her eyes were wide. I had completely forgotten about the charade Rachel and I had played out moments before. Apparently she had bought it. I'd have to correct that, but right now I had some research to do.

"I hate to ask this of you...but I need a favor." I held up the envelopes, careful to cover up Paulo's name. I didn't even need to explain, to ask, to provide detailed information. Marsha knew exactly what I was asking.

Moments later we were standing over the coffeemaker. Marsha had the envelopes in her hand and angled just above the brewing basket. A new, full pot had been made, but she disposed of that while pretending it was an old batch of house blend. We started another round and let the steam rise up and do its job on the envelopes. I actually had thought this was a pretty old-fashioned trick for today's corporate snoop, but the coffeepot rather than a brewing pot of tea lent itself to a more urban feel of espionage.

"I heard the Mariners have quite a team this year," Marsha said loudly. I looked around in hopes of seeing nobody. I thought Marsha was a pro. The two of us chatting loudly about sports was hardly a perfected decoy conversation.

I tried to bring it back to reality. "I don't know much about sports, Marsha. Are the Mariners better than last year?"

She seemed pleased by this response. "Definitely. We should go to a game together. You'd be surprised how fun it is." Marsha looked at her temporary possessions, which were opening beautifully. So I did too.

"Most definitely."

"I just made coffee," Tara said from behind us.

Marsha looked startled and about to break character as an avid sports fan, so I reached for the now open envelopes and quickly headed to the copier room. When I was sure that nobody was coming down the hall, I quickly removed the letters and placed them on the glass. The scan of light flashed side to side. I retrieved the copied pages and placed the originals back in the envelopes. Back at my desk, I used rubber cement to reseal the originals and then slipped them along with the copies in to my coat pocket.

My computer monitor beeped, alerting me it was time to call Cecilia.

"What do you know," she answered with a voice swagger, "the girl can tell time."

I wanted to say "I can shout your name right now. I can put you on conference call with Ken's office." Instead I asked, "Has the situation changed? Do you not need my services anymore?"

She cleared her throat as if considering this carefully. "I do need you. Do you have the package ready to send?"

"*The* package or the package? Because there was a package I picked up a few days ago at the airport..."

"You know what I meant. Unfortunately there is no time to correct your mistake with the scarf and sunglasses. These will do."

"Am I really going to have to ask how you know about my mistake?"

"I have surveillance cameras that are triggered when someone enters my apartment. I had them installed in case my help should decide to help themselves. I asked the security company to alert me of any suspicious activity. I forgot to mention that you'd be picking up items for me, so they notified me that you were...stealing."

"Stealing!" I shouted. "Please tell me you clarified this!"

"Well, if I were you, I wouldn't steal from any high-end department stores for a while. I use the same security company they do."

"If you were me, there wouldn't be a nanny cam installed to watch my 'help.'"

"The package is going 'next day,' right? You got everything...the crystal, the scarf, the letters?" Cecilia lingered on the last word as if to imply insignificance, but instead she gave away the importance of the letters.

I looked over at my coat and saw the edge of the envelopes and the copied pages poking out of the pocket. "The package is going out overnight."

"You might suggest to Rachel that she let up on eating my imported nut mix. I saw her replace a third of the can with Planters. As if I wouldn't know generic."

"Technically, Planters wouldn't be considered generic."

Click.

Thirty-Three

The scents of broccoli and ginger revived my sense of hunger. I'd downed several cups of coffee on an empty stomach. I went from feeling queasy to wondering if the plant in the foyer was edible as I waited for my family at the restaurant. Mom and Cass had probably argued about whether to take the van or negotiate public transportation, Mom being on the side of public transport and Cass being on the side of getting to the restaurant before closing.

I glanced around in case anyone from work was dining here. It was a futile effort since bamboo screens divided the tables and booths from the waiting area. Nobody except the smiling hostess with her hair up in chopsticks could witness the reading of stolen letters. I removed the copied sheets from my pocket and picked away several pieces of red lint—leftover from mittens I owned two years ago.

I skimmed the dates and selected the earliest written one. It was handwritten by Paulo but sent from his law office.

> My Cecilia,
>   It had been much too long since we last spoke.
> I was afraid that our last time together in Brazil

had left you unwilling to communicate with me.
I've missed you and your beautiful smile. Hearing
your voice on the phone brought back many tender
memories.

When I imagine the curve of your lips, I think of
the dewy petals of the crimson lilies on our private
balcony in the winter of 2000.

Well, he should be thinking of collagen.

How delighted I am that we can put our
heartache behind us and work together on this
venture. What we have in common is that neither
of us trusts more than a few confidants, a small
circle of those who have proven their loyalty. And
now this common trait will serve us well as we
trust one another and increase our mutual and
independent interests—my success with the biggest
lawsuit ever to come out of the music industry and
your entry into celebrity PR as an immediate star
with the bank accounts and bankable reputations
of my clients in your capable, lovely hands.

We're both in to win. For this I'm grateful.
Already there is much in motion. Now that we've
located the property, you must establish a series of
delays that will buy us the time we need to sign
on the dotted line. Communicate as soon as you've
made contact.

Let us be as united in business as we are in spirit.

Paulo

Paulo was some letter writer. He was Cecilia's opposite. He drew his prey into his lair with sweet words and enticements. Cecilia roped them in with curses and threats.

A small bell jingled as the door opened. I smelled my mother's perfume and reluctantly put the letters away. I couldn't wait to read the second one—I was hooked on this like Marsha with a Harlequin in hand.

I hugged Nate first. "I miss you," I whispered into his ear.

He held me at arm's length after our hug and said, "We miss you, kid."

"So what are we getting?" I asked my usual.

"Everything...and then some with dim sum," Dad said to complete the routine.

We always ordered family style, which was my favorite way. This translated into lots of leftovers. I wondered if Hudson was finishing off the leftover fried chicken from Levi today for lunch. Last night when I had returned from Cecilia's place, he had presented me with a foil chicken containing three wings, my favorites. "This ain't no swan," I had said, mocking his creation. He had responded, "I worked at a mini-mart, remember."

After reading the letter from Paulo, I was pretty certain Cecilia was trying to line up even more big-name clients to save her job. I wondered if any attention was really being spent on Hudson's situation. Was she using all of her time at the SOS making sure she had a place to jump should she fail to complete this mission? Was I prepared to jump if she failed to complete this mission?

"How's the job?" Dad asked me. We were sitting at a round table so everyone could see everyone else's expression. Mom thought this best for the meal's purpose.

I knew this was actually Dad's way to warm up the group for the main event. We would dine on appetizers of rice wraps and egg rolls and tidbits of my life, and when Nate and Cass were relaxed, Mom would check her watch and begin her session at an exact quarter hour moment.

"It's becoming interesting."

Everyone raised their eyebrows, surprised to hear me use the word interesting in a sentence describing my demotion.

"How so?" Nate asked with genuine support. I smiled over at him warmly. I'd been trying to send him comforting looks since he came through the door.

"Well, my responsibilities keep expanding. The atmosphere is actually better in the office these days. After the loss of some employees and the coming aboard of some others, everyone has settled into a content, focused mind-set."

"And your boss?" Cass said with a bit of tease in her voice.

I smiled broadly. I could feel air on all my front teeth. "He gives me room to grow and space to be responsible. It's a nice feeling."

"That is a huge compliment. Often the new guy, especially one in charge, is reluctant to give over that kind of freedom," Nate responded. "Believe me, I see the opposite in the military all the time. Blaine, did you say? He must really trust you."

Hearing it put this way took my breath away for a moment. "I hadn't thought..."

"It's important for a family to understand what each other is going through. Often we get caught up in our own lives and cannot discern our own messes or successes because our vision is shortsighted or is blurred by the impact of our emotions."

And the clock struck 12:30.

I folded my hands in my lap and stared down at them. I wasn't hurt by the transition because I had expected it. My mind was lost in Nate's comment combined with Mom's introductory speech. I'd been letting my emotions direct me for a long time, and now was no different. But what was different? Before I had wanted to please everyone because I expected something in exchange. I wanted fairness and freedom. And here I was working for a guy who was offering me those things and I still wasn't happy. So what was it?

I sat here with my life coach father and psychiatrist mother and knew I needed help they couldn't offer. "Would you excuse me?" I stood up, interrupting my mother and the waiter who was displaying a platter of fried rice.

"Libby?" Cass was worried I was exiting before the main discourse arrived.

"Forgot to make a call for work. I'll just be a minute."

Not waiting for reprimand or the chance for Cass to plead for me to stay, I dashed out the door with my cell phone in hand. Thank goodness it was now charged. Pulling up the contact list, I pressed a button and started pacing along the sidewalk.

"Please be there. God, please let her..."

"Hello?" Aunt Maddie answered.

"Thank goodness. I need you to help me figure something out."

"Libby? Are you okay?"

"Yes. I mean, I don't know. I thought I was doing pretty well, but then I had this weird feeling as though I was missing something big in my life."

"Back up. What triggered this?" Maddie did share my mother's ability to be matter of fact when a situation required it.

"Do you have time? What time is it there?"

"Just after ten. You're fine. Shoot."

"Nate mentioned how Blaine, my new boss, trusted me. And then Mom was talking about how our emotions often cloud our ability to see our own problems or circumstances."

"Okay."

I was in the middle of downtown Seattle with shoppers, lunchgoers, and street kids walking all around me. I barely noticed them. "Well, I thought about how before this demotion I had really wanted my situation to be fair. I wanted someone to recognize my hard work and honor me for it. And I wanted freedom—to see you, to see the world, to see a paycheck that allowed me to afford my apartment. Those things."

"Ah."

"What's the 'ah' for? I haven't even explained the problem."

"But you have, my dear. The frustration in your voice speaks volumes about your heart right now."

"What's it saying?"

"That 'more' we talked about—you are so close to it, Libby. I can feel it all the way from here. Tell me...do you now have these things?"

"I have versions of them, except the travel, but I'm working on it. Or at least I thought I was. Now I wonder if something else is at play here."

"You are your mother's daughter!" Aunt Maddie squealed.

I stopped to lean against the outside of a Pottery Barn. "Don't say that."

"Your mother is not in the business of giving advice because she wants to control people. Although, I think that is a side benefit, between you and me."

I laughed.

"She has wisdom. And you, Libby, have wisdom. The beautiful thing is that you understand you need God's wisdom to get to that place of fulfillment. Your mother's rejected that, but I'm hopeful. That's another conversation. The other thing at play is what keeps you from all of it—faith, happiness, a sense of self, and contentment."

I looked up across the street and saw a sign promoting shock therapy. A bolt of understanding went through my own mind. I could barely get it out. "Fear?"

"Well, you'd sure be abnormal if that wasn't it. Do you know why you're afraid or what of?"

"I'm afraid that God is like the people around me. I'll trust the process of faith and be let down just like I've been at work and in love. Or I'll misread God, like I've done with my friends lately. What if I give everything over and I'm no better off?"

"That's scary, isn't it? First, faith is a relationship with God. It isn't a cause and effect situation you have in the corporate setting. I know what that's like; I experienced it in formal ministry. Second, you're always better off with faith, Libby. I've hit some low points after this miraculous transition in my life, and I experienced a period of letdown when reality set in. I was scared. I asked all the things you're asking."

"This is not a pep talk yet."

"Then I looked around me. I saw my new situation for what is was—a gift. Everything I'd wanted was right before me in some form. No lie, Libby. And I'm not implying we give God our grocery list and he fulfills it. That's a very distorted vision of faith and religion in general. God didn't give me everything I asked for...but God has given me a heart for everything he was planning to provide. And his version is sweeter, Libby. So much sweeter."

There on the corner I started crying. I got it. I'd been trying to make faith a mystery with a crazy list of steps to get there. I'd forgotten that God knew me—even when I didn't know myself. Aunt Maddie and I hung up and I rushed back to the restaurant, tripping over a patch of moss growing out of a crack in the sidewalk. The hostess of the Ginger Teahouse stepped outside to help me up. We both adjusted my sweater and she examined the cement burns on the palms of my hands. She blew on them and offered reassurance in Chinese as we made our comical way back inside.

Cass was walking toward me with a look of confusion on her face. "Where have you been?" Then she saw the cuts on my hands and rushed to my side. "Libby?"

"I guess this goes with a leap of faith."

"What?"

"I'll explain later. Sorry I abandoned you during your session with Mom."

"It's still going on," she said, laughing. "Nate is moving back in this weekend."

My jaw went slack. "I'll never question Mom's abilities again."

Cass drew her breath in and then pushed it out with big cheeks. "Actually, we've been seeing a Christian counselor at a church in our neighborhood for several weeks. I didn't have the heart to tell Mom. You know how she feels about church."

"Yeah."

"But it all works out. Mom will think she resolved our marital situation, and Nate and I will be healthier as a couple."

We hugged again. "I couldn't be happier for you guys, but you know...I think it'd be good to tell Mom about the counseling."

"Are you crazy?"

"You needed to see faith in action in your life, and same for me. I think Mom needs to see it as well...to recognize it in our lives."

"Maybe you're right. Not today, though, Nate and I are going to politely ask them to head on home so we can work on our family life without distractions."

I grimaced. "Yes, that's enough for one day."

I thanked the hostess and walked back to the table with my sister.

"What food level are we on?" I inquired dutifully rather than explain my absence.

"The mein course," Dad said motioning toward the huge platter of noodles, vegetables, and shrimp.

"Of course," Cass followed.

We slipped back into our family bit, but I knew nothing was going to be routine ever again—at least not for Cass and me.

Thirty-Four

After I got off the bus in my neighborhood, I stopped at the video store for a couple action movies and then ordered some take-out Indian food for dinner. This was all guilt driven. I felt badly for leaving Hudson alone so much. I barely even checked in with him. I had the guy so scared to answer the door or the phone that he was probably feeling a bit as though he were back in solitary therapy at SOS.

I had clocked out early. Partly out of this guilt and mostly because the second letter was burning a hole in my coat pocket. I took two steps at a time up to my lobby. My small but important conversation of revelation with Aunt Maddie had turned things around for me. I still had lots of questions, but I had new food for thought. I was excited to talk through it with Hudson, and I also had a strong desire to share the good news with Blaine. I sensed he would understand my breakthrough and be happy for me. I smiled to myself and a joyful laugh escaped my lips.

"What are you so jolly about?" Newton asked from behind the counter.

I didn't want to look at him to respond, but I did. My happy personal moment inspired me to share goodwill with my fellow man by engaging in polite conversation. That was a mistake. Newton had a toothpick in one hand and a Scrabble tile in the other, and he was looking at me with more curiosity than I would like to generate from such an odd fellow.

"Did you hear that Ray Stricter and Trevor Lawson are going to be in town?"

Dang. That's what I needed to warn Hudson about. I knew there was something urgent. "Who?" I asked innocently and then regretted extending the invitation to prolong the conversation.

"Of the band Torrid? Surely you know Torrid."

"I'm more into jazz."

"Well, they were in Torrid until Jude Shea exited and left them high and dry. Did you know that they all used to live here before they were famous?"

"Interesting," I said, shaking my head and walking toward the elevator.

"I'm hoping they'll come by for a stroll down memory lane. It'd be so great. I've got my camera right here."

I turned to look and Newton pointed to the drawer to his left. He then wedged his toothpick between his front teeth and twisted it.

The elevator door opened and just as I stepped in, he called out, "Your friend left a bit ago. In case that's dinner for two."

I stopped the door with my foot, backed out, and turned around. "He what?"

"He went out a bit ago...maybe half an hour. He looked around the lobby, said 'See ya,' and left. He's more polite than most of the tenants. Speaking of which, you know you'll have to pay $50 more a month if he's staying much longer."

"Which way did he go?"

Newton scrunched up his face in a mode of serious contemplation. The answer was within reach of his little mind if he could just concentrate. "Left."

I headed back out to the neighborhood and turned left. I looked around. What if he'd taken a bus somewhere? I'd never locate him. With every step I took I was getting angrier. How could he risk going out in public like this? I scanned the block up and down and then across the busy street. Panic was rising up in me along with the anger. Now dinner would be cold, and I'd be stuck with two action movies.

Without any direction or plan I kept walking forward. I knew I'd go bonkers if I went back to the apartment to wait. At least I was using up the panic energy this way. *If I find him, I'll hug him and then I'll slap him hard.*

The "Walk" light flicked on at the intersection so I started to walk-run to catch it. He was probably at the market getting a soda. After I hugged and slapped him we'd laugh about it and he'd promise never to...

"Libby!"

I turned around to find Hudson coming out of Easy Street Records and waving. I marched toward him, and his "it's so good to see you" look turned to mock terror. I swatted him several times with the video bag. I pulled him to a spot several yards away from the store and whisper-yelled up at him, "You went there? After our conversations about being extra careful, you go to one of the primary music stores in town? What is up here?" I tapped my forehead hard. Some soup splashed out of the Indian take-out bag.

Hudson laughed but squelched it quickly. "Only for a few minutes, I swear."

"It isn't about the time. It's about the stupidity."

"Hey, hey!" A guy in a black Easy Street T-shirt came running up to us.

I widened my eyes and gave Hudson a huge "I told you so" look and prepared to make up some believable story about how my friend had gone through one of those celebrity lookalike makeover shows and that although this looked like Jude Shea, he was a kindergarten teacher from Renton.

The guy was breathing hard as he held up a plastic bag with a couple CDs in it. "Man, you left without your stuff."

Hudson's smile was full of victory as he thanked the young man.

"See, no need to pour soup all over yourself. What's with you and wearing food, anyway? Is it a condition I should know about? Should a psychiatrist know about it?"

"You are so in the doghouse. Take these." I shoved the bags at him and walked several paces in front of him. He whistled at me a couple times, but I kept my eyes straight ahead, staring only at other pedestrians, the seams in the sidewalk, the potted plants restaurants put out by their stoops to form pseudo-terraces, the awnings of the coffee shops, Blaine.

Blaine!

I looked away quickly. But even as I did, I saw that he had noticed me. I had to return my gaze to him. I was all flustered and excited and guilty about Hudson and Cecilia and tired and still on an adrenaline rush from Hudson's disappearance.

"Libby!" Blaine said this with warmth and happiness, and he said it not only with his voice but with his eyes and smile. But just as Hudson had quickly changed his expression, Blaine's face melted when I said nothing. My lips would not move and my heart was racing.

Instead of saying it was good to see him or that I missed him terribly at work, which was all true, I said, "We were just getting dinner!" and I pointed back at Hudson. It was a stupid thing to say to begin with, but the fact that I said it as though I were covering up doing something wrong made it a hundred times more regrettable.

Blaine seemed surprised, but without missing a beat he nodded and said, "Dinner is good. You deserve it." He extended his hand to Hudson, who was now by my side.

"I'm Blaine. Good to see you. I saw you at the art museum recently."

Hudson was confused, as was I. Had Blaine seen him before? Hudson stuttered as he said hello. He lifted up the bags to explain why he couldn't shake hands. Blaine's hand hovered in the air, unshook and alone, so I shook it. This scene called "Pathetic moment in one woman's life" was playing out quite perfectly. Blaine looked down at our clasped hands and pulled his away to point down the street. "I'm headed for dinner myself. Libby, I'll see you in the office tomorrow. I have a couple days reprieve before heading back out. Don't suppose Cecilia returned today?"

Hudson's eyes lit up with recognition but he played it cool and shuffled his three plastic bags around.

"Nope," I said, loudly. "We might never see that woman again."

"Tomorrow, then."

"I doubt tomorrow. My guess is she is gone for a while longer. Her usual..."

"I meant...I'll see you tomorrow," Blaine said, interrupting me before I continued down the road of further self-embarrassment.

"Yes. Tomorrow. Bright and early. See you, Blaine."

Once he was out of earshot I seethed at Hudson. "This is why you don't go buy the latest Britney Spears CD just because you want to."

"Britney Spears!"

We didn't speak the rest of the walk back to the apartment. I looked so ticked that Newton didn't even make a smart remark about extra housemates.

"I'm sorry. I had to go out. I was having a total craving. It's a carryover from my first round of rehab," he said as soon as we reached the apartment.

I threw my coat down on the couch and glared at him. "A craving? So help me…if you're using, you're out of my place. And you can plan your own comeback."

"For these." He reached into his pockets and removed five Abba-Zaba candy bars. They had wrappers that looked like NASCAR flags. I had seen them all through childhood but never had one. He handed one to me; I pouted. I was above sugar bribery.

"And the record store. You just had to go in for old time's sake?"

"I wanted to see what was new. Libby, I have lived in a total vacuum for months. I wanted to look up a few bands and see what was going on in the industry."

"Here's a news flash for you…Jude Shea is missing. That's right. You heard it here first. The guy tried to jump off the Space Needle, and then he just disappeared without a word. How's that for an update?" I hated that I was overreacting *again* to Hudson. I hated that I sounded just like Marsha in her voice mail about Rachel. But mostly I hated how hurt Blaine's face had looked when I responded so strangely, so indifferently to seeing him after his trip. I wanted to call him, but what would I say?

"I'm sorry."

Sorry would be a good start. I sighed. "Me too. I have this feeling that everything is shifting, Hudson. I don't want to blow it for you." As soon as I said that, I had a surprising revelation. I didn't want to blow it for him, but I was going to have to blow the whistle on myself. After seeing Blaine and having my gut and my heart leap with joy and regret at our encounter, I knew I had to tell him about my involvement in this plan. I wished there was a way to confess my sins and still be a steward of Hudson's career. Blaine would be angry and my private work with Cecilia would be more than adequate cause for dismissal. Now I wished I had asked questions about that dang 401(k).

"Things are shifting. Look." He reached into his other pocket and pulled out a folded piece of bright yellow paper.

I opened up the flyer. It was an announcement about Ray Stricter and Trevor Lawson coming to town for the EMP documentary event.

"Eeeee." I made a Lucille Ball goof up sound. I meant to break it to him.

Hudson picked up on what that meant. "And you were going to tell me when?"

"I just found out. Recently. And then was reminded of it again a few minutes before I went looking for you. You see? It's crucial that you don't go out again. What if you ran in to one of them? And the papers and tabloids will all be rehashing Torrid news because of their return to Seattle. You are on everyone's mind. Got it?"

"I think we need to tell Cecilia about the event. I want Ray and Trev to be a part of the dialogue, and I've told her that all along. This timing, with them in town, feels so intentional. I think this is it. What do you know about the event?"

"Don't even think about it."

"But Mr. Diddle mentioned the great Bob Dylan exhibit."

"I was going to suggest we go this week, but it's too risky. You can't go near that place. I'll be going because Pan has an entry in the competition Ray and Trevor are judging. That reminds me." I snapped my fingers. "I need to call her."

"That reminds me," he said, mimicking my motion. "She called earlier to ask if she could pick me up tomorrow evening and take me to see Max. I'm sure she meant you too. I said yes," he cringed, ready for a scolding, "but before you yell, I want to say this: I can guarantee that there'll not be one tabloid-reading sheep among the herd."

I fell onto the couch with a thud. "I need food."

He was delighted with my nonresponse response. "Me too. I'll fetch the fancy paper plates, and I'll start our evening's entertainment which you so thoughtfully provided. Do you have a preference?" He dug through the movie bag.

"You choose." I was exhausted physically and tired of thinking about all of it...guilt, secrets, plots, disappointments...

"How about *Conspiracy*?"

I nodded. Maybe watching these very things played out on the screen was the cathartic experience I needed.

I woke up to the sound of the DVD player shutting off and Hudson snoring in the bedroom. After watching *Conspiracy*, we had put in *The Usual Suspects*, which we had both seen a few times, so it lost a little something about halfway into it. I'm not sure when I'd dozed off, but I had dreams of Kevin Spacey with long hair.

I peered at the VCR clock, a function of the metal box I'd never been able to utilize unless it was indeed midnight or noon every time I happened to glance at it. Hudson had set my VCR, microwave, and stove clocks during his first full day of solitude. It was 1:30. I sat up, my mind somewhat alert but my body weighed down with exhaustion.

My hand went to my cheek. Etched in my skin was the tweed pattern of my coat. My coat. I turned on the reading lamp and pulled out Paulo's letters.

I had to remember to FedEx the originals to Cecilia as soon as I got in to the office. I reread the first letter. Was it Mel Gibson's onscreen portrayal of paranoia, or did this letter sound a bit more sinister than before? I stretched my body across the arm of the settee and peered into the bedroom. Hudson was sprawled out with his jeans on and part of a blanket strewn across his shoulders. He was sacked out.

I settled further into the cushions and opened the second letter.

> *My Cecilia,*
>
> *Aren't we the devilish ones? It indeed seems fated that you have someone on that end who will serve our needs and who has her own interests in the success of this venture. She need not know the end result of her loyalty for her work to be helpful. In fact, I wish I could keep more employees in the dark. You have a knack for brilliance, my gem.*

The property is secured, delayed, and, after the "accidental" Seattle reunion with all properties involved, the fight to follow should lead us well past the contract deadline. FreeTime will have legal control over them, their image and appearances, and the rights to their music. Meanwhile, the FreeTime band destined to replace Torrid will be able to make their way without being in the shadow of the Jude Shea mystery. Get the champagne chilling. This seems as good as wrapped up. Should we plan a getaway to Belize as our celebration? Or Paris?

I'll see you the day before the fireworks, my good luck charm. I will wear you on my sleeve like the old days, but not until we can be seen together. Did I say old days? It wasn't so long ago was it, my dear? Can thirty years go by in the blink of an eye? I think of that photo of us in Vanity Fair, you walking toward the camera, your eyes lifting to greet the camera and the crowd standing outside Grauman's Chinese Theater...and me stealing glances at you while trying to act as though I was the one leading you into the limelight. But it was you who sparkled.

You've not aged at all. May I be as gracious to myself? I will leave that to you to decide...I see myself only through the veil of a wealthy man's pride. Our reconnection has refueled a sense of our early luster. Thank you for your discretion. Maybe *returning to handwritten letters has value and not just virtue for these times?*

Always,
Paulo

I racked my brain. What had Cecilia originally said when she mentioned Paulo during our phone conversation? She had started her conversation backpedal...a habit I recognized from my many years of trying to get information out of her to write memos. The woman would provide the most intimate details of her love life to a complete stranger on the bus—well, in the first class section of the airplane—but would have to be coddled to provide basic work details. It was her way of control. If I, and later Rachel, knew nothing, we would look like idiots and she would look appalled at our incompetence. Her patterns sure were emerging during her absence. Either that or I was becoming wiser.

That feeling I had in the pit of my stomach about talking to Blaine was now a very loud, all-out conviction.

Thirty-Five

"Do you still have your trip itinerary notebook?" Rachel asked while tossing a staple remover up in the air and catching it on the non-sharp side. Ever since she'd made her decision to exit, she was carefree, happy, and apparently eager to explore untapped talent. I tried not to hold it against her.

"Are you going to mock it again?" I said this to remind her that she'd shown the book to Tara during a coffee break last year. They had leafed through my alpha-order printouts of country highlights, logical flight schedules, day trips, traditions of the locals, and area volunteer organizations to work with for short- or long-term missions/projects. They hadn't laughed at the notebook, but Tara had commented how she would love to give her mother-in-law the gift of a trip to Mongolia to milk a yak for a few dollars a day or 5840 tugrik in Mongolian currency. Then they'd laughed.

Rachel stopped tossing the red mechanism with metal fangs and looked at me, shocked by my accusation. "I never mocked the notebook. I recall saying you should work for a travel agency or a nonprofit. Your itineraries and information are incredible."

"And..."

"Maybe I mentioned that it's too bad you never go anywhere."

I pointed to my nose. "That's it."

"I'd be honored to put your itineraries to the test. May I have the Bs and Ds?"

"Ds?"

"We are going to Denmark after our time in Barcelona."

I gave her a look that probably gave away my feelings of abandonment. The bright side was that after my talk with Blaine today, I'd probably have all the time in the world for world travel. Would I let myself do it? When I cleared away the excuses, did I have the faith and the courage to actually live out these inner longings?

The locked file cabinet on wheels was below my cubicle desktop. We were always baffled by this clever invention. Wouldn't a smart thief just wheel the file cabinet on out of here, should they desperately want the contents? I removed the key from my pen tray and opened the metal drawer carefully. I slid my finger along the notebook tabs representing places I'd only read about. I hadn't looked at my itineraries in so long. I used to update them frequently with side notes and tips I discovered while reading travel books or magazines. Before Ariel started her secret hangout time with Ferris, she and I had watched cable travel shows at her place every week.

I missed my friends. Once all this stuff with Hudson was over, I would plan a girls' night. Or maybe we'd all get together soon for my "sorry you lost your job" party and they could fight over who got to house me once I couldn't pay my rent. I took the A–E notebook out of its space in the drawer and handed it to Rachel, who immediately flipped through the divider pages.

"Is this a new binder? I like it. These photo sleeves are a great idea."

"Thanks." I could tell she was being extra cheerful to make up for my mood. "Sorry. I'm tired. I woke up around one and couldn't get back to sleep last night." I left out the fact that I'd been online researching Paulo Carrera and FreeTime records and the entire music industry until about an hour ago.

"Is that why you're winking at me?"

I rubbed my right eye to see if the stinging would stop. It got worse.

"If that's the case, why are you here so early?" She flicked the wrist of her free hand and checked her red leather and sliver watch. "It isn't even seven thirty. I'm in manic 'Look at me. I'm leaving my job' mode. What's your excuse?"

Look at me. I'm losing my job, I thought, but instead I offered up the actual reason for this extra strange working behavior. "Blaine comes back this morning."

"Ken comes back too. If Cecilia showed up it'd be like old home week."

"I don't think that will be happening."

Rachel leaned in so that her head was well inside the privacy of my cubicle, "What do you know? I'm safe, remember. I take it all with me to Barcelona in a week."

I thought about telling her, but I'd gotten into this mess by going beyond the comfort zone of my conscience. I knew I had to come clean to Blaine first.

"I think I can tell you more later. I'd best prep for Blaine."

Rachel nodded and then patted the notebook. "Thanks for this. Good luck today. You might position yourself to the left of Blaine until that eye can be taken care of. That is, unless you're looking for a sexual harassment lawsuit."

I laughed at this in spite of my fear of the upcoming session with my boss. Pure adrenaline raced through my body, vibrating my foot, my toes, my right thumb. Would this be the last time I'd sit here in this cubicle? I had become attached to its openness, accessibility, and easy exiting. I liked being able to stand up and survey the entire room from my own plot of land. I knew the ache in my gut wasn't about these possible losses. It was about the certain loss of a relationship with Blaine. A working relationship based on mutual respect.

Last night I'd seen a sad look on that good man's face. Today I'd be seeing anger, hurt, and the expression of a man let down by one of his own. I stretched my arms high in the air, arched my back in, and then arched it out to loosen the tight muscles around my neck. My mind raced with possible ways to start the conversation. I didn't know whether to begin by saying I care about him and that my first impulse when I saw him last night was to run and hug him or whether I should begin with "Cecilia is out to ruin a guy who goes by the name Hudson but is *the* Jude Shea and he's been hiding in my apartment so that he can start over, but instead of having a second chance, he's going to get the shaft from his label because the high-powered lawyer Paulo Carrera is in cahoots with Cecilia and there is some important deadline coming soon."

His cologne reached my nose before I heard his footsteps, not because it was overapplied, but because my nose was programmed to take in the scent of Blaine. I shuffled papers on my desk and tried to work up a facial expression which conveyed peace and okayness. My jaw was tight, so I opened and closed my mouth several times.

"I do that during flight to ease the compression. Does it help with work pressure too?" He stood behind me and spoke in his usual friendly manner. I turned around and smiled up at him, but my lips felt lopsided, and I think my eye twitched.

Blaine slanted his head to the side, obviously trying to decipher my new look. He seemed to give up, saying, "Great to be back. It's a good sign that arriving in Seattle felt like coming home, don't you think?"

"I think."

"Did those letters get out?"

"Yes!" I said a bit too loudly. His question had reminded me that I needed to get Cecilia's original letters FedEx'd. "Your letters did go out. Do you have a minute? I need a minute...to do something, but then do you have a minute?"

I could tell right now, sleep deprivation wasn't going to help my cause.

"A minute in a minute. Got it. I could use a pop. Will you want one?"

"I can go get them."

"I brought my own this morning," he said, holding up a six-pack of grape soda. "Figured I'd need it. Couldn't sleep last night. Around one I woke up thinking, brainstorming, worrying and couldn't turn the brain off."

"Grape soda? Are we going on a fifth grade field trip?"

Blaine laughed at that, and I took a better, deeper breath. I quickly pulled a FedEx envelope from the shelf above me, stuffed Cecilia's letters inside, and jotted down the PO Box I had memorized. Per Cecilia's instruction, I wrote VIP in place of her name. I stepped out of my cubicle space nonchalantly and sauntered over to Marsha's outgoing mailbox. She had taken the week off to attend her sister's wedding in Atlanta. I hoped the physical distance I was placing between me and the package would translate to personal distance between me and the entire situation. As soon as I stepped in to Blaine's office I knew I'd be going the distance that only real faith could require and sustain.

Blaine was on his second soda when I knocked on the frame of his office doorway. He motioned with the can for me to come in as though he were welcoming me from a corner table at a local restaurant. It made me feel worse.

I sat across from him and placed the folders I had brought with me on my lap. I fingered the edges of them, and the resulting sound filled the first awkward moments of our unintentional stare down.

"You probably have a lot for me to follow up on," I said to begin practicing the task of making conversation.

"Actually, the way we worked while I was gone was helpful. Most of the follow-up communication happened immediately, thanks to you."

Oh, boy. "Right, thanks to me."

"I was being sincere," he said, interpreting my tone as sarcastic rather than ironic.

"Well, you shouldn't be sincere. I have something quite big to tell you. A lot of little things too. I'm not sure where to start because so much has happened in a short time." With that I began the ramble I had hoped to avoid. *Just because you have bad news doesn't mean you can't be professional. Be brief, Libby.*

Blaine reached out with a soda and I took it, opened it, and downed half of it. The warm, sugary liquid made me gag.

"I forgot to warn you," he said.

I stretched my arm out to place the can on Blaine's desk and sat back. "Warn is a good word. I'm here with confessions and warnings of my own. First, know that I understand the seriousness of what I'm about to reveal, and I understand there will be serious consequences for me and for others because of my choices."

Blaine sat up in his chair and watched me with a look of interest and encouragement. I looked at the files in my lap.

"The first file contains printouts of communication I've had with

Cecilia since she left the office under the auspices of working with an account and later under the assumption of her being at a recovery center. That last one is true, I think. But I'm not sure. You have trusted me with complete loyalty and opportunity, and I wasn't satisfied. Cecilia offered me a chance to get the promotion I felt I've deserved for some time now, so I took that chance by assisting her...behind your back."

I looked up to check his emotions. He had a complete poker face. I bet he wished he could buzz a mentally stable assistant and ask her or him to send security to the office right away. But he was stuck with me, in the office, with the confession.

"Here's the short version," I said, interlocking my fingers together like a child praying before dinner. "While Cecilia was away, she happened upon a very well-known and sought-after celebrity who has been out of the limelight, missing in fact, for quite a while. It turns out he wants to reenter the public eye. Cecilia offered her services—and, indirectly, mine—to accomplish this. She said it'd mean great recognition for Reed and Dunson, for her, and of course, for the sap who helped her."

"Sap," he teased lightly.

"Nice to meet you."

"So your confession is that while I was gone you helped one of our top executives on a project that would bring business, money, and notoriety to this firm. Is that correct?"

I replayed his description in my head several times. "That is a generous spin, but yes, that statement is true." I paused and then added, "Or so I thought."

"This gets better?" Blaine asked. I noticed he reached for a pen.

"Worse. While I thought Cecilia was working on a plan to save this celebrity's career from afar, I've come to suspect that she's really stalling in order to destroy the celebrity's career. The helping her own career would still be true."

"And you know about this twist...how?"

I reshuffled my folders. "File number two contains copies of personal letters sent to Cecilia from a high-powered attorney. These letters indicate that there is more to Cecilia's tactics and more behind her intention than she let on."

"And you got these...?"

I shook my head. I'd protect him from the sordid details.

"Got it. Can you say what you think her plan is? Will it hurt the company?"

I hadn't considered this question before. If Cecilia set herself up with a fabulous new job doing public relations for singers, actors, and other social elite, it wouldn't directly hurt Reed and Dunson. This wasn't a positive revelation to me. Without Cecilia actually being a threat to this firm, nobody would do anything to stop her, and nobody would therefore save Hudson. "No, but she'll hurt the client."

"Her personal client, really," Blaine stated as he jotted down some notes.

I started to panic. I didn't want him to wash his hands of this. We had to do something. "But remember…" I stalled and then it came to me. "Remember that this client trusts her *as* a leader of this company, not as the free agent she aspires to be. He's depending on her to make things right, and it isn't just a PR move for him. He's changed and deserves this second chance. So you see, by Cecilia representing us and betraying him, it *would* destroy our reputation!" I was thrilled that this conclusion would be my ticket to receiving help. It would also undoubtedly be the direct link between me and the conspiracy Ken Dunson would cite in my termination letter.

Blaine put his pen down slowly and quietly. He looked out the window for a couple seconds, but I could tell his gaze stopped somewhere between his desk and the skyline. "Why do you think this celebrity deserves a second chance?"

"He's kind and intelligent. The guy admits to being a jerk before, but he's ready to step up and take the blame, which I find admirable. He knows his career might not be the same; in fact, he hopes it's different because he wants to regain his passion for music. He said…" I stopped speaking as I realized what Blaine had cleverly accomplished.

"Have you had personal contact with him?" Blaine raised his eyebrows with amusement, but his emphasis on the word "personal" was less than jovial.

"He's been living with me." I blurted this as if purging my darkest secret. Once the words were out, I questioned my logic and my sanity. My new vow of honesty needed to be tempered with better timing.

Blaine's jaw dropped. "It's the guy from last night?"

"Yes."

"I thought he was your boyfriend, the musician."

"No, no, no. It was Jude Shea...who could look like Angus a bit from the right side, but I think Hudson is overall more outstanding in looks..."

"Jude, Angus, Hudson? Does folder number three have a flow chart of the men in your life?" Blaine asked, cutting me off. "You've paid them all a lot of attention."

My face grew hot, and I could feel the searing tingle of tears forming.

Blaine looked upward for a moment and then let out a sigh. "Libby, I'm sorry. You're telling me something related to this firm's future, and I made it personal." He sighed again and ran his hand through his hair a couple of times.

Did the hand through the hair reveal frustration with me, himself, or the situation? "I'm sorry," I said to all of the above.

"Is it personal for you, Libby?"

"Yes," I said, nodding emphatically until I saw Blaine's look of disappointment. "I mean, no. Not personal like *that.* I just feel responsible. I've been hiding this guy under the pretense of helping him. If I'm setting him up, I couldn't handle it." I was getting choked up. Guilt, fatigue, and confession melded into one insurmountable emotion.

"I'm in. Give me your folders and a night to figure things out."

"What about the guy?"

"Keep it for a while longer," he said as if talking about a CD. "If that's not too much of a burden?" he added with some uncharacteristic sarcasm.

I stood up and handed him my stack of evidence. For a moment we both held on to opposite ends of the folders. I couldn't seem to let go. My hesitation wasn't because I didn't trust him. It was because for once in my life, I *completely* trusted someone.

Thirty-Six

I opened the door for Rachel after hearing our knock.

"I was really hoping we could have another closet meeting before I leave," she said, both enthused and intrigued.

The truth flashed before me. "I'm going to miss you so much. I didn't realize it until just now." I started to get teary.

"Gee, thanks," she teased. "Don't tell me you pulled me away from the daunting task of cleaning my cubicle just to cry in private?"

I returned to spy mode. "No. I have a serious question. Is there a way into Cecilia's apartment other than through the front door?"

Rachel thought about this for a mere second. "Yes. Should I ask why *you* ask?"

"No. Are you sure there is a second way?"

"I left the security badge at home one night and the queen's guard wouldn't let me through, even though we'd had a perfectly memorable conversation about the best places to eat calamari in Seattle the night before. So I circled the building, climbed up a trellis to the upper floor's hallway through the residents' garden deck, and took the elevator."

I did the math. "Wouldn't that still require you to use her front door?"

"Normally, yes. But then I ran into a neighbor and told her I'd lost the key to the apartment, and asked if I could use her balcony to get to Cecilia's."

"And she let you?"

"She assumed I'd gotten by Goliath at the gate, so I was within the realm of safe and sane. I climbed over the partial wall to Cecilia's back window and wedged a Bic pen and a safety pin into the door jam and slid it up off its rails and set it to the side."

"Did they base *Alias* off of you?" My eye now throbbed as I envisioned a way to repeat this gauntlet in order to review the series of hologram images without activating the security cameras at the front door.

"And the next day I had to hire someone to come up to her place and reattach the sliding door. Thank goodness I figured out how to dismantle her security cameras. All it takes is a magnet…a strong magnet. That keeps the camera from moving. It basically records the static image of the fake palm plant by the front door."

"What?"

Rachel smiled at me mischievously. She knew that's what I had wanted all along. "Did you think you really knew something I didn't know?" Rachel rubbed her hands together sinisterly. "What are we up to anyway?"

I rolled my eyes and started to braid the edges of my hair—a nervous habit of mine. How much should I tell my friend? "Can you keep a secret?"

"Yes!" She motioned locking her lips and peered at me with wide brown eyes.

"Cecilia is up to something," I whispered.

Rachel tilted her face upward and started to laugh hysterically.

"No, I mean really up to something. A plot even."

Rachel kept laughing and then put her hand over her mouth to stifle the sound. "No kidding? That's a shocker." She paused for a moment, took in my serious face, and then swallowed the rest of her giggles before saying, "Got it. This is different. I'm listening."

For the next forty-five minutes I filled Rachel in on my life's adventure. With every turn she met my news with the appropriate looks of surprise, shock, and even envy. There was a point in which I felt amazingly in control; this is when I started crying.

"Libby, what is it? I'll help. It'll be fine."

I sobbed louder. Stress was erupting in a pathetic display of sadness. Rachel sat beside me on another bucket and put her arm around my shoulders. I felt ridiculous. "I completely let Blaine down. I didn't know how much that mattered until I saw the expression on his face when I told him I'd been hiding Hudson at my place."

Rachel ruffled my hair. "Oh, silly, naive Libby. That wasn't disappointment."

"Then what was it?" I took a stuttered breath in to regain my composure.

"Jealousy, my dear. You've been so focused on secrets that you couldn't see the blatant, and I mean blatant, big like Blaine has for you."

"Big like?" I asked.

"If I said love and you did screw up this entire relationship before it started, you'd be crushed, destroyed, and emotionally crippled forever. But now it'll just be a 'big like' you once could've had."

I squinted my eyes to help my mind focus on and follow her words. "Love?"

"Ah, you missed my point. Stay with big like. It's for your own good."

"I forgot a pen. Do you have one?"

I reached into my backpack and pulled out a pen I had swiped from my bank. I put it back in the black hole of my bag and scrounged some more.

"I'm not picky, but I am holding up half of a sliding glass door. By myself."

I retrieved another pen. "Sorry, but that one was my smoothest writer. Other than the beautiful one Blaine got me. That one I'll have to take really good care of. It's expensive and... well, now meaningful. I thought about what you..."

"Did I mention this is glass, and heavy, and breakable?" Rachel's face became a darker shade of red under the duress.

"Hey, I carried my laptop for the whole Kilimanjaro climb up here." I wedged the meaningless pen into the top tracks of the door and sure enough, the door popped out. I grabbed my side so it wouldn't fall atop both of us and we shuffled it over a few feet to lean it against the outside wall.

"Who's home watching the important package?"

"We had plans with Pan, so I sent him on alone. I hope I didn't goof up."

"You said your friends didn't recognize him at your birthday party, right?"

"Yeah, but Pan's mind is all focused on music, music, music. You'd think she'd connect the dots. She did say he looked kinda like Jude Shea. Maybe that is all she'll think. I mean who would believe Jude Shea was hanging out in my apartment?"

"Gotta give Cecilia credit. She knew where to hide him."

I nodded and walked into the beautiful apartment through the balcony opening.

"I love big, open apartments like this. It feels like the set of a Doris Day movie."

"Yeah. It reminds me of Mary Tyler Moore's first apartment."

"Exactly," I said. "Are you really going to leave me?"

Rachel gave me a "Don't start that" look. What she didn't say with her expression, but we both thought, was that I wouldn't be at Reed and Dunson either...not once all this came out in to the open. I shut up and set up my computer while Rachel got the hologram television remote set to run the slide show.

From my Favorites window on the computer, I pulled up two sites that featured photos of Paulo Carrera. One was his law firm's website, which looked a bit more like an ad for plastic surgery with a slide show of actors and pop stars running like movie film over the top of the screen. The other was *Vogue* archives from the mid-1970s. It showed a photo of a very dashing, young Paulo at some Hollywood premiere.

Rachel clicked through the photos and stopped on the one of Cecilia and the handsome Latin man and pressed pause. "Got it."

I looked from screen to screen. "We got ourselves a match. Come look."

Rachel walked over to the bar where I had my laptop plugged in and looked at the image on my computer and then to the one frozen in full dimension. "It's the sexy crinkle around the eyes. I love that. Maybe I'll fall in love with a beautiful, brilliant, rich Spaniard, and I'll never come back."

I looked closely at her. She'd thought of this life plan before. We all carried personal fantasies with us. I'd let mine weigh down the God-given dreams of my heart. Had I ever truly desired the scenario I'd envisioned every year at review time of career advancement and the perfect man about to propose? Or had it just seemed like the right dream for a woman of my age and my unfortunate job situation? It all felt generic now that I wanted only the assurance that I was doing what God made me to do. More and more I was relating to Aunt Maddie's personal faith choices. From Mom's perspective, her sister was crazy and irresponsible and destined for destitution. From God's perspective, Maddie was a faithful servant bound for the riches of a fulfilled life.

In spite of Rachel's comment, I knew I'd survive the loss of the Big Like as long as I believed God would make good of my failings, but at the thought of losing Blaine, my heart skipped a beat. This getting my life on track wouldn't be so easy. I looked again at the hologram. I felt bad for Cecilia. She had been that bright light in her heyday, and even now could be the most engaging, captivating person; no wonder she wanted to continue to shine. As envious as I could be of her career, former starlike qualities, and her wealth, I realized that she represented everything I was hoping to avoid—a life lived in fear that I'd never be good enough.

"Maybe Cecilia was faking her need for assistants all this time," Rachel called out from another room, bringing me back to the moment.

"Why?" I yelled back.

Rachel emerged from Cecilia's office with a bright red folder. "She has her own filing system at home."

"Amazing. She once threw a bottle of nail polish remover at me because I suggested we could save time if she returned account files in alpha order."

"She's not into alpha except alpha females, of course, but she is into color coding. And guess what red is."

"The new black?"

"That too. Red means hot, hot, hot. You can thank me later."

Rachel walked over to me, pulled up a bar stool, and removed the contents of the "urgent" folder. Paulo's name and law firm's LA address were at the top of a fax cover page. In the handwriting I recognized from the letters, a note was scribed which read, "Got 'em!" I quickly scanned the rest of the fax, which was a twenty-page music contract for Torrid. I ran my finger over the last page to the elegant signature of Jude Shea. This was signed the same year I started the training program. How weird that five years later our life paths were intersecting. For the first time I felt a deep reassurance that my time at Reed and Dunson wasn't wasted and wouldn't be a blemish on my life's résumé. There were reasons I might not ever understand for this time in career purgatory.

"I thought you'd hit panic mode, not nirvana when you saw this," Rachel said and pointed to a paragraph half a page up from the signatures.

My eyes followed her finger and I read:

```
       Should the signing band with its signing mem-
   bers prove unable to provide a market-length album
   recording every eighteen months during the life of
   this contract to FreeTime records, the band and
   all signing members will be in breach of their
   contract and will thereby relinquish all rights to
   their music published through FreeTime records or
   any of its subsidiary labels and will be prohib-
   ited from signing with another label for the dura-
   tion of this contract's timeline plus two years.
```

"What is the contract's timeline?" I asked aloud.

Rachel reviewed the pages. "Here it is. They have another year on their contract."

"They wouldn't be able to record with anyone for three years. Some music careers don't even last that long. They'd be ruined."

"And look at these addendums with the dates of all their recordings. In two and a half weeks it will be exactly eighteen months since they submitted *A Sinner's Ruin*, their last CD, and my least favorite, if anyone's asking. It was so dark. It gave me the creeps."

"*A Sinner's Ruin*. My gosh…I'd forgotten what the name of the CD had been." Jude hadn't only visited the edge of Seattle's landmark. He'd been on the edge of total despair. No wonder he ran.

Thirty-Seven

The sound of laughter filled the hallway outside my apartment. The smell of farm soon followed, and then Pan and Hudson emerged with mud and grass caked on their shoes.

"Stop there!" I raised my hand to halt my friends and went to find something to put down on the floor in front of them.

"I'm so sorry I stood up for Max's right to art at Libby's birthday party," Hudson said, letting out an authentic laugh. He wasn't holding back at all. For a brief second I was jealous that Pan could bring that out of him. We'd had fun conversation and deep conversation, but there was something different about him tonight.

"Who knew watching sheep was more fun than Disneyland?" I muttered as I placed newspaper sections and paper towels down before them.

Pan wiped tears from her cheeks. "I was a bit self-righteous that night, wasn't I?"

"I had higher expectations after your salt, pepper, and butter knife preview."

She giggled and shoved him away from my makeshift foyer. His dirty right boot came within an inch of my fingers. I rolled my eyes and wiped up bits of field from my beautiful hardwood floors. To think that I just spent an evening breaking and entering to save this guy's career while he was out cavorting with sheep. And now my friend was falling for a guy she could never have—in her documentary or in her life.

I didn't like being ignored. "I said, who knew watching sheep was more fun..."

Hudson reached for my hand and pulled me up. "You should've come with us, Libby. You would've found it hilarious."

Without smiling I said, "I can crack myself up just by recalling his satin jumpers. Even thirteen-year-old girls stopped wearing satin jumpers two decades ago."

They laughed even harder.

I went to the bedroom and grabbed a pair of Hudson's jeans and my terry cloth robe with bright orange flower appliqués along the sleeves. It had been a gift from my mother. She sent it with a "get well soon" card after I'd missed one of her important lectures—I'd been taking a college final. My apartment was filled with passive-aggressive gifts from my mother and the gift shop owner she counsels.

"Here, you two." I said, bringing out the dry clothing. My cell phone rang. "I'll be in the bedroom. You can fight over the robe."

Again they laughed hysterically. Again I rolled my eyes.

"Hello?"

"Where on earth is the mail I asked you to send?"

My hand went to my forehead. I rubbed my temple to ease the pending migraine. Had I only just mailed those letters from Paulo today?

"Cecilia! I'm sorry. Those will arrive in the morning. Somehow they didn't make the original package. You'll have them tomorrow first thing. I promise."

"I don't know if I should trust you. You're friends with Rochelle, right?"

"Who? Rachel?"

"Whatever. She's quitting. Can you believe it?"

"Much stranger things have happened," I said pointedly. It was lost on her.

"It's betrayal, that's what it is. Corporate betrayal."

"Did you study drama in college?"

"Whatever made you think...oh. Ha, ha. Very funny. You won't be

laughing if that mail is not here first thing. I will awaken, have my cappuccino with a light dusting of chocolate, and then I will head straight to
the mail center to check my PO Box."

"They let you leave?" I asked. It would be a mistake to let her know
that I assumed she was probably in a five-star hotel penthouse with Paulo
by now.

Cecilia was silent for quite a while before saying, "For good behavior."

"Do you have a plan update for me?"

More silence on her end. But the laughter from the next room was
rising more than falling. I tried to muffle the receiver, but it was too
late.

"Where are you?"

"My apartment."

Cecilia now laughed. "Where are you, Libby?"

"My apartment!" I said, indignant.

"And where is the package?" she asked sternly.

"He's the one laughing."

"Hmm. Maybe I had better speed up the plan after all."

"That would be very wise. And now I'd better go tone down the
package's laughter or a neighbor might come over and expose us all."

"Oh, dear. Go!"

Click.

I looked at my phone and then the door to the living room, better
known as comedy central. I got up, pushed the door almost shut, and
then returned to the bed where, with a racing heart I scanned my contact
number listing and selected Blaine's name.

"Libby?" Blaine answered.

"How'd you know?"

"I have you...on my phone. In my phone."

"Oh," I said, pleasantly surprised. And surprised by the pleasantness
of the surprise. "I'm sorry to call you after hours."

Blaine cleared his throat. "No problem at all. I went through the files.
Have you ever considered private eye work?"

"I'll be needing a new field," I said in jest, but the proceeding silence made me mean it. "We found a copy of the contract. I think you should look at this right away."

"We? Found?"

"Rachel. I told her today because I needed her help. She found the contract by cracking Cecilia's filing color code."

"Red for hot priority?" Blaine asked, amused.

"Okay, smarty, do you want to look at this tonight or not?"

"Tonight?"

Too forward. "Or first thing in the morning. The contract changes the urgency of the timeline for our plan. Something needs to happen soon, Blaine."

"I'll be right over."

"Well, not to be pushy, but Hudson and I have company."

"And I now understand after reading these files that Hudson is code for Jude. But how wise is it for you two to be entertaining guests?"

"It's my friend, Pan. She doesn't know." I lowered my voice a few notches and glanced at the door. Through the slight opening, I could see Pan trying on Hudson's leather jacket. I should have warned Hudson about Pan's feelings. This was going to snowball into an emotional disaster. When she finds out Hudson isn't interested, she'll be upset with herself and Hudson. When she finds out that Hudson isn't Hudson, she'll be terminally peeved at me.

"Come over. I'll send a cab to your place. Is ten minutes enough time?"

"We live in the same neighborhood. What's the address? I can walk."

"Can we please do some of this my way?"

Some of what? I glanced at my sad outfit in the mirror and said, "Give me fifteen." We hung up and I spent twelve minutes changing clothes and applying mascara, two minutes questioning the final selection, and one minute telling Pan and Hudson I had to go to my sister's house for an impromptu family meeting.

Hudson perked up. "We'll be fine. Do you mind if we watch the rest of *The Usual Suspects?* That is, if Pan wants to?"

"Yes!" Pan said and then promptly slapped her hand to her forehead. "Dang. I've got to go home and let the dogs out."

"I'll go!" Hudson said. I shook my head at him.

"Really?" Pan asked full of nerves and a crush.

"Oh, actually I just remembered I have some work to do tonight. While I'm away from the office, I have to send through a lot of reports." Hudson revisited our old lie.

"Sure, I understand." Her face fell and so did his. I realized that Rachel was right. I was so used to secrets lately that I was blind to real things happening right in front of me. Pan's like for Hudson was mutual!

"Another time," I said convincingly and gently prodded Pan, in my robe, to walk out the door with me.

I stepped to the side of a brown carton in front of Blaine's apartment and knocked twice on the cherry wood door. His building looked a lot like the Regal Queen after a million-dollar renovation. I was studying the detailed fish design on the doorknob just as it turned.

"Hey!" Blaine said, startled by our close proximity.

I straightened up. "You have a delivery." I pointed to the box.

"I was hoping this would get here." he leaned over and picked up the box with ease and motioned for me to go on in to the apartment.

"This is beautiful," I said, taking in the tidy and stylish dwelling with modern, comfortable furniture; tasteful, large-framed prints and photographs; and floor to ceiling windows. The view was of moonlit water and the roof terraces of other apartments.

"Our apartment buildings were designed by the same architect."

"I was just thinking that this looked like my place after it won the lottery."

"Make yourself comfortable. Need a drink?" Blaine put the carton on his dining room table, which was a style Pan and I had both picked during one of our fantasy shops through Parkers furniture store showroom a few months ago. Since we both barely existed on tight budgets, this was our alternative form of shopping.

"No, I'm good. Coat?" I asked.

"Let me take that." Blaine stepped behind me and took my waterproof suede coat from my shoulders. I passed the red folder from my right hand to my left so he could slide the coat off. He hung it on a hanger and then on the hook beside his front door.

"Your other special delivery," I said, handing him the folder.

"I'd better get this started first. Have a seat." Blaine stripped the brown mailer tape from the carton and removed a ball of wrinkled clothes.

"I hate to be the bearer of bad news, but when you send out your laundry, they're supposed to *clean* your clothes—not play rugby in them and then wad them up."

He laughed. I loved that I made him laugh.

While I waited in the living room, he talked to me from the laundry room down the hall. "I had so many files from my meetings that I decided to load up my travel suitcase with business and mail my laundry to myself." His voice was eventually drowned out by the sound of water rushing in to a front-load washing machine.

When Blaine returned to the living room, I was lying back on his comfy couch.

"You see, that's what I like about you. To some people 'make yourself at home' is a mere pleasantry. But you perceive it just as it was intended...an authentic invitation."

"Well, only because we have the same architect am I able to truly make myself at home. How do you know this little tidbit, anyway?"

"Is this the folder?" Blaine returned to a more professional tone as he retrieved the red folder from beneath my sock-covered foot. My shoes were beneath the coffee table.

I sat upright to make room for him on the couch, but he chose a chair across the room from me. His eyes stayed glued to the contract. Only once, when he got to the vital page 18, did he look up.

"I know. This is big news, right?" I decided not to be offended.

"I wanted to be hopeful, but he has to be told. It's probably too late."

"There has to be a way. There has to be a reason I got..."

"That empty file on Paulo at work now makes sense. It probably had info related to all this in it and was never meant to be a new account."

I nodded. "I'm sure that's it."

"Cecilia's absence really makes sense. I couldn't understand why she'd put her job at risk. The label is probably making it well worth her while to delay Jude."

"Speaking of whom, Jude is waiting for me. I told him I'd be at my sister's house. I'd better go." I wanted the flow of encouraging words, not the clog of reality.

"You just got here." Blaine looked right at me as though he had more to say. But there was only silence.

"It's late. I want to process all of this and figure something out."

He took his cue and got up to retrieve my coat. He held it open for me while I put my shoes on in slow motion.

For a moment his hands rested on my shoulders. "Libby?"

I turned around to face him. My pulse still pounded from the contact. "What?"

"He needs to know the truth," Blaine said and handed me the red folder. "Unless Torrid magically reunites and records an album in two weeks, he'll need a new gig for a few years. The guy took time off. Maybe that was a good choice."

"We can't let his career end because he trusted us...me." My voice was shaky. The guilt and frustration were so overwhelming. "I couldn't handle knowing that my willingness to believe the wrong person could bring him down."

Blaine reached up and held my chin with his right hand for a lingering moment. Then he looked straight into my eyes. "Give yourself grace, Libby. Jude did this to his career. He was a spoiled rock star who couldn't stay disciplined."

"You're too hard on him."

"He sold out and then he regretted it."

"That has a familiar ring to it," I said, ashamed.

"Exactly. Yet you're so ready to give him a chance. Extend the same grace to yourself. I would."

"You have," I said earnestly and turned and left.

Because of the cart between us, I could not pat her shoulder as would be the socially correct thing to do. So I encircled her with repeated compliments. "It's pretty. Really pretty. Really." After a solid minute of this I realized with horror that Marsha never hit the button for the Reed and Dunson floor. This moment wasn't going to end soon. "Your polish is fabulous!" I amped up my volume to snap her out of her mood.

"I want to be married. That's all. Is that too much to want?"

I shook my head with empathy. "Not at all. You should want that."

"You're mocking me because you don't want that."

"I'm not mocking you. And who said I don't want to get married?"

"Everyone."

The doors opened and my eyes lit up. Marsha pushed "close doors."

"Everyone? Everyone around here has nothing better to do than talk about whether or not I want to get married?"

"Everyone I talk to," she said.

Since the woman was in charge of my immediate fate, I didn't point out that she was the common denominator in those conversations. She was the only one talking about my love life. "I want to get married. Someday. It just not my top priority in life."

She teared up again.

"I'm sorry. I didn't mean to imply that it was your priority."

"It is my priority. What makes me mad is that the women who don't want it get all the possibilities." She looked at me pointedly. Not that there was anyone else to look at in the confined space, but I knew she directed the general comment at me specifically.

"I've never received a proposal of marriage."

"But you could. That rocker follows you around like a puppy dog, and we've all noticed how Blaine looks at you. So if you don't like the hot, bad-boy type and you aren't into a completely nice, handsome, corporate guy, what do you want?"

Out of this elevator. "The rocker is not in the picture. And why does everyone think Blaine likes me? He's just a nice guy."

"See...you've heard people talk about Blaine. And Sasha saw you walking around with the leather guy last week. You don't even know how lucky you are."

I wasn't about to get into explaining who the "leather guy" really was.

Thirty-Eight

The main floor elevator of our business complex opened just as I stepped up to it. I saw this as a good sign until I got in and a hand with fuchsia-colored nails kept the doors from closing.

"Hi, Marsha," I said and then inched my way as far back as I could to make room for her and the large load of copier paper she had on a roller cart. "Did we run out of paper upstairs?" I asked the obvious.

Instead of turning the cart and backing in, Marsha pushed her load forward so that she stood facing me when the doors did finally close. I looked away, I read the copier paper wrappers, and then I had to concede to Marsha's unspoken request for attention.

"I like the hair garden thingy," I said and pointed toward the browning lavender buds that encircled her head.

"Hair garden?" she said with total disgust.

"I meant flowers. Did you get those at the market?"

"This is the very expensive floral wreath I wore in my sister's wedding."

"The wedding three days ago? Could you hit the floor button for us?"

"I love it," she said adamantly and then started crying.

"Marsha, I don't know how love works. I do believe God gives all of us different desires of the heart. But you can't expect every guy you meet to be the one. That's not real or ideal."

She wiped her eyes and nodded. "I do kinda force it."

"We'd better head up."

"Yeah." She pushed the button and adjusted her wreath. "I can't believe I'm so late."

"Nobody'll notice," Marsha said, yawning.

"See...people don't pay attention to me."

"Not when Cecilia's back in town."

"Wha...?"

I walked a zigzag pattern around cubicle central while popping my head up over the mini-walls every few feet scanning for Cecilia. I didn't want my initial encounter with her to be in front of coworkers. All I could think was how grateful I was that I had confessed to Blaine when I did.

"I just talked to her last night. What is she doing here?" I whisper-yelled at Blaine after rushing into his office, shoving the door shut, pulling the blinds to the hall-facing windows, and sliding down to the floor with a thud.

He dropped a stack of forms. "Libby! You could give a man a heart attack."

"You can't give someone a heart attack. They have a heart attack."

"I beg to differ." He rubbed his chest before leaning forward from his roller chair to pick up the papers. We were eye level. He looked at me and started laughing.

"This isn't funny." Neither was the crick in my neck. I shifted to all fours and crawled over to Blaine's couch in a small, windowless inset.

"It's a little funny. It's like watching a live version of *I Love Lucy.*"

"Well, Ricky, say something. Who's she meeting with? Did you talk to her?"

Before coming over, Blaine used his intercom to buzz my phone. "Hold all my calls, please," he said in jest.

"I thought we had more time. Do you think she knows that we know?"

"No. She was smart to appear sooner than later. With Ray and Trevor coming in for that EMP event, they'll have all three Torrid members in Seattle at the same time and can slap them each with the lawsuit." Blaine sat down on the couch. We were angled to face one another. "It's perfect timing for her and Paulo. Besides, Ken was fed up."

"I don't get that part. Why would they *want* Torrid members to be in the same place?"

"My guess? That's probably a fluke, but maybe FreeTime is working it to their advantage and hoping for a scene. There's gotta be a lot of animosity between the band members. The hype of an all-out conflict could mean more CDs sold and more money straight to FreeTime's bank account."

"Jude would never fight," I stated.

Blaine shook his head. "I didn't mean a brawl, but I imagine there'll be some choice words exchanged either in person or through the media."

"So what's Cecilia saying to Ken?"

"While I was there, she was downplaying her absence as an extended work trip."

"Ken's buying that?"

"He doesn't know about all the espionage going on, but no...he's not buying it, and Cecilia's not really selling it. Let's face it. She's all set for her move. This last week or two will be a formality. If she had some sense of decency, she'd be giving Ken official notice now, but that would raise questions. Speaking of raising questions, how'd Jude respond to the truth last night?"

I waved that question away with my hand.

"Couldn't tell him? You're running out of time."

"I almost did." I paused a moment "Instead of sleeping last night, I came up with a plan. I'll tell him everything tonight."

"Libby, you can't save him. Be honest with him, yes, but even if he'd never met Cecilia, all this other stuff would be happening. You didn't create this mess. He did."

"So you keep saying. Does that mean you're out?"

"Out?"

"You're not going to help me?"

He sighed deeply and threw up his hands. "I don't personally care about Jude's career. And I don't think this will end up hurting the firm's reputation. But I do care about you…I don't want your job to be in jeopardy should Jude decide to take action against the firm. I'll help."

"Thank you," I said. And then added, "He wouldn't do that."

"How are we going to help this saint of a man?"

"The band will regroup and record a new CD before the deadline so they won't be in breach of their contract."

"That's the plan? The two musicians who've had no career for the past eighteen months because of Jude will just forgive and forget *and* record an entire CD in a week?"

"Yep."

"You do have faith."

"I'm a slow learner, but I'm getting there."

"Me too." He smiled, and it was such an open, vulnerable smile that I looked away.

A knock saved us from an awkward silence. Blaine got up and opened the door slowly and then fully when he saw who it was. His hand motioned toward the area where I was and Rachel stepped in. She looked as though she were about to burst with news.

"I have things to discuss with Libby," Rachel said as way of apology to Blaine.

Blaine nodded and pointed to a chair.

"This is trivial work news. Libby and I can go out to her office when she's done here. I'll just wait out there." Rachel stepped backward a few feet.

"He knows everything, Rachel," I said. "Have a seat."

She seemed relieved. "I'm on a mission. Cecilia is looking for you, Libby. Philip told her you were in. She sent me in search of you. Are you ready to face her?"

"Is anyone?" I asked.

"I'm almost sad to be leaving. I might miss how all this ends."

"Don't worry. Libby has a plan," Blaine offered with false sincerity.

"You do?"

I snapped my fingers at Blaine. "Either you have faith or you don't. There is no room for a skeptic, even if this is his office." I was full of confidence in my idea.

"What's the plan?" Rachel asked.

"The band will get together and record a new CD so that the big breach of contract will be avoided and they can salvage the rights to their material and careers."

"The two guys who now have no career because of Jude will just forgive and forget *and* record an entire CD in a week?"

"That's exactly what I said," Blaine commented.

Only then, staring into my spy partner's look of pure fascination, did my plan seem borderline idiotic. "There has to be a way to right this wrong," I cried.

"First you need to assure Cecilia that all is well with her plot, because she looks like a mad cow with a great facial. She's scaring everyone. Go make her feel secure. Up." Rachel waved me to a standing position and led me by the hand out of Blaine's office.

"Let me know how I can help. I mean it," Blaine said in my ear before Rachel delivered me like a bounty hunter to Cecilia's door.

Thirty-Nine

Cecilia was lying back in a leather swivel chair, her long, tan legs propped up on the matching ottoman, and a slender silver cigarette holder with amethyst adornments balanced in the V of two fingers. The woman had always been dramatic, but she had clearly gone Hollywood in mind and manner.

It made me mad. "It must feel good to be gone so long and not have it matter."

She peered at me through her for-show Chanel bifocal glasses, which did not help her read my mood. Her legs gracefully retracted to a proper business angle while her head went back and her lips expelled a fume of smoke into the air.

"You could've mentioned on the phone last night that you were returning today." I didn't realize how much I had changed. Fear always muted my frustration in the past. But now I had no internal filters big enough, strong enough, or willing enough to transform my true feelings into polite professionalisms for Cecilia.

"Sit," she said with such force that I abided. "I came back because our past few phone conversations alarmed me. Apparently your nunnery has turned into the land of parties for dummies. I was afraid for Hudson's welfare. Besides, it's time for me to be here and to fulfill the promise I

273

made to…him." Cecilia rested the tip of the cigarette holder in a crystal ashtray and held out her hands, palms up, to me.

"What?"

"You are released. As soon as he is in my care, that is. Libby, don't think your loyalty has gone unnoticed. I'm sure that having a man like our Hudson sent you all atwitter, yet you seemed to have managed the situation better than I could've hoped. When your three-month review comes up for your new position, I will be certain to speak to Blaine and Ken about getting you in to the account executive training program."

I laughed my fake laugh, the one I usually did behind her back. It was refreshing to do so to her face in the glow of her trendy track lighting. "That's rich, Cecilia. You mean you have enough clout to get me into the same program I've been in for five years?" *Under your tyrannical tutelage.*

"I meant to say I would get you into an AE position, darling. Need not get your…whatever that is you are wearing…in a bunch. What is with everyone around here? One assistant had illegal substances growing in her hair."

"This is a suit—an expensive suit, Cecilia. And Marsha happens to be wearing a lovely floral wreath." I glared at her miniskirt and wanted to yell, "Meanwhile you're wearing fabric swatches." But instead I smiled and lifted my hands, palms up.

"What?" She asked.

"I'm releasing you of my presence so that I can get back to Blaine."

She looked at me intently, eyes narrowing to slits, and she retrieved the cigarette for a theatrical puff. "How's that all going? You and Blaine?"

I headed for the door without responding. She didn't deserve to say Blaine's name, let alone ask about him.

"I want to see the package tonight. I'll come by at eight."

I headed straight to my cubicle and dialed home. The machine picked up. I'd warned Hudson to never answer. "It's me. I have important things to discuss so I'll be home by four. You mentioned writing new music, right? Just curious. We'll talk. Don't open the door for Tupperware salesmen, paperboys, or Girl Scouts, and don't order in. I'll bring dinner. Good job not answering the phone. Unless you're out of the apartment, then bad job." I hung up wishing he'd broken the phone rule so that I knew he was okay.

I juggled a large bag of fish-and-chips and used my shoulder to push open the stalled door of the bus. With Cecilia's early return, I knew this would be one of the last nights I'd have a legitimate excuse to carry two orders of take-out food home. I slowed my steps. I'd miss having Hudson around, but there was also an underlying excitement about what might happen next. The smell of lemon wedges and malt vinegar was rejuvenating, and I was excited to tell him the truth and make things right. Cecilia would interrupt the evening to spin her lies, but otherwise this night would be about coming clean, helping Jude find his way out, and ensuring a more authentic life of my own.

As I crossed the street, I noticed Levi pacing at the western corner of the block. I was in a hurry to see Hudson, but Levi seemed troubled. He was also the key to my master plan. He was the only one who could arrange a meeting with Jude, Ray, and Trevor, set up a sound studio, and oversee an entire album recording in a week. I scrolled through that list again. Yes. It was good I was seeing Levi now.

I ventured right instead of left, maneuvering through a thicket of Seattleites waiting outside of Easy Street Records for a CD release. When Levi saw me break through the crowd, his pacing stopped and he motioned with his hands for me to hurry to his corner. I would have emphasized that I was the one carrying a greasy bag brimming with food, but he looked distraught, so I quickened my steps up the incline and arrived at the corner breathless and worried.

I handed Levi the food and bent over to catch my breath.

"Libby, there is no time."

"No...time to breathe? It is required for living."

"You can't go in the front way. Jude said you'd be coming home about now. I've been watching for you so I could sneak you in the back."

"There is no back."

Without a word, Levi started along the sidewalk in racewalk mode.

"Don't drop that bag. It's a special meal. Jude and I don't have many more nights to hang out." I was rambling and ambling now. I looked around to be sure nobody heard my reference to Jude. "I don't know what's going on, but I have a lot to tell you, Levi. There's no plan to save his career. My boss lied. But now I have a plan that requires your help and connections. I have faith we can pull off this plan before the deadline. There's a deadline, that's something else I need to tell you about."

Levi stopped and turned back to look at me with worried eyes. "People know, Libby. We must hurry."

I didn't have to ask what they knew. And there was no time to find out how they knew. So I stopped talking, started jogging, and followed the old man and the seafood. We had walked two sides of the block and were nearing the main entrance street for the Regal Queen. "Unless you have a system of cables and pulleys, I don't see how we're getting in the back of the building, Levi."

The little Pac-Man figure turned a sharp left and headed for the front door of my church. The church I meant to be mine, anyway. "What are you doing?" I yelled.

"It's okay. This is my church."

"You go here?"

Levi unlocked the door with a set of keys on a rope key chain. "I'm the pastor."

I stopped in my tracks and mentally fell down.

"Come. Come," he said and ushered me into the darkness of the sanctuary.

When he shut the front door behind us, the faint glow from strands of twinkle lights along the back wall illuminated worn wooden pews, mismatched runners, and a frayed friendliness. It was very comfortable and safe. What had I been afraid of?

Levi led me down the one aisle to the altar and then opened a narrow door on the left. He pulled a piece of string above our heads and a small lightbulb flickered on and cast our shadows against a white curtain. Levi pulled the curtain aside for me. "Watch your step. This is the baptistery and it might still be wet from earlier this week."

"Do you know how many times I've almost come here?" I asked incredulously.

"Not for sure. But I've watched you wait outside many a-Sunday."

"Why didn't you say anything?"

"Now go through that door," Levi instructed. "And, by the way, I recall inviting you to church."

"Yes, but I didn't know it was this church or that this church was *your* church. This door? I feel like Alice in Wonderland." I opened yet another small door and a set of steep stairs filled my view.

"Flashlight to right, by foot."

I reached out my hand and sure enough, there was small flashlight resting on the first stair. "I think I'd like your sermons. You are a man of precise words."

The stairs creaked and complained as we made our way up to the opening. A sliver of light greeted us at the top. My eyes could make out angled walls and dark shapes. "You can take the lead now, Levi. This is a bit creepy. Where are we? I'm all turned around."

"This is the Regal Queen attic. If I remember correctly, we walk about fifteen long strides to be directly over my apartment," Levi whispered.

"Then what? We knock three times, Tony Orlando?"

Levi laughed. "As a matter of fact, we do." The spry man counted out the steps on tiptoes, so I followed in the same manner. He did indeed knock three times on the apartment's ceiling. Two feet ahead of him, a square yard of attic flooring dropped down and the sunlight traveling through Levi's apartment below projected a funnel of light in the darkness of the dank attic. It looked like a scene from *Poltergeist,* which I knew only because Hudson had made me watch it twice during the past few days.

Levi handed down the food and then pulled me by the hand over to the hole in the floor. "Sit with your legs dangling down, reach to the other side, grab this ridge, and swing down into the room. They'll get you."

"They? You first."

"Are you sure you'll follow?"

"I didn't leave a trail of bread crumbs, so I have no choice."

"Okay. Watch me." With ease Levi followed the instructions he had given me and a moment later the agile man was standing in his apartment, cheering me on.

I hesitated. Then Jude came in to view below. "I'll get you, Libby."

I closed my eyes and swung down. Jude grabbed me at my waist and let me down to the floor slowly. I opened my eyes and stared in to his. "Jude, I have so much to tell you. Things are not as they seem."

"You'd better hear me out, Libby. I messed up everything. But first, I want you to meet my friends Trevor Lawson and Ray Stricter." He turned me to face two thin but handsome men.

"Libby." Trevor nodded.

"Hi, Libby." Ray reached out to shake my hand, which was shaking on its own.

"Friends?"

Jude smiled. "Yeah. Thanks to Levi. You'd better sit down for this."

I willingly obliged and took a seat on the long, green couch. It looked like it belonged in a 1950s dentist office. Only then did I notice Newton tied to a chair by the hallway. He had on huge headphones. I could hear Frank Sinatra emanating from them.

"Newton!"

Newton started to open his mouth but Levi shushed him with one stern look. Newton closed his mouth and pouted. I kept staring at the captive and then at Levi.

"Libby," Jude said as he sat down next to me, "I went against your rules."

"Ya think?"

"The feeling that I needed to reconnect with Ray and Trevor turned into urgency. I just knew I had to come clean with them personally, without Cecilia. And then if they forgave me, we'd find a way to go on. If they didn't forgive me, then whatever Cecilia has planned as my big reemergence into the public arena wouldn't matter. I wouldn't consider doing that unless Ray and Trevor knew all about it."

"Good instinct."

"So after Cecilia called this morning to tell me she'd explain her plan tonight..."

"Cecilia called you?"

"Yeah. It was about an hour after you left and an hour before you called with your message. But by then I had already come over here, to Levi's place. I knew that if anyone could locate Ray and Trevor behind the scenes, it would be Levi. I also knew he'd be willing to help us work through the situation."

I nodded toward Newton.

"I'm getting to that part. Ray and Trevor came over here, not knowing that Levi had invited them so that they'd have to face me."

"And no blood was shed?" I asked.

Ray spoke up, "I thought about it. We spent the first seven months of

Jude's disappearance sure that he'd gone off to do something stupid and dangerous. We were afraid we'd lost our friend. Then there were rumors of sightings and bits and pieces of information coming in to us that pushed us from worry to anger."

"But we've had time to cool off. Ray and I have been working on our own projects. Heck, Ray even got married. The break's been good for us. Jude's gimmicks got the attention, but we were all out of control. Ask Levi. He had to save our hides over and over," said Trevor in a surprisingly quiet, gentle voice.

"And drive us home from more than a few bars after last call."

I nodded toward Newton again.

Jude sighed. "After the initial shock, it was like when we lived here before...we were just great buddies. Then Levi gets a call from John Meier."

"That name sounds familiar."

"He covers the local music scene for the paper and several online publications. Somehow, he'd received word that Ray and Trevor were seen entering the Regal Queen and that I might be here as well. John knew Levi lived here, so he immediately called and asked what was going on. Of course, Levi denied anything and everything, but the rumor still got out there, thanks to..." Jude pointed to Newton.

I followed the point and scowled at Newton. "Newton, you and your darn tabloids." I returned my attention to Levi. "Actually, I was afraid he'd pick up on who Hudson was even sooner."

Levi cleared his throat. "Newton mentioned Hudson looked like Jude one day when I picked up my mail, and I totally scoffed at that comparison to derail any further ideas. But when he saw Ray and Trevor walk into the lobby this morning, he was on the phone within minutes of their arrival."

"So that crowd outside Easy Street?"

"That's for us," Ray pointed to Trevor and himself. "We have a scheduled appearance in..." he checked his watch, "half an hour. There's also a group forming outside of the apartments in case the rumor about Jude is true."

"What's stopping them from coming up?" I asked, panicked.

"Levi called in four club bouncers who go to his Bible study."

"There's an image you don't get every day," I said and thought about it for a few seconds. "Call me crazy, but wouldn't the sudden appearance of four large men be a pretty good clue that the rumor was right?"

"That's where we're stuck. We had to keep people away, but now we're trapped up here and fueling the story all the more. How badly do you think I messed up Cecilia's plan?" Jude asked with such sincerity that I regretted, yet again, ever believing that Cecilia was looking out for anyone but herself.

"I don't suppose any of you three have a copy of your contract?" I asked.

The three bandmates simultaneously pulled out copies of the contract from their pockets and presented them to me for inspection.

"I'm impressed. So you know all about the timing?"

"Did you really think none of us knew our careers would be sealed in a week?"

I shrugged, my stereotype of musicians quickly deteriorating.

"That's the main reason Ray and I agreed to be a part of the EMP event this weekend. We want to be visible during this contract dissolution. FreeTime might own us more than ever after this week, but our fans should know that we didn't sell out completely. We got enough flak for our last album. If we disappear without a word, we've totally lost all chance for respect," Trevor stated with passion.

"I'm the only sellout," Jude said. "I couldn't see a way out, so I just made one. This is all my doing. That's why Cecilia's offer to step in and help me undo the damage was perfect."

Levi smacked his lips to express his aha moment. "Cecilia Mitchum?"

"Yes!" Jude and I said at the same time.

"I know Cecilia from way back. You'd better brace yourselves, boys. I'm guessing Libby's news is not good news. Unless Cecilia had a dramatic conversion this decade?"

"No dramatic conversion," I stated and headed into my pathetic confession.

Forty

"I'm not at all surprised Paulo and Cecilia are teamed up again. It's perfect, really," Levi said, scratching his chin. He was reminiscing.

"You know him too?" Jude asked, scratching his own chin as he watched Levi.

"The LA and Seattle music scenes were competitive but also linked by common promoters, investors, and legal counsel. I met Paulo at several events and Cecilia was always close by."

"In what capacity?" This was getting most interesting.

"His assistant. But only in the beginning. Soon she built a name for herself in public relations. Paulo would represent affluent clients in court, usually get them off on a technicality, and then turn them over to Cecilia. She did reputation clean up for the executives who lived the high life but didn't stand on moral high ground. When Jude told me a little bit about his encounter with a local PR pro, I didn't even think of Cecilia."

"He probably used misleading words like 'kind' and 'helpful,'" I said. "Why *did* she leave that industry?"

"The last reputation she had to clean up was her own. She succumbed to the darker side of that high life and began a tour of rehab centers. That too was a very celebrity thing to do at the time. But Paulo didn't like the burden of her problems, so they parted ways romantically. Cecilia needed a new life, so she got in on the ground floor with Ken Dunson. He was the PR 'it' kid back then and had a solid image for creativity with scruples. It was a great move for her, actually."

I finished the story with my information. "But she fears losing her status in a company she helped build and along comes Paulo. She misses him and the status, and shifting to Paulo's circle is a professionally acceptable way to exit Reed and Dunson. When she happened across Jude, she probably couldn't believe her luck."

"Do you really think, after all you know about her, that her encounter with Jude was accidental?" Levi asked.

Jude and I both looked at each other with opened mouths of pure astonishment.

"Really?" I hadn't thought through a deeper level of deception. "Man, she's good."

"No, wait. How would she have known where I was?" Jude asked, reluctant to believe he had been sought out rather than discovered.

"Paulo has probably had you investigated and followed for months. All of you."

"I need a bathroom," Newton said with a wheeze.

Levi stood up from where he was seated by the kitchen table and walked over to grant Newton temporary freedom. He pointed down the hall and then positioned himself by the front door.

"Libby?" Jude asked in a rather quiet voice.

"What is it?"

"I really like Pandora."

I smiled. He was so sincere. "You mean like, like?"

"I'm captivated by her. But she's going to find out about all of this. And then the fact that we both kept this big secret while she's working on her documentary and we said nothing...I knew after the first time she and I talked that I shouldn't keep the secret from her, but I didn't want to blow the plan. I'm still learning how to trust my instincts."

"Me too," I admitted. "I'd love to say this'll all work out, but I don't know anymore. Pan is stubborn and private and vulnerable. Her pride might overrule her heart."

"Her heart? So you think she has feelings for me?"

I nodded.

Jude let out a big sigh of relief. "Well, then it's worth risking her initial reaction if I think I stand the slightest chance of regaining her trust. After all, Trevor and Ray have been great about a much bigger deception."

"Sorry to burst your Pollyanna bubble, but a musician slighted is nothing compared to a woman scorned."

"I get your point. I've got to talk to her now. Can I use your phone?"

I handed it to him and then pulled it back. "You can't tell her this on the phone. And if you bring her over, she'll know everything that's going on."

"I want her to know everything. In fact, I think she should be able to film us. She could have an exclusive interview with me and the guys." He turned to face the others and raised his voice. "Anyone care if I try to make good with the woman of my dreams by offering her an exclusive interview with us?"

Ray and Trevor looked at one another, shrugged, and smiled. "Go for it."

Levi interrupted the conversation. "What would she do with this film? Think through this, guys. It's a make-or-break moment in your careers. You don't want to do anything without a plan."

Trevor looked out the window to the street below. "There are more people. Ray, we're going to have to head over to Easy Street soon. We have to act like nothing different has happened. We'll just say we came here to visit Levi and keep it at that."

"The last thing we should do is keep your reunion a secret. That's exactly what FreeTime records wanted. The more fans who know, the more difficult it will be for the label to write you guys off as former icons and usher in their group du jour. Could you record an album in the next week?"

Trevor started laughing, as did Levi, who was now escorting Newton from the bathroom to the front room.

"All right, I get it. Stupid suggestion. But what if you guys record a new song, and we get it out there? The demand will be too great for them to ignore. They'll start seeing dollar signs."

"Jude's been sharing some of his new stuff. We could easily choose one and get it recorded," Ray offered up to the process.

"Do you have to have a studio?" I asked.

"We can use the church sanctuary. It has great acoustics."

"What about instruments?"

They laughed again.

"What?"

"Levi has a two-bedroom apartment and sleeps on the couch so that he has room to house his collection. Instruments will not be the problem," Trevor said. He looked over Newton's head at a clock in the shape of a guitar and stood up quickly. "Ray, we gotta go. Believe it or not, Jude, we trust you with how this will play out. Heck, I figured the EMP event would be the start of early retirement, not the beginning of a reunion tour."

"Pan can film us recording the song. We'll make our music video on the spot and Pan can debut you at the event as part of her project. She'll have to forgive me with that offer. Right, Libby?"

I nodded. "You may have just found a way around the scorn."

Jude became emotional as he looked at his two friends. "You guys, I can't believe you have forgiven me. I was so self-absorbed."

Ray gripped him by the shoulder. "Man, we all were. Like I said, not one of us was healthy. Jude, the fact that you were the most narcissistic ass of all and a confused mess of a man is probably what saved the rest of us. And you know I say that with great affection," he said, laughing to avoid the deeper sentiment.

Levi placed a short stepladder under the hole in the ceiling and motioned for the guys to follow him back through the attic. He was the last to pull himself up. When he looked back down into the apartment, he said, "I'll be back as soon as they get out of the church safely. Maybe we could start setting up the sanctuary and be ready to go by seven thirty."

"Wait. We can't drag the equipment through your bat cave. How can we possibly set up?" Jude asked. "There are too many people outside, even though most of them will probably head over to Easy Street once they see there's no action here."

The reality set in. We'd be trapped here until someone famous came out of the Regal Queen. "Ray and Trevor have to come back," I stated. "They have to go through the front door. That was the whole excuse to have your bouncers posted out front." I walked over to Newton and wagged my finger at him. "This is your fault. You had to interfere. You had to be a fan of tabloids and want to be a part of the show!"

Levi rolled his eyes. "You're right. Guys," he called into the abyss, "you two get to leave the normal way."

Jude helped Ray and Trevor and then Levi back down. "This doesn't resolve the equipment dilemma," he said. "I still can't just walk out that door, especially not carrying a guitar case and a drum set."

"We need a decoy," Levi suggested.

We all looked at Newton. His eyes were fixed on his own feet until he felt the weight of the stares and looked up. Once we got a second glance at his features and sad posture, we knew this was a dead end. "Naww," Jude said.

"I've got it!" I said, filled with the excitement of possible resolution. "Newton, you'll make another call to John Meier and tell him that the guy *you think* is Jude has left the building and headed to Clem's."

"The bar? How will that help? There won't be anyone there," Levi asked.

"Oh, he'll see someone. And as far as he'll be concerned, the mystery will be solved, at least temporarily."

"And ours will just begin?" Jude asked, completely lost.

"Who will he see?" Levi asked as he and Jude's bandmates headed for the door.

"Trust me," I said with a grin. I reached for my phone and pulled up my contacts. His was the first name on my alpha listing. Good thing I hadn't deleted my ex.

The door shut and Newton, Jude, and I remained. Jude politely started to talk with the snitch about the history of the apartment building while I waited with the phone to my ear.

After several rings, a breathless Angus answered the phone. "Yo!"

Boy, had I ever made the right decision. I placed him on speaker phone and spoke into the mic. "Angus, are you alone? What are you doing?"

"Those are two questions former girlfriends are not allowed to ask anymore." Angus said, laughing. "But yes, I am alone. I was just polishing my boots."

"Who do you often get mistaken for?"

His voice reverberated through the end of my cell phone. "Most often? Jude Shea. Why?" he said nonchalantly and quite pleased.

Jude turned from chatting with Newton and raised his eyebrows.

"Who happens to be in town right now," Angus continued, surprising us all.

"How'd you...why do you think that?"

"I'm in the know. In fact, there were ridiculous rumors about him being at your apartment building, but I told everyone I would know if that were the case."

"So where is he?"

"That I don't know. He's underground. Someone is hiding him. The guy's stayed out of the public eye this long—he won't reappear until he wants to. But I can tell you this, as soon as he does, I'll be one of the first to know."

"I believe you. In fact, I'm calling about Jude."

"Oh, yeah? You gonna tell me that you spotted him too? What? Was he with that creep who plays checkers with his donuts at the front desk?" Angus asked sarcastically.

Newton opened his mouth to protest, but I shook my head firmly.

I laughed too. "No. That would never happen. He doesn't play checkers, but he's right here with me."

"What is this...'national pick on your ex' day?"

Jude spoke up. "Angus, it's Jude Shea."

"Mick Jaggar's on the other line, can you hold?" Angus said, laughing.

"It is Jude, Angus. And we need you to get over here to Clem's bar in the next thirty minutes as a decoy. John Meier and maybe some others will be there looking for Jude. They'll see you and then realize that the creep who plays checkers with donuts never saw Jude at all. He saw *you*."

"Ariel told me you were being very odd lately."

"Ariel?"

"Oops. Cat's out of the bag."

"You're seeing Ariel?"

"Don't get off the subject here. What are you up to? Just tell me."

"How can I get you to believe Jude is right here?"

"Stickin' with that story, are you? Okay...let's see. I would need your *Jude* to play the intro to 'Waco, Texas.'"

"'Waco, Texas'?" I asked, clueless.

Jude was already on his way to retrieve a guitar from Levi's bedroom.

"It's from their first album," Newton clarified.

"Who was that?" Angus asked.

"Long story."

"So we can get off the phone now? I need to finish these boots and get over to Easy Street."

"Good luck. It's packed. Ray and Trevor just headed over there."

"They did, did they? So you hang with Ray and Trevor too, do ya?" Angus said with more frustration than good humor.

From behind me, the first sounds of a somewhat familiar song were being played. "Oh, I do remember this song. It's called 'Waco, Texas'? That's sick."

Jude played with flair while I held up the phone. Then I heard Angus' voice holler through the small speaker.

"What?" I asked, pulling the phone closer to me than to the guitar.

"Libby, how stupid do you think I am. I'm a bit surprised you have a copy of that album, but I did teach you a few things about good music while we dated, so it's possible you went out and bought it."

Oh, great.

Newton spoke up. "It's acoustic. It couldn't be the album. Sing, Jude."

"Good point, Newton. Angus, did you hear that? This is acoustic. Hit it, Jude."

So he began, with a voice that was rough, mellow, and very soulful. It made me weak in the knees. He was beautiful, and he was an artist. How had I missed the full reality that I, Libby Hawthorne, had been housing and hiding this amazing musician?

I let Jude play for several moments before I raised the phone back to my ear and switched off the speaker. "Well?" I asked.

"I don't understand any of this or what you've gotten yourself in to, but I'll go to Clem's. What do I tell John? We've met before. I can't pretend to be Jude."

"I want you to be yourself. He just has to believe that someone saw you and thought you were Jude. We have to dismiss the rumor that Jude is here until we're ready for people to know. When John leaves the bar, call me and then wait another fifteen minutes before heading over to the Queen Anne Community Church. I'll meet you there."

"Levi's church?"

"How'd you know that?"

"Libby, every musician with any sense of Seattle's legacy knows Levi."

"Oh, right. Of course," I paused and then said in a serious tone, "You're in this thing officially, Angus. Don't tell anyone. I'm trusting you."

"So am I, dude. Thanks for doing this," Jude called out with a deeper than usual voice.

"I figure I owe you, Libby."

"Why?"

"I don't think you realized what I was going through when we first met. And that's because I never explained to you how down I was. When we met at Elliott Bay that day, I was lower than low. And you had this great spark, a real wonder about you. I knew we wouldn't last because you are this perfect, sweet, good person and I'm...I'm not. I just wanted to be with you for as long as I could. The months we dated helped me get back on track. You really influenced me. I figured you'd always see me as a wannabe with no future, so I never came clean with how I was feeling. But I loved you for what you brought me through." Angus stopped talking and I remained on the line, stunned and a little choked up.

I coughed the tickle out of my throat. "That is the sweetest thing anyone has ever said to me, Angus. For what it's worth, I never gave you credit for your discipline to music or for your talent. And you're a good person. I've messed up a lot lately. I don't have any claims on goodness, and I'm far from perfect, but I am trying to figure life out."

Jude nodded and pointed to himself. "And so is Jude," I added. "That's why his return to the limelight is so important. He's really changed, and he wants things to be better this time."

"Sorry I didn't tell you about Ariel. It's a recent thing. I guess I didn't want you to tell her to stay away from me."

"I can see you two together."

"You're not with...?" Angus said as the startling thought occurred to him.

"No!" I laughed. "I'm so not with Jude. I'm not with anyone," I said bravely, but my sadness was evident.

"Who was that guy at that art show? That looked serious."

"Like I said, I've messed up a lot lately."

I hung up, reviewed my contact list, and pulled up Pan's name. "Here. Don't tell her anything except to be at my place at seven fifteen. And ask her to bring her camera. And your next call had better be to the florist and the pet shop."

"Roses for forgiveness? And...a dog collar?"

"Doggie treats for her clan. And hurry up...Newton has an important call to make."

Fifty-One

"Something smells really good," Levi said, sniffing the air when he returned from escorting Ray and Trevor out of the building and over to Easy Street records.

"I forgot. I brought fish-and-chips for Jude and me. Let me heat that up and we can all eat. The portions are huge, anyway." I grabbed the greasy sack and walked over to the microwave. "How are Ray and Trevor?"

"After seeing that crowd, I think that recording a single is the way to go. The fans will insist on a new album. FreeTime would be crazy to drop them and prevent them from releasing anything new. I'm just not sure how we'll transport the equipment without being noticed."

Jude said, "Maybe we should go to an actual studio."

"I trust guys at the studios, but we could still be spotted," Levi said.

"There's another way," said Newton.

We all turned to the captured man.

"Another way to what?" Jude asked.

"To the church from the apartment building...to take the equipment."

Levi sat down and leaned with his elbows resting on his knees and his full attention on Newton. "How?"

Newton's skinny shoulders reached toward his big, red ear lobes.

"Don't get coy with us, Newton," I said. I came out of the kitchen with the scariest utensil I could find, a meat thermometer. "Do you want dinner or not?"

He swallowed and nodded.

"Then tell us. And don't pretend for one moment that this day is not the most exciting day of your life. You should be kissing our feet."

"You're right," he said with more confidence. "This is the most exciting day of my life." He actually smiled, and I noticed he had bright blue eyes. He was always looking down or to the side. "In the basement there is a sealed door that leads to the church's basement. We can use the elevator to carry the equipment."

Levi was shaking his head. "No. I've lived here forever. There is no basement button on the elevator. I'd have noticed it."

"There's an old freight elevator at the back of the building. Originally it was built because the owner had a wheelchair and needed a bigger elevator. Later they used it to bring in food supplies when this was a hotel with a small restaurant in the lobby. You wouldn't know it now, because my dad is too cheap to restore this building, but this was a wonderful place. The architect was very well known later in his career."

"He's the same one who designed the Vista View," I added.

"Yes! How'd you know?" Newton looked at me with the same surprised look I was giving him. All this time I had written him off as a complete bubble head.

"Blaine…a friend of mine mentioned that his building was by the same guy. He just told me that yesterday. Small world."

"Oh, that guy. I told him about the architect. That's how he knows."

"When would you have talked to him?"

"He used to come in and stand by the lobby door, trying to get the nerve to ring for you. I finally asked him to stop loitering and he told me he was watching out for you, so we started talking about the building, blah, blah, blah."

"I can't believe he used to watch for me. Why didn't you tell him to buzz me? Or just send him up? All you have to do is look at the guy to know he's…" I stopped myself.

"He's what?" Jude asked. He raised his eyebrows a couple times, teasing me.

"He's amazing," I admitted.

"Well, at first I told him you were shy and it might scare you that he was being so forward. Then once he came in to the picture," Newton pointed a bony finger at Jude, "I told Blaine that you were living with a guy. Nobody ever believed the cousin story."

"So your dad knows a lot about the history of this place?" Jude asked.

"He doesn't know anything except it was a cheap piece of property when he bought it right before the real estate market started its climb. It's just an investment to him. I tried to tell him that it was a landmark, but he doesn't listen to me. I studied architecture in college for a couple years. The only reason I took this pathetic job was to be close to a respectable person's work."

"Newton, you get the biggest portion of fish-and-chips." I got up and prepared some plates of food while the guys discussed the building and planned how to get the equipment set up in the next hour.

After I had served dinner, I gave myself some space by sitting over by the window facing the street. There were no longer any fans or hopeful reporters camped out on the sidewalk. I opened up the window a crack to let some of the evening breeze in. A French fry rested on my tongue. The salt dissolved and the malt vinegar made my mouth tingle. I daydreamed about Blaine coming by to see me. When Jude and I had run in to him out front a few days ago, Blaine had probably just been here. No wonder he seemed so flustered to see me with a guy. I realized how badly I wanted to believe Marsha and Rachel about Blaine's feelings, but why didn't the one person who mattered say anything? He was willing to be a stalker but not willing to tell me that he liked me?

Just then a nice-looking car pulled up, and a pair of legs followed by blond hair and a long leather coat emerged. Cecilia! I had totally forgotten that she was coming. My phone rang. Cecilia's name appeared on the small screen, and I could see her placing her earpiece in as she looked around. I shifted back from the window and yelled to Jude, "Get to my apartment now. Cecilia's here. Newton...can we trust you?"

"Yes," he said in a believable tone.

"Then get downstairs and greet her. I'm going to answer this, but you need to stall her for a few minutes before sending her up. Levi, you'd better stay out of sight. I'll let you know as soon as we can load the equipment."

Jude and Newton stumbled over each other and out the door. I answered the phone. "Hello?" I asked innocently.

"Which hovel do you call your own?" Cecilia barked.

"Who is this?"

"One guess."

"You're early."

"I'm also busy with a million details for the big unveiling. So unless you want to let your new best buddy down big-time, you'd better let the master puppeteer in."

"Oh, when is he arriving?" I taunted the woman to slow her progress.

"I don't have long. What number are you in? I promised to check on Hudson."

"Who'd you promise?" Aha. She basically admitted she wasn't working alone.

"I'll ask the little man with the red ear lobes to direct me to your apartment. Don't bother cleaning. I wouldn't be impressed either way."

Click.

I walked into my apartment and saw that Jude was gathering up all the paperwork and files we had that were relevant to Cecilia.

"She'll be here in a moment," I said. "Remember, be as grateful as ever and ask lots of questions or she might be suspicious why we aren't asking for details."

"Good point. I'm very curious as to what she is going to pitch to us."

"Throw at us is more like it."

The place was clear of evidence by the time we heard Cecilia's heels dragging on the snagged carpet followed by the sound of her tripping. I opened the door.

"This isn't carpet. It's a bouclé sweater. Why can't you live on the lake or downtown like functional people do?"

"Oh, Cecilia...are you offering me a raise?"

She gave me a dirty look but then her eyes and mouth widened into an approving smile when she spotted Jude standing in the apartment.

"Well, it certainly wasn't the overdose of mint tea that had me thinking you were dreamy. Clearly you are."

My phone rang. It was Angus' number.

"Don't answer that," Cecilia barked.

"I have to. It might be Blaine. He's always making me work overtime."

"Yeah. I'll bet. Fine. Can I have something to drink? Something in its original, identifiable container."

"Hello?" I answered the phone and pointed toward the kitchen.

"Libby. John Meier believed the story and has left."

"Meet me outside the church in thirty minutes. If I'm not there, just wait."

"Got it. See you there. Thanks, Libby. This is pretty awesome."

"You're welcome." I hung up and turned back around.

"Church?" Cecilia laughed. She sounded like my mother. Suddenly a lot of things made sense about my work and family relationships. There'd be time for therapy later.

"I forgot I had Bible study tonight."

"That explains so much," she laughed again in a condescending tone and sipped a Sprite without touching her lips to the can. I could see Jude was annoyed with her, so I gave him a fake happy smile and he smiled back.

"Cecilia, have a seat. We're anxious to hear the plan. I know it'll be great with you at the helm. That day we met was such a blessing."

"A blessing? Oh, you poor, sexy, dear man. You've been at the convent too long, I can see that. I should've saved you sooner. But no matter. Things are in motion."

"I knew you'd have a good plan. Libby and I are all set for it."

"Unfortunately, this is where Libby exits the scene and it's just you and me, kid."

"How can she not be a part of the plan?" Jude asked, coming to my defense.

"Jude, darling, it's for her own protection. The less she knows the better. You don't want her to lose her good standing with her adoring new boss, do you?"

He shook his head.

"You have fifteen minutes until the car service comes back around," she said as she looked at her watch like a coach with a stopwatch.

"Then what?" he asked.

"You're coming to my place. It's senseless for you to punish yourself with another night of this." Her eyes lit up. "Unless you want another night with Gidget?"

"All my stuff is here, and I've been writing music. I'm inspired by being back in this neighborhood. Cecilia, I want to know more about the plan tonight. I've been patient, but this is my life we're talking about. Libby and I both deserve some information."

Jude's strength surprised Cecilia. She nodded slightly. "Tomorrow night is fine. At least we'll have one evening to enjoy each other's company." Her finger reached out like an iguana's tongue and flicked along Jude's jawline. He looked genuinely repulsed.

"Why, what happens after tomorrow night?" I asked innocently.

I watched her eyes get big as she caught her own slip up. "One evening after another, I meant, until my plan is ready. And then you, Jude, are going to have a fabulous outing. A concert. A big one, with media, fans, and an after party beyond anything you've ever seen, and…" Cecilia's voice faded and she sipped the soda awkwardly. Her lack of even a good pretend plan was so obvious.

When my phone rang again, Cecilia didn't miss a beat. Instead of complaining, she saw it as her chance to exit. "You'd better take that. It's probably Blaine again. Okay, Jude, darling, tomorrow you're with me. We'll get you back out there." She wasn't used to pretending optimism and she certainly wasn't used to holding a can of soda. "What do I do with this? Do you reuse these or something?"

"I'll take that," Jude offered and reached for the can. She held on to it teasingly for a moment and then quickly departed.

I answered the phone. "Pan? Can you still meet us in half an hour?" I stepped back into the apartment and shut the door.

"Yes. What's going on, Libby? Hudson seemed strange."

"You should know something about Hudson," I said as Jude tried to grab the phone from me. "Hudson is strange. But it's a good strange. Can you meet us outside the Community Church instead of my apartment?"

"Church? And I'm bringing a camera? You're making me nervous. I wasn't kidding before...marrying your cousin is illegal and most undesirable."

I laughed. "I promise you that I'm not marrying my cousin. The church is empty. We're just hanging out there. See you in a few." I hung up the phone and then said, "Jude, could you help Levi start transporting the equipment? And have him call Ray and Trevor so they know things are on for tonight at the church. I'm going to run an errand. I'll meet you at the church, if that's okay? Levi will need to let Angus in. He'll probably get there before Pan does and before I can make it back."

Jude saluted me and headed out. He didn't need to ask where I was going.

Forty-Two

I buzzed Blaine's apartment for the third time. My stomach churned with nerves. Even though he'd been acting strange lately, he was still responsible for Jude having this chance, and I wanted him there with me, with us.

"We don't give out candy," Blaine said from behind me. He was approaching the door with a big bag of groceries in his arms.

"More laundry?" I teased.

"Funny girl. Here, my keys are in my right hand." His cheeks were red from the cold and his eyes were bright.

I let us in. "Can I go on up with you? I have some news."

"Sure. Follow me."

"Everything's going to work out. At least I hope so."

"I'm glad for you."

"Be glad for all of us. We made this happen. That's why I need you there tonight."

"There?" He stopped walking, turned, and looked over the bag of groceries at me.

"The band is going to record a new song, and it's going to be documented. You were right about the album idea—they laughed at that—but they did forgive Jude and they like the new stuff he's been writing. There's a chance that if the public demand for that one song and the story of the band's reunion is great enough, FreeTime will have to pay attention." I finished my ramblings and stood breathless and anxious. Blaine nodded a few times. Then I realized he wasn't nodding; he was motioning toward the door. I had the keys still. "Sorry!" I unlocked the door and Blaine exaggerated the heaviness of the grocery bag by staggering to the kitchen island.

"Libby, you don't need or want me there. I'm happy that this is working out, but you have much more invested in Jude than I do."

I walked over to him and stood close. Closer than usual. Even though "we" were not a "we," I knew "we" were off-kilter. And it made me sad. I wanted it to be right. Blaine was the first boss who ever cared about me and my potential career. I couldn't stand it if we left things strained and awkward. "You're wrong."

"Really?"

"Yes. I don't want you there as a support for Jude. I want you there with me and for me. You gave me the chance to continue with all of this craziness in spite of your feelings about Jude's guilt and probably in spite of your feelings about my sanity. I need that kind of support tonight."

Blaine took a deep breath. I could tell he was preparing another argument against going because he wouldn't look at me. I knew I had to go the way of personal or I'd always wonder why he stopped supporting me. I asked the big question—"Why do you stand in my apartment lobby and never come up to talk to me?"

He stepped back as though I had pushed him. In a way, I had. "I..." he started to talk and then looked at me with a baffled "how did you know?" expression.

"Did I let you down? I know I messed up, but did I let you down so much that we can't work together or be friends? I need to know." Tears were forming in my eyes. This was my cue to step back, not to give him a chance to disengage from the conversation, but to give myself a moment to compose my emotions.

"I reviewed employee files and backgrounds a month before I came to Seattle. I knew before we met that you weren't going to be my assistant for long. But then Cecilia disappeared and the timeline changed. Ken wanted Cecilia's transition in place before following my recommendation that you be promoted to creative."

"Why are you telling me this now? To make my inevitable firing more pathetic?"

"No, Libby. So you won't think I'm a jerk of a boss who uses his influence or perceived power to manipulate..."

I interrupted him. "I'd perceive you as a jerk for helping my career?"

"No, for still being your boss and doing this..." he stopped talking and the most serious expression I've ever seen on his gentle face passed over his features.

Just as I was going to ask "what?" he closed the gap between us.

He kissed me. A beautiful, full, lovely, take-your-breath-away kiss. My head went numb and my arms tingled and my ears grew hot. Is this how these things happen? Can my life be such a mess and still have the gift of a good thing? Was he nuts? Could he even know me and what he was getting into after such a short time?

Blaine pulled away from the kiss but did not step back. I could smell my coffee breath. I could smell his grape soda breath. And it was still a perfect moment.

"Be quiet," he said in a hushed voice and his finger gently traced the line of my brow to the top of my nose.

He did know me.

I leaned in and kissed him back. This time my mind wasn't invaded by a litany of reasons why he was mad or why I was daft or why the world was probably going to end tomorrow because I finally found someone. There was only the sound of happy chimes, the kind Aunt Maddie had experienced on the day she finally let herself believe in more.

We held hands the entire way to the church. I kept trying to steal glances at his profile, but his face was turned toward me. It's a miracle we ever reached the church without getting hit by a bus or a stop sign.

"Here we are, Libby," he said and smiled broadly.

"What's so funny?" I asked, noticing for the first time that he had longer lashes than I did. It was too late to hate him.

"It felt really good to say your name like that."

I cocked my head to the side, bewildered. "You always call me by my first name."

"Not like that."

I replayed his comment in my head. "You're right. Never like that. Everything's different."

"Everything's better. I may even start to like Jude and his music."

I teasingly poked his arm and then kissed him on the cheek. He tried to open the door to the church, but it was locked. We could hear someone playing the drums, but that was it. I knocked loudly.

Levi first opened the door a crack and then fully. "Blaine? Come in."

"Hi, Pastor Levi," Blaine said warmly.

"How do you know each other?" Levi, Blaine, and I all said at the same time.

"We work together," I said, explaining Blaine and me.

"And we're together," Blaine added proudly.

"Levi is a neighbor in my apartment building. And he's Jude's mentor," I explained to Blaine, who raised his eyebrows with a "what do ya know" look.

Levi shook Blaine's hand and asked, "Do you remember the first time you came to church, Blaine, and we talked about how hard it was to move to a new city and how hard it was to get connected?"

"Yes, I remember it well. You told me that God had set things in motion for my life here, and that I needed to trust that."

"That's it. And see how connected we all are in such a short time?" His voice dropped to a whisper. "Well, I actually thought of Libby right away for you. I'd seen her stand outside the church numerous times, and I knew that as soon as she stepped foot in this church, I'd introduce you. And here you are, Libby, but this is even better."

A knock interrupted our conversation. Puzzled, Levi inched back over to the door and opened it a crack. "Angus?"

"Oh, let him in. He's late, but so are we," I said looking shyly at Blaine. He returned the glance.

Angus came bustling in, full of apologies as usual. Levi stared at him and then at me. "You *two* know each other? Libby, I'm starting to think you are the new Kevin Bacon."

"We do." I kept the explanation light out of respect for Blaine.

Angus seemed to catch my tone. "We've been friends for some time."
He reached out and shook hands with Blaine. They nodded respectfully
to one another.

"I saw you briefly at that art show," Blaine said.

I finished this long round of connect-the-dots for Blaine's benefit,
though I don't think he cared. "Angus knows Levi through…" I was about
to say the music industry but Levi completed my sentence with a twist.

"Bible study."

"What?" I asked.

"Oh, man… I never 'out' people like this. My apologies, Angus. This
is a crazy day."

Angus turned up his hands and shrugged. "It happens."

I gave him a halfhearted slug in the arm. "That's great, Angus."

"Quite the *Oprah* moment," Blaine said.

"It is," Levi agreed. "And I'm afraid we have a more extreme *Oprah*
moment in process. There's been a bit of an incident."

"Incident?" I tried to calm the negative thoughts in my mind—the
thoughts of "if one thing is good, the next thing will be bad."

"Nothing serious. Don't worry. Libby, you're probably the one who
can help. Follow me to the reception room."

Blaine, Angus, and I formed a line behind Levi and made our way
down the very short hall to a separate room filled with folding tables and
chairs. A gathering of several older ladies with vintage hats hovered over
something. I could smell the rose-scented perfume they seemed to share.
"What happened?" I asked.

"Your friend…she passed out."

As the group of women shifted, and their matching blue silk dresses
with polka dots swayed to one side, I spotted Jude leaning over Pan. He
was gently patting her face, which was very pale.

"Oh my gosh!" I hurried over to Jude's side and kneeled next to him.
"What happened? Is she sick?"

"I told her," he said and then emphasized, "everything."

"Yes, I figured. What did she say?"

"She said something about killing you and then she fell backward.
Thank goodness May and Adele were right there to ease her fall."

"May and Adele?" I looked up into the concerned, orange-cheeked faces of the women around us. Two of the ladies raised their hands slightly to claim their names.

Jude continued touching Pan's face. "These ladies are the church choir. Levi forgot they were having their photo taken tonight for the church directory."

I looked again at the faces. None of them would know the band. We were safe.

Pan started to mumble. Quick on the draw, four of the women pulled paper fans from their purses and began to whisk their wrists back and forth. In the forthcoming breeze, Pan's hair extended from her face as though she had placed her hand on an electric sphere in science class. I kneeled down next to her opposite Jude.

All of a sudden a tug on the neckline of my shirt brought me down to Pan's face. My eyeball was merely two inches away from hers. She had a hold of me and would not let go. "You've never been good at secrets. Why start now?"

I raised my hand in to the air and motioned the okay sign with my fingers. I tried to say, "She's fine," but I could barely breathe.

"Pan. I'm so sorry about all of this," Jude said, fanning her with his hand.

My friend released her hold on me and focused all her energies on staring into Jude's eyes.

"She's fine, she's fine!" I called out.

Adele turned to the others. "Ladies, we should sing a song for this young lady."

"That is a splendid idea," May said, clasping her hands together and looking heavenward. "Let's go, girls." She and the rest of the choir headed out the door to the main sanctuary.

In a few minutes the ladies, accompanied by the musical talents of Ray and Trevor, started to sing.

> The Lord has promised good to me,
> His Word my hope secures;
> He will my Shield and Portion be,
> As long as life endures.

Yea, when this flesh and heart shall fail,
And mortal life shall cease,
I shall possess, within the veil,
A life of joy and peace.

Pan stood upright with the help of Jude, Blaine, and myself. She was groggy, but her mind did not wander long. After she made sure her camera was fine, her thoughts and statements kept returning to my growing list of shortcomings as a friend. When she could walk a straight line she excused herself and me to the back of the sanctuary lined with bulletin boards promoting Sunday school, reading groups, Bible studies, and potlucks.

"Couldn't you extend a little lifeline of fact to a friend before she made a complete idiot of herself? You knew all about Jude at the time I told you about the documentary, and still, those pretty lips of yours never revealed..."

"It was painful to not tell you..."

"Wait a minute...those pretty lips are hiding something."

My hand went to my mouth. "Blaine and I are together."

"Your boss?"

"He won't be my boss for long, so it isn't a weird thing."

Pan hugged me tightly and then withdrew suddenly. She held me away at arm's length. "You haven't been dating him all this time without telling me, have you?"

I laughed. "No. This is news as it is happening. We *just* admitted our feelings for one another. Speaking of which, how did you feel when Jude told you *everything.*"

Pan looked away, restless and frustrated. "Stupid. All this time I was gaining a crush at adolescent speed and I was talking about Seattle's music scene like an expert while I'm rubbing elbows with *the* man, *the* story of a lifetime, and I missed it. The fact that I got to hang out with him takes a bit of the sting out, but you owe me so much."

I shook my head. "He told you everything, right?"

"What else is there? The guy I made go watch sheep rotating in a pasture for two hours is Jude Shea."

"Jude!" I called out to beckon the cop-out rock star.

He hurried over. "You're okay, right, Pan?"

She nodded and looked down at her feet.

"Your explanation seems to have some missing blanks for Miss Garrett." I motioned with my hands for him to proceed.

He put his hands in his front pockets and then his back pockets and then in his jacket pockets. He wasn't looking for anything other than courage. I pulled him close to me and whispered, "Let me help you here. Did you tell her you like her? Did you tell the woman she gets to interview you and receive a slam dunk for the competition?"

"To my defense, she passed out before I could tell her the rest," Jude said loudly.

"There's more?" Pan's eyes grew wide.

"We want you to interview us and film our first recording. You can show it at the event to unveil our reunion...if you want to, that is."

Pan reached for my arm to steady herself. "Yes, I want," she said. "Are you sure you want people to find out through me? Won't your label get mad?"

"Long story," I explained without explanation. "Speaking of long stories...this story isn't over. Jude has something else to say. Should I leave?"

"No!" Pan and Jude said in duet.

"Pandora, I've really enjoyed our time together. I even liked the time staring at the sheep. Don't ever tell anyone about that, by the way. I think you are kind, smart, incredibly interesting, and beautiful. You like to laugh, but you don't like to give away your emotions. That I can relate to. Oh, wait." Jude spun on a heel and headed to a pew, where he grabbed a bouquet of flowers and a white bag and brought them back to Pan.

"Flowers for you. Biscuits and chew toys for the dogs. Will you go out with me?"

"You want to go out, go out. Like date?" she asked, incredulous.

"I do. But there is a stipulation. You have to go out with me, not Hudson."

"I kind of liked Hudson. Is this Jude guy just as nice, smart, and sweet?"

"He is," Jude said shyly. "I'm glad I found you."

Pan smiled and nodded profusely to the sweet sound of being found.

> *Amazing grace! How sweet the sound*
> *That saved a wretch like me!*
> *I once was lost, but now am found;*
> *Was blind, but now I see.*

Forty-Three

The wind gained force and whisked all around Jude and me as we walked from Eighth Street toward the water and in the direction of the bookstore.

"Got the pastries?" I asked. "Did you take a bite of that marionberry one?"

"Yep and yep," he affirmed.

"I knew it. Mr. Diddle won't know where to start with this pastry buffet!"

"He'll pick the blueberry one. It has the most icing."

"You've gotten to know him rather quickly."

"Underneath the few words and the seemingly limited life, the guy's an open book. Pun intended. I can't believe you are playing hooky."

"I don't think I can officially call it playing hooky if my boss approved it, can I?"

"We will today. It's more fun that way. That's one nice guy. You'd think that after what you two embarked on last night, he'd want you with him."

"Maybe I'm too much of a distraction for what the poor man has to do today."

"He's not confronting Cecilia, is he?"

"No, but he's telling Ken everything. He can't keep her misuse of corporate reputation and finances a secret."

"Will Ken blame him?"

"He's more worried about how Ken will perceive me."

"Just think. If Ken says 'fire that girl,' this could be your life every weekday."

"Because I would meet a sugar daddy or win the lottery in this scenario?"

"I could support you. If all goes as planned, I'll keep receiving my royalties. That's plenty for a while. You could be my urban missionary project."

"I'll get back to you on that. Maybe Pan won't want to share your wealth with a woman who does her mission work from a bench at the coffee shop or the floor of her favorite bookstore."

The wind picked up and we hurried our steps toward the familiar doorway.

I stopped a couple of feet short of the door and craned my neck forward with shock. "Mr. Diddle's an open book, you said?" I pointed to a small handwritten sign taped to the lower corner of the window which read "For Sale."

"Wow. Most unexpected."

"He can't sell. He and this bookstore are part of this city. This store is that special hidden treasure just waiting to be discovered by the right person at the right time. Open that door. I have hot coffee and a hot temper."

"Right this way, then!" Jude let me inside to the space that had been my refuge on so many Sundays when I didn't have the courage to go to church, but I knew I had to be somewhere meaningful in the morning.

We didn't even have to look for Mr. Diddle. He was perched on a stool behind his cash register desk. He didn't actually have a register. He used a shoe box and a receipt pad. He looked up at us and smiled warmly. His eyes lit up when he saw the white pastry bags we had in tow.

"Sell? Sell!" My earlier arguments had faded and only my disbelief came forward in spurts. "Why? Sell? No...I won't allow it."

"Libby. Did you think I'd be here forever? Besides, you won't be coming back here as regularly."

"Why not?"

"I figured it was about time you went to the other place on Sunday mornings."

"I don't know how you know that," I said, pouting, "but I agree. However, look at this. It's a Friday, and I'm here. I need 80 Days. It is part of my routine in this city."

"Jude, do you hear this lovely young woman? She thinks she's the only one who gets to make a change." Mr. Diddle laughed and rummaged with delight through the bags. He reached for the blueberry pastry and licked the top.

Jude gave me an "I told you so" look. "It does sound like she's implying that."

"Whose side are you on?" I demanded.

"Everybody's," Jude said. "Why don't we celebrate Mr. Diddle's next step. Which is?" He pulled up two stools for us across from Mr. Diddle.

"I'm traveling," Mr. Diddle said with typical simplicity.

"Traveling? That doesn't mean you have to sell," I protested while smearing cream cheese on my onion bagel.

"I want to leave things open. You see, I've met someone."

Jude and I both stopped mid-bite. I released my jaw first. "How?"

"Libby!" Jude said.

"I didn't mean it that way. I meant…How? You don't leave the store."

Mr. Diddle laughed heartily. He was enjoying every minute of this. "The girl is right, Jude. I don't exactly get out on the town. But the miracle of today, as you two should know, is that one can correspond with potential dates with email."

"You used an online dating service?" I asked both intrigued and appalled. "You didn't tell some woman that you are thirty years old and drive a convertible, did you?"

"Ye of little faith," Jude said with dismay. "Libby, give the man some credit. Who is she, Mr. Diddle?"

"It's an interesting story, how I met this woman. Libby, you are the one responsible for this event in my life."

"She's good at that."

"What do you mean? Is she a pastry chef or something?"

"Her name is Madeline Ruth Kingston." He smiled and waited for my reaction. He didn't wait long.

"You went from pen pal status with my aunt to online romance?"

Jude's eyes grew wide. "*The Practice of the Presence of God* aunt? The nun?"

"Ex-nun," Mr. Diddle and I said together. Mr. Diddle pointed to Jude. "It is her."

I was in shock. "She never mentioned this development. I talked to her last week and..."

"I know. She told me." His eyes twinkled when he said this.

"Unbelievable. So what? You're going to Croatia, I suppose?"

He nodded and reached into the bag closest him on the counter. His hand withdrew clutching a maple bar.

"You get to go on the trip of *my* dreams to see *my* aunt?"

"Mm-hmm," he confirmed with a full mouth.

"That's a great story!" Jude said, apparently missing the pain this was causing me.

"When do you leave on my trip?"

"As soon as I sell this place. Maybe now I should use those marketing ideas."

"No way. Too late, Mr. Diddle. I'm not going to help you sell this bookstore," I said adamantly. I took a few deep breaths and realized I was being very selfish. I loved Mr. Diddle. I loved my aunt. This was a good thing. "I'm happy for you and for my aunt, though I will give her a piece of my mind about keeping this a secret."

"Because you *never* keep secrets, right?" Jude pointed out.

He was right. I had to laugh at myself, but I was still upset about losing this important place and about watching this dear man pursue the trip I had planned many times.

"Why wait? I have an email started to her right now. You may tell her just what you think about all this." Mr. Diddle motioned toward his back office.

"I think I will. Do you mind, Hudson?"

He raised his arms in submission. "I wouldn't dream of standing in your way right now! What was that about a woman scorned?"

He and Mr. Diddle chuckled like two gossiping old men. I turned around quickly so they wouldn't see me smile, and I headed for the computer to tell my life's role model congratulations.

I walked circles around my living room. Every few minutes I glanced out the window to the street below. Cecilia had sent a cab for Jude. I hated to say goodbye. Even with Jude and Pan becoming a couple, I knew things would be so different after he was back in the limelight. I felt as though I were losing a longtime friend. I heard the zip of a backpack and the snap of a suitcase latch before Jude surfaced from the bedroom. He placed his things by the door and came over to stand near me by the window. We both looked out over his old neighborhood. It was easier than looking at one another.

"Libby."

"I know."

"This is so strange," he said in a muted voice.

I looked at him. "But not as strange as it would've been a year ago."

He smiled and hugged me close. "I hate to say this, but I will have to thank Cecilia for everything. This is exactly how everything needed to turn out."

"I'd like to think an authority beyond Cecilia had something to do with it," I said, laughing. "But I know what you mean, and I agree."

"Well, that's a given."

"Before the cab comes, let's go over tomorrow's plan."

"Good idea." He turned from the window and walked the track I had just paced. "Cecilia will leave for the EMP event, likely leaving me behind in her apartment so that Paulo can have his guys serve me with legal papers. But I'll sneak out as soon as she leaves, take a cab back here, pick you up, we'll go over to the event together and await Pan's turn to present her proposal. Then voilà…the world will know. That it?"

"Be sure to take all your stuff with you that evening. Once Cecilia's plan crumbles, I don't think she'll be inviting you back to her place."

"That reminds me, I have this." Jude reached in to his back pocket and retrieved my copy of *The Practice of the Presence of God.* "It's yours."

"No, you keep it. Most of the margin notes are yours, anyway."

"Are you sure?"

"Mr. Diddle owes me. I'll get a copy before he leaves town. Before he leaves me."

"Thanks, Libby."

A cab pulled up. We watched as Newton went outside, peered in to the passenger window and motioned for Jude to come down.

Jude looked at me as if reading my mind and said, "We'll hang out, Libby. I swear. Besides, I'm in love with your best friend. How far away do you think I'll go?"

"You're right. We'll see lots of each other. But don't talk to Pan between now and the event. Cecilia might hear you and catch on."

He held up a cell phone. "It's hers, so she can call me right before the event. Don't worry. I'll be discreet. Besides, she'll be at the editing suite all night and probably most of tomorrow, and she has no phone there."

"Jude, I really hope Torrid gets a second chance."

"And I hope Ken shows you mercy."

"I'll know soon enough. Blaine and I are getting together tomorrow morning."

"Not tonight?"

"No. I didn't want to emotionally deal with Ken's response tonight, not after your departure. Blaine and I agreed to meet up with a fresh perspective tomorrow."

The cab driver honked a couple times.

"If you ever need a job reference for...I dunno...hiding people or a personal reference for a roommate, let me know." Jude kissed me on the cheek, gave me a wink, and headed out the door with his belongings.

I decided not to watch out the window as he left. I went to the kitchen to make some coffee. I wasn't hoping for genius. I just knew I wouldn't be sleeping tonight.

Forty-Four

A knock at the door the next morning startled me. "Who is it?"

"The guy who never goes past the lobby," Blaine called through the keyhole.

I smiled and went over to let him in. We stood awkwardly for a moment, staring at one another, and then Blaine hugged me to break the ice. "I've missed you," he said.

"I've missed you too."

"Breakfast for two." He held up a McDonald's sack. I could smell the hash browns and began to salivate.

"Take a seat anywhere. Do you want coffee?" I headed to the kitchen for paper plates and fresh coffee.

Blaine took off his coat and rolled up his sleeves. He sat tentatively on the couch. "Yes to coffee." He was silent for a moment before stating, "I hope things go well for Jude. I wish the best of luck."

"That's good of you. I know you are still not impressed with him."

"That's not true. After the night at the church, I realized I was quick to judge him. There's no reason a guy like him can't experience transformation. I actually liked the new song. It was basically about redemption. I was surprised."

I returned to the living room and sat beside him. "It surprised me too.

After the ladies in blue sang 'Amazing Grace,' Jude changed the name of his new song to 'Mortal Life' since it's about the hardness of being human and the hope of change."

Blaine considered this. "I like it."

"Now give it to me straight. On a scale of one to ten, how mad was Ken."

Blaine held up ten fingers. I put my face in my hands and groaned.

"But only at Cecilia."

I looked up. "Really?"

"Mostly he was disappointed. He gave Cecilia a chance after Paulo had basically messed up her life years ago. He genuinely cares about her and hates to see her get messed up with Paulo again."

"Is he worried that tonight could mean bad media for Cecilia and for the firm?"

"Well, he did have issues with how that could play out, but again it was more out of concern for Cecilia. He's afraid she'll never recover once her reputation is dragged through the mud again."

"He can't talk to her. It will ruin everything. She's too involved in this from start to finish. If Ken informs her about what is going to take place, she'll tell Paulo, and he'll influence FreeTime and the EMP board. He could pull Ray and Trevor from the judge's panel and they have to be there so that Torrid can perform 'Mortal Life'..."

Blaine grabbed my hand to calm my nerves. "I understand. I think all of that needs to happen, but I'm also wondering if Ken isn't right too. That seems wise to me."

I thought through it or at least tried to. I didn't see a solution. I stood up, full of energy and anger. "Dang that Cecilia! She makes me so mad. After all the garbage she puts me and others through..."

"Yes?"

"I still want to help her."

"Good woman. I know this is hard. First, I want you to know that I will not put Jude at risk either. You have to trust me. I didn't give him a fair perspective before. I was jealous, basically."

"You were?" I sat back down. "You were jealous of Jude?"

"Of course. First of Angus, then of Jude...once I saw the rocker image you seemed to gravitate toward, I thought I didn't stand a chance."

"That's so sweet!"

"Jealousy isn't so sweet. I don't like to be that kind of guy."

"Don't ever be that kind of guy again. But now that we've cleared the air...I can say that I forgive you, and you're pretty darn wonderful to also want to help Cecilia. She hasn't exactly made your life easy, either. But what can we do that won't destroy Torrid in the process, not to mention destroy Pan's chance at that funding?"

"I'm glad you asked. Come in!" Blaine called toward the door.

"Nobody knocked," I said, turning to look at the door just as Levi walked in. "Oh, boy. I smell a new plan. Pastor Levi, are you always in the middle of such controversy?"

"Not since my band days. And please call me Levi. I'm not much into titles."

"What did you find out?" Blaine asked as Levi took a seat across from us in my papasan chair. To me, Blaine explained, "Levi spoke with a friend of his who works with FreeTime records."

I shook my head.

"Don't worry, Libby. I didn't reveal anything. However, I did get some good news. Remedying all of this may be quite simple. Tyler, my old friend and contact at FreeTime, shared some reassuring information. I told him I was concerned for my friends Ray and Trevor that maybe FreeTime would have it in for them with the approaching contract deadline. And he said that FreeTime has hired a big gun, which we happen to know is Paulo, to pursue a lawsuit against Ray and Trevor to hold them to the contract, *but* that it was all really a ploy to get Jude to surface." Levi sat back as though that explained everything.

"Why is this good? Of course they want him to surface. They want to sue him."

"No. They want Torrid to be up and running. Everything they've done has been to draw Jude out from hiding. They have no intention of destroying the potential of this group. If Jude doesn't come out of the woodwork, then Ray and Trevor will be held accountable for the broken contract, but that isn't their focus."

This still didn't add up. "Help me out here, Levi. FreeTime hired Paulo, who hired Cecilia...so FreeTime knows Jude has surfaced. Cecilia has had him indirectly in her custody for weeks now. If Tyler is telling the truth about what they want from all this, then they already have it. There would be no reason to threaten with the lawsuit. FreeTime has a band they are going to promote big time...to replace Torrid basically. Isn't that what they want?"

"That's yet another ploy to draw Jude out. Tyler even mentioned it. There is no band. They are trying every angle possible to get the group back together. They figured Jude and his ego would not allow for another band to steal their tour schedule and their fan base."

"But they have Jude. Cecilia has him in her apartment right now."

"You're forgetting two very important things. One...we know Jude and the bandmates made up, but FreeTime does not. They assume there would be loads of bad blood between them all and that the pending lawsuit will unite them out of fear and financial obligation."

"Makes sense," said Blaine. "What's the second thing?"

"How do lawyers make money?"

"Lawsuits," I said.

"Litigation," Blaine corrected.

"Exactly. Paulo and Cecilia are acting out of their best interest. And in *their* best interest, Jude would not surface in time, would not have a chance to reunite, and Paulo could go ahead with legal action against Torrid."

I gasped. "FreeTime doesn't know about Jude?"

Levi shook his head. "I'm sure they don't. Tyler is high up, and he was honestly certain that it looked like this would go the way of litigation."

"Oh, my. Paulo and Cecilia...what are they going to do with Jude?"

"They won't cause him physical harm. But I think they'll go to the event tonight, present Ray and Trevor with the lawsuit in front of the media, bask in the glory of the attention, return to Cecilia's and tell Jude that they tried to negotiate with Ray and Trevor but that they want nothing to do with him...and then make up some story about how they will help Jude by sending him back in to hiding. And of course...that is exactly what would help them, not Jude."

"This is exhausting!" I screamed.

Blaine patted me on the back. "I'm seeing how this is the best case scenario for us. As soon as Pan stands up there and presents her documentary, the whole world will know that Jude and the band are reunited and Paulo and Cecilia's plan will be moot."

I started to breathe at a more regular rate. "Okay. That works. So we're good? We're good. And Torrid will get their second chance without any trouble from FreeTime. The only problem is saving Cecilia. Although the more we learn the less deserving this woman appears to be."

"Maybe this time, she'll use a second chance for good," Levi said in a pastoral tone. "Everything can go as planned, except we'll pull Cecilia out of that media moment tonight. The industry knows Paulo and some probably remember Cecilia. There's no way their presence will go unrecorded. Cecilia's going to look bad no matter what."

"The only solution is to keep her away from the event," Blaine said.

I laughed. "She's been plotting for months. You can't keep her away."

"What does Cecilia love more than she loves Paulo?" Levi asked.

I thought a few seconds. "Attention. Flattery. Herself?"

"And that's exactly what will trap her. It's for her own good."

"She won't see it that way."

"She will in time," Levi promised.

"How do you trap a trapper?" I asked my puzzle without having the answer.

"We'll have someone call her posing as a reporter and say that an informant at FreeTime revealed she's behind this monumental lawsuit. They'll ask to do an advance research interview and photo shoot with her today so that they can emphasize her rather than Paulo when the story breaks tonight or tomorrow."

"We don't have time to do a photo shoot," I said, dismissing all this work.

"Stay with us, Libby. There won't be a shoot. We're telling her this so she will ask Paulo to go on ahead without her tonight. She'll slip away on her own to meet the reporter, and the reporter will detain her until this is all over."

"And this is doing her a favor?" I asked jokingly. "Who plays the reporter in this off-off-Broadway production?"

"Newton," Levi said confidently.

"She'll take one look at him and leave."

"May I?" Levi pointed toward the coffeepot. I got up to pour him a cup so he'd continue. "I'll be with Newton too. Cecilia knows me and knows my ties to the industry. Newton will explain that I am there to provide juicy details about Ray and Trevor. We'll do a mock interview, detain her, and then when the time is running out, we'll offer to take her to the event, but of course we won't. We'll pretend to get lost or whatever it takes to keep her far from the scene."

"What if she really loves Paulo. This would end things."

Levi smiled sweetly. "I love that you thought of that, Libby. But the man would have used her as his scapegoat once this all fell apart."

This did seem possible. It really was as simple as detaining Cecilia. "Unless this reporter is supposed to be from *Hobo Monthly*, Newton had better borrow one of Blaine's suits."

Forty-Five

When Jude walked through my door, I hugged him. I was so relieved that he'd made it out of Cecilia's apartment with all of his belongings and with his life. Frankly, after Levi revealed the actual plan behind the plan, I feared that Cecilia and Paulo would resort to physically harming Jude. Or holding him captive.

"That's quite a greeting! It's only been a day, Libby."

"I hated the idea of you in Cecilia's control."

"So did I." He took off the old disguise of a cowboy hat and I took a long look at my friend. He was dressed in a pair of very expensive designer jeans and a tight, knit black sweater. A large platinum ring flashed. "How is this for a return-to-life outfit?"

"Perfect. How did it go?"

"As planned. Although Cecilia left the apartment over a couple hours ago. I didn't think she'd leave me unattended like that, but of course she thinks I'm relying on her to make my return happen. She took a call, spent an hour getting dressed, and headed out. Oh, and she said to stay away from her expensive almonds and to stay put until she and a friend returned later to tell me the rest of the plan."

I smiled at the confirmation that Cecilia had taken the bait. I'd decided not to tell Jude the rest of the story. He had too much riding on tonight, and I didn't want to raise his level of concern.

He continued. "I was able to sneak a call in to Pan. She knows this will be my first sober appearance in a long, long time."

"I didn't think about that."

"I've been so eager to return to the creative process that I didn't think about it much, either. I can't wait to start building a solid foundation here in Seattle. No more hiding behind a life that was never my purpose to begin with."

I knew the feeling. "Let's not keep your new life waiting."

Levi had arranged for someone from EMP to let me and my guest in through a back door. We headed to the closed-off Dylan display, where we could see the presentation stage and also stay hidden from the view of the growing crowd. The place was packed with supporters of the competition and those curious about Ray and Trevor.

"I have butterflies and I don't have to do anything," I said, wringing my hands.

"You should've come to this event with Blaine and just enjoyed it as a date. There was no need to have you babysit me. I'm good, really. Is it too late to call him?"

"He thought it best to keep representation from Reed and Dunson to a minimum."

Jude laughed openly. He was a completely different person in such a short time. "That's wise of him. You know you got yourself a very good man, Libby."

"He is great, isn't he? I can't wait to be in a real, grown-up relationship."

"I feel the same about Pan. Maybe grown-up love only happens when you're ready for it."

"Well, that and we probably missed out on it a few times when we weren't ready for it."

"True. Look, there's Pan. Isn't she pretty?"

"She is. Oh, and there's Angus...with Ariel. That's going to take some getting used to."

"Ariel and I had quite a good conversation at your birthday party. I could see her and Angus hitting it off. I think she's ready for her own grown-up love."

"And maybe Angus is too. After this past week, I saw him in a new light."

While the emcee discussed the rules of the competition and the importance of the Experience Music Project, Jude and I roamed around the Dylan display, reading pages of lyrics and examining articles. "This is what being a musician is about. Dylan was a wordsmith who connected with people's stories and lives. Do you think I'll get there?"

"From the sound of 'Mortal Life,' I think you are there, Jude."

"I invited Mr. Diddle. I hope he'll come."

"I'll bet he does. That man took a liking to you right away. Everyone does. Hey, can a good guy last in this business?"

"Apparently he can," Jude said, pointing to a photo of Dylan.

"Apparently."

A loud round of applause drew us back to the railing where we stood to watch the show. I saw Paulo right off. He was just to the right of the judges' area...the perfect spot to pounce on Ray and Trevor once the award show was over. Paulo checked his watch several times, clearly becoming aggravated at Cecilia's absence.

The first two presenters were already seated back in the audience. That left two, including Pan. "I'd better get back down to the stage area. Do you think I can get away with it with the cowboy hat?"

"You might get beat up, but you won't be mistaken for Jude Shea."

"Wish me luck. We'll talk soon." He gave me another quick hug and headed down the stairs. I considered joining the crowd after a few minutes but decided the best view was right here. Another round of applause kicked in for the next to the last presenter as he stepped down, leaving only Pan on stage. She looked excited and poised.

The emcee quickly shuffled over to the microphone. "Now we welcome our final presenter. Pandora Garrett has been in the film and production industry for more than twelve years. Her documentary on Seattle's education system was honored with the Morrison Film award last year. This year we are pleased to have her introduce the last submission of the evening. Pandora Garrett, everyone."

The crowd responded with a polite clapping. Little did they know that Pan was about to introduce the biggest news possible. She walked across the stage to the mic stand. She took a moment and then said,

"Thank you. I know you're all eager for the after party. The creators of tonight's event have a wonderful gala prepared, so I'll get right to it. My documentary, if funded..." Pan paused and glanced over to the judges and smiled. The crowd laughed as she said, "...is called Music Transformed. Seattle is recognized for its ability to give birth to music that transforms the industry and each generation. Our musicians are known for bucking trends and evolving not to suit the corporate industry, but to make statements, change that corporate industry, and set the stage for new sounds and new experiences. Without any further explanation, I bring you my documentary short. Tonight, you as an audience will be a part of a transforming moment in music history."

Pan positioned a remote in her hand toward a projector and the screen went black, then gray, and then the black-and-white image of the church sanctuary appeared in focus. I watched the perplexed faces of the crowd. A few folks walked toward the back, no doubt planning to be the first in line for the party.

The darkened images of two men walking to the front of the sanctuary gave an eerie feel. The camera remained far enough back and the focus was loose enough that nobody would know the two men were Ray and Trevor. Their voices were low and inaudible. Trevor got in position behind the drums and Ray strapped on a guitar. They played the beginning of a famous Torrid song and the crowd did a double take to the judges' table. Ray and Trevor kept their eyes fixed on the screen, so the crowd followed their cue. On film, the two stopped playing. But the sound of a guitar off-camera began. The camera panned over to the sole guitar player's hands in motion. I recognized the song as 'Mortal Life.' For a minute the audience watched the player's deft handling of the guitar strings. When he stopped, the camera pulled back to reveal the face of Jude Shea and the crowd went crazy.

From two stories away, I had to plug my ears with my fingers. I started laughing with absolute happiness as I watched a black cowboy hat make its way through the crowd and back behind the stage. In the commotion, Ray and Trevor also snuck back behind the curtain. People were yelling, "Be quiet!" as Jude began to talk on screen.

I quickly scanned the back of the crowd for the distinguished gray hair of Paulo. As I suspected, he was heading for the main exit doors.

Pan's interview with the band captured the complete attention of everyone in that room. Those who had shifted to the other area had returned to catch the momentous recording of Torrid's reunion. The film short ended with the same shot of Jude as in the opening—only his hands and a portion of the guitar were in view and the faint beginnings of 'Mortal Life' were heard. Pan raised her hand and the remote once again and the film screen began its rise up into the rafters. In its wake stood the three members of Torrid. Jude continued playing in sync with where the film version left off. Chills were rushing up and down my spine. It was so exciting to watch the perfect way for Jude to make his return unfold. Tears stung my eyes and I let them fall gladly.

Some guy I didn't know on the next level down yelled up at me, "Shall we join them below?"

"You go on without me!" I said, laughing and clapping along. I couldn't wait to call Blaine and tell him he missed the show of the year.

Forty-Six

My alarm went off right next to my ear. I jumped out of bed and hurried to the closet, where I had my outfit for this morning hung up on the back of the door. I wasn't nervous anymore, only excited about what this choice would mean for me.

I dressed and primped in a record fifteen minutes and had plenty of time to eat a scone and sip some fresh coffee before Blaine knocked on the door.

"Good morning," I greeted the handsome man in a breathtaking suit.

"You've been posted," he said, pulling a sticky note from my door.

I read the note aloud. "Cecilia safe, sound, and roarin' mad. Is this the Sunday you break your routine? More later. —Levi."

"Did you tell him we were planning to go to church today?" I asked.

"Nope. This is good news about Cecilia." He started quietly laughing.

"What?"

"I wish I could've seen Newton struggling through a fake interview for an hour. That had to be something. It was probably even a better show than your Jude put on. No offense. I know you told me how fabulous it was last night."

"It was amazing. Pan outdid herself and so did the band. Oh, and Paulo was so mad. You should've seen him storm out of there. I hope he doesn't try to reach Cecilia."

"I did get a call last night that I forgot to mention to you," Blaine said, looking guilty.

"What? You need to confess before we go to church."

"We aren't Catholic."

"Are you trying to get out of honesty?"

"Levi called me last night and said that Cecilia worked herself up in to such a fit that she hyperventilated. They had to take her to the hospital and admit her."

"Is she okay? Is she there all alone?"

"She's fine. They gave her heavy sedatives, and Levi told them that it might be best to keep her um...comfortable...through this afternoon. I called Ken, and he went over to be with her."

"What a good man. I wish I knew him better."

"I joined Reed and Dunson because of Ken's legacy in the field."

"We should probably get going."

"Yeah, I hear the pastor gives you drugs if you get out of line."

"Oh, so now you're handsome *and* funny."

"You think I'm handsome?" Blaine puffed up his chest like a comic strip character displaying his magnetism.

"I did, but actually it's just the suit. It reminds me of my ex."

"This looks like Angus?" Blaine's face fell.

"Newton," I said, unable to hold in my laugh. "Gotcha!"

I stood in the spot that was more familiar to me than even my favorite aisle at 80 Days. Blaine kept walking but my feet were planted five inches from a patch of grass growing out of a crack in the sidewalk and seven yards from the front of the church.

Blaine noticed I wasn't by his side once he opened the door like a gentleman for me. I smiled and waved from my post. He tilted his head to the side and examined his new girlfriend. She had issues.

"I'm not good with long-distance relationships," he said, trying to resist making fun of me completely.

"This is a momentous occasion. Let me do it my way."

Blaine shut the door and stood to the side to allow a normal couple to go in.

"What are you doing?" I asked.

"I'm waiting. Libby, I'd wait for you any day of the week and twice as long on Sunday."

I leaned my weight on my heels and then on my toes and looked around me. The usual Sunday activity was in full motion. The nine o'clock bus pulled up behind me and the doors opened and closed. I could smell the fumes as it took off down the street. This was the usual point in time when I would turn and begin my trek toward 80 Days.

I watched Blaine smile and nod to a few more people. He pulled his coat collar in closer as the breeze from the bay funneled up the street.

"I'm almost ready," I said, still in my spot.

Blaine perked up, but he didn't seem bothered by my behavior at all.

An older man came by and motioned for Blaine to go on ahead. "Oh, no thank you, sir. I'm waiting for Libby." Blaine pointed to me and the man waved.

I waved back and started walking.

"Are you ready for this?" Blaine asked kindly.

"I think I've been ready all this time. I just didn't know it. And Blaine?"

"What, Libby?"

"Thanks for waiting for me."

I looped a roll of red streamers over Rachel's cubicle while Marsha wrapped her chair with bright yellow. We'd decided to go the way of Barcelona's flag colors to help say goodbye to Rachel and to celebrate her new life of travel.

"We don't have much more time before Rachel will be in," I warned Marsha, who was now wrapping Rachel's stapler in the yellow paper.

"I told her to come in thirty minutes late to give us more time. She didn't argue. Hey, Libby."

"Yes?" I stopped what I was doing and looked down at her.

"Thanks for the elevator talk the other day. I wasn't in a good place after my sister's wedding, and I appreciated all that you said. I needed to be reminded that a relationship needs to happen in good time, but also the right time for me. I have so many other interests that I neglect because I'm worried they'll distract me from...I dunno."

"The hunt?"

"Yes. How sad is that?"

"Hey, I have two friends who recently voiced their interest in having a relationship and they didn't have any prospects. Then bam! They are both dating guys who seem like really good matches. Oh, one's the rocker."

"Who's the lucky girl?"

"One of my best friends."

"Does it bother you that she is dating your ex-boyfriend?"

"Angus was more of a friend, a project, a phase? But probably not ever a true boyfriend. Neither of us was ready for that."

The roller chair creaked under my boots, so I stood up straighter. Ken was walking down the hall. He looked up and saw me. His eyes were friendly.

"Libby, could you meet with me in five minutes?"

"Sure," I said with confidence I didn't have. No wonder he was pleased to see me. He was excited to cross my firing off his to-do list.

"What's up?" Marsha stood up. A strip of yellow paper hung from her hair.

I shrugged and finished my office decor. Maybe I could do this for a living once I was ousted from public relations for good.

Blaine walked toward me. "We're meeting with Ken together."

I placed my hands around my throat in a choke sign. Then I said, "Marsha, can you and Sasha finish up? I could be a while."

Marsha put the finishing touches on a large bow and stood back to admire her handiwork. "We'll be fine. So will you, Libby. You're the best employee this firm has. Even if you do have a thing for rock stars." She winked at me and returned to her masterpiece.

My mouth opened in shock. I didn't give Marsha enough credit in the past.

I wandered down to Ken's office and caught my reflection in Cecilia's office window. The back of my jacket was flipped up. "Good catch, Libby," I said. I had to take small victories where I could find them.

"Ken is expecting you," Tara said as soon as I rounded the corner. She stood up and knocked lightly on Ken's door before opening it and letting me in.

Ken stood up and motioned me toward a chair next to Blaine. "I understand you've had quite the busy past few weeks. Blaine mentioned your concern over Cecilia. I want you to know that she is doing well."

"And Paulo?"

"Paulo left on a midnight flight the night of the EMP event, thanks to your friend's documentary short."

"I certainly hope she won," Blaine said.

"She didn't. In all the excitement, we forgot the conflict of interest with Ray and Trevor being judges. Minor detail. But the exposure her documentary short got that night is already getting attention. It should seal her fate as a well-financed filmmaker."

"Glad to hear it. I'm sorry to transition so quickly to the task at hand, but I think it's best," Ken said.

I braced my arms on the chair and my heart on the inevitable. "Certainly."

"We'll be facing changes related to your position in this company. Blaine recommended you for a promotion to the creative department when he started here. Cecilia's behavior sidetracked us all, but here we are finally, and you have a decision to make."

"I do?" This was going along much better than I had planned. Was the man offering me the promotion I've wanted for five years? I felt my pulse quicken instantaneously.

"There's an associate position in creative, which according to Blaine, is not high enough for your abilities, but it is all we can offer right now. It's still a jump in status and money from the position you're in."

"So what am I choosing between, exactly?"

Blaine spoke up. "Libby, while I'm recommending you for this promotion, Ken has also discovered some of your other talents. There is another position open that would be served well by these skills."

"Oh, back there. The decorating with streamers thing?"

"No. It's better than..." Ken started to address my sarcasm with realism.

"Her humor takes some getting used to, Ken." Blaine sat back and shook his head, laughing.

"I see," Ken said with an almost smile. "Libby, last week Rachel and Tara brought me this." He reached behind his chair and pulled up my travel itinerary notebook.

"I swear I didn't do that on company time. I did use our three-ring paper hole punch because my little one hole punch at home broke when I got to F through K."

"You mean there are more of these?"

"Is this about a position with Annie, the corporate travel coordinator?"

Ken opened up the notebook and flipped through the pages. "No. This position is with our humanitarian foundation."

I was stunned. "I thought that was something made up to threaten Cecilia."

Blaine and Ken looked at one another for a brief second before Ken said, "It's real and a big part of the business model I've tried to create here."

"I'm very interested, Mr. Dunson. Those notebooks reflect more than organizational skills. They reflect my desire to travel but also my hope to serve others while traveling. My aunt does humanitarian work in Croatia, and she's my role model."

"The position is not as desirable as the other. We need someone who will help us evaluate programs to support."

"I'd love that."

"It'd involve some travel for research. Probably not to places this exotic," he said raising the notebook, "but there is potential for that in time."

"I'd love that."

"There's more. It's part-time because the foundation has also undergone some changes after the merger. To create full-time status for you, we'd need to give you another fifteen hours. The only kind of position that suits that limited number of hours is, unfortunately, an assistant position."

I gulped and thought about this for all of ten seconds. It all still felt right. "I could do that."

"And the only spot we have available for that number of hours is with Cecilia."

I looked at Blaine in case this was a joke. No joke. I gulped again, "She still works here?"

Ken adjusted his tie. "At the hospital yesterday I promised her a limited part-time position until she retires. Call me crazy."

"Crazy and then some," I said without apology and then saw Blaine's look of horror. "But nice. I know you and Cecilia have a professional history. I respect that."

Ken seemed a bit surprised by my giving him permission to do his job. "Thank you. So about the position options...what are your thoughts?"

"I want it. I want the humanitarian foundation position even with the...other responsibility."

"You realize it's not an actual promotion. The other position pays more."

"Will I still have medical and the other benefits?"

"Definitely."

"Then I'm in. I'd love it. In fact, it's better than I could've hoped for." Ken and Blaine shared another glance.

"What was that look about?"

"Blaine knows you well. He said you'd take the foundation job. I took one look at your performance record and was convinced you'd take the promotion."

I looked over at Blaine this time. He was such a good man, and he knew me. "This year I read a book that helped me understand that you can do great things in the least of positions. You can understand your purpose no matter where you are. I know this is right. There's no need to discuss it further. Thank you for this opportunity, Ken." I stood and shook his hand. I didn't want to stay around for any more options or discussion. For the first time in my life, there was no second-guessing.

"Thanks, Blaine." I shook his hand too and excused myself.

Funny how leaving that office, having just accepted a demotion and a secretarial position felt so very right and intentional. My mother would wish herself dead and then roll over in her grave, once again, if she knew about the choice I had just made.

I went back to my cubicle and picked up the phone to call Cass with the incredibly good news.

Forty-Seven

I tripped over a dip in the cobbled road and started to laugh. How many times had I tripped at that very spot on my way to see Mr. Diddle, Nomad, and those walls of books at 80 Days? Knowing this could be my last journey along this particular side street, I took in the details. Buildings with shared walls stood in varying shades of gray, green, and blue, not unlike the bay on any given day. Bike racks, newspaper dispensers, parking meters, bus stop signs, and enduring maple trees dotted the sidewalk.

I glanced down at the white box I had in my hands. Today I brought a large cupcake for Mr. Diddle and a couple of organic dog treats for Nomad. It was a special day, but a sad one. The door was slightly ajar. With my foot, I pushed it all the way open and ventured in. My eyes searched the narrow space. Maybe I should have talked Mr. Diddle into leasing it to me. With Ariel's help I could turn this into a reasonable apartment. I smiled, knowing myself too well. I wouldn't leave the Regal Queen now. It was much too convenient to my church…and to Blaine. As hard as it was, sometimes saying goodbye was the only way to invite something else into our lives.

My entrance scattered dust and a few runaway pieces of paper from the counter. Nomad stirred on his large purple pillow in the corner near a rocking chair. He stood with some effort and made his way to me gently and sweetly. My throat tightened. I would miss this welcome, but I was thankful I would not have to miss Nomad. Pan had agreed to add him to her family while Mr. Diddle traveled. I personally planned to wear down Newton and his "no pets" rule so that I could take Nomad in as my own.

"Hey, buddy." I leaned over and scratched the top of his head.

"Do I smell sugar of a wonderful kind?" Mr. Diddle came out from his office carrying a backpack in his hand.

"My, aren't you the traveler. Look at you!" I laughed as he turned several times so I could take in the full effect of his travel attire—a sweat suit and running shoes.

"It's what the smart travelers wear. And take a look at this bag. I ordered it online, but it turns out this company is right here in Seattle. All this time, I watched Rick Steves on television and didn't know he was a neighbor."

"I'll bet he didn't know about this lovely little travel and used bookstore, either."

Mr. Diddle pointed his finger at me. "You can't start with that marketing speech now. I have a plane to catch." He checked his watch.

"Here, have this first." I handed him the cupcake box and he promptly handed the dog bones to Nomad, who now stood between us with an upturned chin to catch the action and the treat.

"It's good!" Mr. Diddle bit into his treat and approved his finale. Chocolate frosting covered his front teeth.

"Will you have a security company check on the place or do you need me to come by every now and then?" I asked while walking the maze of shelves one last time.

"Didn't you notice the sign?"

I shook my head absently.

"I have sold 80 Days! Just about a week ago. Can you believe it?"

"You sold it?"

"You look depressed. Wouldn't you rather have it be available to the next Libby who comes walking along, looking for something, someplace?"

"What if they turn it into something like a dry cleaners or a souvenir shop?"

"I can't be bothered with 'what if' as long as I'm doing what I'm supposed to do. Same for you, Libby."

I nodded. He was right. Three weeks ago I allowed myself only one day to question "what if I had taken the promotion instead of the humanitarian organization job?" I knew I was headed in a right direction for myself, even though there were many unknowns ahead. A deeper faith meant a greater freedom to trust God's leading, wherever that took me.

Okay, maybe there was one additional moment of questioning how God works. Two weeks ago, Marsha answered her phone on the other side of the fabric and bracket wall and then screamed at the top of her lungs, "I won! I won! I get to go to Italy with the author of *Temptation in Tuscany*!" I'd never know if Marsha won because of the bookstore contest form I filled out in her name or because of the one she filled out a week prior. It didn't really matter. I knew I wasn't supposed to go right now or in that way. Just the way I had known I wasn't supposed to leave everything behind and hop on the plane with Rachel. The waiting didn't feel easier, only more intentional.

A breeze brushed over the tops of the shelves, scattering more dust. Mr. Diddle's voice rang out. "You almost missed us. Libby's here now."

I peaked around the corner and saw Jude standing in the doorway. I ran up to him and we hugged. I hadn't seen him since the big unveiling. We'd spoken by phone a couple times, and Pan had kept me informed about how he was doing now that he was back in the spotlight of public adoration. He looked great. I told him so.

"You too, Libby. I guess love and a new job can do a lot for a woman's inner glow. Or maybe you and Cecilia are sharing facial secrets?"

I hit his arm playfully. "That isn't funny. Besides, Cecilia was given an additional month off for mandatory counseling before she returns to her post at the firm."

"Wow, corporate level forgiveness. This could be the wave of the future."

"Are you here to get Nomad? I could've taken him for a few days. Newton owes me that, at least. I can't believe you let him sell a story to the tabloids about his discovery of your undercover persona."

Jude shrugged. "The guy loves those magazines. He'll get his moment in the sun. And it hasn't hurt his attitude, either. He's actually cordial when he calls."

"You let him call you? Who's the nicest celebrity ever?"

"I want to stay grounded. Oh, that reminds me. I wanted to show you my new contract. I'm glad you're here." He glanced at Mr. Diddle, who started whistling some happy tune before handing me a two-page document.

"I don't know much about music contracts, but I think you got ripped off. This is a few chapters short of your earlier contract."

He smiled and placed the papers in front of my face. My eyes finally focused in on the first line. "Deed of ownership for 561 Bay Street, establishment: 80 Days Bookstore."

"You bought the bookstore!"

"I told you I wanted to establish real Seattle roots. I'm expanding it to include used records. Select records, that is. I hired Angus to run it when I'm touring."

"Angus?"

"He's a good guy. I met him the night of our filming at the church."

I nodded. "You know you'll have to change the name."

"No way. It's like you said. It's a part of Seattle's hidden treasure culture."

I shook my head as though I was frustrated, but, of course, I was elated with how this had all evolved. God knew what he was doing.

"And my first act as new owner is this. Drumroll, Mr. Diddle." Jude pointed to Mr. Diddle, who decided to tap out a beat with his new silver-and-orange shoes. His fingers were busy peeling back the transparent wrap on the cupcake. Jude removed a hardcover book from his pack and handed it to me.

I knew without looking at the title what it was. "Thank you." I hugged him again.

Mr. Diddle cleared his throat. Jude piped up, "Okay, it's from both of us."

I hugged Mr. Diddle and he held on for a second. I knew that I'd been a lifeline for him as he had been one for me. He stepped back and patted me on the head as though I were four. Well, four with a driver's license. "Where's my limo?" he said.

"Just up the street. You can practice walking in your fancy new shoes with your fancy new pack." I laughed and looked at Jude. "He's in for a treat. I borrowed Pan's old clunker."

"Ah, the memories of our ride from the airport that day."

Mr. Diddle picked up Nomad and nuzzled him before handing him over to Jude. "I'll be back for you, my friend." He patted his dog as he had patted my head seconds before. Affection was universal.

The airport security lines were short and Mr. Diddle was about to cross over into the land of travelers only. He looked back at me and waved.

I waved and called out, "Tell Aunt Maddie that Blaine and I will be there soon for a visit! We'll see you then too, friend!"

"Friend!" The security officer motioned Mr. Diddle on through the gate. I watched him walk down the corridor and toward a Croatian sunset. Mr. Diddle, Marsha, and Rachel would use my itineraries before I did. But that made me feel good.

I left the airport through the automatic doors and walked to Pan's car in the short-term parking lot. Once I got in, I pulled the book from my purse. Even with this different edition, my fingers went straight to my favorite section about Brother Lawrence:

> *Before he had experienced God's swift help in his affairs, he had attempted to plan every detail, doing the job in his own strength. Now, though, acting with childlike simplicity in God's sight, he did everything for the love of God, thanking Him for His guidance. Everything he did passed calmly, in a way that held him close to the loving presence of God.*

The car ignition turned without any problem, and I was thankful. Purpose was taking me in a different direction than I had planned. I wasn't even sure where I was headed, exactly. Nevertheless…it was a great feeling simply to get started.